THE TUNNELS OF EARTH

#15

*To Wayne
Enjoy the Book
Best Wishes*

FREDERICK CARPENTER

Copyright © 2020 Frederick Carpenter
All rights reserved
First Edition

Fulton Books, Inc.
Meadville, PA

Published by Fulton Books 2020

TXu002202369

ISBN 978-1-64654-847-7 (paperback)
ISBN 978-1-64654-848-4 (digital)

Printed in the United States of America

Contents

Part I North Atlantic 5

Part II Enzo 53

Part III Delegation 137

Part IV Rescue 203

Part V Hide and Seek 236

Part VI Inquisition 270

Part I
NORTH ATLANTIC

It was a warm September night; pinpoints of light dotted the sky. The stars seemed so close you could reach out and grab a handful. The reflection of the moon on the flat ocean surface offered up a shimmering quality.

In the main dining room, large banners were hung that read "Bon Voyage" and "Homeward Bound." The passengers were celebrating their last night at sea.

The small cruise ship *Mist of the Atlantic* was on the final leg of its voyage. Its complement of 450 passengers and 340 crew members began their voyage in New York City one week earlier. It was a New England to Canadian Maritime's cruise.

When it left the pier, that late summer afternoon, *Mist of the Atlantic* traveled north to visit ports of call along the coast of the United States on its way to Nova Scotia. The first leg of the journey included stops in Newport, Rhode Island, and Boston, Massachusetts.

From there the *Mist of the Atlantic* sailed on to its last US port of call, Portland Maine. From Portland, it was on to Nova Scotia, Canada, overnight. The ship remained there for two days. On the second afternoon in Halifax, it did an evening departure turnaround for the Big Apple.

The party started early as the *Mist of the Atlantic*, a modest 560-foot cruise ship, powered back toward New York. The atmosphere was euphoric as the passengers intended to finish the cruise in grand style. Music drifted through the corridors and burst out onto the airy decks. The partying was difficult to avoid, but some people tried.

Some passengers on their last night shipboard were not interested in celebrating. They simply enjoyed a casual stroll on the deck. Others relaxed in deck chairs covered with blankets, breathing in the cool salty air.

It was getting late, and on B deck, one passenger, a man by the name of Miller Goff, leaned out over the railing talking softly to his companion.

"This has been such a wonderful vacation. I can't remember having so much fun on a cruise. I feel so relaxed. We need to do this again, perhaps next year!"

As they rehashed highlights of their cruise, another passenger standing nearby excitedly pointed off to the eastern sky. This broke Goff's concentration and drew his attention to strange lights moving high in the distant sky. Distracted by his lady friend, he dismissed them as bright stars or an airplane flying at high altitude. He quickly changed his mind when a beam of light shot straight down to the ocean's surface from the point high above.

He was curious now, watching intently as a tiny object clung to the beam, seemingly riding it down. The object dropped at a blurring rate and appeared to finish its descent, crashing into the ocean. At least that's what he thought. It was not like any crash he would have imagined. No one heard a sound. It wasn't a catastrophic event; there were no signs of an explosion when it disappeared, presumably making contact with the water.

Word quickly spread throughout the ship attracting more people to gather at the railing to see what had just happened. Passengers listened intently to witnesses' descriptions of the strange event. Many were afraid and confused. Even so, they listened to the bizarre accounts related by those who saw it.

An announcement from the bridge confirmed what the gathering passengers had seen. The captain came on the intercom and declared that the *Mist of the Atlantic* was going on high alert and would approach the crash site to search for survivors. A request for medical personnel to report to the main dining room was made to prepare for the arrival of any survivors. It was clear to everyone that the party was over.

A passenger close to Goff said to a man standing nearby, "Dr. Stack, did you hear that announcement? They need you in the ballroom."

Not seeming very happy, the man responded. "Yes, I heard."

Slightly annoyed, the doctor turned and walked away.

Powering toward the crash site, more mysterious lights appeared in the distance.

"It must be another ship," proclaimed one of the passengers. "It's heading this way!"

As the lights closed in on the *Mist of the Atlantic*, it was clear that they were not from another ship. There was nothing on the surface. To everyone's dismay, the lights were on a collision course. The passengers braced for impact.

Looking in astonishment, the lights were moving toward the *Mist of the Atlantic* below the ocean surface! As they came closer, the submerged lights formed a series of dots in a circular pattern, hundreds of feet around. To the horror of the spectators, the lights were about to pass directly under the ship.

As water was displaced by the object beneath them, it left a wake, lifting the cruise ship, causing it to violently surge up and slam down, leaving passengers holding on for their lives. After passing under the ship, the lights continued east, toward the US Mainland.

After the lights traveled under the *Mist of the Atlantic*, the cruise ship entered the suspected crash site. Floodlights scanned the water for debris, but none was detected. It became very clear to Captain Stephen Larsson that this was no crash site. This was something entirely different. Whatever came down the beam was moving underwater toward the continental United States.

"What kind of vessel is this?" Larsson, speaking to his first officer in Swedish. "Call the Coast Guard and tell them that we made contact with some kind of undersea vessel... Oh, and, Tommy, don't be too specific if you know what I mean. Just tell them we spotted something unusual under the water heading toward the coast. I would be afraid to tell them anything more."

As First Officer Lars Thomason reached the radio room, another beam of light plunged down to the ocean. To his horror, the *Mist of the Atlantic* was within the perimeter of the beam. Looking up at the night sky, he saw something sliding down the beam, growing in size.

It was coming fast. Approaching at high speed, the waters of the ocean churned and parted below the cruise ship opening a cavernous hole. It was as if Moses was parting the Red Sea in the middle of the Atlantic Ocean.

The *Mist of the Atlantic* momentarily lurched and then dropped like a stone into the hole. Passengers screamed as the unknown object followed the cruise ship into the breech. As the object dropped below the surface, water returned filling in the hole, leaving the ocean surface empty.

*****

City by the Sea

On the south coast of New England, Aquidneck Island rises out of Narragansett Bay. As part of the State of Rhode Island, it is recognized as a popular vacation destination. Three long bridges connect it to the mainland. With a number of smaller islands scattered around the bay, Aquidneck Island stands out as the largest.

The island's history extends back to the earliest European settlements in North America. In early 1600, Aquidneck Island was a hunting ground and summer residence for the Wampanoag Indian tribe. The translation of the word *Aquidneck* comes from the Algonquian language, in English meaning, "at the island of peace."

Europeans, including Roger Williams, the founder of Providence and Ann Hutchinson, a historic excommunicated religious leader from Boston, secured the island for settlement in 1638. This first settlement in the northern part of the island was named Pocasset. Like the rest of the state of Rhode Island, it was settled based on religious freedom. Other settlers followed, forming communities that still exist today.

THE TUNNELS OF EARTH

Roughly forty-four square miles in size, the island is wedged in on the south east quadrant of the state. It borders the open Atlantic Ocean to the south. The island covers an area about twice the size of the island of Manhattan in New York.

Modern Aquidneck Island contains three towns, all possessing their own unique characteristics. The city of Newport is the focal point of the island and is located in the southeast corner. It was founded by a breakaway group from Pocasset, including William Coddington and Nicolas Easton. They separated from Hutchinson's settlement and moved their group south. Over the centuries, Newport grew to become a bustling community with a considerable year-round population.

In the nineteenth century and early twentieth century, it was a getaway for the nation's rich industrialists. Mansions and massive summer cottages were built by these millionaires of the time, and they remain to this day as monuments to their incredible wealth.

At present, Newport is one of New England's most popular tourist spots. Well-known as a playground for the rich and famous, it serves as an important recreation center for the yachting community and has maintained an outstanding yachting reputation throughout the world.

A summer destination, Newport has beautiful Atlantic Ocean beaches. It also serves as the home to the International Tennis Hall of Fame. A bustling community, it has streets lined with hotels, shops, and restaurants.

Middletown is the central island community that wraps around Newport to the north and east. It houses a large middle-class bedroom community. It also has ocean beaches that rival most other beaches in New England. As historic Newport's neighbor, Middletown has the islands commercial area. Military and defense contractors maintain a visible presence making their homes in Middletown.

The northern most community on the tip of Aquidneck Island is Portsmouth. Formally known as Pocasset, this bedroom community is the largest of the three towns. It has two bridges extending north and east that offer access to the region's important cities, Fall River Massachusetts and Providence, the capital of Rhode Island.

*****

Day of Smoke

It was late summer; Labor Day had come and gone. It was a quiet afternoon with diehard beachgoers, unwilling to let go of summer, packing up for the day.

With his beach chair and his newspaper under his arm, a forty-nine-year-old vacationing office equipment salesman, Morris Wellman, trudged slowly through the sand. He was returning to his car in the parking lot at Easton's beach. He was an avid sun worshipper that tried to squeeze in as much beach time as possible. He hated to see summer end.

Whenever possible, he would find a nice spot on the beach, set up his chair, read his newspaper, and enjoy the beauty of nature. No one took greater pride in their deep bronze tan. It wasn't a Florida tan, but he worked hard to achieve it then maintain it through the summer.

Reaching the parking lot, Wellman heard a strange whistling sound overhead. Being naturally curious, he turned to see what it was. He was surprised by the sound, coming in from the open ocean. He thought it strange because there were no boats or ships in sight offshore.

Before he saw what it was, he thought, *It must be someone using a drone over the beach*. He was mistaken. As he watched, a gleaming silver projectile dropped out of the sky, crashing onto the beach with a thud. It was two hundred feet away, closer to the sea.

Some people panicked and ran away, while others inquisitively looked on. Like Wellman, they had no understanding of what just happened.

This strange object that created such a disturbance was now partially buried in beach sand. Everyone thought the excitement was over, but after a moment, the projectile gave off a puff of white smoke. Wellman was sure that he was witnessing a drone crashed, catching fire on the beach. He wasn't alarmed but thought it was strange that the smoke was pure white.

Calmly, he removed his cell phone from his bathing suit pocket and dialed 911. When the operator answered, he gave the dispatcher a description of what he was witnessing. He received an acknowledgment that there was a problem because fifteen other beachgoers had also made the same call. She said that the Newport Fire Department was en route.

Still fixed in a position where he could see, Wellman heard the sirens in the distance. The big red fire truck drove into the beach parking lot. Ladder One pulled up to the edge of the beach.

A young fireman jumped down off the truck to drop the chain across the beach access. In no apparent rush, the truck entered the beach and drove down the firm sand to the alleged fire. As they closed in on the smoke, many curious questions were raised among the firemen about this unusual fire.

The truck stopped within fifty feet of the fire, and the fully equipped four-man crew jumped down to investigate. They could see the billowing smoke but saw no indication of flames. Captain William Burke arrived shortly after, in his big Ford Expedition. He drove down the beach and stopped adjacent to the truck, close to the scene where the smoke rose into the late afternoon sky.

Curiosity seekers were gathering, lining the short barriers at the edge of the parking lot, looking down the beach. Some curious bystanders climbed over the barrier and began to walk down toward the smoke.

Arriving police dashed in to hold back the gathering onlookers. To prevent a group of gawkers from moving closer to the smoke, one officer blew his whistle, stopping them in their tracks. It didn't help the situation that it was past five o'clock at the local drinking establishments, giving the scene a carnival atmosphere with the bystanders expressing themselves loudly.

At dusk, people at the scene saw the red lights flashing in the mist and the firemen milling around the smoke. The captain approached the site where the fire crew was discussing how to deal with this unusual cloud of smoke.

One fireman, walking around the billowing smoke, was struck by a small puff that flew out at him. He felt a sting on his arm and let out a yelp. The rest of the crew thought this was funny and laughed as he shook it off.

When he examined his arm closely, he noticed redness and blisters in that spot. Reporting this to the others, he revealed that the smoke was caustic. Everyone took a step back.

Chief Randy Doyle was the next firefighter on the scene. A decorated forty-year member of the fire department, he had seen just about every situation dealing with fire, or so he thought. He looked at the scene and scratched his head.

Wellman, still hanging around in the parking lot, described what he witnessed to one of the police officers. The officer dutifully jotted down every detail in his little notebook. "It was a cylinder about four feet long." Wellman said. "I would say that it was much like a scuba tank rounded on both ends."

He then related that after a few seconds, smoke was generated from this large capsule. "Once that started, all of the projectile details were obscured."

Taking command of the situation, Chief Doyle said, "Guys, get the hose over here and knock down this fire."

The crew prepared the hose as he and the captain walked around the smoke looking for flames. After closer examination, he found that whatever was causing the smoke was not from fire. They also observed that the smoke was slowly extending outward, burning the sand. It was growing in size, extending away from the capsule!

Doyle thought, *What's the fuel source?*

The crew, ready and in position, pointed the hose toward the base of the smoke. The lead fireman working the nozzle was ready to douse the plume. When he pulled back the lever, the water streamed out, hitting the smoke at its base. This caused particles to jump in every direction.

The device was partially exposed to the firemen but was quickly covered up again. The particles that splashed away from the device grew into new smaller plumes growing separate from the main. In the pressurized flow of water, the main column of smoke curled around the stream from the hose and continued skyward.

The chief waved his arms and shouted, "Stop! It's only making matters worse." The main plume was unaffected, and eight new baby plumes were rising in close proximity to the original.

Doyle scratched his head again and said, "Get out the shovels."

The crew proceeded to retrieve shovels from the truck and again stood waiting for directions. The chief walked around looking for a suitable plume to smother, deciding on a smallish one on the right side of the main plume.

Doyle pointing at the selected plume said, "Okay, boys, cover this over with sand and see what happens."

A senior fireman, standing by the truck, gestured to the rookie next to him to follow the chief's orders. Obediently, he approached the smoke and scooped up a shovel full of sand and threw it on the plume. The reaction was like oil hitting water. The smoke dispersed out in a series of new separate plumes.

Things were getting complicated. There was one plume of smoke when they arrived, now there were eighteen, including the large mother plume with eight small and nine tiny but growing plumes. The firemen backed away again.

"Captain Burke," Doyle said, "call the airport and get the runway fire equipment over here. We need the foam truck."

The call went to the airport fire house, and after a short while, the truck arrived with the foam equipment. The driver looked down the beach and saw what he thought was a dozen bonfires. One seemed to be forty feet wide and burning out of control. Smaller fires were all around it. He thought to himself, *This must be a downed aircraft leaking volatile jet fuel, thus causing the intense smoke.*

Fireman Brad Jones got out of the foam truck, proceeded to put on his protective suit, and uncoiled the thick hose. The foam used by this truck was specialized to smother highly combustible aircraft fuel fires.

Before he began foaming the fire, he spoke to the chief, learning that this was not an aircraft or a boat or anything like that. It was an unknown projectile from the sea, fueled by an unknown propellant.

The chief said, "We tried the standard methods to extinguish the fire, but nothing worked."

Jones nodded and said, "I'll give it a shot, Chief."

He approached the smoke and began hosing the foam over a small three-foot-wide plume. The foam covered the smoke completely. Everyone thought that this was going to do it, but within seconds, the foam jiggled and bubbled, followed by the smoke bursting through, rising skyward again. This method, like all the previous methods, failed.

Clearly frustrated, the chief grabbed one of the shovels. The fireman casually leaning on it nearly fell over when the chief ripped it out of his hands. Wielding it around, Doyle walked over to the smallest plumes.

Without hesitation, he scooped the sand deep below the smoke and lifted it up into the shovel. Doyle walked carefully toward the water line, carrying the smoke. His head bobbed left and right, attempting to avoid contact with the fumes. Unfortunately for him, a quick gust of wind blew a burst of smoke squarely into his face.

Crying out in pain, he continued to carry the smoke toward the low surf. Upon reaching water's edge, he dropped the smoke into a small wave. In agony, he collapsed to his knees in the ankle-deep water. The sea lapped up on his body as he gasped for air. The fire company rushed to his aid, seeing his face burned, bright red, and covered with blisters.

A rescue squad that arrived just minutes earlier provided crucial first aid, treating him for burns and placing an oxygen mask over his mouth and nose. While the paramedics cared for the chief, Jones turned and walked back to the spot where the chief removed smoke from the beach. That spot was still billowing upward as if nothing had happened. Then he walked over to the spot where Doyle dropped the contents of the shovel in the water. There he noticed the small pile of sand on the bottom, fizzing up under the surface. He picked up the shovel from the surf, inspecting the part that was in contact with the smoke. He saw that it was scored.

As the police formed a tight line excluding the public from the scene, another smoke missile struck the beach five hundred yards to the west. With the landing of the second projectile, Captain Burke determined that they were dealing with a new kind of threat.

The captain said, "We need help!"

*****

Tiger Shark

At the Castle Hill Coast Guard Station, the *USCGC Tiger Shark*, a Marine Protector-class Coast Guard cutter, was immediately called out to investigate the source of the projectiles coming from offshore. Located at Castle Hill, it was very close to the action. The Coast Guard station was in a small cove just around the bend on the western shore on the East Passage of Narragansett Bay. It lay four miles southeast of the first two strikes.

When the call came in, the cutter was off the dock and powering out of the sheltered cove. Once it cleared the cove, the Coast Guard cutter turned south into the open Atlantic. The *Tiger Shark*, an eighty-four-foot coastal patrol boat with twin diesel engines, turned east southeast to investigate the source of the incoming smoke missiles.

The *Tiger Shark* would not be alone on this mission. A Jay Hawk-class helicopter was coming out of Cape Cod, and another cutter, the *USCGC Monomoy*, a 110-foot Island-class Coast Guard ship, was on the same heading out of Woods Hole, Massachusetts.

It was 2000 hours. Darkness would soon cloak the ocean south of the mainland. After dusk, the only lights the officer of the deck Ensign Ron Norwood could see were the tiny lights on the western shore of Martha's Vineyard, an island seventeen miles south of Massachusetts. He didn't know that that island, too, was in the same situation as Aquidneck Island. The cutter continued into the night under a peaceful night sky.

Cruising southeast with resolve, the *Tiger Shark*'s attempt to locate the source of the smoke missiles had failed. The cutter was moving into the area known as Cox Ledge, twenty-three miles south of Aquidneck Island. Cox Ledge, a favorite fishing ground, is in the Atlantic Ocean between Block Island RI and Martha's Vineyard.

Maintaining course to intercept the smoke, smoke projectile contrails were visible high overhead in the sky. Wispy contrails could be seen in the moonlight accompanied by a whooshing sound streaking through the clear night sky. On radar, monitoring the missiles origination was clearly a problem.

"Sir, we can't get a clear picture of what's ahead," the radar officer stated. "The radar is being jammed. If we continue on this course, we will be moving blind."

The captain said, "Stay on course. We need to find out who is doing this."

Powering late into the night, it was hours until sunup while on the radar, there was a large mysterious splotch covering the screen, thirty miles east to west by twenty miles north to south, and the *Tiger Shark* was now entering it.

Looking through binoculars, the crew scoured the sea for any sign of a vessel.

Patrolling the splotch, one guardsman spotted a dark shadow just on the horizon. He called out, "Contact on the horizon, sir! It looks like an island."

Calling the crew's attention to what he spotted in the distance, it was big, and like a land mass, it was darker than the ocean surface at night. It couldn't be land; there was no land for thousands of miles on this course. Whatever it was, it was partially below the horizon out of view.

The Coast Guard cutter's present position was now fifty miles southeast of Block Island in the open ocean. Another twenty miles they would be at Block Canyon, where the sea floor dramatically drops off to over six thousand feet.

The *Tiger Shark* slowed but maintained its course toward the dark oasis on the horizon. Crew members passed the binoculars around trying to explain what they were looking at. It was still too dark to see it clearly.

As dawn approached, the dark shape was taking form. The object transformed into what appeared to be a low vessel floating on the surface of the ocean. It was of unknown origin. Other than that, it was the biggest ship they had ever seen.

Below deck, the crew was pouring over ship identification charts. It wasn't Russian, and it wasn't Chinese. Nothing came close to matching the description of what they were looking at. As the sun rose in the sky, light now reflected off this strange vessel.

After studying the charts, it became clear to the crew that they were not looking at a catalogued ship. It was also clear in their minds what they were really looking at. However, no one was willing to say it out loud. No one spoke about what they were all thinking. They were thinking that they were looking at something from beyond this world.

Shortly after identifying something that was not a ship, the crew realized that this unknown vessel wasn't floating on the ocean at all. Not only was it not floating on the sea, it was not in contact with the water. It was floating in the sky.

As the *Tiger Shark* moved closer, the unidentified object grew larger, drifting higher in the sky. From their position down range, the crew could see its enormity. It was difficult to gauge just how large it was because it was still miles away. It was floating in the sky, farther down range than originally thought. Judging from their line of sight, with the horizon around five miles away, that would place this bogey at least three to five miles beyond that.

As the *Tiger Shark* approached, the unidentified ship seemed to ascend skyward. In reality, it remained perfectly still, hovering high over the ocean. Details started to appear.

The craft was saucer-like, slightly convex on the bottom with a similar shape on top. The difference was on the top, there was a narrowing conical rise in the center. It was capped with a slightly rounded peak. It was jet black in.

At the outer edge of the vessel, there were low arches that stretched around its entire circumference. The thin band of arches formed a pattern, circumventing its midriff. It was impossible to tell what the composition of the ship was, but it looked to be made of a flat black metallic material.

On the bridge of the *Tiger Shark*, the captain, Lt. Commander Mel Jackson, was grilling his crew for more and more information. He knew the radar was acting screwy, so he called the radio operator for a status report.

"Radio's out, Captain, can't raise anyone."

"Keep trying and let me know if anything changes."

Turning to the helmsman, Jackson ordered, "All ahead, slow."

His thoughts raced. There was no way that this hovering craft could not have noticed their arrival on the scene. He had deep concern about putting his vessel and crew in harm's way.

Jackson said to another crewman, "Are we getting this on video?"

"Yes, sir, ever since first light."

"Good, keep rolling. We'll send it to command when the interference clears."

After thinking about the situation for a moment, he revised his plan.

The captain said to his executive officer Russ Franks, "Has the Monomoy come on station yet?"

Lt. Franks replied, "Yes, sir, we have a visual of it about four miles northeast of us. We can't raise them on the radio, too much static."

The captain said, "Send a small boat across to the Monomoy. Request that they move back out of the interference zone so we can relay our communications through them to shore. Send our position and the position of the bogey. Send all the video as well. We need to stay in communication with the mainland starting now. Tell them that the *Tiger Shark* will stay inside the static zone. We will shuttle the small boat back and forth as long as we can."

Bearing down on the unknown craft, new features appeared. Of those new features, within the arches around the body of the ship was a series of ports. While looking through his binoculars, Jackson examined one of the ports when a projectile shot out. After the launch, the band around the craft slowly rotated to the next opening.

Another missile fired from the newly aligned tube. The band rotated again, readying the next door to launch. Putting the time between missiles on the stopwatch revealed that the missiles fired at the rate of about two per minute. Soon that number would increase.

*****

Day 2

The fire department remained on the beach all night, unable to stop the spread of the smoke. First, they built a fire break around it, then a high sand berm, but nothing impeded the expansion of the smoke. The original area of smoke expanded dramatically, covering an additional 40 percent of Easton's beach, from the waterline up to the pavilion stairs.

Down the beach where the second smoke projectile struck, the area could not be contained. Over the course of the preceding night and morning, numerous smoke projectiles flew overhead, landing around southern Newport.

Police officers reported from the beaches in southern Middletown that smoke started to impact there too. At the Newport Fire Headquarters, acting chief Rick Gerrard received endless phone calls reporting new hits throughout the area. More aggravating to Gerrard were inquiries from state and federal agencies.

Chief Doyle was at Newport Hospital in guarded condition with chemical burns on his face, throat, and bronchial tubes. Fortunately, his lungs were clear, making the prognosis good for a complete recovery.

Gerrard was waiting to hear from a bureaucrat in Washington, DC, about what kind of assistance was becoming available to help with this unusual situation. He also wanted to hear from the Coast Guard regarding the origin of the smoke projectiles. On top of that, the governor's office was calling every hour for information to forward to Washington.

Gerrard thought to himself, *I want to be chief, but not under these circumstances.*

Ed Capello, Newport's police chief, barged into the room, moving to the table where Gerrard stood. He shifted things out of his way and rolled out a large city map. There were black Sharpie marks on all the places on the map where smoke had impacted.

It was curious because everywhere it landed was away from populated areas. Beaches, vacant lots, parks, ball fields, and parking lots were all marked in black. All the strikes so far were only detected in open areas in the south of Aquidneck Island.

To this point, there were no reports of any civilians being harmed. The only known casualty was the fire chief. Gerrard and Capello determined that it was important to keep it that way, so they agreed that people living near the beaches were to be evacuated.

Shifting winds off the ocean were starting to send the smoke to unexpected places. The toxic fumes damaged everything that it touched. Buildings near the impact sights showed damage after making contact with the blowing white smoke. Structures with vinyl siding were literally melting. Brick and concrete showed signs of discoloration but suffered no structural damage yet. Mortar was becoming brittle.

Because of the volatile nature of the smoke, a joint public safety declaration was issued from the mayor and public safety officials. It said, "Because of the possible danger to public safety, evacuation is the only answer we have for the time being."

*****

Goat Island

Coast Guard Command moved into the Coddington Hotel on Goat Island across scenic Newport Harbor. On short notice, their whole operation was abandoned at Castle Hill, forcing them to join other state and municipal agencies already in position. This was the perfect location because of its proximity to the action.

This tiny island lays across from the boating and retail center of downtown Newport. Its marina enclosed the west side of Newport harbor. Super yachts adorned its docks but on a slightly smaller scale. With the old fort, Fort Adams on the southern side of the harbor combined with Goat Island and downtown Newport, a spectacular harbor is formed. Being a large protected harbor, it enjoys notoriety all over the yachting world.

Across the water from Goat Island, Thames Street in downtown Newport runs along the coastline on that side of the harbor. A major summer shopping and vacation center, this section of town contains an abundance of hotels, shops, and restaurants to draw seasonal crowds by the thousands.

Goat Island, too, is a popular destination. It is connected to Newport by a short four-hundred-yard causeway, giving the main island access to the attractions on the smaller one. Located on Goat Island sits the Coddington Hotel, residential condominiums, and several marinas. On the west side of Goat Island, there is access to the open bay. No docks or public access exists there, but the west side of the island is available for a quick response or a quick escape.

Near the Newport Bridge on Aquidneck Island resides the Newport Naval base. One of its features is the prestigious Naval War College, now on full alert. During the Nixon Administration, funding cuts diminished the importance of the Newport Naval Base in the overall scheme of national defense. At present, no war ships were tied up to its underutilized docks.

Across the bay in North Kingstown sits another underutilized naval facility, Quonset Point Naval Air Station. When the need for this base no longer existed, Quonset transformed into the home of the Rhode Island's Air National Guard. The guard maintained the airport with a number of aircraft and helicopters. Near where the main gate used to be of this former navy installation was the home of the famous Fighting Seabees.

The prestigious Seabees were famous for their exploits in combat construction during World War II. When the Seabees left the region, in its place grew an industrial park and shopping plaza.

As a memorial to this once prominent feature at Quonset Point was the Seabee Museum.

Because the smoke attacks on Newport were considered an attack on the sovereignty of the United States, units from the naval base were dispatched to Goat Island to help local authorities alleviate the growing workload.

The administration building on the Newport Naval base supported government personnel and bureaucrats that were arriving every hour. They were all descending on the city by the sea. These agencies included the Environmental Protection Agency, Homeland Security, Department of Defense, Department of the Interior, and various other more secretive US government departments.

In the chaos, all the agencies demanded special consideration. National officials put in their requests for offices and administrative support. Local authorities were spread thin trying to make things work.

*****

Retaliation

The first message finally arrived at the command center from the Tiger Shark. If they weren't confused by what the message Captain Jackson sent, they were shocked by the video. The room was quiet as the video revealed the earliest dramatic shots of the strange flying craft. Much to the dismay of the analysts, the vivid scenes showing the source of the smoke ended abruptly. The reason given why it ended was to allow the *Tiger Shark* to send something quickly ashore in case they came under attack.

As part of the message, Captain Jackson said, "We cannot identify this ship. We would appreciate any guidance going forward."

Navy Admiral Ronald "Butch" Reynolds, the ranking officer, was on the scene from the northeast command. In the room, there was an urgency that swift action needed to be taken. Unfortunately, the northeast region of the United States was no longer an area of frequent naval activity. With most of the base closures, Newport and other bases nearby cut by government were undermanned and underequipped.

Admiral Reynolds got on the phone to locate any single ships scattered around the New York, New England area. Finding a number of ships in the Atlantic Fleet, he had little luck finding many in range.

There were, however, a few individual ships potentially in range of the target. One destroyer, leaving Boston, preparing to go to sea on a shakedown cruise, was rerouted to the scene south of Martha's Vineyard. Another destroyer traveling west in Long Island Sound had to reverse course for a rendezvous with the *Tiger Shark* and the other Coast Guard vessel.

The conflagration of man and the unknown was about to take place off the coast of New England. On the charts it was south of Cox Ledge in Block Island Sound.

*****

The Offensive

It was early morning on the third day when the crew of the *Tiger Shark* watched as two naval destroyers entered the scene from the west. Captain Jackson thought that his ship's position at the moment was precarious at best. The Coast Guard cutter was drifting under the hovering craft. Anticipation on the bridge of the Coast Guard cutter was high as the navy moved in for a fight.

It was a short encounter. Arriving on station the naval ships wasted no time attacking the intruder. Moving at flank speed, the destroyers fired RIM-174 ERAM missiles at the bogey. The assault lasted twenty minutes.

Spotters on the *Tiger Shark* craned their necks to see impacts on the UFO high above. They noted the blast fragment warheads had no effect on the craft. As a matter of fact, they couldn't determine if there were any hits on the structure at all.

It became apparent that these destroyers were not up for the fight. To make matters worse, each destroyer was carrying limited ordinance when called in for the assault. Their reduced capabilities prevented them from maintaining any kind of sustained attack.

With their missiles gone and conventional ordinance having no effect on the strange craft, the hapless destroyers were sitting ducks and clearly in range of their target. They waited for retaliation, but none came.

It was like a bear ravaging a beehive for honey and ignoring any attempts by the bees to defend it. The *Tiger Shark* played no role in the attack and continued to maintain a low profile in the waters below the craft. Captain Jackson hoped they wouldn't be held responsible by the ship above them for the failed destroyer attack.

The smoke projectiles continued without pause as four Air Force F-22 Raptors approached for the next round. Once again, the prey didn't attempt to defend itself. The air attack commenced and should have been devastating, but like the destroyer assault, it fizzled out without noticeable effect.

Pilots found that they developed control problems, closing on the target. The closer the Raptors got, the stronger the interference in their electronics was detected. This caused engines to sputter and their maneuvering capacity to fail. The anomaly would remain consistent until the jets reversed direction and moved away from their target.

When the aircraft recovered, they circled around for a renewed attack, but realizing that they couldn't get close, they fired from a greater distance. Still within striking range, the incoming AIM-120 AMRAAM Slammer missiles mysteriously flamed out. They failed to impact the craft, dropping into the turbulent sea. The round was over.

The *Tiger Shark* stood fast on station. It continued to relay information by small boat to the Coast Guard cutter standing by outside the static zone. Their diligence continued to play an important role in the flow of information back to headquarters.

*****

Day 4

The next morning brought new uninterrupted missile strikes on the southern end of Aquidneck Island. Historic Ocean Road was now open only to official vehicles. Normal traffic was restricted. Businesses, homes, and multimillion-dollar mansions were being evacuated.

Located a very short distance from Easton Beach, Salve Regina University was evacuating. No canisters struck the campus, but for student safety, administration was sending them home and closing down the college. Strikes occurred at the Newport Country Club, Brenton Point Park, and other large areas west of Easton's beach. Even the abandoned Coast Guard Station at Castle Hill had a strike land within a hundred feet.

A classified message came from the Pentagon to the command center at Quonset clarifying the worldwide situation. After reviewing satellite feeds and communicating with intelligence agencies around the world, the islands east of Newport were also under smoke attack. That report included Martha's Vineyard and the Elizabeth Islands including Cuttyhunk, Nashawena, Pasque, and Naushon Islands. For some unknown reason, Nantucket had been spared from the siege.

Government officials felt some relief knowing that it was a localized event in this small region tucked in the southeast corner of New England. They only had to focus on this one area. The attention of the government, military, and soon the world would be watching the events taking place on this small patch of earth's surface.

At Quonset Point Naval Air Station, Scientists began to arrive to analyze the toxic smoke. No conventional storage worked to encase the smoke so special containers, obtained from the nuclear energy commission had to be brought in by aircraft. They were being flown in from Amarillo Texas.

*****

The steady stream of smoke projectiles from the sea continued to land in open spaces around Newport and Middletown. The bombardment was methodical. Existing columns of smoke on the ground were growing and expanding, linking up with other plumes. Even populated areas were now on the verge of being engulfed in the growing number of smoke plumes.

The evacuation was slow and agonizing. People begrudgingly left their homes, bringing what they could carry. No one seemed panicked, but the anxiety of being forced out of their houses made them angry.

Citizens thinking that the smoke was too far away didn't understand why they had to leave and shelter out of town, off island. Some had time to go back to their homes two or three times to collect personal belongings. They didn't comprehend the danger represented by the smoke.

As days passed, all that changed. The locals were abruptly prevented from returning to their homes by roadblocks, flashing red lights, and armed military personnel.

The smoke was now congealing into a solid mass across Newport and Middletown. Open areas around the south of the island were consumed. The falling smoke projectiles increased and crashed to the earth in larger numbers. What started out as a single strike with long intervals between projectiles transformed to many landing in a shorter period of time. Only now did the evacuation take on a greater urgency.

*****

Day 5

Southern Aquidneck Island was becoming impassable. Smoke closed down the clearings and engulfed everything nearby. It was impossible to safely negotiate any neighborhood as smoke encroached them.

In a few cases, residents decided to barricade themselves in their homes. These hopeful people believed they could somehow wait out the crisis. This, however, was not an event that would end well for those who stayed.

There was no waiting out the smoke; it was all consuming. No living thing could survive in its toxic environment. The casualty list started to grow with locals missing and presumed dead. In almost every case, their homes became their tombs.

*****

Day 7

The entire city of Newport was shrouded under cover of thick white smoke. The projectiles that increased on the third day were now in what seemed to be a systematic pattern of coverage, moving up the island. Evacuation had become more frantic, while the three bridges, the Mount Hope Bridge, the Sakonnet River Bridge, and the Pell/Newport Bridge, became clogged with cars and pedestrians trying to escape.

Time was running out to use the southernmost bridge, the Newport Bridge. That two-mile span took evacuees across the east passage of Narragansett Bay to a neighboring island, Conanicut Island. Once across that island, evacuees would travel on Route 138 to the Jamestown Bridge. Traveling another mile and a half over the west passage of the bay, they would finally reach the mainland.

The other bridges on Aquidneck Island weren't under the same amount of traffic pressure. They were both at the northern tip of the island away from the smoke. The Mount Hope Bridge went north off the island to Bristol heading toward Providence. The Sakonnet River Bridge carried traffic east toward Fall River.

In the northern part of the island, Portsmouth braced for the smoke to arrive. It was creeping north, leaving Newport and parts of Middletown fully involved. Citizens of Portsmouth with forethought gathered their belongings and left the island early. However, there were still many people that hesitated and found themselves caught in the long bottleneck on the bridges when they ultimately decided to leave.

Day 9

The last of the population of Newport that were going to leave were now off the island. The only people left close to the problem were those in their official capacity on Goat Island. Portsmouth was now included in the siege of smoke.

Animals, too, were retreating. Deer, coyotes, and other small animals were seen all over the north end of Portsmouth. Normally shy around humans, it was not apparent when wild deer crossed the Mount Hope Bridge side by side with fleeing automobiles and pedestrians.

When there were no visible features of Newport and Middletown left to see, Goat Island was still there. All the different local and federal agencies were packed into the Coddington Hotel. Smoke was up to the edge of the causeway on the Newport side, but it stopped there. No smoke missiles hit Goat Island in the first eight days, and with their perceived accuracy, it seemed that it would be spared.

******

The Navy was gone. Command closed the Newport Naval Base and moved across the bay to the now fully operational Quonset Point Naval Air station. The Coast Guard also moved across the bay to Point Judith lighthouse with supporting units up the bay in Providence and on Block Island. Patrol Boats rotated in to Point Judith so they could keep an eye on the waters around Aquidneck Island.

*****

End of Watch

It was the end of a long arduous cruise for the crew of the *Tiger Shark*. They had been on station for two weeks. The things that they observed were far from ordinary. *Tiger Shark* left Castle Hill a couple of weeks earlier but now had no port to return to. Its home base was under a veil of smoke, smoke issued by the vessel that hovered high above their heads. It was an extraordinary ship, uncaring about why they were there or what they did.

During their time on station, the crew watched as the flying craft increased the output of smoke projectiles, unafraid of anything the military had to throw at them. They watched as two naval destroyers sent missiles at the UFO from outside the static area and watched as the missile engines failed, falling harmlessly into the sea. They watched when conventional artillery shells bounced off its exterior to no effect.

The crew of the *Tiger Shark* witnessed fighter jets enter the area and barely make it out under their own power. Jet engines sputtered and nearly flamed out when they got close to the bogey. Missiles from the fighters could not lock on to their target and fell innocuously into the sea.

Finally, they observed the UFO moved at incredible speed jumping from place to place to escape facing any further attacks but still carrying out its mission of delivering smoke to Aquidneck Island.

*****

Reconnaissance

The FPI Cougar entered the restricted area from the north, crossing the empty Mount Hope Bridge. It moved down the main road, south on Route 114 along the western side of the island. Stone and the four other National Guardsmen in the vehicle were making observations out of the windows and shooting video of the scenes around them.

After several minutes on Route 114, they reached Memorial Drive. There they did a drive through the Portsmouth High School parking lot. School was out.

Under normal circumstances, classes would be in fall semester with the seniors looking forward to their final year of high school. No one had been there for two weeks. Ever since the first smoke bomb landed in Portsmouth, classes were suspended.

The armored car drove out of the school driveway and took a left continuing down Route 114. Cruising residential areas, they observed everything looked normal. The only thing missing was people.

Grass in the yards had grown long, which was uncharacteristic for this area. The normally manicured lawns were something of the past. Other than the lawns, the neighborhoods looked undisturbed. Back on Route 114, they drove into other neighborhoods where some homeowners took the time to board up their windows, securing their properties.

Stone thought of the irony, the pride that the residents took in their homes. This carefully maintained neighborhood, as well as all the surrounding neighborhoods, will be gone in a matter of days.

Continuing down Route 114, they took a right onto Stringham Road leading down to the bay and the Melville Boat Basin. Entering the boat yard, the Cougar drove between the buildings and sheds, admiring the expensive yachts, winterized and stored on their stands. They had seen there last summer yachting season.

Over the years, twelve-meter yachts of America's Cup fame were maintained and stored here. That was back in the glory days of the competition when it was held every four years in the Atlantic Ocean just off the Coast of Newport.

Those were the glory days when the US was invincible, never losing the cup. Since then however, the Cup had been won and lost by other competitive sailing countries around the world, as well as returning to the possession of the United States. Neither the race nor the cup ever returned to Newport. The twelve-meter yachts went down in history as well, replaced by a much faster high-tech racing catamaran.

THE TUNNELS OF EARTH

Completing their spin around the deserted marina, the Cougar turned back north to finish its patrol. It was still reasonably clear around the vehicle for hundreds of yards in some places and hundreds of feet in others. However, the smoke projectiles were unpredictable, falling randomly on the town. No one in the Cougar felt safe.

The houses, the businesses, the schools, and all the community buildings were targets. To the surprise of the crew of the armored car, a smoke projectile crashed onto a house fifty feet away, smashing through the roof. After a moment, smoke slowly drifted up and out of the hole that the missile created.

That strike on the roof hastened the decision to leave. With no radio contact, reduced visibility, and an unnerved crew, Lieutenant Paul Alves, the National Guard officer in charge, made the decision to get out of Portsmouth while there was still time.

The sergeant driving the Cougar steered off Route 114 and entered the ramp to Route 24, the highway just north of the high school. They were moving at a faster pace now. Just ahead, there was a plume of smoke on the highway directly in their path. The vehicle slowed, turning onto the median grass crossing the highway to the other side to stay clear of it.

Wump! Another smoke bomb landed where the armored vehicle had been just moments earlier. The situation was becoming critical, with no one in the Cougar feeling confident that the toxic agent equipment would protect them from a direct hit.

On an empty Route 24, the patrol sped toward their destination. With the Sakonnet River Bridge in sight, a soldier looking out the rear window saw a white van bearing down on them. A half mile back, it was weaving its way around the fresh smoke that had just landed. It was kicking up dust as it gained ground.

The guardsman observing this said, "Sir, there's a van back there!"

The lieutenant responded, "Stop the truck! Let's make sure they clear the bridge."

The driver reluctantly pulled the big heavy vehicle over and stopped. In that position, exposed to the sky, they waited for the van to pass and make its way over the bridge. It was only seconds, but it felt like an eternity for the van to reach them. *Wump!* More smoke fell one hundred feet to the right.

As the van closed the distance to the Cougar, two men with desperate expressions on their faces were visible through the broad front windshield. They were getting close when—*wump!*—another streak fell from the sky and landed ten feet to the left of the van. The van driver turned the wheel sharply to avoid it and swerved away, escaping the plume. Erratically the van kept advancing with tufts of smoke clinging to its side.

Racing forward, it surged by the armored vehicle, nearly sideswiping it, dropping nose first into a gully by the side of the road, where it came to a stop. The two men forced open the doors and jumped out, frantically coughing and brushing off their clothes. One of the occupants clung to a white pillowcase that was leaking cash. On closer examination, there was wrapped coins and jewelry as well.

Alves directed the guardsmen to assist the dazed men. They moved quickly to help them out of their smoldering clothes and checked for wounds. Both were burned slightly, but they were partially protected by their coats. There was no time for a thorough examination, so they were hustled into the now cramped armored vehicle. Once everyone was inside, the military vehicle dashed for the Sakonnet River Bridge and safety.

Alves said to the sergeant, "Let's swing by the Tiverton police station and drop off our new friends."

*****

Goat Island

It was amazing that Goat Island, over the short causeway from Newport, had been spared. Not being directly affected by what was happening, it became the number one strategic location in the region.

The local hotel was filled to capacity with scientists, government officials, and military personnel, all trying to analyze accumulated data. The Coddington Hotel had been off limits to civilians and unauthorized personnel since the first week of the smoke. Makeshift laboratories were springing up both in the hotel and the surrounding buildings.

To move outside of the buildings, protective suits were worn to protect individuals from the caustic environment. The suits, like the one worn by Brad Jones, the airport firefighter, was standard clothing outside. This suit, good for fighting aircraft or chemical fires, was also found to be suitable for individuals in the vicinity of the smoke. It didn't deter the caustic smoke, but it protected the individual from the fumes.

Fumes drifting across Newport Harbor were strong but not strong enough to damage the buildings or harm personnel in the protective suits. When the wind was out of the west, which was most of the time, no fumes would cross over to the island, making life a little easier for everyone.

In the hotel, the rooms on the west side away from the causeway were the most sought after. They were filled with equipment and personnel from the various investigating agencies.

Coddington manager Maurice Millius had been on sight since the beginning. He had been an employee of the company for many years. His new job was to support the incoming government guests in any way that he could. He was also there to protect the interests of the corporation, the large hotel chain that employed him.

He was directed by management to help any entity in the hotel that needed it. That meant that he would act as the liaison with the outside world. Of course, there were considerable fees involved. The Goat Island Landmark was becoming the most profitable operation in the corporation.

There were frequent turnovers of individuals and organizations that came into the Coddington. They would come in, perform experiments, and then leave. Earlier that month, a construction crew came in, built a special testing lab in a ballroom, and then left. Government and military agencies cordoned off areas where classified activities were being conducted.

Although he managed the hotel, Millius was restricted from many areas in it. The kitchen was open, operated by the US

Army. Millius had no authority there. There was no housekeeping department anymore because the Army handled the day to day operations such as housekeeping, laundry, and transportation. For the most part, he was a caretaker, there to keep an eye on things—at least things that he was allowed to see.

For the military, the hotel had become a secure government facility. Their mission was to test tools, clothing, and equipment that might be smoke resistant. Scientists tested many of their ideas to find ways to retard the smoke. Presently they weren't having very much luck. Special containers were being developed that would allow samples of smoke to be brought into the lab for testing. Some scientists were trying to enter the smoke across the causeway wearing early stage biological suits, but soon they all came running back. There was a first-rate burn center at the hotel. For now, there was no proven way to deal with this very caustic material.

*****

There was one important lifesaving factor that was discovered during all the turmoil. It was learned that the bodies of water covering areas on Aquidneck island were completely undisturbed, free of smoke. Small ponds and larger reservoirs were clear to the sky. Island Park, at the northeast corner of the island, near the Sakonnet Bridge, had acres of island land nestled in the ponds, unaffected by the smoke.

There were situations where people, surrounded by smoke, found themselves safe. They could move out, away from the shore to one of the small islands in one of several coves in Island Park. If they swam or had a boat or clung to a log, they could easily reach an island and be rescued by a patrolling helicopter.

On Spectacle Island, the largest in Island Park, a small aid station was set up and manned by courageous volunteers to help people trapped by the smoke. In the early days, it was a viable means of escape, but as time passed fewer and fewer people were rescued. The aid station remained open until no more refugees appeared.

*****

The Island of Smoke

Newport, Middletown, and Portsmouth were no longer a collection of viable communities. They were, in turn, covered by the funeral pyre of alien smoke. In a matter of weeks, it roiled up and covered the entire Island. It had reached the point that no life could survive there.

Populations around Aquidneck Island, Tiverton, and Bristol were evacuated in anticipation of the smoke spreading to those towns. It never did. It stayed nestled within the confines of the island.

There was a sweet toxic smell to the smoke that was enough to keep people away from the surrounding communities. The western shore of neighboring towns, Tiverton and Little Compton, were permanently closed to the public up to a mile inland.

The narrows of the Sakonnet River were closed with Fish Road as the boundary in the northern part of Tiverton extending down Route 77 until it reached Meetinghouse Road in Little Compton. These areas were deemed uninhabitable.

Beavertail and the southern end of Jamestown were also permanently closed. Blown by the wind, fumes kept the small village at Hull Cove empty of residents. Outside of these boundaries, neighborhoods were declared conditionally safe.

Fort Weatherall also on Conanicut Island was less than a mile from Newport across the East Passage. It was evacuated north to Hamilton Avenue and west as far as Southwest Avenue. There was never a threat to this area, but government officials deemed it necessary to keep it closed.

In other communities around Aquidneck Island, people returned to their homes in areas that were declared nonrestricted. After the shock wore off from witnessing a large island consumed in a thick layer of smoke, things returned to normal. The locals learned not to think too much about the island across the bay. Their lives were restored to a state of normalcy, as much as it could be. Residents tried to pick up where they left off.

Their lives could be compared to populations living at the base of an active volcano. They knew it was there, and they knew it was dangerous, but they tried not to let it interfere with their lives. As time passed, people returned to the surrounding towns. They became those towns at the base of the volcano. The danger was real, but it was perceived to be manageable.

Children would be born and would grow up with the smoke as a backdrop. To them, it would be a routine part of their lives. Their logic told them that they would be insulated from the danger by the bay. Besides it was an amazing sight, miles of smoky coastline drifting skyward over the waters of Narragansett Bay. It was spectacular!

*****

On an afternoon in late October, a small group of government employees were transported to the Coddington Hotel by helicopter. They were there on behalf of the federal government and were looking for rooms.

When they found the manager, Millius told them, "I'm sorry, but there aren't any rooms in the hotel available at this time. Every agency in the government has booked them up for six months."

The self-identified leader of the group flashed his NSA badge and said, "We need rooms! We're here on official business, so you are required to make room for us."

He glared and waited for Millius to reply.

"Well, let me think," Millius said. "For the time being you can take my room, and I will stay in my office."

Ed LaBrea, the chief agent, asked, "Which is larger? We need the larger space. There are four of us."

Millius said, "My office has two small rooms and a bathroom. That would be the larger room. The room where I sleep is probably the smallest accommodation in the hotel."

"Good! We'll take the office," LaBrea abruptly said. "Get what you need so we can move in."

Flustered by La Brea's attitude, Millius said, "I'll have to get some help. I have a ton of paperwork that I'll need access to."

"Leave the papers for now, I want to see them before we turn them back over to you."

Millius cried, "But I need those papers. It's all hotel business!"

LaBrea turned to a young agent and said, "Frederickson, give Mr. Millius a hand getting his personal effects. We need to be in place *now*."

Dean Frederickson was a twenty-five-year-old agent who had been with the NSA since he got out of the Army two years earlier. This was his first assignment away from Washington, DC, and he was eager to do his part.

NSA was here to oversee any research that could be useful to the federal government. Primarily they were here to help crack the code of the smoke, but anything that could be used elsewhere in the government, they would be in the right place to appropriate it.

LaBrea said to Millius, "By the way, I want a list of all of your past, present, and scheduled future tenants and their location in the hotel where we can find them."

Before Millius left with Frederickson, he said, "Some of these tenants have super-secret clearances, even I can't enter their workspaces."

LaBrea replied, "Don't worry about it. Get me the list and just get your stuff out of our rooms."

Millius was not used to being treated in such a harsh manner. He shook his head, turned, and walked to his office with Frederickson to get whatever the NSA would allow him to take.

*****

Cottage Industry

Even though Aquidneck Island was inaccessible to the public and under complete government quarantine, patrol boats had to keep personal watercrafts hundreds of yards off the coast. There was a no-fly zone over the island as well. No airplanes other than military were permitted over Narragansett Bay east of Jamestown, west of Tiverton, and south of Bristol.

No boats were allowed in the narrows between Portsmouth and Tiverton. There was a tight network of military security focused on the island twenty-four hours a day, seven days a week, three hundred and sixty-five days a year.

Despite all the security, enterprising charter boat captains continually ran the thin blockade and brought paying customers as close to the island as they could get. If they managed to get by the security boats, the passengers experienced the spectacle of smoke, up close and personal. These thrill seekers gladly put themselves in harm's way to feel the excitement of getting dangerously close to the island of smoke.

Another way of testing fate was to fly a glider over the island. The atmosphere formed a chimney fueling powerful updrafts, making conditions challenging. The updrafts allowed gliders to do loops and rolls, staying airborne for a long time.

Entrepreneurial companies created a booming cottage industry building custom gliders. The made to order gliders had longer reinforced wings. This modification was to make them stronger and more stable in the increased turbulence.

This new enterprise out of central Massachusetts challenged the Coast Guard and Air National Guard because the gliders, attached to light aircraft, would come in low from a variety of directions, making them hard to stop. It was easier to glide over the Massachusetts islands, but the real challenge was Aquidneck Island.

Once released by the plane, quite often glider pilots were shooed away before they could get the satisfaction of a perfect ride. Often, pilots were taken into custody by authorities, but if they successfully avoided detection, the thrill seekers got the ride of their life.

Other enterprising individuals ran skydiving excursions over the islands. This service, even more dangerous than gliders, offered adrenaline junkies a death-defying jump high over the islands. In the case of Aquidneck Island, if all went as planned, the jumper would leave the plane over the windward side of the island, open their parachutes, drift high across the wide island to land safely in Narragansett Bay beyond the smoke on the leeward side.

In the water, they would inflate their life vests and wait. Fast pickup boats recovered the daredevils, who then attempted to elude the Coast Guard patrol boats. It was an illegal operation, and if caught, boat captains and sky divers were subject to arrest and prosecution. The money was so good that it meant getting arrested was a small deterrent.

*****

Death by Smoke

Over the years, there was a new saying coined: "death by smoke." This in fact was due to the mounting number of deaths of thrill seekers and unlucky citizens. Occasionally, a boat would stray too close to the smoke, where it would wreak havoc on its unprepared passengers.

Death by smoke would come about under various conditions on the bay. It could be a dark night or a foggy day. Boat occupants would inhale the toxic fumes or disappear into the windswept smoke offshore. Once contact was made with the smoke, survival was improbable. Hideous burns destroyed flesh, and inhaled fumes did quick work on the frail human lungs.

Several times, groups of skydivers would miscalculate the direction of the wind. Jumping from the airplane, instead of traveling the full distance across the island, they would drift down onto it to die a horrible death, alone, never to be recovered.

Around the world, alien smoke cults sprung up. Junkets to Aquidneck Island and the outer islands were popular. Cultists would come from all over to worship what in their minds was the representation of an alien god. In some instances, they would come to join the deity. The latter came with backpacks ready to travel to another place. In human terms, some did—they traveled to their deaths. No living soul will ever know what they found.

It was one of these voyages to the alien side that took a yacht full of worshippers to the inlet at Castle Hill, the location of the former Newport Coast Guard Station. With a patrol boat in hot pursuit, the large luxury powerboat rushed into the inlet, vanishing in the smoke.

Muffled screams and coughs could be heard on the Coast Guard Cutter standing offshore. When the tide changed, the partially melted fiberglass boat drifted out of the inlet back into the bay. All passengers, eighteen people in all, were dead. Characteristic burns blackened their flesh.

*****

Breakthrough

During the early years of smoke, little advancement had been made technically. Now after eight long years of intense research, a protective suit was ready to be tested. MIT was the driving force behind the research, development, and testing of the prototype. Its qualities were the creation of a working corrosive-resistant suit. It was developed to do more than just survive in the smoke.

Many preliminary tests were performed before actual volunteers entered a specially constructed chamber on the edge of the causeway on the Newport side. To test the suit, smoke was pumped into the chamber and volunteers would enter to evaluate its protective qualities. The progress of the suit was slow in development. Over time, its ability to protect the person wearing it allowed them to function normally.

With each test, the suit improved. Finally, it was perfected to the point where no further adjustments were necessary. At long last, there was a suit made to stand up to the harsh environment on the islands hidden in smoke.

Aquidneck Island was where the testing was to be done. Because of the ability to easily test them at the Goat Island facility, it was used as the step-off point. Brave local Army National Guard units were to be the first to go in.

First and foremost, the early missions were to find out what was concealed under the deadly white curtain. Weapon durability tests were also scheduled on the list of things to do. Rifles would be carried, secured in special bulky anticorrosive sacks.

No visibility was possible in the smoke; it was too concentrated. Vision would be achieved through a combination of computerized technologies. An array of devices were located on a heads-up display in the wearer's faceplate. These devices were built into the suit with a wide variety of detection capabilities. Embedded spectrographic technologies in the heavy oversized helmets included infrared, radar, heat, and ultraviolet sensors. When the faceplate was in the down position, the wearer could see color-filled outlines of fellow soldiers and anything that might be hidden in the terrain. In the smoke or out, there was no actual seeing when the visor was down. The time for the field test had arrived.

First Test

On the day of the test, six soldiers walked across the Goat Island causeway in their new bulky suits to the entry point on the far side. On the edge of the causeway, the smoke was boiling up right in front of their faces.

The roadway at the end of the low bridge was gone. It was where automobiles and pedestrians crossed to get to Goat Island eight years earlier. On the Newport side, the road and underlying supports had corroded away by the toxic elements.

Each soldier would have to climb down what was left of the girders, only to step onto the unknown alien surface. The soldiers were tethered together with corrosive resistant rope so no one would get separated. From the command center in the hotel, the soldiers were visible, preparing to start the test.

Balconies and windows were jammed with spectators as the team historically moved to enter the unknown. Several more steps and they would be out of sight. The first guardsman leaned on a low girder then awkwardly jumped down from the partially corroded cross piece, still gripping something under the causeway.

He braced himself for a fall. It never came. The surface was solid, smooth, with a slight slippery quality to it. He took a few steps; his footing was secure. From the hotel, the partially visible soldier could be seen giving the thumbs-up to his companions.

Sounding unlike Neil Armstrong in his space suit on the first dramatic moon landing, the first soldier said, "Come on down, but watch your step."

One by one the patrol members climbed down off the causeway and disappeared. When the final soldier entered, all communication with the outside world stopped. They were out of contact instantly. They were isolated and on their own.

*****

Over the next six months, scheduled patrols penetrated the smoke. Each patrol went in at various entry points to survey assigned quadrants. In every case, the result was the same. A smooth, flat, slippery surface, nothing else.

Months of exploration and mapping failed to reveal any details. Patrols scoured the island blindly and found no signs of change. Now in their second year, the incursions were routine. It was just smoke, solidified ground, and extreme desolation.

Newer more advanced suits were being manufactured. They were refined to reduce the bulkiness and weight. This made the patrols practical as new composite materials made weapons more resistant to the smoke. Communication was the only area that lacked progress. Walking in the smoke was getting easier.

*****

While the events were playing out in the islands off New England, the world didn't stop turning. From the first days when the island was consumed by smoke to present day, the Middle East continued to boil over. In the Mediterranean Sea, the islands of Cypress and Crete became entangled with Islamic jihad. After a series of important confrontations, the US and British armed forces quelled insurgencies on those islands. Terrorism continued, but the expansion of the Islamic State had been slowed dramatically.

In the Caribbean, a new power entered the world stage in the form of the South American Alliance. The SAA formed in 2020 in Venezuela, and by the end of 2022, Columbia and Panama fell into line. When the flame of communism went out in Cuba 2021, reconstruction became a problem when factions of that nation aligned themselves with the SAA.

With US and international business returning to Cuba, the Cuban Liberation Army or the CLA tried to disrupt foreign influence. At first, the CLA was considered a nuisance and not making inroads in the Cuban government reorganization. In 2022, they invited the SAA to come in and help take over the country.

Caught off guard, the US hurried to form a fighting force, consolidating units from its existing peacetime army. The American Expeditionary force landed, splitting the island of Cuba in two. This strategy caused the SAA to immediately try to negotiate a cease-fire. Having the advantage, US command wouldn't hear of it. Forces swept across the entire island, securing it.

Meanwhile a second American invasion force was in route to Venezuela. This maneuver worked brilliantly, causing the conflict to end when the US landed twenty thousand troops on Venezuela's home soil. The SAA ceased to exist.

*****

2025

In the year 2025, the National Guard's tour of duty at Quonset Point came to an end. They were being replaced by a unit made up of elite special forces. Army Rangers, Navy SEALs, and Marines, freed up after the conflict with the SAA, had been in training for months for this assignment.

"Attention!"

Everyone in the mess hall came to attention as Major General Robert Ray, USMC, entered the room. Assembled in the Quonset Point Naval Air Station cafeteria was the newly formed unit replacing the National Guard unit that was standing down.

It was a choice unit from top to bottom, made up of carefully screened volunteers from the Army, Navy, and Marines. Their primary objective was to monitor the area and investigate any incident within local jurisdiction. Their designation was Eagle Corps.

"Eagle Corps!" General Ray bellowed. "You're here to assume the important responsibility as custodians of the smoke-filled islands. You are members of a rapid response team, not only to monitor the day-to-day activities in the smoke but also to be the first to defend the United States from any unknown adversary. Perhaps under better circumstances, you will be the first to communicate with citizens of a distant planet."

General Ray had been the commanding officer of Eagle Corps since the beginning of training. An important part of his responsibilities was to integrate the members of the different services. He noticed right away that he was dealing with highly disciplined members of the different branches.

Although there were some interservice rivalries, over a condensed period of time, they meshed into a cohesive military force. They were ready for whatever this assignment offered.

Eagle Corps spent hundreds of hours training together. Their training involved familiarization with their new specialized equipment and tactics in the smoke. They were ready to implement what they learned.

Eagle Corps had equipment that was far superior to what the National Guard worked with. The fabric was thin, durable, and more comfortable than the older suits. It offered better protection to the servicemen wearing it. There was an upgrade to the electronic displays in their helmets, reducing its size and weight.

Communication was still a problem in the smoke, but it, too, was improving. Weapons, ammunition, and tactical gear were now completely impervious to the caustic nature of the smoke. Carrying cumbersome weapons bags was no longer required.

*****

Discovery

On station for four months, Eagle Corps was used to the routine of daily patrols. On this day, something was different. A small seismic event was detected in the center of what used to be Newport by scientists on Goat Island. It was brief, and it noticeably registered on the seismometers.

After walking the same monotonous terrain for all these weeks, E-Corps detected a blip on their instruments.

Marine Sergeant Nolan Sweet, walking point, spoke into his headset, "I've got something here, sir!"

The patrol abruptly came to a halt and waited.

"What do you have, Sergeant?" the officer in charge said in a slightly surprised manner.

Sweet replied, "Don't know, sir, but it's something new."

"Hold your position, I'm on my way up."

Approaching Sweet's position, the team leader, Ensign Alex Klein, could clearly see the blue outline of a shape on his face shield array. On all the previous patrols, when he passed these coordinates, nothing was there. Something had happened, and it happened recently.

A structure of some kind was standing in the barren wasteland. It was a solid shape that had materialized on the smooth barren surface. It appeared to be a cylinder, roughly fifty feet in diameter and about two stories high. The rounded walls rose up at a ninety-degree angle to the flat top.

Its perimeter was clearly displayed on the sensors on the left side of the faceplate array of the commander's helmet. The structure looked like a short can of beans. According to telemetry, it was about twenty feet high with smooth sides. No other features could be identified.

The sensors didn't register a base around this pillbox; the ground seemed to disappear under it. The structure seemed to be floating above the surface. Members of team Osprey slowly circled the outside of this new terrain feature. They were careful not to get to close to the empty space displayed on their screens. Studying the layout closer, it appeared that there was a drop-off around the center structure. It was moat-like.

Ensign Alex Klein directed the lead team member to approach the edge of the trench to extract some readings. Sergeant Sweet carefully approached the area where he thought the edge was located. When he determined a drop-off, he stopped. He raised a distance meter over the side, pointing it straight down. It did not return a reading.

He continued to move slowly and carefully along the edge of the drop-off, taking readings. Time after time he couldn't register the bottom. After painstakingly testing in eight different locations, he finally got a reading.

Sweet's device registered a depth of eighty-five feet. Moving to his left five paces, he got a reading of seventy-two feet. Again, after another slight move to his left, the device revealed another depth; this time it was sixty-eight feet.

Checking again after intervals of five paces, he found no higher levels, but the readings went in reverse until they disappeared again. They seemed to have found a high spot inside this trench. It was about sixty-eight feet down suspended in what seemed a bottomless pit.

This was a good day's work. The patrol returned to command to let the civilian section of Eagle Corps figure out what it all meant.

This section was made up of scientists, physicists, and unknown government types.

Every move the patrol made was recorded and later scrutinized. All data from their recording tools would be analyzed to accumulate and compile details of this new information. Maybe some of these new pieces of the puzzle will fit into place. Once analysis was done, Eagle Corps Command would decide what to do next.

The "pillbox" was a breakthrough. GPS determined that it was located at 41° 28'30.98" N and 71° 18'28.13 W. On an old city map, the co-ordinance of the pillbox was precisely located at the corner where Bellevue Avenue met Narragansett Avenue. It was right in the heart of Newport.

There was a flurry of activity on Goat Island going over every piece of data submitted by the patrol. Sorties into the smoke were stepped up, concentrating on finding more structures. After a week of enthusiastic searching, no additional structures were found.

*****

Contact

One month after the original contact, another patrol entered the smoke to find the configuration of the trench had physically changed. It seemed that on one side of the pillbox, a section was lowered. They noticed that it formed a bridge across the trench to the hard ground. After carefully examining it and testing its weight-bearing strength, the patrol crossed over to the solid structure.

One team member, Marine Corporal Paul Baker, using corrosion-resistant rope, scrambled up the side to examine the rooftop. After a hard climb with all his gear, he looked around, checking for an entrance leading into the tower. He carefully walked around what presented itself as a flat surface.

In his search, he found a manhole-size opening in the roof near the rounded outer edge. Examining it closer, he detected another flat surface, six feet below his position on the roof. It was just inside the side wall.

After thorough inspection, Baker climbed down, determining he had found a way in. It was an arched doorway about six feet high and five feet wide. He couldn't distinguish any kind of door or hatch; it was just open.

"Sir, this is Baker. I think I found a way in."

"Can you see inside?" the officer responded.

"No, sir, it looks like a passageway of some kind."

"Baker, move forward slowly and tell me what you see."

On receiving the order, Baker, breathing heavily, advanced a few steps into a corridor. Walking in several feet, he discovered that the smoke was dissipating. Shuffling a little deeper, the interior corridor was clear enough to view with the naked eye. Baker raised his protective visor and turned on LED lights on either side of his helmet. He saw smooth black walls running at a downward angle.

He clicked on his camera and began collecting video to send back to headquarters. With improved systems and less interference, the transmission allowed HQ to see what Baker was seeing in real time. After years of static, engineers were able to filter out most of the glitches in communications.

Improved electronic tools of all kinds were now available to the patrols. Baker dutifully stayed just inside the opening until he was relieved of duty. His team was done for the day. His oxygen was getting low. He didn't want to leave, but his reduced life support was the reason he had to go.

The next patrol came on sight "loaded for bear." Every member came in overloaded with specialized equipment. They had cameras, scanning equipment, and sensors to detect movement. It would be difficult to avoid detection by Team Hawk, Eagle Corps.

A small LITTLEBIRD drone was also included to investigate down the stretch of passageway. Orders from headquarters were to release the drone if the opportunity presented itself. This time two-team members entered the corridor, just beyond the point where Baker had stopped. They descended slowly down the angled walkway.

THE TUNNELS OF EARTH

When they discovered that it was a continual downward spiraling passage, it was time to release the drone. LITTLEBIRD was small, lightweight, and very responsive to controls. It had video capabilities and sensors similar to the helmets. Navy Petty Officer Richie Earhart unpacked the drone, tested the controls, and prepared to release it.

The drone was compact. It had four horizontal propellers, making it a quadcopter. It was fully equipped for just this kind of operation. Earhart threw the switch, turning it on, and then released it from his hand. He watched it proceed down the corridor and out of sight.

It advanced slowly with a low audible whirring sound. When Earhart lost sight of it, he switched over to his handheld monitor. After about four minutes of downward flight, the tunnel opened into a large cavernous chamber. LITTLEBIRD's sensors went crazy measuring the space, recording all findings.

Thinking about it for a moment, Earhart switched off the lights to minimize possible attention from anyone or anything that might be there. It moved around the large open space recording and taking readings. Readouts indicated the chamber was about one hundred feet wide and thirty feet high. Radar, infrared, night vision, and ultraviolet were all on as the drone made slow loops around the interior, recording everything and sending all the information back to base.

From a position above and outside the corridor, the balance of Team Hawk noticed that the walls of the corridor were slowly closing in around the two men inside. The second team member in the passage, Marine Corporal James Kelly, lowered his visor, tapped Earhart on the shoulder, and started backing out into the smoke.

Slowly retreating upward, Kelly said, "Come on, we need to get out of here. The walls are moving in on us."

Holding his position, Earhart gave Kelly the high sign then continued to maintain contact with the drone. He coolly manipulated the two joystick controls with his thumbs to rotate the drone 180 degrees to start back up to the surface.

Outside on the roof of the pillbox, he could hear someone say in a loud voice, "Bogeys at three o'clock, moving this way, moving fast."

Team Leader Navy SEAL Lieutenant Roger Buckley crouched down next to his technology specialist saying, "What do see, Staff Sergeant?"

Staff Sergeant Rico Torres said, "Sir, I have four unknowns moving this way. They're not human. They're not giving off any biosignatures."

Looking over Torres's shoulder at the display, Buckley barked out orders to the team, "Weapons ready! Bogeys are coming in from the north."

Watching the monitor, he saw four small white blips on the screen gliding across the surface outside the pillbox, moving in their direction. With zero visibility, Team Hawk waited blindly, relying only on their sensors. As the bogeys approached the drop-off; three of them disappeared, vanishing from the screen. With three of the objects gone, one kept coming, across the bridge, straight up the side of the pillbox wall.

Buckley cried, "There's one coming right at us!"

The men were waiting, blinded by the smoke. They knew there was something coming, but they couldn't see it.

Torres yelled, "It's on top of us!"

Buckley, looking up, said, "It's flying right over us! Earhart, get out of there!"

As the walls continued to close in, the drone still hadn't reached the corridor from the open chamber. Earhart increased forward pressure on the stick, forcing the drone to race toward the exit. Concentrating on retrieving the drone and backing out of the corridor, he felt something hit his shoulder.

Whatever it was knocked him off balance and down on the deck. He jumped quickly to his feet and glanced over his shoulder. Finding that whatever knocked him over was gone. Thinking fast, Earhart manipulated the stick on the controller, directing the drone to stop in place and catch whatever was coming on video.

Preparing for whatever entered the chamber, he flipped a switch and said softly to himself, "Lights on!"

Whirring motionlessly, the floodlight on the LITTLEBIRD flashed on. Its cameras were trained on the lower passage entrance. Earhart hoped that when the bogey burst through the opening, it would be clearly visible to the cameras and video recorder on the drone.

Watching the monitor, Earhart said, "Wow, I hope they're getting this."

Earhart backed out of the passage right before the sidewalls sealed closed, cutting off the transmission to the LITTLEBIRD. Powerless, it dropped to the floor with a total loss of contact with the outside world. The signal could not penetrate the wall with the corridor closed. The drone lay dormant on the deck. With the excitement over, Team Hawk maintained station until they, too, were relieved.

Headquarters was abuzz with images sent by the drone's sensors. General Ray anticipated what the camera captured before the signal was lost. Watching the high-definition monitors, the feed from the drone displayed a dark chamber at the end of a short tunnel.

Employing the night vision settings, they discovered that it was a dome at the bottom of the ramp. It was lined with interior supports that worked their way from the floor to the ceiling. The far side of the dome was revealed as an opening to some other place.

No sensor readings from beyond that opening were transmitted back to HQ. Interior walls and floor were hard to visualize on the video monitors. The supports to the ceiling could be distinguished by darker shadows running up the wall, but that was it. Nothing else was revealed about the chamber.

The next thing anticipated was seeing the mysterious bogey moving down the passageway entering the dome. To the surprise of General Ray and the others watching, the bogey burst into the chamber and was gone in an instant. There was about one and a half seconds of clear video, but that was enough to freeze frame this strange entity.

On examination, the being was pearl white with arms and perhaps legs. They couldn't tell because it seemed to be floating or riding on something. If it had a head, it was just a narrowing of the upper body that extended about ten inches above its pseudo shoulders.

There was a split at the top of the head which suggested it had horns or perhaps antennae. The difference was that the upper parts of the horns closed in toward the middle, stopping with a three-inch gap between tips.

Investigators guessed and surmised that the identity was that of a strange robot. In reality, General Ray and the scientists had no idea what they were looking at. It didn't look alive.

More analysis was needed. The information that they got from the drone filled in some gaps in their knowledge, but it left them with even more questions.

The celebration in the control room was short-lived. General Ray emphasized, "We need to get back in there! The teams need to be ready to go long term, at a moment's notice."

"We have our team rotation set for the next two weeks. For today, Falcon team will take the next patrol. Condor will follow them four hours later, and finally Osprey team will take the third watch. Harrier team will be on standby."

After such an exciting day, the subsequent patrols came back somewhat disappointed. The corridor remained closed. To add to the insult, later that day it was discovered the bridge to the tower no longer spanned the trench. From that point on, few structural changes were detected. Because of the smoke, they couldn't get a clear image of what was happening at the site.

Part II
ENZO

Early in September 2026, there was a major event effecting the northeast United States and Aquidneck Island in particular. Hurricane Enzo was the fifth hurricane of the season. It was an act that no army of scientists could have predicted.

Over the years, a number of hurricanes came close to Aquidneck Island, but it was one near miss after another. This one was different. Weather satellites tracked Enzo as it entered the western hemisphere. Rolling over the Virgin Islands, it curved northward into the Atlantic Ocean. As it moved north, it glanced off the outer banks of North Carolina before returning to sea, heading up the East Coast.

Several computer models forecast that it was leaving the coast and going out to sea, but as it approached the tip of Long Island, it abruptly turned north. Not a single model was right. It passed over Montauk Point, crossed Block Island Sound, and roared straight up Narragansett Bay.

What was different about storm number five was it advanced up Narragansett Bay and hit Aquidneck Island head-on. It was the worst hurricane since Hurricane Gabe in the northeast US in 2022. Moving due north, Enzo surged directly into the state of Rhode Island, also skirting parts of eastern Connecticut and southeastern Massachusetts. It was devastating, and it created enormous hardship for local citizens in its path.

Sitting on the southern end of Narragansett Bay, Aquidneck Island received a direct hit. It was a category four hurricane, leaving massive destruction in its wake. On the mainland, damage to personal property was staggering. Enzo pushed up into the mainland, and by the time it reached Providence County, it was downgraded to into a tropical storm.

After the storm, many people were stranded and out of luck. Hundreds of homes were destroyed. Many of the problems were caused by storm surge.

On Enzo's departure, people in shelters came out of hiding to breathe the fresh air and to see the clear blue sky. Everyone was looking for relief. The air had an incredible crispness to it. Those that could see Narragansett Bay couldn't believe their eyes when they looked in the direction of Aquidneck Island.

The smoke was gone; the island was clearly visible. Once more, an island rose out of the bay, and for the first time in ten years, amazed citizens could see it. Wisps of smoke rose to the sky, but they were fading away.

*****

The Barren Black Island

Immediately, the military stationed at Quonset Point went into action. Air reconnaissance flew over the island and determined what they already knew. It was a vast featureless landscape. There was a specific location, however, that command really wanted to see. Over the years, many of the patrols concentrated on this location. It had been patrolled many times but only entered once.

The reconnaissance pilot said to his copilot, "Finally we're going to get a good look."

He had been flying over this island on and off for three years and never saw the surface. This day would be different; he was looking for something specific. Standing alone in a south-central location on the island was the pillbox. It looked like a version of a wheel of cheese. It revealed the known dimensions, and it was as black as the surrounding landscape. The one great unknown was the now fully exposed trench surrounding the tower.

Examining the mounting number of photos, intelligence officers could see details, fascinating details. The trench looked like a circular medieval moat, surrounding a castle tower. The major feature about the castle was it was in the center of the moat in a deep depression in the earth.

The trench dropped straight down. The early photos couldn't determine its depth. When there was high sun, pictures finally gave the investigators a clue. Flying directly over the trench and directing the cameras straight down, they determined that the bottom was out of sight on three sides. But on the fourth side, the pillbox dropped vertically in the center of the moat then curved into the side wall.

When it curved into the wall, it leveled off horizontally. This explained some of the drone data about the ramp going down deep into the tower then opening into a large dome. Scanning the photos, experts looked for another way in. None of the photographs gave them any clue of a possible entrance. Scanning equipment focused on the pillbox, the trench, and even the surrounding area outside the target zone.

"Which team is ready to go in, Captain?" General Ray asked the duty officer.

"Hawk, sir."

General Ray said, "Get Team Hawk on the helicopters with the Navy boys. I think we have a real opportunity here. We might just get inside."

Team Hawk assembled in one of the large hurricane-damaged hangars at the Quonset Naval Air Station getting ready to deploy. This was the moment that they had trained for. They had been going into the smoke for six months, and now they were going to be able to see where they had been and what was there.

One of the other hangars was being used to house refugees that were left homeless by Hurricane Enzo. Hangar 11, normally used by Eagle Corps, was hardly in use anymore.

Routine patrols had been curtailed because of lack of progress in gathering new information. Nothing new had been discovered in months, so the hangar used for preparation was going to be opened to the suffering disaster victims. After the news the island was now exposed, quick action had to be taken by base command. They had to shuffle hangar usage, so Hanger 11 was operational once again.

*****

Team Hawk

The conflicts in the Mediterranean and South America shaped the members of Eagle Corps. One of the most experienced teams was Team Hawk. Battle hardened and dedicated to the defense of the United States, they were the prototypes of what Eagle Corps demanded.

Team Hawk was made up of seven military operatives from three of the four branches of service. There were four Navy SEALs, two Recon Marines, and a Navy corpsman. Navy Lieutenant Roger Buckley was the team leader. A fourteen-year Navy man, he had been a SEAL for ten of those years. Eight months earlier, after receiving his promotion to lieutenant, he was assigned to E-Corps.

An experienced Navy SEAL, he served in Cuba in special operations. He was late on the scene to see combat in Venezuela but wound up being temporarily assigned to headquarters in Caracas.

He was a cerebral warrior spending hour studying military history, tactics, and weapons. Although he was of slight build and had the look of a computer programmer, he was a former All-State wrestler in high school who demonstrated he was a tough and capable leader.

Marine Staff Sgt. Richie Torres, the team's second in command, served eight years in the Corps and specialized in intelligence and communications. He was in Force Recon for seven years and stormed the beaches with the American Expeditionary Force of Eastern Cuba at Banes before being selected for Eagle Corps.

Navy Petty Officer Second Class Richie Earhart was a ten-year Navy man from Groton, Connecticut, with a specialty in electronics.

He joined Eagle Corps as part of Team Hawk, carrying all the useful gadgets that could detect just about anything. He was a member of the second American invasion force to route the South American Alliance in Venezuela.

Marine Corporal James Kelly and Navy Petty Officer Second Class Randy Brewer were the team's weapons specialists. Highly trained in the art of killing, they were more than just grunts, they were trained operators with talent to use all the Eagle Corps' specialized equipment needed in this twenty-first-century military.

An experienced marine, Kelly spent his time in military operations including a MED (Mediterranean) cruise deployed to Crete where he was a fire team leader. He also spent time fighting in Cuba.

Brewer, a member of Navy SEALs, spent his time during the conflict reconnoitering beachheads as a diver clearing obstacles in advance of the military invasion. When that job was done, he parachuted into Guantanamo Bay to join the southern invasion force.

Navy Petty Officer Second Class Ed Stiles was the ordinance mate with a specialty in blowing things up. He liked doing it too. A veteran of the Cuban conflict, he was a veteran of Afghanistan as well in his twelve-year career.

The final member attached to Team Hawk was Navy Corpsman Chief Petty Officer Rachael Cooper. She was small in stature but very strong. The members of Eagle Corps didn't mess with their only female member because she didn't take any bull shit from anyone. Behind her back they referred to her as Mom because she was about ten years older than most of the team. She spent little time in combat situations and reached Cuba at the end of hostilities.

The Mission

Three Navy Seahawk helicopters waited outside the hanger with their rotors spinning. In single file, Team Hawk members walked out of the hanger and mounted up on the closest helicopter. The other two helicopters were loading up with support personnel,

Navy technicians, technical gear, and a National Guard security team. Once loaded, the Sikorsky Seahawk (SH-60) helicopters took off and headed out over the bay on an east-southeast course. It would be a quick hop to their destination, the corner of Bellevue and Narragansett.

Team Hawk was in full protective gear in anticipation of the smoke returning. They wore gear that included helmets, complete with heads-up displays. Heavy gloves covered their hands to seal them into their protective suits. They were armed with corrosive resistant weapons including rifles, pistols, and explosives.

Each team member had a backpack weighing roughly forty pounds. They were traveling light today. Many times, they would be expected to carry much heavier loads. In the pack was everything they would need for up to twenty-four hours, food, water, and ammunition.

Flying in from the western shore of Narragansett Bay just above the water, the navy helicopters flew fast and low. On the approach to Aquidneck Island, the team saw a surreal sight. It looked like everyone that had a boat was heading toward the island.

The overwhelmed Coast Guard didn't have enough patrol boats to stop the onrush of civilians crossing the bay. Passing over the shoreline, E-Corps could see a growing number of civilians moving inland. Returning their focus to the job ahead, the helicopters moved closer to the target area. The tower came into view in the distance.

The unbroken black surface passed below them. Only after reaching the landing zone did they realize that the terrain around the pillbox was graded. It gradually sloped downward, so the top of the tower and trench were below grade. It was impossible to see it from a distance at ground level. The structures were literally constructed in a recess. The excavation was like a circular shape sloping downward, leveling off just before the spot where the trench dropped off.

When the Choppers landed, the team wasted no time disembarking and moving toward the structure. Team Hawk examined the exterior of the pillbox from across the moat and saw no visible entrance. Realizing they couldn't just walk to the tower, they brought grappling hooks and ropes to bridge the gap.

THE TUNNELS OF EARTH

After seeing the trench, Lt. Buckley realized that the moat was too wide to successfully fire the grappling hooks over it. The collective thought was, it would be a very lucky shot to fire over this moat and find something to hook onto.

They would have to look for entry in other places first. Buckley leaned over the edge of the trench and took a good look. The lighting was not very good at that time of day, but he could just about make out the curve of the tower in the deep shadows.

Buckley ordered Petty Officer Brewer to unfurl his rope and drop into the trench, onto the elbow in the tower. Kelly prepared his rope as well. Ropes fell and glanced off the tube of the central structure falling to either side. The ropes hung limp off the sides of the horizontal tube. The two men wasted no time repelling down to the horizontal section where the tube entered the wall.

On the ropes, the two members of Team Hawk walked themselves up to the top of the curved tube. They shined lights all around the structure. The high-powered beams did not reveal anything but smooth rounded walls on either side. From their perspective they had a better chance of hooking on the tower with grappling hooks than finding an entrance at this level.

When Brewer reported his findings back to Lieutenant Buckley, he called Staff Sergeant Rickie Torres over.

Buckley said, "Hitch a ride on a chopper over to the pillbox and see if you can find a way in."

Moments later, Torres, attached to a rope, suspended from the SH60 flying overhead. Ninety seconds later, he was standing on the pillbox, a place he had been before but in thick smoke. He began to scour the roof area.

Kelly and Brewer were useless standing down below, so they decided to climb to the top of the pillbox. Loading a grappling hook onto his weapon, Kelly yelled up to warn Torres to stand clear as he fired. The shot from the specially rigged rifle blasted up and over the highest point. The hook traveled over and caught on the far side of the pillbox. As the corporal pulled, trying to catch a lip, it slid off to the side and down past the men and into the darkness.

With Torres standing off to the side, the Navy SEAL was next. Brewer got as far back on the tube as he could then shot in the same general direction. He knew immediately that his hook was set on the top of the pillbox. Torres ran over and planted it deeply as Brewer gave it a strong tug. Convinced that the rope was set, he started to climb. Kelly, tied in with a safety line around his waist, watched as his companion started the ascent.

Brewer, a powerful climber, made it look effortless as he moved up the wall. Once he gained a foothold on the top, he gestured to Kelly to come on up. Kelly, using the safety rope connected to Brewer, climbed the rope in an easy fashion just like his Navy SEAL counterpart.

On the summit they kept the ropes attached to prevent the possibility of that long, deep drop to nowhere. Now with three members of Team Hawk on the top of the pillbox, they looked and found no entryway. They found the drop-off where the original team made their entry and saw only a flat sealed wall in front of them. Torres looked to his CO and gave a negative shake of his head. Buckley gestured to the team to stay put.

Learning that there was no way in, Buckley walked over to a naval officer with a clipboard standing next to the second Seahawk helicopter. From the top of the structure, at a long distance, the three members of E-Corps could see him talking and gesturing to the other officer. The officer nodded and turned to his crew standing close by.

The next step was in this unknown officer's hands. He barked out some orders, and his crew jumped into action. They removed three large cases from the second helicopter. A group of enlisted men carried the cases over to the officer's position. They placed them in a line in front of the pillbox and knelt on one knee next to them. Other personnel assembled what looked like an instrument panel.

When the instrument console was assembled, the boxes were opened, and navy men pulled out three small unmanned aircraft from them. Several more cases were handed out to waiting technicians. The drones were placed on the barren black terrain and were left unattended for the moment. A fourth larger drone was unpacked and placed closer to the console. Three technicians were setting up their stations, doing a final instrument check.

Team Hawk on top of the pillbox watched as the officer gave an order for the single drone to be brought into play. On the naval officer's command, it sputtered and then came to life. The engine whirred as it reached launch speed. The show was about to begin, Kelly squatted down to get a good look over the side into the pit. The three men on the pillbox had the best view of the action.

The drone lifted off and shot straight up thirty feet, hovering momentarily. Leaning forward, it zoomed toward the trench. Reaching it, the drone stopped, hovering a moment so the technician could get his bearings on the instruments. Once that was complete, it dropped straight down, out of sight. Kelly watched from his unique position as the drone moved down past him into the blackness.

The show was over almost as soon as it started. The only individuals still totally involved were the technicians working the controls. As it descended, the drone's floodlights switched on, lighting up the interior walls of the moat.

Three monitors recorded the proceedings as light filled the void. The display read the depth as well as how far the drone was from the walls. Information streamed topside to the monitoring crew, who relayed it to the officer in charge.

Word was passed along that the drone was approaching a depth of two hundred feet. This was where the tube started to turn in a similar manner as the tower above. It only took three minutes for the drone to drop to the base of the pit. At the curve, the drone leveled off and proceeded down a horizontal tube. The technicians couldn't understand why the depth couldn't be recorded initially. They just shook their heads and refocused on their jobs.

The strong floodlights displayed the scene clearly on the monitors as it proceeded forward down the tunnel. The cameras showed a featureless interior with no breaks in the walls. After an uneventful reconnaissance several hundred yards in, the officer determined that it was almost time to turn around and resurface. Fuel was still at a safe level to get the drone out of the hole. It continued traveling another three hundred yards before being recalled, detecting nothing of interest.

*****

Side Show

The situation topside was getting interesting. Attracted by the helicopters and the growing military activity, civilians that had crossed the bay to see the island up close were making their way on foot toward the commotion. The small security force that joined the first group could not anticipate the large number of people arriving from every direction. Reinforcements were required immediately. The unprepared National Guard security officer hastened together plans to ship over a larger force to secure the site.

The first civilians reached the flimsy perimeter and demanded to see what was going on. At first, a threat of force was enough to keep the curious citizens away from the pit. As their numbers grew, the confidence of the crowd was bolstered. Guards were being slowly pushed back toward the edge of the depression, toward the operational zone.

The officer in charge thought, *Where are the reinforcements?*

Just as the crowd reached the lip of the depression, several helicopters arrived with more soldiers, coming in to fortify the perimeter. National guardsmen leaped from the landing choppers and ran to positions alongside their beleaguered comrades. Reaching the crest of the depression, they joined their fellow guardsmen in an attempt to push back the growing crowd.

Finally, the National Guard stopped the advance, but for the time being the mob was not going to be pushed back. It was a stalemate; all movement, forward and back, ceased. With the standoff in effect, the lucky people in the front enjoyed ringside seats to all that was taking place.

*****

Phase Two

The drone surfaced and was guided back to the console area where it came to rest on the charred surface. It was time for phase two to begin. The officer that was seen to be in charge had hoped that this next step would not be necessary. Unfortunately for him, nothing would replace the presence of human interpretation in this kind of situation.

The crew unloaded the next tool that was stored on the CH60. The jet pack came off the helicopter and was brought to the staging area. This would be a piloted craft, and the man giving all the orders was going to be the pilot. No side passageways were detected by the single drone, so using the jet pack would perhaps offer a clearer picture of the tunnel layout.

The jet pack was a modernized version of the Bell Rocket Belt, designed originally by Wendell Moore in the late 1950s at Bell Laboratories. Early in its infancy, there was a flurry of interest by the military, but over the decades it became nothing more than a novelty. The rocket belt had been featured at air shows and in adventure movies for more than sixty years.

In 2022, there was a new interest in the rocket belt. Reengineering, using lighter materials and better fuel efficiency, its application was more feasible than it was back in the mid-twentieth century.

Once again, the military bought a bunch of the newer models for use in the different branches of the service. There were several jet packs sent to Quonset Point for the purpose of maneuvering around the smoke. They sat there for a year waiting to be put into service, but to this point they were only a training tool.

Navy Lieutenant Ed Vacek was ready to go. The officer in charge of the drone team was also the trained specialist on the belt. His second in command moved in to take over his position at the console while he put on the protective flight suit. No one knew if there was breathable air in the trench, so similar precautions had to be taken as those entering the smoke.

Team Hawk was in country less than two hours and were in the best position to watch the whole operation up close. They couldn't find a way into this mysterious alien structure, so for the time being they had to settle on being spectators.

A second jet pack was brought in by a heavy lift helicopter. Once the hole was secured, the extra jet pack was available to support teams that would follow Vacek into the underground.

Before he entered the tunnel, Vacek approached Lt. Buckley to enlist his help. His plan called for Team Hawk to be in position at the bottom of the trench when he arrived on the jet pack. After clearing his plan with Buckley, he moved away, focused on his job.

He walked over to the trench looking for his point of entry. He spent several minutes walking and stopping, looking down, then walking and stopping and looking again. He had plenty of room to drop into the trench; his only concern was the neck below the tower. It traveled across the opening, connecting it to the outer wall. Whatever else worried him about dropping into the tunnel; he would soon come face to face with it.

A heavy lift helicopter, a Sikorsky CH53K, would be used to drop men, equipment, and supplies down to the bottom of the trench. It was equipped with a triple-hook cargo handling system and heavy lift winches. This one was also hastily rigged with powerful lights. The CH53K set down just outside the security perimeter less than two hundred feet from the trench. It was quickly blanketed by armed security.

Vacek's crew was busy around the console hooking up the second stage electronics and testing them. With the help of his crew, he donned the heavy jet pack and then topped off his outfit by slipping on the helmet. Buckley was out of earshot, but he could see him talking nonstop to his crew while adjusting his equipment.

Lt. Buckley explained the insertion plan to Team Hawk while hooking up to the rope. They were attaching to the world's premier heavy-lift helicopter, the CH-53K King Stallion, now hovering one hundred feet above. Sitting on the charred ground next to him were six jerricans full of jet pack fuel.

The wash from the rotors kicked up the black earth, making anyone without the special suit very uncomfortable. The black sand managed to do what the National Guard could not. It forced the crowd to retreat from the stinging grit, giving the guard some breathing room and a moment of peace.

The plan was for the team to be lowered to the bottom of the trench using the special patrol insertion / extraction system (SPIE). Once at the bottom, they would set up a secure area. When in position, Buckley would notify the surface for Lt. Vacek to start his descent.

When Vacek entered, he would drop down the vertical shaft then make the slow turn to advance down the tube as far as possible. If all went well, he would return, refuel from the jerricans and attempt to extend his run deeper into the tunnel.

The insertion would be executed in two phases. First, Team Hawk, hooked in on ropes, would be lowered down the vertical shaft. Once secured in place at the elbow at the bottom, the fuel would be lowered.

*****

Insertion

The Navy team members at the console were ready to begin. Team Hawk was harnessed in on two of the cables. Buckley gave the thumbs-up to the helicopter pilot indicating the team was ready. Moments later the craft lifted the team members two at a time. The big heavy CH-53K swung over to the tower, hovering long enough to pick up Torres, Brewer, and Kelly.

Once harnessed in, all the team members gave two thumbs-up. Seeing this, the helicopter pilot lifted the CH-53K vertically gaining enough clearance to maneuver away from the pillbox. When positioned over the trench, two winches hummed and began lowering the human cargo. Team Hawk would be the first to enter the unknown.

The trench was over two hundred feet deep. The journey down seemed like an eternity. The winches played out at a slow and deliberate rate, too slow for Buckley's liking. He didn't want to give someone or something time to pick them off while on the cables.

After the first drone returned with nothing eventful happening, Vacek was confident that the danger was minimal. Seven fully equipped members of E-Corps were going to be waiting at the bottom of the trench for him.

What could go wrong? he thought.

On touchdown at the base, E-Corps detached from their harnesses and in pairs, moved into position to give Vacek plenty of room to get through. Buckley directed the team into tactical position, forming a line with Kelly and Brewer in the center, Stiles and Earhart on the flanks with Communication Specialist Torres, Corpsman Cooper, and himself, slightly to the rear.

The tunnel was expansive, at least fifty feet in circumference. It was as tall in the tunnel as it was wide at the surface. The floor curved up at the base of the conduit.

Team members cursed as they struggled to move in their protective suits. They were hot; the faceplates of their helmets were fogging up. Under the protective fabric, their bodies were drenched in sweat. There was nothing they could do but complete the mission. Buckley thought, *Just do your job and get out.* That was foremost on his mind.

Earhart pointed his grenade launcher down range. In his pack he carried an assortment of explosive devices. Stiles had his choice of weapons, a standard issue M4A1 rifle. Brewer had the rifle/grenade launcher combo where Kelly had his old reliable sniper rifle. All were equipped with night vision goggles, spectrum array, as well as radio headsets.

*****

The Main Event

Many more curiosity seekers had gathered along the perimeter to watch what was going to happen next. The guards settled for holding the masses in place so they couldn't interfere. The word on the perimeter was when more reinforcements arrive on the line, they would walk the crowd back out of sight of the trench.

The onlookers had already seen too much. Security was struggling to hold the line. They worked hard to maintain the human fence around the pit with the small force they had in place.

*****

When the fuel cans were delivered down the cable, SSgt. Torres relayed a message to the surface that Team Hawk was now in position, standing by. Two enlisted men steadied Vacek in an upright position when the engines on the belt came to life. Directed by the lieutenant, the assistants stepped back. Several seconds later, a startling blast of flame shot downward lifting him off the ground. He wobbled and then thrust straight up. When he gained total control, he leaned forward, guiding the belt toward the trench. Uncteremoniously he moved over the abyss. When he reached a position twenty feet over the precipice, he throttled up. Although the newer belt's flying time was upwards of twenty minutes, Vacek didn't want to waste fuel.

Lt. Ed Vacek, commander of the Bell Rocket Belt, gave a theatrical thumbs-up to the spectators and then plunged down into the trench. Team Hawk could hear the loud engines of the rocket belt roaring and popping in the distance heading in their direction.

The most striking difference between the rocket belts from the past and the one Vacek was attached to was the rocket belt controls were autonomous, working all functions of the mission. For the most part, Vacek was a passenger. He was trained in manual controlling the belt if required to do so.

Team Hawk waited patiently for the belt to reach the point where it could make the turn and power down the tunnel. It didn't take long—light from the rocket lit up the vertical tube. When it reached the bottom, it momentarily slowed, took an awkward turn, and then lurched forward proceeding down the tunnel.

Buckley thought that this was quite an impressive sight. After the belt made the turn into the tunnel, something else caught his eye in the bright illumination. It was behind the team, at the base of the upward curve of the tunnel. It was back in the shadows, but on closer inspection, he found what he thought was a vent.

It was about three feet high, and after shining his light into it, he discovered that it went into the curved wall for some distance. He mentioned it to Torres and Cooper but promptly returned his focus to the mission. In his mind, he thought it was an important find.

With luck it could lead to an entrance to the underground dome. There was nothing he could do about it now because his job was to protect the man down the line. He could further investigate it after this stage of the mission ended.

Vacek, rocketing down the tunnel, was eyeballing everything in front of him. As a backup to human observation, everything was being recorded and transmitted to the surface. He continued to look high and low, but he saw no deviations in the smooth walls.

The one thing he did notice was there was an occasional black mound scattered randomly around the deck of the structure. He couldn't examine them closely because he was moving too fast. Besides, his fuel would soon be running low. He had to consider when he should turn around, refuel, and then proceed deeper into the tunnel.

Over his microphone, Vacek announced to Buckley that he was returning for fuel. He slowed his forward progress in order to swing around to go back to the base of the tube. As he began to rotate, he caught a glimpse of something moving deep in the tunnel. He stopped his turn and hovered, directing his floodlight toward the movement. Whatever he was looking at seemed to be standing erect on two legs. It was light in color and stood out clearly against the black backdrop. It was impossible to identify at such a great distance. It was little more than a speck.

Vacek said into his mic, "I have contact with something down here, something moving. Unfortunately, I have to return for fuel before I can investigate."

He thought, *This is a very important discovery, but I have to break away.*

THE TUNNELS OF EARTH

Refueling would only take a few minutes, so he reluctantly turned to leave. Buckley heard Vacek's message and heard an acknowledgment from the surface. He prepared the team for refueling the rocket belt. They were preparing for his arrival in about three minutes.

Vacek didn't like turning his back on this anomaly, but he had no choice. He moved off as quickly as his equipment safely allowed. Moving back toward the entrance, a chill went through his body. He was acutely aware that he wasn't alone.

Vacek heard a *pop!* followed by a loud whirring sound coming up behind him. He sensed strong turbulence closing in on him. Now spooked, he switched the belt to manual and punched the accelerator, racing to get out of the tube.

The disturbance was quite a distance down the tunnel, but PO Earhart saw the speck, that was Vacek coming. "What's rattling this guy? He's going way too fast."

In a strained voice, Vacek said in his mic to the team waiting at the end of the tunnel, "Eagle Corps, take cover if you can. Something big is coming up behind me!"

Vacek was on the edge of losing control. By now everyone saw him coming down the tunnel followed by the increasing sound of a freight train bearing down on him. Buckley could only see a dark figure in the middle of a ring of light coming toward them.

Vacek, roaring down the tunnel, struggled to stay ahead of the fast-moving storm. As the belt approached Team Hawk, the roar got louder.

Buckley recognized that they were sitting ducks in the path of this oncoming threat. Alarmed, he remembered the low vent behind them, knowing that it would be their only hope. They needed to move inside as quickly as possible to shelter themselves from the danger.

Buckley shined his flashlight on the vent and shouted, "Everyone, inside! Get in as far as you can! Get in, now!"

Without panic, the team scrambled into the vent. The fuel cans were abandoned as they entered one at a time. They were ducking down as low as possible or crawling to get out of the tunnel. It was a cramped entrance, but they were highly motivated. Ten feet from the entrance, the opening increased to the point they were able to stand up.

The roaring storm was gaining on him. Vacek knew the danger as he was almost at the turn. He felt that he would survive only if he could make the upward turn toward the surface.

The wind was coming too fast. Fighting to get inside the vent, Team Hawk members were still unprotected. Vacek flew by, and then the windstorm hit, knocking the team forcefully to the deck, pushing them deeper into the vent. There they hunkered down in the midst of this superstorm. Buckley wasn't positive that everyone made it inside.

The belts engine roared louder than the storm as it made the turn. On the upward leg to the surface, Vacek could see his shadow elongating on the curved floor by the natural light from above. Not confident that he could maintain control of the belt, Vacek prayed that he had the ability to do so.

He turned upward, going too fast, hitting the far wall. Bouncing off the wall, he battled the handgrips to keep control and stay upright. On contact with the wall, he lost speed and came to the realization he could no longer outrace the wind. He kept going but was waiting for the hit.

The wind turned the corner and surged upward, catching up to and then engulfing the jet pack pilot, pushing him forcefully toward the light. Vacek struggled to remain vertical in the belt while being pushed toward the sky. Looking up, he saw the tower looming directly above his head in the center of the tube.

He was on a collision course. He was going to hit the pillbox! With all his concentration and will, he gunned the engine forward. In doing so he surged, hitting the wall again as he rocketed past the tower into the daylight.

The swirling windstorm pushed Vacek high out of the pit and then fell away. The belt pilot, moving skyward erratically, struggled to maintain control. He knew he was in trouble, so he gunned the engine to slow his descent. Stalling the craft, he careened in for a crash landing.

He hit hard, landing feet first, twisting and then crumpling down on his side. Jerricans landed all around him, bursting open, spreading highly flammable fuel everywhere. Servicemen with fire extinguishers moved in to control any fire that might break out.

Vacek was bruised, shaken, and he had two crushed and bleeding hands. His ankles and knees ached from his hard landing. Most of his injuries were from hitting the wall than from the crash landing. He was grateful to be out of the tunnel and alive.

He thought to himself about the aviation proverb, *Any day you can walk away from a crash is a good day.*

His crew gathered around Vacek and peeled the jet pack off as carefully as they could. Medical personnel rushed in to offer treatment.

*****

When the powerful wind receded, Buckley looked around to take a head count. Including himself, he counted six people. "One short!"

He anxiously moved around shining his flashlight on the team members lying on the deck. He thrust the light on a face. It was Kelly. Another face was Brewer. He shined the light on all the team members in turn. They were coughing and trying to prop themselves up against the tunnel wall as Buckley passed from one person to the next. He saw Cooper, Torres, and Stiles. He turned the flashlight and shined it up and down the vent.

Buckley called his name, "Earhart!"

No response. Petty Officer Earhart was not there. He didn't get inside when the high winds passed. Now distressed, Team Hawk clamored out of the hole in the wall to look for their colleague. The jerry cans filled with jet fuel and other equipment left outside were no longer there.

Earhart was nowhere in sight. There was nothing but a dense curtain of dust particles sinking back down onto the tunnel floor. It would have been impossible to breathe in the dust had they not been wearing their protective suits.

*****

Topside, the onlookers on the security line witnessed basically the same things that the people inside the perimeter saw. They heard a rumble from the pit, saw the man with the jet pack propelled out of the hole surrounded by forceful wind and dust, then watched as he struggled for control, crashing in a heap.

They watched servicemen running to his aid. What the people on the inside of the perimeter didn't see was the man without a jet pack catapulted out of the pit heading skyward, arms flailing. They didn't see him fly over the perimeter and they didn't see him land hard beyond the crowd.

Some civilians rushed to the place where the man fell. Others tried to alert the guards about the casualty. The guards weren't listening. They were more interested in seeing what happened to the pilot of the jet pack. Only after the crowd dragged the shattered body to the guard position did they realize the seriousness of the situation.

It was the crumpled body of Richie Earhart. He was in his special uniform with what looked like a space helmet still in place. His side arm was undisturbed in his holster on his duty belt while his backpack and Grenade launcher were nowhere to be found. Petty Officer Earhart, member of Team Hawk, was a reminder to those on the surface that the rest of his team was still down in the pit.

Before he was stretchered off, Vacek's second in command knelt down next to him to check out the condition of his boss. Vacek wasn't interested in that; he ordered him to implement the next phase.

Vacek said, "There is something alive down there. It attacked me and used the windstorm directly against me. Clear it out."

He lay back on the stretcher and noticed to his left there was one of those black mounds from the tunnel lying next to him. He reached out, but it was too far away, so he said to a nearby sailor, "What is that?"

The sailor reached down and picked up the object and said, "It's a dead rat sir, a big one."

As the operation continued, the crowd kept growing, developing into a circus atmosphere. The people within sight of the pit were more than satisfied with their vantage point. Every action that took place inside the ring was within their line of sight.

More helicopters were shuttling in personnel and equipment. The perimeter was becoming more secure with each flight. The latest flight included more than just security personnel to beef up the perimeter. It also included Team Falcon, another section of Eagle Corps.

Team Hawk was down below, still trying to ascertain what happened to Earhart when they heard the voice of Marine Captain Ronald (Rex) Steel in their earpieces.

"Lieutenant Buckley, this is Captain Steel, can you hear me?"

"Yes, sir, I hear you loud and clear."

"What is the status of your team?"

"We got hit by a tornado or something down here, but Hawk is still functional. We are searching for a missing team member."

Steel noted, "It looks like we have a casualty from your team topside, Lieutenant."

"Petty Officer Earhart, sir?"

"I think so. He was blown out of the hole during the event."

"What's his status?"

"He's dead, Lieutenant. It looks like he was killed after falling from a great height."

"I can't believe it. You mean the wind blew him out of the tunnel?"

Buckley felt devastated; he had never lost a man under his command before. He forced back his emotions and did everything in his power to maintain control in front of the team. He had to stay strong for them. It was easier said than done. Steel spoke again, bringing Buckley back to reality.

"Lieutenant, I'm going to send down the cables to get your team out of there. Word is that there is going to be a drone strike coming your way in a few minutes, so we don't need any more casualties."

Having information that was too important to overlook, Buckley responded, "Sir, we found a passage down here I want to investigate. We were forced into it when we sheltered ourselves from the wind. I think it might be a way into the main structure. If I'm correct, we can go in and be out of this tunnel when the drones deploy."

"All right, go with your gut, Lieutenant, but maintain radio contact. Only go in as far as it takes for you to determine where it goes."

"Yes, sir, I'll contact you when we figure that out."

"Team Falcon will be in the hole after the drone strike."

"Roger that." Buckley signed off.

Refusing to be carried off the field, Vacek, dazed and hurt, gave the order to activate the drones. Navy Lieutenant, Junior Grade, Seth Grabowski ordered the Troika drone system to deploy. Troika was a three-drone system that positioned each drone to continuously support the other two. His staff was readying the console to accommodate the new drone configuration.

The drones were small but heavily armed. Each one was equipped with identical weapon systems. They carried sensors, lasers, and small cigar-sized missiles that could clear out a small enemy force.

Going into a large space, the tubular tunnel—they were going to fly in formation—was shaped like a vertical triangle. One of the three quad copters would ride high toward the peak while the two companions would ride low and wide toward each side. If one was damaged or destroyed, the others would detect and then destroy their target all while relaying information and video back to the surface.

Much had happened since those first helicopters landed at the site. First while on the surface, Team Hawk searched unsuccessfully for an entrance into the tower, and then a single drone uneventfully trekked down the tunnel. That was followed by the manned jet pack traveling deep into the tube just to be run out of the tunnel by powerful turbulence.

One member of Team Hawk was killed in support of the incursion of the jet pack pilot, and the remaining six members were going out of contact to explore an opening in the wall. This could be their break to locate the tower entrance or maybe something else.

*****

Troika

The Troika lifted off the ground and flew toward the pit. Each drone had a controller on a console for mission deployment, but as the operation developed, each flying destroyer acted independently.

The show continued for the people observing the operation. Their excitement grew, and the scene became electrifying as they watched the new drones lift off, flying three abreast toward the pit. Once again, the object of the crowd's interest disappeared down the moat. As noise levels diminished, the crowd settled down with anticipation of the next act.

Grabowski, drinking a mug of black coffee, had his own monitoring station, with screens that showed feeds from all the drones. He could see strong lights spreading out in front of the formation, giving him a good forward view of the scene.

Automatically the drone configuration shifted into battle mode. One moved up to form the peak as the other two spread out laterally. The Troika was established. Now the task was to find this "standing" object down the tunnel. There was no hint of caution as they proceeded.

The principles ruling the troika program is to draw out the enemy and neutralize it. Having been attacked by an unknown enemy made this mission straight forward. No last-minute decisions would be needed. They would eliminate the target.

Only a very clear indication of surrender could possibly stop the attack. Otherwise the mission would be executed as planned. The Troika moved forward in search-and-destroy mode. Deeper and deeper, they advanced down the tunnel.

Reaching the point where Lt. Vacek turned around, they pushed forward. The sensors showed no activity, revealing nothing.

Grabowski realized that if the mission continued this way, he would have a problem. The drones were approaching their point of no return, and they hadn't discovered anything. He had to make a decision.

He ordered the technicians to stop the drones and have them hover in place. His logic was that they would be able to hover there for about five minutes as opposed to proceeding down the tunnel for less time. He informed the technicians to keep their eyes open.

The signal went out from the technicians that brought the drones to a controlled stop, hovering quietly. Floodlights from the stationary unmanned aircraft bathed the tunnel, fore and aft. One minute went by and then another, then a third minute passed. Almost simultaneously, Lt. JG Grabowski was about to send the recall transmission when the drones activated. Grabowski pulled his hands back away from the controls and let the drones do their work.

Looking closely at his monitor, he saw a figure. It looked like something standing up at the side of the tunnel. On detecting movement, the drones switched to attack mode. They were cycling through their task menu independently. An attack was imminent.

Observed by the console technicians, drone one, at the peak of the formation, switched on its missile system. Next, weapon targeting put crosshairs on the target, followed by the missile activating and launching.

It took a fraction of a second for the missile to reach its target and detonate. On Grabowski's monitor, the form disappeared from the screen in a flash of light. In the brief lull after the blast, the drones cycled out of attack mode. All seemed calm; it was time to recall the drones.

Grabowski was about to order the recall of the drones when on his monitor a visible blue streak of electrical current formed at the target's location. One stream of electricity turned into two then three. Swirling electric waves formed and danced in the air moving toward the drones. That was the last information transmitted by the troika. The screen went to static and then black. The console controls went dead.

Stumped, Grabowski demanded to know what happened. Controllers scurried around checking circuits on and. under the console, doing diagnostic tests. Two minutes passed, the console was still dead. and none of the technicians had a clue to what went wrong.

At that point. they still didn't know the status of the drones. Were they operational. or had they shut down? Every indicator showed that they were not functioning. Four minutes passed, and there was no sign of drone activity.

Grabowski pondered his next move. He knew that whatever they fired on was destroyed, yet the drones seemed to have been destroyed as well. *What can I commit next?* The question was answered by Capt. Rex Steel.

Steel said, "We're going down into the pit and kick some ass while we have the chance."

Grabowski replied, "Captain, I don't recommend it. We don't know what happened to the drones yet."

I'll make that call, Lieutenant." Steel pointed to his bars showing that he was the ranking officer on the scene.

"That would be crazy. It's a big unknown down there. You could be walking into a trap."

Steel sneered and said, "Just the way I like it." He walked away.

Grabowski under his breath muttered, "Stupid jarhead."

Rex Steel was a career Marine. He was a mustang. He joined the Corps at seventeen as a private and worked his way up to his present rank of captain. As an enlisted man, he spent tours of duty in Iraq and Afghanistan.

As a buck sergeant in Afghanistan, he received a field commission and was promoted to second lieutenant. His promotion came following acts of bravery that stemmed from an incident where his platoon leader was hit by gunfire. Without any concern for his own safety, while protecting the wounded officer, he led the rest of the platoon through hostile gunfire to safety.

His promotion gave him command of a combat platoon of Marines. Highly decorated during his tours in the Middle East, on his return to the states, he applied to BRC (Basic Recon Course) at Camp Pendleton in California. Successfully completing recon training, he led Marines in the Cuban Conflict with the Second Recon Battalion out of Camp Lejeune North Carolina. Through his impressive service in Cuba, he was promoted to his current rank of captain.

*****

Drone Strike

At the nine-minute mark, a sailor at the edge of the pit yelled, "Hey, there's something coming up the tube!" The staging area jumped to life. Those with weapons grabbed them and trained them on the pit. They were preparing to battle whatever was surfacing.

Slowly and deliberately, the three drones, under unknown control, surfaced in line. Their props whirred as they rose out of the pit. They paused momentarily and then proceeded toward the command console. Grabowski was dumbfounded as his three technicians frantically tried to regain control of their drones. They were now within twenty feet and closing. Grabowski could only watch.

The last thing the young naval officer saw was the three drones lined up directly in front of him. He sensed what was going to happen and tried to run for his life. Before he could make a move, he heard the missile system switch on. The rockets fired. The workstation and all personnel nearby were obliterated.

In response to the attack, the armed sailors, marines, and soldiers raised their weapons targeting the drones, but before anyone could fire, the drones switched off, went limp, and crashed to the ground.

That didn't stop the military force from putting dozens of rounds into the immobilized drones. Recklessly firing at the dormant devices, personnel were falling from stray rounds and ricochets. Unbeknownst to those suffering from friendly fire; the drones went inactive the moment the rockets were launched.

*****

The Vent

Team Hawk collected themselves and moved deeper into the vent. They had no idea what had just happened in the tunnel or on the surface. Communication problems made it impossible to contact the outside world. As they hiked into the new passageway, all radio communication just stopped. The thickness of the walls and hundreds of feet of earth between them and the surface, stopped them from talking to anyone.

After hiking in for about ten minutes, they came upon an intersection, with adjacent passages traveling in different directions. Buckley stopped the group to get his bearings. There were two tubes leading off the main. One went up at a thirty-degree angle back in the direction that they came. One went straight, continuing on the same course, and one went down at a thirty-degree angle opposite of the one going up.

Essentially cut off from the world, Team Hawk was moving blindly. The decision to go on depended on the needs of the group. Going down would take them farther away from the surface, and to Buckley that didn't seem like a logical choice. He chose to reverse course and go up. This, he thought, would be in the direction of the tower. It was an educated guess because none of the navigation equipment worked.

Buckley said, "We need to go this way, up, toward the surface. We may find the chamber that was viewed by Earhart's drone."

He thought about what he had just said and realized that Earhart wasn't with them. He was dead on the surface. Buckley felt a rush of guilt with the thought that he had failed him.

Their hike increased to a steep angle. Team Hawk labored upward with the hope they would soon find a way out. When they reached the highest point, they saw nothing but a continuation of tunnel ahead.

Buckley said, "Take a five-minute break. It looks like we could be at this a while."

*****

Aftermath

On the surface, it was a gruesome scene. All the controls at the elaborate console and one of the helicopters were totally destroyed. Along with the shock of what happened, there was terrible confusion. In this mission, the tables were turned; their own weapons were used against them.

Medical workers tried to assess the chaotic scene. Medics and corpsmen moved around assisting the wounded. First aid supplies were hastily being unpacked, passed out, and used to treat the wounded.

Eight men were dead, killed by the drones. Several others were injured by friendly fire. Many of the unharmed personnel were in shock.

Among the dead was Lieutenant JG Grabowski, who died at his post. He didn't know what hit him as he was blown to bits by the missiles he was supposed to be in control of.

When General Ray arrived on the scene with reinforcements, morale could not have been lower. He arrived by a different mode of transportation. With the surface of the island smooth, flat, and stable, it was decided to bring in larger aircraft. C130s started landing north of the site, and with that, the pillbox and trench area were quickly secured with a new overwhelming force.

The first C130 had no problems landing. It was utilizing an extra mile of the flat surface to land. At first, it was thought that the surface would be too slippery for winged aircraft, so the lead plane landed at full throttle. The logic was that if the surface was not stable enough, it could lift off and fly around again. Fortunately, a touch-and-go wasn't necessary. The plane landed uneventfully, using most of the distance allotted, to come to a complete stop.

More E-Corps units arrived and found Captain Steel in his small makeshift command area. He was more than ready to go, but after the drones attacked, he had to wait. Now with the availability of Army Ranger Condor team and Navy SEAL Osprey Team on the scene, he had to wait and coordinate with them.

There was only one team that was not on the scene. Harrier team was on liberty, and their leader was out of town. That was fine with Steel because Navy Lt. Cmdr. David Collins, Harrier Team leader and E-Corps commander, was the only member of E-Corps that outranked him. Steel liked being in charge and knew he was qualified to lead this highly skilled unit. Some of the leaders of the other teams were of equal rank to Steel, but he was the senior man with more time in grade, placing him in command.

*****

The Dome

After a much-needed break, Team Hawk continued down the tunnel. It took another fifteen minutes to finally reach an outlet. Corporal Kelly, who was walking point, observed a dimly lit area up ahead. Buckley thought, *Was this another junction, or was this the end of the passageway?*

As they advanced up to the opening, Buckley indicated that he wanted Brewer to take up a position just outside the passageway to provide cover for the moving team. Brewer advanced to a spot and dropped to a prone position where he could see into the lit area. He scanned it, discovering that they were entering a large expansive area. When he was satisfied that the area was clear, he gave the signal for the team to move up.

Cautiously, Team Hawk advanced into the opening in single file. They quickly discovered that they were on a high walkway that clung to the structure's outside wall. Buckley directed the team to move into the shadows.

Crouching down, he slowly moved to the edge of the walkway, getting a glimpse of what was around them. They had entered a large circular room. Buckley could see that walkways went all the way around the perimeter. He also saw that there were two walkways below their position and one above. Seeing that the top was rounded, he concluded what they were in was a dome.

The lighting was subdued, emanating from long vertical recessed fixtures on the wall. In the low light, he could barely distinguish where the floor met the wall. It blended perfectly with the surroundings and gave off no reflection. Buckley could see to the far wall; it, too, was obscured by its flat black texture. He estimated the distance and guessed that it was over a hundred yards across and, judging the vertical distance between walkways, was ten to twelve feet. He estimated the height of the dome was 100 to 150 feet.

Buckley directed in a low voice, "Kelly, bring up the Barrett and set up cover for us."

Kelly replied, "Aye-aye, sir."

Corporal Kelly, USMC, came up next to the lieutenant and stretched out in a prone position at the edge of the walkway. He took the front cover off his scope, then he removed the back. His weapon was a Barrett fifty-caliber rifle. The fifty cal. was a powerful sniper rifle that could stop enemy personnel with accuracy at great distances.

It was a deadly weapon, an antipersonnel weapon, but it could deal with more than just the flimsy human body; it could also stop vehicles by damaging the engine block with armor-piercing ammunition. It also had the penetrating power to hit targets shielded behind cinder block walls. A round from the Barrett could kill an enemy hiding behind it.

Kelly put his eye up to the scope and swept the area. When he was satisfied that it was safe to proceed, he gave Buckley the high sign. On that signal, Buckley returned to the team and told them to follow him.

With Kelly in support, Team Hawk moved to the right on the walkway high above the floor. As they moved in unison, small details were revealed. There were ramps that ascended to the upper walkway, and farther along they discovered a descending ramp. Several passageways were scattered along the walkways going into the side walls.

Buckley nodded for Brewer and Stiles to move down the first ramp. At the bottom, they looked around. When they determined that it was safe, they signaled the team to come down. Kelly was

THE TUNNELS OF EARTH

summoned forward to the edge of the next ramp, where he took up his next support position.

As the unit advanced down the ramp toward the base of the structure, they observed upright and angular supports that held up the ramps and walkways. The dome was made of the same flat black material that they found everywhere.

Moving quicker now, Kelly had to hustle to cover the team as they moved around and down the next ramp. Team Hawk was now descending to the floor. Moving down to the base of the ramp, they clung to the walls in the deep shadows.

Kelly moved down to the first walkway where he took up his next position. Team Hawk was now moving across the floor. There was a different indirect light coming from one side of the structure. The lighting was much brighter, revealing details.

Hawk moved as they were trained, slowly and quietly. They combed the area, finding it empty. The dome was devoid of equipment, personnel, and anything else you might find in a space this size. After exploring one end of the dome, they started moving back in the other direction.

Withdrawing up to the first raised level, the group started to circle around to the other side. While proceeding around the walkway, muffled sounds could be heard coming from the lighted area. Someone or something was entering from a ground-level passageway.

Alerted by the movement, Team Hawk quickly hurried into the shadows, out of sight. Kelly looked down the high-powered rifle scope in anticipation of a big target. From his new position, Buckley could see that the lighted side of the structure was a massive opening.

This new opening was a tunnel located on the south east side of the dome. It had an arched ceiling overhead. From their location off to the side, they couldn't determine any details other than it was the source of the sound and the brighter lighting. Remaining quiet, Team Hawk waited, preparing themselves for what was about to enter.

Located on the west side of the arch, they watched as an unusual hovering vehicle entered from the tunnel. It looked like a plain rectangle, maybe a small school bus without wheels. Turning right, it moved toward the eastern sidewall. Its movement was in the opposite direction from where Kelly watched. When the strange vehicle came to a stop, more details appeared. Copper in color, it was boxy and did not look aerodynamic at all, yet it hovered about a foot above the floor, with no measurable sound.

Next out of the tunnel came unusual beings, riding on individual vehicles that also hovered above the floor like the boxy truck. Five humanoids, riding on hovercrafts, pulled up next to the rectangle as two other humanoids exited the boxy vehicle. From his location, Buckley couldn't tell if they were living or not.

The humanoids had some human traits, but there was a notable difference. They were pearl white with appendages similar to arms but longer. They were most likely robots. If they had legs, they were short and concealed on the hovercraft. No separation was detectable between the head and body. Perhaps they were robots that could go and work where their masters could not.

When on the hover vehicles, they moved effortlessly, but when they dismounted, they moved mechanically and painfully slow.

The humanoid group assembled at the far wall. A hidden door rose up in the wall, and half of the group walked slowly in. From across the dome, Team Hawk couldn't tell what they were doing. Buckley thought that it was important to the mission to get some data on these beings. He indicated to Petty Officers Stiles and Brewer to work their way around to the left, along the walkway.

Buckley said, "Be careful and stay close to the wall. Use the supports for cover. Secure some pictures, video, and whatever readings you can pick up. Keep your weapons ready, but use them only as a last resort. We're not here to fight."

Acknowledging the order, the two men moved off cautiously. They worked their way around the platform to get in a good position. Brewer was a weapons specialist, but he was also carrying a video camera on this mission. Stiles was organizing some of his sensors thinking about which detection device he wanted to use first.

The slight movement of the SEALs caught the attention of an observant humanoid on the floor. It, too, had sensors that made it aware that something was moving on the walkway. Stiles and Brewer were moving, unaware that they were now being observed by an alien onlooker.

Focusing on the walkway, the humanoid moved slowly in the direction of the intruders. As it advanced, it concentrated directly on the area where Brewer and Stiles were. It was checking sensors, trying to identify the life forms that it made contact with.

With their tasks in the dome complete, the humanoid workers mounted their vehicles and receded down the main tunnel. Kelly saw what was unfolding and had the single humanoid stalking the team lined up in his sights.

Suddenly a new group of faster and more agile humanoids appeared in the dome. They moved aggressively toward the hiding pair, holding what looked like weapons. From the tip of these weapons, red light beams bathed the area.

These new arrivals were smaller, white in color with bulky upper bodies, holding their weapons with more humanlike arms. Laser light bathed the area. They were hunting.

There were now four alien beings involved in the search. They didn't have a lock on the exact location of Team Hawk. They were seventy-five feet away moving in a search pattern. Buckley signaled Torres and Cooper to back off toward the ramp to upper levels.

Stiles and Brewer, now very aware of what was happening, abandoned their investigation and started to drop back from their position. The initial and closest humanoid detected their movement and ramped up its weapon level. It went from a wide scanning laser to a compressed beam. Seconds later it fired.

Hit by the beam, Stiles's body jerked back slumping to the deck. Brewer dropped down next to him to assess the condition of his friend and saw a terrible deep cauterized burn on his chest. He knew that Stiles could not have survived the blast. He tried to remain as still as possible, attempting to target his assailant. Another beam hit Stiles's lifeless body again, making a sizzling sound.

Unnerved and no longer concerned about stealth, Brewer aimed his weapon, returning fire. The shot was precise, hitting the humanoid in the head section. Its body rocked backward, collapsing down on the deck. It laid there for a moment but then slowly started to raise itself to an upright position.

Unaware of what had happened to the other robot behind them, the other humanoids were stalking Buckley, Torres, and Cooper. They hadn't found them yet. The team stayed low and moved to get higher, away from their pursuers. Kelly, seeing that Brewer was being targeted, aimed for a kill shot. With the single damaged humanoid in his sights, he squeezed off a single round.

With the humanoid struggling to stand up, it was knocked to the deck again; Kelly's shot split its head in half. It continued to move erratically, convulsing on the deck, unable to stand. In futility, it fired its laser harmlessly in random directions, not able to target Team Hawk. Kelly, still on the first level, said to himself, "One down, three to go." He chambered another round in the Barrett and looked for his next target.

The three remaining humanoids were hot on the trail of the three retreating team members. Brewer saw his chance and got up to move again. He kept an eye on the position of the pursuers across the dome.

Kelly was patient, waiting for a chance to take another good shot. He could see his team moving up the ramp above him, and finally he had a bead on the lead humanoid. It crested the second level as Kelly lined up the shot. The second one, lower on the ramp, was coming up directly behind the first. The Marine sharpshooter took the shot. He hoped for a double hit with the powerful fifty-caliber round. He got his wish; the bullet struck the first humanoid, passing through it, slamming into the second.

The round struck the lead humanoid in the upper torso. Instead of downing it and hitting the second in the head, there was a massive explosion that rocked the dome. The first humanoid was fragmented, while the second one right behind was engulfed in flames. The third humanoid coming up several feet behind fell back down the ramp, out of sight.

Kelly turned and watched as the team reached the third level, disappearing into the passage. He looked across to another level and saw Brewer making his way back toward the team. Moving up to the third level, Brewer slipped out of sight into the side passage. Seconds later, he observed Brewer reappear out of the tunnel to take up a position covering him so he could get back to the group.

Lieutenant Buckley moved into position next to Brewer. He saw that he was visibly distraught and shaking badly.

Fearing the worst, he said, "Where's Stiles?"

Responding, Brewer said, "He didn't make it, sir; He was hit by that ray gun. He was burned, burned badly, sir."

Buckley grimaced at the thought of losing another team member. He sighed and said, "We have to bring him out. If it's all clear down there, we need to get him."

Brewer continued, "I think we got all the bad guys, sir."

Buckley turned to the other team members crouched inside the passageway. "Doc, you and Sergeant Torres, get down to Stiles's position and bring him out."

Turning back to Brewer, he said, "SEAL, are you okay to set cover so we can get Stiles back here?"

"Yes, sir."

Buckley, to Torres and Cooper, said, "Okay, go get him."

Moving resolutely, Torres and Doc Cooper moved down to recover Stiles's body. Still on high alert but sure the danger had passed, Kelly put down the fifty cal. and removed the more versatile Heckler and Koch from the sling over his shoulder. He needed to find out what happened to the third humanoid. With his weapon pointing in the direction of the destroyed humanoids, he approached to see if he got them all.

With a sense of urgency, Torres and Cooper arrived at Stiles's location. They smelled burned flesh permeating the air. Doc Cooper took a moment to confirm there were no life signs. Torres lifted the weight of Stiles's lifeless body over his shoulder and struggled to gain his footing. He regained his balance and started up the ramp toward the passage.

Kelly cautiously approached the destroyed humanoids. He was aware of everything around him as he flipped the selector switch on the H&K to automatic. He lifted it, putting the sights on the ridge in front of him.

Torres moved slowly under the weight of Stiles climbing the ramps. Through great effort he succeeded to reach the third level. He and Cooper carried Stiles's lifeless body into the passageway.

Doc Cooper turned and gave the signal to Kelly to return to the group. Kelly held up one finger indicating he needed a minute. Turning back to the destroyed and burning humanoids, he moved in to get a closer look. Looking back once more to see that Brewer was still covering him, he continued forward.

The first humanoid was ten feet away, its chest blown apart. It looked like it was made of a heavy plastic material. The second was destroyed by the blast and was still burning. It was propped up at a forty-five-degree angle against the wall. The third was still over the crest of the ramp out of sight.

Brewer watched his partner's approach to the edge of the ramp, raising his weapon ready to fire in Kelly's support. Before any target came into view, he saw a burst of red light and the third robot charging over the crest. Kelly fired his weapon, set on automatic. Losing his balance his aim became erratic, missing his target. Trying to regain his footing, he was hit by the red laser blast. Wounded and reeling, Kelly glanced off the edge of the walkway and fell to the dome floor.

Brewer fired his weapon set on semiautomatic. Rounds flew out of the muzzle as fast as he could pull the trigger. The first-round hit, then the second. They were both headshots. The third hit the upper torso, but the fourth did the job. It was a body shot. The humanoid exploded much like the first one Kelly destroyed. What was left of the humanoid fell and slid down to the bottom of the ramp.

On hearing more shots, Buckley rushed out of the passage and lay prone next to Brewer. The petty officer was frantic. He just watched his sidekick killed right in front of his eyes. Not to mention being with Stiles when he was killed.

Buckley yelled to Cooper, "Come on, Doc! We got to get down there fast!"

Buckley thought that they were pressing their luck, but they had to try. Buckley and Cooper sprinted down the ramps to the floor where they found Kelly's lifeless broken body. Torres was now covering the action. Brewer was so upset; he was unable to do so.

THE TUNNELS OF EARTH

Doc Cooper checked his vital signs and determined Kelly, too, was dead. They were now close to the edge of the large tunnel opening in the side of the dome.

Once again, a fallen team member's body had to be carried up the ramp to the passageway. Buckley, lifting Kelly's body over his shoulder, proceeded up the ramp. Cooper hesitated; like Kelly, her curiosity got the best of her. She took the twenty or so steps to the side tunnel.

She glanced down the tunnel and saw what seemed to be an endless passage. It was straight while angling downward. It diminished over what seemed like miles. The arch was large and menacing. It was big enough to fly small aircraft through. It gradually extended downward at about a ten-degree angle.

On the sidewalls she saw ramps ascending to walkways running along the stretch of tunnel. It was different from the dome. One major difference was this tunnel was well lit. There were bright lights recessed into the matte black walls. The ramps and walkways on either side of the tunnel were spaced out at various heights. Along the walkways were hatches. They had doors with portholes, big enough to drive one of those rectangular vehicles through.

Cooper was lingering too long, captivated but not afraid. It was a fascination with this subterranean world. She knew it was time to break away and rejoin her team.

Suddenly, before she had a chance to withdraw, a hatch on the far side of the tunnel opened and humanoids poured out, moving toward the dome. Her alertness returned, and she feared her opportunity to leave had passed. They were on the far side of the tunnel moving up the slope to the dome. The chief petty officer could only hope that she hadn't been detected.

After seeing the humanoids weapons in action, Cooper knew she wouldn't have a chance if they found her trying to retreat out of the tunnel. She dropped to the deck and crawled slowly and cautiously in the opposite direction. She was crawling downward into the tunnel away from the dome.

Dozens of humanoids were now in the dome. She didn't dare look back. She feared for her team, now wondering what happened to her. She was also afraid the humanoids would ambush them. Moving deeper, Cooper prayed that Lt. Buckley and Team Hawk made it to safety.

The tunnel was quiet, but back in the dome there were loud battle sounds. There was gunfire and loud explosions rocking the distant section of the dome. Still moving, Cooper tried to figure out how she could reverse her course to escape. She kept crawling downward, farther away from the action.

As she moved deeper and deeper in the tunnel, she moved farther away from Team Hawk. She tried to remember her training on evasive maneuvering, but her training was limited, much less extensive than the Special Forces members of Eagle Corps. She was a Navy corpsman with little survival education.

The passage continued to angle down. At that moment, she had the feeling it would go on forever. If it didn't end soon, it could only mean that it would continue to travel out under the Atlantic Ocean. She mustered enough courage to turn around and look back toward the dome. To her surprise, she saw that she had advanced much deeper into the tunnel than she thought.

The dome was hundreds of yards behind her. It was almost all tunnel to the rear and to the front. She stopped and listened. She could hear the hum of what she thought was machinery down lower in the passage. It was definitely time to turn around.

Feeling more confident, Cooper started to walk back up the tunnel. She moved in a manner so as not to make any noise. The dome was growing in the distance, and she thought with a little luck, she was going to make it.

As she got closer, she could see the humanoids rounding the corner, returning to the tunnel. They were moving fast, riding on their hovering vehicles. Cooper thought that they would soon discover and kill her. She turned and proceeded back down the tunnel once again.

Now running, Cooper saw there were passages behind open doors in the side wall. She knew that she was passing through well-lit areas, but at no time was there any indication that she had been seen by the humanoids.

THE TUNNELS OF EARTH

Weighing her options, she chose to get out of the main tunnel. Without hesitation, she went through an open door into the first passageway she came to. She discovered that this particular passageway ran parallel to the main tunnel. She stopped at the door and peeked around the corner, trying to get a glimpse of the fast-moving humanoids. They were closing in on her position.

Cooper decided to go up the parallel tunnel to get by the humanoids. She started running again. As she ran, the passageway started flat but then rose, spiraling upward.

She realized immediately that she had made a terrible mistake going this way. She knew that she couldn't go back, so she went higher in the upward spiraling passageway. She moved up until the passage ended on a flat platform in a new domed area. This dome was much smaller in size than the first. It was different because it had large openings on two sides running parallel to the main tunnel.

Cooper wasn't in this new dome long before she heard something coming from one of the openings. She ducked back into the passage. To her amazement, she saw a flying vehicle traveling up the passage, passing through the dome, and then disappearing through the higher exit. She thought, *What is this, a bus stop?*

Moments later, another vehicle went by, moving down the passageway. It was empty. No one was driving, and there were no passengers. It was an enclosed vehicle with windows all around. She had to believe that the vehicle was self-operating.

Returning to the platform, she moved down to the end where it widened out. Piles of what looked like building material was stacked in the narrow space. She thought, *This must be a drop-off point in the tunnel.* From what she could tell, this was a depot where trains would drop off its cargo then return for more.

Cooper realized that she was tired, overwhelmed with fatigue. Feeling safe for the moment, she decided to rest her eyes. She thought that she could hide in the stacks and close her eyes for a few minutes then escape the way she came in. Not part of the plan, she fell asleep.

When she awoke, she felt the helmet pinching uncomfortably against the back of her head and neck. She thought to herself, *I'm taking this damn thing off.* She unlatched the helmet, took a deep breath, and then lifted it over her head.

She took a short breath, followed by a bigger one. The atmosphere was heavy but breathable! Realizing this, she hurled the helmet to the back of the pile. Next she thought about how she was going to deal with this uncomfortable suit.

She was hot and sweaty, but she had to live with it. She didn't have a uniform underneath her suit, and she didn't want to run around in her skivvies. Anyway, it was better without the helmet.

Somewhat rested, she looked at her watch. She realized that she slept three hours. Optimistically she thought that the others must be on the surface by now, trying not to think the worst that could have happened.

*****

Team Hawk had not been heard from for hours. Steel needed to find them. He also wanted to go down the main tunnel and confront whatever hostile entity caused all the mayhem topside.

Team Condor's Army Spec 4 Arthur Benson touched down at the bottom of the pit. Almost simultaneously Captain Steel's boots touched down lower on the curve. One by one, Falcon, Condor, and Osprey team members reached the base of the pit. It was a force three times larger in strength than normal.

Steel's group moved quickly and quietly down the tunnel. He ordered lights out using night vision, infrared, and ultraviolet to maneuver. Eighteen men moved as one. Their objective was to get to that point where all the bad things happened.

They passed the place where Vacek activated the angry wind. Then they approached the spot where the bolts of electricity took over the drones.

Steel thought, *What will be waiting up ahead?*

They were tired, but they kept moving. Their training prepared them for this. Anticipation grew as they got close to the target area. Advancing down the tunnel, team members periodically stepped on, kicked, and tripped over dark obstacles on the deck.

Steel made an arm gesture. Everyone stopped then crouched down. Steel called up the sniper and had him cover the first team moving in. He used his night vision scope to scan the tunnel out front. Steel indicated for Condor to move forward.

Without hesitation they advanced. After a short distance, they stopped and crouched down again. The next thing that happened was the point man breaking radio silence.

Moving just ahead of his team, Army Ranger Sgt. Vince Blackwell reported, "I found what's left of the bogey."

Steel replied, "Status?"

"It's in a lot of pieces, not living, not dead. It's some kind of machine. It's humanoid in structure, but no way, can't be alive."

*****

Steel snarled into his mic, "Keep moving. We're coming up behind you, stay alert."

Steel waved his hand forward, indicating to the team to move out. Standing up, they were moving again. The last member, the sniper holding his ground, continued to scan the darkness.

Blackwell broke silence again. "I found a door."

Steel said, "Hold your position and cover your angles, we're coming up."

Blackwell's team Condor joined him at the door with their weapons ready. They covered the area down the tunnel as well as the closed door.

Steel reached the scattered humanoid parts and ordered Osprey team to collect what they could and bring them back to the shaft. He continued advancing down the tunnel. Condor team had moved about a hundred feet ahead of them.

Steel felt the hairs on his arms stand up straight as an electric charge was building up around him. He could see the bluish electrical streams churning up ahead where he knew Condor team was positioned. He heard shots and then saw a bright bluish explosive flash. The field of electricity immediately dropped off to zero.

Steel yelled, "Let's move!"

Falcon team sprinted forward. They came upon a battle scene with members of Condor team lying on the deck, being treated for injuries. Steel looked for First Lieutenant David Uber and found that he was unconscious near the door. Falcon Corpsman Doc Eric Forster needed no direction to help the casualties. Steel looked for second in command, Master Sergeant Delbert Brown. He found him applying a pressure bandage to a gash on one of his soldier's head.

"What happened, Top?"

Master Sergeant Brown replied, "Sir, the door opened, and we were engulfed in electric current. A thing was inside the door. It was standing there directing waves of electricity toward us. Before we were immobilized, Sergeant Weber shot him or it, whatever it was."

"The problem was when he fired, the thing exploded taking out those of us closest to the door." Steel looked up and saw the door was still open and said, "Falcon team, follow me."

Finding Blackwell unhurt, he said, "Blackwell, take point."

Steel said to the team corpsman, "Doc, you stay here and help Condor get out of here."

Doc Forster, not fancying the idea of leaving his own team, followed orders and reluctantly replied, "Yes, sir."

Falcon team rushed through the door and found a smaller tunnel moving away. Steel's blood was up, and he was looking for a fight. They moved rapidly into a corridor running parallel with the tunnel. As they moved, the passage rose up and away from where they came. A hundred feet down the corridor, Steel stopped the group and tried to get his bearings. It was dark, and there was nothing he could identify.

While trying to decide his next move, he stepped on something. He flashed his light on the object and saw a carcass of what looked like a dead rat. This made him recall the objects that they were tripping over in the main tunnel. *Were those rats too?* He looked closer and confirmed that it was a large dead rat.

"Where did it come from?" With all the toxic material on the island that would kill any living thing, how could a rat get here?

"Flores," Steel said, "stow this thing in your pack so we can take a look at it later."

THE TUNNELS OF EARTH

He continued, "Okay, people, let's keep going."

The passageway that Falcon team was in was a maze. The first passageway ended but there was a side one off to the left. That tube went on for a while and then stopped abruptly in a dead end. The team backtracked and found another way to go. It too was a dead end.

Frustrated, Steel said, "Let's find our way out of here. These tunnels go nowhere."

Steel made the decision to return to the main tunnel. He thought they might be able to help with Team Condor's casualties.

*****

The CH-53K heavy-lift helicopter slowly cranked up the cable from the depths. Over the last several hours it repeatedly hovered over the pit and executed the thankless job of hoisting the casualties out of the hole. Another body was being hoisted out of the pit as well. It was the body of Ed Stiles being lifted to the surface.

Lt. Buckley, PO Brewer, and SSgt. Torres were already on the surface. Sitting quietly together in the sun, a messenger approached and requested Lt. Buckley report to General Ray.

General Ray was situated in his newly constructed command tent. It was his mobile headquarters. On entering the tent, Buckley saw a group of enlisted men setting up an office, preparing to take care of the general's administrative business. It looked like he was here to stay.

General Ray saw him enter the tent and summoned him into a chair in front of his desk. He said, "Lieutenant, what the hell happened down there?"

Exhausted, he would try to find words to explain to the general what had transpired.

"Sir, Team Hawk went down into the tunnel in support of the Bell Rocket Belt pilot Lieutenant Vacek. We were waiting for him to return from his run down the tunnel when we were caught in a situation. The belt had to escape the pit by outrunning a windstorm. During the windstorm, we sought shelter in a vent on the backside of the tunnel. When the storm was over, we realized that Earhart hadn't made it into the shelter and was thrown from the pit.

"At that point we needed to find our way into that structure and find a reason for all that happened. With permission from my superior, Captain Steel, we followed the opening until eventually it led us to other tunnels. From there we managed to work our way into a subterranean dome.

"On entering that chamber, we encountered alien robots. Some seemed to be workers, but others were aggressive. That's when it all went south. We tried to remain hidden, but they discovered us. That's when Stiles was killed. Cpl. Kelly stopped three of them with his sniper rifle, giving us a chance to recover Petty Officer Stiles's body. We evacuated Stiles and then Kelly became our third casualty when he, too, was attacked. Brewer neutralized the last alien."

Expressionless, General Ray said, "Then what happened?"

Buckley continued, "We had to get Kelly out, so Doc Cooper and I went down to evacuate him. When we got there, he was dead as well. I started to carry him up to our secured location, but when we reached the first level we came under heavy attack by a larger force of humanoids. Under Kelly's weight, I couldn't outrun them, so I had to leave him.

"I thought Doc Cooper was right next to me, but when I told her to run, she was nowhere in sight. I couldn't go back because the aliens were climbing the first ramp fifty feet behind me. PO Brewer and Staff Sergeant Torres covered my retreat with concentrated fire. I didn't turn around, but I could hear the explosions behind me, and I knew the humanoids were being slowed down.

"I made it to the escape tunnel entrance, and the three of us moved inside. The aliens kept coming, and we kept firing, firing at anything that appeared in the entrance. Torres was able to use some of the explosives we had to turn them away. He tossed a satchel charge outside the entrance, and then we dropped back and set another one, twenty feet inside the tunnel. It blew up a few of the humanoids, but more importantly it stopped their advance."

Now seething, General Ray spoke in a low voice, "You lost four members of your team? Three confirmed dead, and your corpsman is missing."

Buckley nervously replied, "Yes, sir."

General Ray tried to hold back his anger. He said, "How could this happen?" You weren't down there to start a war. You were there to find a way in. Did you find a way in?"

Buckley replied, "Sir, in my opinion, what happened couldn't have been avoided. I saw the humanoids and felt that the situation needed to be investigated. After all, sir, it took over ten years for us to see what we were up against. We found out quickly that they had sophisticated weapons and detection equipment. We observed living or mechanical beings down there, and the most important thing we found out was how to stop them."

Buckley paused then said, "Sir, yes, sir, I think we found the way in!"

General Ray responded sarcastically, "I hope your lost troops appreciate that fact, Lieutenant."

His voice changed to a softer tone. "We're dealing with the unknown here, Lieutenant. I can't fault you for taking the initiative. Under similar circumstances, I would have done the same thing.

"Make out a detailed report and have it on my desk tomorrow morning. Now, get the rest of your team out of here. Take them back to Quonset, and Lieutenant, put everything that happened down in your report. I have other teams to worry about now."

What General Ray didn't tell him was that Capt. Steel's team had not reported in from their patrol down below.

When the general was done with him, Buckley returned to where his team waited. He saw one body bag after another being carried up the ramp into a C130.

He saw Doc Forster from Falcon team and said, "Doc, where is Captain Steel?"

"He's still down there, sir. I came back with the casualties of Team Condor. Falcon team found an open door and kept on going."

Buckley watched as nine body bags were carried into the aircraft. He didn't know what had happened up here on the surface, but he thought it must have been a war. Yes, he knew about his team's casualties, he knew what had happened to them. What happened to the others? Who are they? And finally, the most disturbing question was, What happened to Cooper?

Buckley hurried Brewer and Torres aboard a helicopter leaving for the mainland. They were out of the action for now.

Buckley was shaken by the experience. He had been in fights before, but he'd never lost anyone in battle. What bothered him most was the thought of Doc Cooper moving next to him one moment and gone the next. Not gunned down, just gone.

The Seahawk helicopter lifted off with Lt. Buckley, Navy SEAL and leader of Team Hawk, leaning back with his head supported on the bulkhead, staring off into space.

*****

Hitching a Ride

Cooper stood on the platform studying the movement of the unusual trams in the tunnel. She timed the intervals between them and made the decision to board one going north, going up the tunnel. She hadn't seen any of them stop at the platform, so she planned to get a running start and jump aboard the exterior and hold on.

She returned to the area she thought was the boarding zone. Cooper checked her watch in anticipation of the next car. It seemed like a long time, but she could hear the whooshing sound coming up from below. Cooper poised herself to get a running start, but she heard the tram slowing down.

Alarmed, she jumped behind a support and watched the tram come to a complete stop. Cooper thought something was amiss, so she remained hidden until it moved again. She thought about it for a moment and wondered if her presence on the platform triggered it to stop.

She waited for the next tram and then stepped out onto the platform. Once again, the tram stopped. In the rear portion of the car, a door slid open. This time Cooper went to the door and poked her head inside the car looking for occupants. She saw no signs of life, so she stepped in, moving to the rear of the tram, away from the door.

On examining the layout of the car, she noticed there were no seats. There was an open floor plan on either side front to back. In the middle of the car, there was a small standing space with what looked like a set of upright supports every four feet and two horizontal bars running the full length of the tram, front to back. Cooper thought to herself that this reminded her of the city bus she used growing up to get around San Francisco.

The tram surged forward and entered the upward bound tunnel. Just as she started to relax, Cooper realized that she picked the wrong ride to get back to the dome. Looking ahead, she saw the end of the tunnel and experienced the sick feeling of entering a roundabout.

Cooper realized that she made another grave error when the tram looped around and proceeded back down the tunnel. Thinking quickly, she went to the rear door as it approached the station where she boarded. The tram didn't stop. It just kept traveling down the tunnel.

She thought it over and realized. *I have to use the front door to exit.*

Moving toward the front of the tram she waited, hoping that the next station was close. *When will this tram reach another station?* she thought.

Plunging down the tunnel, the black enclosed walls opened up into the side of the spacious main tunnel. She suspected that if she could get off, she would be able to walk right up the tunnel to get out. The problem was the tram was moving too fast to jump off. She considered it but concluded that it would be crazy. She reminded herself that the key was having the ability to "walk" out of the tunnel.

She tried to remain patient while waiting to reach the next station. She prayed that it would be empty. Looking out into the tunnel, Cooper saw machines, big robotic machines on tracks working high, shaping the arched ceiling. There were no operators, and they seemed to work efficiently and independently. She could see that part of this tunnel was not complete.

After what seemed like an eternity, the opening in the large tunnel narrowed down to a smaller one being enlarged. She continued riding downward.

Just when she thought that there were no other stations, the tram surged into a side tunnel big enough for just one car. It began to slow. She made sure to position herself at the front door this time so she could exit when the door opened. Concentrating on the door, she was surprised to see the platform filled with a dozen humanoid robots.

Cooper dropped to the floor hoping she wasn't seen. Her mind raced, thinking that she had to get to the back of the tram behind the entrance door. Staying low and moving fast, she made it to the rear of the car.

She was behind the door when the tram stopped. She didn't feel safe because she remained fully exposed to all parts of the car. The door opened, and humanoids quietly proceeded to enter on their personal hovercrafts. Cooper now understood the reason for the layout of the tram car.

Humanoids entered in single file and advanced to the front of the transport. One after another they advanced as far forward as they could and then stopped. When the column on the right was filled with passengers, touching front to back, the second column began to load.

The process slowed down when a damaged robot hobbled onto the tram. The damaged robot moved forward on the left side and stopped in the front to back position they all assumed.

Cooper's attention was drawn to this robot because it had severe damage. The head was split in two. She panicked; this was the robot in the dome that killed Stiles. Cooper could easily identify bullet impact points on the robot.

She saw what it did to Stiles, so she thought, *Please don't turn around.*

When two thirds of the left side were full, the door closed and the transport continued down the tunnel. Cooper stayed completely still, but she soon realized that there was no looking around or interaction of any kind by the mechanical commuters. She relaxed a little, thinking that these are machines and don't realize that she is in their presence.

The tram glided back out into the main tunnel, continuing in a downward trajectory. Cooper looked out of a small window behind her and was fascinated at the various stages of completion of the arched tunnel. Work was going on in many different areas. Twenty more minutes passed when the tram veered into the wall again. Cooper thought that this would be another stop. She was right.

More humanoids were waiting to enter the shuttle. The door opened, and before Cooper could make a break for it out the back door, more humanoids entered and filled in the remaining slots. The tram was full. She thought that any overflow was going to come back into her area.

The vehicle started moving again. Panic was setting in; she knew that she was too deep in the tunnel to walk out. Cooper would need to find another way to get back to the surface.

With no more room on the tram, it approached yet another stop. The platform was full of the same type of humanoids, but it still slowed and stopped. No humanoids left the tram, and none tried to enter. However, something other than a humanoid came aboard and walked up the center section to the front.

Were Cooper's eyes playing tricks on her, or was this a human being? It was an adolescent, a boy. She wanted to call out to him and see if he could help her, but her instincts told her to remain silent. She would wait. The tram glided on.

After what seemed like hours, several more stations, and no more riders, the tram came to a stop. Ahead there was a large well-lit opening. Cooper thought she was seeing beyond the tunnel but wasn't sure. It had to be near the end of the line.

At this stop the humanoids started to get off. Single file and one column at a time, they exited in an orderly fashion. The tram emptied out, except for the boy. He remained in place when the tram started up again.

Cooper remained frozen in the back. Soon after the tram proceeded forward, the boy started to look around. She couldn't hide, so when he looked toward the back, she was in full view. He got excited and started to move to the back of the car.

He exclaimed, "Are you here from Zome?"

She didn't know what to say. He was speaking English. What did he mean Zome?

He said, "It's about time you arrived. We've been waiting for you a long time." He approached her still asking questions.

Cooper spoke in a soft voice, "What do you mean am I from Zome? I'm from Earth."

Excited, the boy said, "We have been waiting for you."

"I am sorry to disappoint you, but I don't think you were waiting for me because I didn't know that you were here."

His enthusiasm waned, and he said, "You mean you're not from the planet Zome? Why are you wearing that space suit?"

"I'm afraid not. I just arrived here from the surface. This suit is just protection against the elements down here."

The boy looked confused as the tram slowed and stopped.

He said, "This is where I get off."

Cooper confided in him, "I'm lost. Can I get off here with you?"

Now a little disappointed, the boy responded, "That's up to you."

Exiting the tram and still confused, he said, "What surface are you talking about anyway?"

"Earth's surface of course."

"Really. That's where I originally came from, but it's been so long I don't remember much about it."

"How long have you been down here?"

"I can't remember that either."

"You're not down here alone, are you?"

"No, no, I'm not alone. There are hundreds of us."

Cooper's mind was racing. She didn't know what to make of this. How could this boy, not more than fourteen years old, survive in this environment underground surrounded by hostile humanoid robots?

Leaving the tram, Cooper couldn't believe her eyes. She was at the edge of an enormous cavern. It was high, deep, and well lit. It was nothing like the dome or the tunnels that she traveled down.

Cooper and the teenage boy were standing at the wider rounded end of an enormous cavern. Looking down the length of the opening, she could see it taper off with light dimming at the far end. At the narrow end, it was so dark that she couldn't determine where the cavern ended. It just faded away into darkness.

The cavern looked like it was made of natural seabed. Not the endless black material in the tunnels but in a variety of colors you would expect of rock formations. They had different hues of brown, gray, black, and even streaks of white.

There were several openings to various structures, and to her amazement, in the distance, there was an ocean liner. It was gigantic, but it didn't take up more than a small percentage of the cavern. It was high and dry propped up against the cavern wall. She noticed that it was damaged with an enormous gash at the base of the hull near the bow. Looking closer, she determined that this was something else. It was the entrance to the ship from the cavern floor.

Cooper said, "Wow, what's that ocean liner?"

"Oh, that's where I live. It's the *Mist of the Atlantic*."

"The *Mist of the Atlantic*!"

Cooper had heard about this ship. It disappeared in the North Atlantic ten years ago. No one knew what happened to it. It disappeared mysteriously on its return voyage from Canada. After a long thorough search by the Coast Guard, they finally gave up when no clues of what happened to the ship were ever discovered. That was all she knew. The disappearance happened when she was just out of Naval Medical Corps School at METC (Medical Education and Training Campus) in San Antonio Texas.

Cooper and the unidentified youth progressed along a walkway, a type not unfamiliar to Cooper's experience back in the dome.

Pointing to a courtyard, the boy said, "If you're lost, you should come with me."

"Thank you." She had little choice. Cooper then asked, "How did you get here?"

"We came here when the Aalzad accidently captured our ship in a beam as they descended from the sky. It was many years ago. Our cruise ship was dragged down into the ocean about to be destroyed when it was rescued by the Aalzad. We have been down here ever since. My guardian told me that this is a naturally formed air-filled cavern. I was also told that it's the only one of its kind on earth.

"That's why the Aalzad specifically came to this place because they knew that this cavern would be a safe haven. It just wasn't always this big. I can remember a time when there was very little room to get off the ship. For a long time, our motion was restricted, even when the cavern expanded. But over the years, the worker robots shaped this cavern into what it is today.

"The robots are smart. They take care of their jobs, and they take care of us too. Without them we would have perished years ago. As a matter of fact, they saved those of us that died in the shipwreck."

Puzzled, Cooper said. "What do you mean died?"

"People died when we were forced under the surface of the ocean. We were caught in a light beam that opened the ocean under the *Mist of the Atlantic*. When the Aalzad realized what they had done, they captured the *Atlantic Mist* in a protective cocoon of light that stabilized us. But before we were saved, we had dropped in free fall many feet. Many of the passengers had terrible injuries, and others were killed in the fall. When they caught us, we were saved, but it was too late for a number of passengers."

Cooper couldn't believe that she was talking to a young articulate adolescent. He spoke like a mature adult but in a fourteen-year old voice.

"So some people died, right?"

"Yes. They died, but the Aalzad brought them back to life."

Walking with the young boy, they were getting close to the large cruise ship. Cooper saw humans sitting in the courtyard under the looming ocean liner. They saw her but showed no interest.

She stopped the boy and asked, "What's your name? My name is Rachael, Rachael Cooper."

The boy replied, "My name is George Field."

They stopped before they reached the improvised hull entrance.

George thought for a moment with a concerned expression on his face and asked, "Rachael, why are you here?"

Cooper, trying not to reveal their firefight in the dome, said, "We found an opening in the surface of the earth. A group of explorers including me came down to investigate. I got separated, so here I am."

George replied, "I know I have been here a long time. I mean a really long time. I know that my body has not changed. It's the same with all the others too. I never grew up, and they never aged. If the *Mist of the Atlantic* made it to port that night, I would be almost as old as you. Those that died are alive and are the same age they were when they got here. There's a difference though.

"Those that died were brought back to life by artificial means, but their minds were empty. Over time they learned as an infant learns. They learned the things that they lost at death, but all their personal memories were wiped clean.

"They grew into different people. Married couples that died and were revived did not remember being married to each other. Sometimes they got together again because there was a strong attraction between them, but sometimes former couples were not the least bit interested in each other."

Cooper continued, "What are the people doing now?"

"The people have few demands, so they lounge around or sleep for long periods of time. Some of the passengers have the need to lead constructive lives. Those people that feel that way work on the tunnel system helping the robots. Some work in the kitchen preparing food for the people. Of course, their work is limited, but they help in ways that they can."

Inquisitively Cooper said, "I see some people here in the courtyard. They don't seem very interested in the arrival of a stranger. Are they okay?"

"They're okay. They have seen many things that are beyond normal human experience, so you aren't very interesting to them. For the most part, they have no motivation from long periods of inactivity."

Cooper changed the subject. "Why were you on the tram?"

"I am an explorer too. I like to travel around the tunnel system and see what's going on. I go to many parts of the tunnels and chambers and ride the shuttle as often as I can."

"Do any of the robots bother you?"

"No, I have never had a problem going anywhere within the tunnel system. Robots just do their jobs. Occasionally they come back to the base to recharge or for repairs. All they do is work. They are all programed. They know one job, and they stick to it."

"Can you get me out of here, back to the surface?"

"I wouldn't know where to start. The system is a vast underground network with dozens of hubs. My exploring has only revealed the lower part of the system. I will ask my guardian if he can help you."

"Guardian? You mentioned that before. What's a guardian?"

"They are robots, but they are nothing like the worker robots. They are hovering brains. They are spherical beings that float around and talk to us. We learn from them about the Aalzad culture, and they learn things from us."

George continued, "When we first made contact with the guardians, they couldn't communicate with us. Through continuous contact, they learned our language and now they talk to us in English. Some of the passengers speak other languages and their guardians have learned to speak their languages as well. This ship has a Scandinavian crew, many of them speak Swedish. It's funny to hear the guardians speaking Swedish to each other."

"Where are the guardians now?"

"They don't stay here with us. Mostly, they come and go from the Aalzad ship. If they need to know something or we have a need, they appear. I'm surprised Max hasn't shown up yet because of your being here."

Concerned at what George said, Cooper responded, "Max? He knows I'm here?"

"That's what I named him. I think he knows you're here because of all the contact you had with the workers."

"Will I be a problem for you, my being here?"

"I don't see why you would be. You're not a threat, are you?"

"They might think I am. I have to tell you that we had trouble with some of the robots when we entered the tunnels. They attacked us."

George pointed. "Look, he's right over there. Let's ask him."

Cooper looked in the direction that George indicated and saw none of the familiar shaped humanoids. She did see what looked like a large elongated stainless-steel balloon floating above the walkway. She thought to herself, *How can I explain what happened?*

George greeted Max as if he were human. "Hello, Max, I have a new friend."

Max was a spherical being, no longer than thirty inches high and eighteen inches across. Rounded at the top and bottom, he had no perceptible arms or legs, but there were two big eyes or sensors in the upper portion, and it had a panel of lights and sensors around its midline. Those were its only discernable features. He approached George and Rachael Cooper.

Max, in a clear, cheerful human voice, said, "Yes, I can see that. Welcome, we have always wondered when people from the surface would finally reach us. You are the first. George Field calls me Max, so I will introduce myself as such. What is your name?"

"My name is Rachael Cooper."

"Rachael Cooper, there was a disturbance at the other end of the tunnel. Have you any knowledge of that?"

Rachael was nervous; she felt she could not lie, so she said, "Yes, I was with a team of explorers when we were attacked by some of your humanoid robots. I was separated from my group and got lost in your tunnel system."

Max acknowledged, "Yes, I heard some of our workers were destroyed. By what means do explorers destroy worker robots?"

"My companions carried weapons as a safety precaution and had to use them in self-defense."

Asking with the appropriate inquisitive inflections, Max stated, "Where are your companions now?"

"I hope that they have returned to the surface."

"We have knowledge that there are other explorers now. What do you know about them?"

"I know that other teams were available, but I don't know about anyone else entering the tunnels."

"We will know soon enough. In the meantime, I want to welcome you on behalf of the citizens of Zome.

"The Aalzad come from a faraway galaxy and have come to earth to mine resources from your planet, that you have in such abundance. They did not come here to harm the inhabitance of this planet. Since our accidently bringing the *Mist of Atlantic* into our society, there has not been any contact with the outside population until today. We have been undetected for over forty earth years.

"The original craft that came from Zome set the stage for deep water access to the open cavern we are in right now. Here on the Atlantic Ocean in an area halfway between Cox Ledge and a place where the shelf drops thousands of feet at Alvin's Canyon, we found this natural dry air-filled cavern. It has suited most of our needs, so we established this spot for our operation.

"Once the Aalzad started the work of making a base on Earth, they left all of the work to us. There are no Aalzad citizens on earth now. However, we are in preparation for their return."

Reluctantly, Cooper asked, "What will you do with me?"

"Do with you? You are welcome here. I believe that you are not here to harm us. You are free to move around as you please."

"I am not here, as you say, to harm anyone. On the contrary, I am a healer. I take care of sick and injured people."

Max, in a dismissive voice, said, "We have no need for anyone with your skill here, but you can remain with us as our guest."

Max turned and began floating away when Cooper realized how hungry she was.

She hollered, "Hey, Max! What do people eat down here?"

Max turned and said, "We have food, food delivered by the robots. Are you hungry?"

"Yes, I am."

Max spoke to George, "George, take Rachael Cooper to the Tropos Magra and show her where she can get something to eat. Show her what you eat and give her a choice of food. I will let the kitchen know you are coming."

"I'll take her there now. Goodbye, Max." George said that with real affection as Max moved away.

Cooper became nervous about this arrangement. She was too hungry to worry about it though.

George said with real excitement, "Rachael, come with me. We're going up to the spaceship."

Cooper didn't know what to think about that. *I'm going to a spaceship!*

They walked away from the shadow of the *Mist of the Atlantic* and toward the side wall of the cavern. Located on the wall was a long ramp that led to a large smooth object imbedded in the overhead rock. There was clearly an opening in the seafloor, and this smooth object rested on top of it. It was gigantic. She could only assume that the Atlantic Ocean was directly above this alien craft.

As they approached the top of the ramp, there was a large door. It was open, and George was heading inside. Looking up toward the center of the smooth artificial underbelly, Rachael saw a circle etched on the craft looming above the cavern. It had to have been at least the size of two football fields side by side. Directly below it on the cavern floor was another circle, embedded in the floor. It was a mirror image of the underside of the Tropos Magra. The only difference was, on the outside perimeter of the floor circle, it was lined with a series of holes, possibly drains.

Reaching the entrance of the Tropos Magra, Rachael Cooper followed George through the big door. Walking into what looked like the hangar deck of a monstrous aircraft carrier, they were entering a quarter section of the ship. There were various vehicles around the bay. To one side there was what looked like a stack of canisters. They were familiar to her because in training, she had access to dud smoke projectiles. These devices were unused and had obviously been stored there for a long period of time.

Passing through another door into another quarter section, there was what looked like a manufacturing facility. Cooper saw robots working on the far side of one of the rooms. To the left there were shelves filled with small boxes. George proceeded over to the boxes, reached inside one, and took out what looked like a large stuffed wrap.

He turned and said, "Here, Rachael, try this."

Skeptically, she looked at what he was holding in his hand. To Cooper, it looked like a doughy rectangular pastry with a soft powdery surface.

"What is that?"

He said, "This is food. Don't you know food when you see it?"

"I have never seen food that looked like that before."

"It's delicious, watch!"

George proceeded to take a big bite out of the pastry, covering his mouth with the white powder. Then he gestured Rachael to do the same. Only because she was starving, she reluctantly picked up the thick pastry and took a bite.

Her instinct was to be repulsed by it, but then she tasted it. It wasn't bad. It tasted like pasta. She ate it and asked George for another.

George laughed and said, "I told you it was good. There is a large assortment of meals with many different tastes. Whatever you like, the Aalzad can create."

"Does everything look like this?"

George just nodded.

Cooper started to relax a little. What seemed like imminent peril now was becoming an interesting adventure. She had a million questions for George on how all this had come about.

Walking back to the *Mist of the Atlantic*, George started to weave the tale that would seem impossible to the other inhabitants of Earth.

George explained, "Our ship was accidently captured when this giant spaceship came down on top of us midocean. I was in our stateroom, but from what I was told, it carried us down below the surface. When they realized that they trapped us, the Aalzad ship cocooned us in a giant air bubble, protecting us until we reached the bottom of the sea."

Pointing to the smooth circle on the underbelly of the spaceship, George said, "The *Mist of the Atlantic* was taken inside that hold. My faint memory of that event was that we were brought aboard the Tropos Magra and remained there for an unspecified period of time. We stayed there while work of expansion began on the cavern.

"When the hollowing-out process reached a point where the cavern was large enough, the *Mist of the Atlantic* was moved into the position it's in now. That's when the passengers moved in, setting up housekeeping back on the cruise ship. None of the humans seemed upset, and none expressed that they wanted to leave."

Cooper said, "How do you move a five-hundred-foot ship?"

"I don't know, but the Aalzad have many amazing abilities. That hole in the seafloor is just one of them."

Continuing, George said, "I remember that living Aalzad beings arrived with the initial landing, however, we had no contact with them. All the contact we had was with special robots that kept us alive. To the best of my knowledge there are no living beings from Zome here now.

"When we could communicate with the robots, we were told that when the Aalzad arrived, they brought two ships. These ships were filled with special equipment and engineering robots for digging and manufacturing."

Continuing their walk back to the propped-up cruise ship, they were not stopped or greeted by any of the humans they passed. Cooper thought, *They seem drugged.* Perhaps not having fresh air and sunlight for this long had something to do with it. For the most part they were pale and underweight.

George went on, "They left this spaceship here at the bottom of the ocean and raised the other ship to terraform some surface land for their use. I have no personal knowledge of this, but the guardians would tell us what the Aalzad spacemen were doing.

"The work was also getting underway to transform the ocean bed into a work and living space. After several weeks we never saw the spacemen again. It was assumed that they left on the second ship to return to their home planet."

Cooper still tried to figure out why the people were so despondent. Perhaps they felt hopelessness about their situation, or perhaps there was something in the atmosphere they were breathing that altered their mood. Either way, they didn't seem to be concerned about anything.

George, still gabbing away, said, "Robots do all the work. There were manufacturing robots that constructed the interior of the chamber. There were general worker robots that did almost everything else. There were the liaison robots that we call guardians that speak to us and fulfill our needs."

The boy seemed unaware of the security robots, the hostile robots that attacked Team Hawk in the dome. Even though Cooper was very aware of their existence, she kept it to herself.

George rattled on, "Worker robots do not need direction from other robots. They work independently. They just do what they were built for."

Talking now about the ship's company, George said, "For the passengers and crew of the *Mist of the Atlantic*, there was no death, at least for the people recovered by the Aalzad. When the giant disk-shaped spacecraft came down on top of us, we fell into an abyss. The helpless ship was shaken and twisted until it was captured in the very beam that opened up the sea.

"People died. they were crushed by flying objects or thrown great distances just to slam into immovable objects such as bulkheads, overhead support beams, and in the case of the crew, engines and galley equipment. I heard from Max that sixty of the four hundred and fifty passengers on board were killed. Fourteen poor souls were never recovered after being thrown from the ship.

"The passengers and crew did not remember a lot about what happened, but they did recall dead bodies on the deck, passageways, and in the crew work areas. They remembered their own injuries, broken bones, deep bleeding wounds, and other types of trauma. They also remembered the panic, thinking that death would soon end their personal nightmares."

George continued, "All went black for us. When we awoke, we were on the spaceship. Some of the people hypothesized and tried to explain how long we were comatose, but they had no reference of time. No one had any recollection of what happened beyond the fall into the hole in the ocean.

"Some people became religious and felt that this was the afterlife. That didn't seem right to most of the passengers. They thought something more bizarre than death was happening to them. Those that were hurt were no longer hurt. There were no scars or evidence of their injuries.

"The people that had died were there, alive again but definitely not themselves. They were mentally blank. At first, things that a child could do, they couldn't. It became apparent that they could learn because in a matter of weeks, they started to learn the basic things. Learning came quickly because they had mature healthy brains, not infant brains. Over time they became fully functional again, but they had no memories before the night they died.

"There was an understanding within the community that whoever looked over us had enormous power. The people knew they were saved by beings with superior intelligence and technological abilities. They fixed people and restored life.

"They were acting beyond all known human limitations. They waited for an explanation from the Aalzad, but none came. Those restored to life are now living normal lives. They had years in the cavern to rehabilitate."

Cooper and George reached the hull entrance to the ship. She hesitated and stopped at the entrance while George was starting up the stairs.

George notice that she wasn't following, so he said, "It's all right to come to my room. My parents are there, and I will introduce you to them."

Cooper hesitated and didn't like the thought of meeting these strange people. However, she knew that she had no place else to go. She finally came to that realization and agreed to follow him inside.

George's family was on one of the decks high above the water line. That meant very little because the ship was high and dry. They had a long way to climb. There were no working elevators, so they entered through the hull and climbed many stairs to his deck. The lighting in the stairwell was dim at best, and the passageway was void of passengers.

On reaching George's cabin, Cooper reluctantly entered. It was a cabin the size of a small narrow hotel room with a bathroom, two double beds, a desk, and a straight back chair. George's parents were in one of the beds and appeared to be sound asleep. George said that his parents slept most of the time.

"They sleep for long stretches at a time and waste away the rest of the day. Their existence encompasses sleeping, eating, and little else. It's rare that I come back and find them awake."

"Why don't you sleep as much?"

"I don't know. I guess I'm too busy to sleep. I need very little. I'm not sure, but I think it has something to do with my age. There are other young people here, and they don't seem to sleep very much either. They don't have my energy though. If you need sleep, you can sleep here in my bed. I will be around if you need anything."

Cooper declined the invitation but found that after a while, she was nodding off in the hard-back chair. George helped her to the bed, where she fell into a deep sleep.

When she awoke, George was lying in bed next to her. She sat up quickly and checked to see that she was still fully dressed. She smiled slightly and relaxed a little, thinking, *I guess George is harmless.* She didn't know how long she had slept, and she didn't know if it was day or night topside, but she felt somewhat refreshed.

With everyone still asleep, she exited the room and climbed down the stairs, moving outside into the walled courtyard. She didn't know what to do next.

She thought, *Should I try to walk up the tunnel to get out of here, or should I stay put?*

She sat on one of many cube-shaped rocks and looked around. In the distance, she thought she saw George's guardian, but then again, Max was the only guardian that she had ever seen. It was coming right toward her.

She discovered that it was Max, as he spoke directly to her, "Rachael Cooper, I would like you to come with me."

Cooper became unnerved. "Where are we going?"

"I would like you to come with me to the Tropos Magra."

"Why?"

"Some of the guardians would like to talk to you. They are curious about where you come from. They would be pleased to answer any questions that you may have as well."

"Should I be alarmed about meeting more guardians?"

"No, I don't believe so. They have not met a human from the surface before. The passengers from the *Mist of the Atlantic* are the only people they have had contact with. Their feeling is, however, that these humans have been living in an unnatural environment. The guardians feel that they are not demonstrating normal characteristics as those living on the surface.

"For the ten years we have observed them, they have changed, from being active, inquisitive beings into people that lack the drive needed to live and work. They no longer possess the energy and motivation needed to create and maintain a thriving community.

"They feel that you are different. This is the reason why they are very interested in meeting you."

Cooper reluctantly agreed to accompany Max to meet the other guardians. They proceeded up the ramp to the massive ship embedded in the roof of the cavern.

Max led the way up the long ramp through the door and into the massive deck. Passing through familiar locations George had taken her earlier, they entered a new area of the alien ship that had smaller chambers. The guardians were waiting for her in one of those chambers.

The spheres were crammed in very tightly, leaving only enough room for their guest. The room was about eight feet high with curved exterior walls rising to a flat ceiling. The room was in the shape of a pie section. In the curved outer section was a large rectangle shaped like a window. Within the rectangle it was blacker than the walls in the room.

Cooper didn't think that it could possibly be a window, but as soon as she came to that conclusion, she was startled by strong headlights of an undersea craft coming into view. It was in the distance moving toward the Aalzad ship. With the spacecraft embedded in the seafloor between the open-air cavern below and the Atlantic Ocean above, this chamber was higher than the water line.

Refocusing her attention, Cooper stood before the packed room, full of spheres that had the same elongated metallic beach ball shape. None of these entities in the cramped space resembled life. They hovered about two feet above the deck and were absolutely silent.

Max introduced Rachael Cooper to the strange group. One sphere directly in front of her spoke to her in English.

"My name is Richard. I was given my name by the person I serve. That is Dr. David Stack from New York, New York. It was his son's name. In your world, he would be an orthopedic surgeon. He was on vacation with his wife when he came to know me."

A second sphere introduced itself as Trixie; her companion was a woman that was part of the ship's company, an entertainer and professional dancer. A third was Jethro, and a fourth was Ava. The spheres in turn politely introduced themselves.

She was patient with the group, listening intently to each speaker. Cooper was fascinated with the diverse makeup of the passenger manifest. She was also amazed at the care that these objects had for their human companions. They spoke with warmth about their humans.

All the spheres introduced themselves to Cooper except one. She waited for that introduction to come, but Richard, who was the speaker for the group, skipped over the last sphere and began speaking again.

"We found your people ten earth years ago. Since that time no one has aged and, except for those lost at sea, no one has died. Although your people had no bearing on time, they knew that time had elapsed."

The guardian's voice reproduction had a slight electronic New York accent to it. It sounded natural with some discrepancies in cadence.

"Old people did not age, and children did not grow up. We guardians were specifically manufactured to support human life here in the cavern. We aren't alive by your definition, but we have the ability to learn from our human companions."

THE TUNNELS OF EARTH

Cooper listened carefully as Richard went on. "At first contact we learned to communicate using simple mimicry, and over time communication in English became established.

"Over time we processed enough spheres to serve all the passengers. We can speak English, French for the French-Canadian passengers, and Swedish for the ship's crew. There were less than eighty Swedish speakers on board, and all could speak English to some extent. Their companion spheres learned Swedish just to make them feel comfortable.

"When we established a base here in the cavern, things started to develop. Work was being done by worker robots, who never interacted with the humans in their midst. They did interact with the guardians who ultimately dealt with the humans. The learning seemed right across the board.

"You seem to be different from the passengers. Are you a different kind of human?"

Cooper said, "I don't know what you mean different? The difference that I would see is that I am conscious and alert, where the people that I have been in contact with down here show a lack of energy and awareness. There is one exception. The boy that I met early in my visit, he seems normal to me."

Max spoke, "She means George, my companion. He is a special case. He is filled with curiosity, and he needs to stay active. Time and the cavern do not seem to have affected him like the others."

Richard continued, "You are dressed in strange clothing. It is almost like a suit the Aalzad would wear in space. Do you travel in outer space?"

"No, I have never been in space. This suit does protect me almost as much as a space suit would."

Jethro asked, "We knew that your people would come someday. Now that you have found us, what will you do?"

"I don't know. I have no power to speak for my people. My team had a confrontation near the surface with your worker robots. My people will expect to be attacked again. I think that the best way to meet them is in friendship, not as adversaries." Cooper paused. "Perhaps I can help you get the answer to that question."

"In what way can you help?" Jethro replied.

"I'm not sure. I might be able to tell my people on the surface that you mean no harm. You don't mean us any harm, do you?"

Richard spoke for the group, "Of course we don't wish to harm anyone on your planet. We are a highly advanced civilization compared to the people of your world. We could have destroyed you at any time. We do not wish to do so."

"Why did your robots attack us when we entered the tunnel?"

Richard answered Cooper's question, "I can only say that their attack was not a conscious act. They use their lasers to exterminate small animals that enter through our hidden vents on your unpopulated islands. Their attack on you was a mistake."

Cooper questioned, "How could small animals survive the smoke when nothing else could?"

"They were from islands that were not covered by the smoke. Disguised vents were in many places not affected by the smoke.

"Many of your rodents found their way in from the smaller islands and made nests in the tunnels to reproduce. At one point we had a serious infestation of rats, as your people call them. They were everywhere. They were even in the Tropos Magra, where we store all the food. We had to start exterminating them. A maintenance program was put in place and has existed ever since."

Seething, Cooper raised her voice. "Exterminators! We were attacked by exterminators? Do I look like a rat to you? They tried to kill all the members of my team and succeeded in killing two of us."

Cooper's emotions were getting the better of her.

Incensed, she said, "What about that tremendous wind that forced us out of the main tunnel? Was that part of your extermination program? What about Earhart blown out of the tunnel by the wind? Was he being exterminated?"

Knowing that Cooper was very upset, Richard carefully replied, "I know nothing about a third member of your party dying or a tremendous wind you speak of, but I can tell you this: had any of the guardians known about the attacks before they happened, they would not have occurred.

THE TUNNELS OF EARTH

"The wind? I can only think that must have been a backflow test of our air intake jets. To date we have never officially done one of those tests."

Still showing anger, Cooper fumed, "That was no test! It forced us out of the main tunnel and killed one of our team members. Someone meant to attack us."

Richard replied, "Very interesting. The jets have been constructed to intake air from the surface. Tests were scheduled since the tower has been completed, but none were carried out. If one did happen, sensors would have detected movement in the tunnel and would have shut it down. This anomaly should not have happened. I can understand your anger."

Jethro, to the left of Richard, spoke up, "There can only be one explanation for the attacks. Years ago, there were stories of a special type of robot, a worker, known as the gatekeeper. It was said to be indistinguishable from a normal worker, but its main purpose was to protect the upper tunnels from intruders.

"While it would normally act as a common tunnel worker, it had the ability to act independently when necessary. After hearing your account of what happened, it appears the stories are true."

Richard gestured to the unidentified sphere; it turned and entered a hatch at the far wall.

Richard continued, "I need to correct you on the number of casualties that were inflicted on your team in the upper complex. This includes the man that you say was killed by the wind. There were only two fatalities."

Cooper snarled, "There were three, I saw two of them die in the dome!"

Overcome by emotion, she slumped down on one knee. All the strength that she had mustered was now leaving her body in a rush. She couldn't listen anymore.

She said, "This can't be happening. I'm going insane. I have to get out of here."

The chamber was quiet and unemotional. None of the guardians understood the outrage they were experiencing. The spheres just waited silently.

She turned to rush out of the room, but before she could, Richard spoke, "There were only two deaths, Rachael Cooper. Go to that door and open it." He was directing her to the hatch where the unidentified guardian passed through.

Cooper froze, afraid to take a step to see what was behind that door.

Richard continued, "Believe me when I tell you that had we known and had the chance to save the two members of your team, we would have. Go to the door and open it. I want to prove to you our sincerity is real."

Regaining her composure, she slowly turned back and walked to the door. The unidentified guardian ushered her into the room. The light was low. Cooper saw a window in this room as well. She could still see the undersea vehicle moving at the bottom of the ocean.

She saw a shadowy figure sitting in the corner of the room near the window, looking the other way. He was human, dressed as she was. She was overcome with fear, but somehow, she found the strength to move toward him. It was Kelly!

Cooper had seen his lifeless body on the floor of the dome and had no doubt that he was killed. As a Navy corpsman, she had seen dead bodies before. She had seen several while attached to Marine combat units, and she knew that Kelly had been killed. He turned and looked sheepishly at her with no sign of recognition.

Richard quietly moved up in a position behind Cooper's right shoulder. He said in a soft, caring voice, "He won't know you. His mind is clear. We have found a way to successfully bring the person back in every way, but we have never been able to restore memories. He is a functioning adult male that needs to relearn everything—language, customs, and relationships. It will take time, but he will be Kelly again."

Richard was now talking about the unnamed guardian. "This is a guardian assigned to you to help restore Kelly into a normal healthy individual again. Your friend will start with language skills and common tasks. After that, he will learn about other human things that are important.

THE TUNNELS OF EARTH

"Some humans have said sports are important to males. I have no reference for it, but I do understand the principles of sex, the perpetuation of the species and male-female dynamics. Why don't you give this guardian a name? It will need one so it can introduce itself to Kelly."

Very confused, Cooper said, "How do you determine what their name should be? Should I give the guardian a male or female name?"

Richard replied, "If the guardian is for a male, then he should have a male name. If the guardian serves a female, then she shall have a female name."

Cooper thought for a minute and held in the smile. "His name will be Roger." Another Roger—Roger Buckley will be running rough shod over Kelly again soon.

Cooper, softening a little, said to Richard, "I believe you now, that you didn't come here to harm us. I thank you for saving James Kelly. I also believe that my other colleagues would be alive today had you been aware of what happened to them."

"Thank you for your trust. Trust is an important thing. The Aalzad have trusted us for many years. We do flawless work for them, and we expect nothing in return, except trust. Now that we have gained your trust, we need your help."

Surprised, Cooper said, "How can I help you?"

"I need you to return to the surface with the revived human, Roger, and myself to communicate with your leaders about why we are here. We will leave immediately."

Cooper was excited. She was going back to the surface and wouldn't have to sneak back up the tunnel. Not only that, she will be getting an official escort.

*****

Riding in one of the hovering rectangular vehicles, the small group traveled quickly up the tunnel on their way to the surface. Cooper referred to this strange vehicle as a boxcar because of its shape. It was a smooth and quiet ride, but it had none of the comforts you would find in your typical Humvee. It was more like sitting in the bed of a pickup truck.

The boxcar moved fast, but it took close to an hour to get to the dome. Cooper was back where she started her unscheduled journey. The dome was coming into view when the Box Car veered right, into a side hatch.

The vehicle slowed down and then stopped. Stiffly, Cooper got out, followed by Richard. Roger guided Kelly out of the vehicle and, under his control, had him follow the group. Cooper didn't understand how Roger was able to guide him. There was no way for her to know.

They walked a short distance to another passageway. When they came upon a hatch, they entered a small compartment. Inside, there was a bump, and the space began to rise. Cooper realized that they were in some kind of lift device—an elevator! After several minutes, it stopped. It came to a halt just below a low roof.

Waiting in position, the roof quietly slid to one side, exposing the deep blue sky. A blast of cool air reminded her that it was late fall outside; the air was crisp. It was the first time Cooper had seen the sky since she entered the underworld with Team Hawk. Who knows how long ago that was? She could only guess how long she slept in George's cabin. The lift rose several more feet and stopped. It was concealed in a deep crevice just below ground level. To reach the open air they had to climb up a rocky incline for the short distance.

The sky was expanding over Cooper's head. She shielded her eyes from the sun in the perfect cloudless sky. It was a beautiful day. Exiting the opening, they could see the familiar flat empty landscape. Other than the depression in the earth, the terrain where they assembled was a similar layout to the area around the tower.

When the rest of the group made it to the surface, they started to move. Cooper was walking, Richard hovering next to her. Kelly was under the guidance of Roger. In the distance, Chief Cooper could see activity around the pit, or so she thought. The pit was far away, but it seemed closer because of the flatness of the environment.

As the group got closer, she noticed aircraft. Not the helicopters she came over with, but C130 aircraft parked on the smooth surface.

THE TUNNELS OF EARTH

Beyond the airplanes was a city of camouflage tents and military vehicles. Progressing toward the camp, Cooper saw something kicking up dust, heading their way. Once it got a little closer, she identified it as a jeep approaching with a driver and three soldiers, one in the front and two in the back seat.

Cooper said to Richard, "Don't speak. I will introduce you when the time is right."

"I will follow your directions." He then spoke to Roger to do the same. Roger maintained silent control over Kelly.

When the jeep pulled up, there was an army staff sergeant packing a side arm in the passenger seat. Not familiar with driving on the black surface, the jeep skidded as it pulled up next to the strange-looking travelers.

The sergeant hopped out of the vehicle and in an authoritative voice said, "You are in a restricted area. Who are you, and why are you here?"

Cooper responded that she was the corpsman with Team Hawk, Eagle Corps.

She said, "We have returned from the tunnels below this island. I need to talk to my commanding officer or an officer in charge."

The sergeant probed, "Why are you dressed like that, and what are those things with you?"

Cooper coolly responded, "That's classified, Sergeant. It's important for me to talk to someone in charge, now! Do you understand?"

A little unnerved by her response, the sergeant said, "Get in the jeep. I'll take you to headquarters."

The two soldiers reluctantly got out of the jeep, making way for Cooper and Kelly to sit in the back seat. Then the spheres that looked top secret would hover into the short storage area in the back.

Kelly had trouble getting into the jeep, and one of the soldiers said, "Hey is he all right?"

"He has a head injury from a firefight we were involved in, down in the tunnels," Cooper responded.

The soldiers' attitudes changed; they showed more respect and approval because they had heard about a fight deep in the earth. It was a rumor that had grown to legendary proportions, men versus aliens.

When everyone was securely seated, the jeep turned around and made its way toward HQ. The other two soldiers, not having a ride, began to slog back to base. The jeep raced into camp and pulled up to one of the dozens of camouflaged tents.

The sergeant jumped from the vehicle and said, "Wait here."

He got out and walked into the tent. After a moment, a young second lieutenant flipped open the canvas flap and approached to the jeep. He immediately started to question Cooper and then tried to question Kelly.

The cocky young officer said, "You just came out of the earth?"

"Yes, sir, that's why I have to talk to my CO or someone in authority as soon as possible."

He turned around and said, "Come into my office and get out of the chill."

Cooper, helping Kelly out of the jeep, walked toward the tent. She saw that the spheres had slid in and moved behind them. When they entered, the tent heater was blasting. It felt good for a few minutes but then it became uncomfortably warm. There was a table, several chairs, and a file cabinet. A smaller table was next to the entrance where an admin clerk would normally sit.

They were offered seats near the larger table. The officer stepped behind the table and sat down. He looked over the humans and spheres and said, "What are those things?"

Cooper replied, "I am not at liberty to tell you, Lieutenant."

The lieutenant, taking a hard line, said, "Look, you need to tell me what's going on here! I will take this to the next level once I'm satisfied."

Standing her ground, Cooper said, "With all due respect, sir, this is above your pay grade, and it's above mine too. Unfortunately, I have the information my superiors need. That would involve my commanding officer, Navy Lieutenant Buckley, his commander Lieutenant Cmdr. Collins, and whoever else is in a position of authority over them. It's that important. Do you understand, Lieutenant?"

The officer didn't respond to what Cooper said but did seem to grasp the gravity of the situation. He stood up, walked around the table, exiting the tent. When he returned, he sat back down and silently waited behind the table. The tension was incredible, but after ten minutes, the occupants of the field HQ heard the rotors of a Seahawk helicopter approaching.

When it landed, the officer moved to the entrance, held back the flap of the tent, and said, "Your ride is here."

Cooper and company shuffled out of the tent and boarded the Seahawk helicopter. Kelly struggled to board but managed to get in with Cooper's help. The spheres remained silent and made no impression on the crew.

On takeoff, Cooper looked out the open door and identified the pillbox in the middle of the city of tents. There weren't many familiar sights remaining from before she entered the world down below. She saw buildings up ahead, close to the black island. They could only be going to one place; they were heading for Goat Island. Chances are, they were going directly to the hotel there.

The Coddington had been in use continuously for ten years by various government agencies. Organizations came to Goat Island, set up shop, fulfilled their contracts, and then packed up and left. The height of activity happened in the early years of the smoke, but it tapered off when outcomes from the initial research showed little in the way of results.

When protective suits were improved, companies returned to test them out. When smoke analysis got better, the researchers returned. Now with the smoke gone, the resurrection of the Coddington was complete. High officials, both military and civilian, were moving in again.

In all these years, there was one staple feature to this place, Maurice Millius. Millius was the enduring manager of the Coddington Hotel from the day it went out of business back in 2015. He was always there. Assisting where he could and overseeing the hotel when activity slowed. He was growing old at the Coddington.

The helicopter landed on the big white H painted in the parking lot. The occupants were quickly shuffled off the chopper by security personnel and guided to the main entrance. Met by Millius, he greeted them pleasantly and guided them to a vacant conference room.

Millius, Cooper, Kelly, and the guardians rode the elevator to the third floor and entered a dark empty meeting room. There they waited for about forty-five minutes when a pair of military officers and one civilian entered the room. Cooper saw her CO Lt. Buckley, and she recognized Lt. Cmdr. Collins, but the civilian was not a person she had ever seen before.

Relieved and concerned, Buckley approached Cooper and said, "Doc, I can't believe that you are alive. The last thing I saw when I was carrying Kelly was the attacking robots. When I left the dome, I was absolutely sure you were dead."

She responded, "I'm okay, sir."

Cooper then turned and nodded toward Kelly sitting quietly in a row of seats near the wall. Buckley looked in the direction indicated by Cooper and could not believe his eyes.

Visibly shaken, Buckley said to Cooper, "This can't be. I had to leave his lifeless body in the dome. I was sure he was dead!"

"He was dead, sir."

"What? What kind of miracle is this?"

Ecstatic, Buckley approached Kelly and spoke, "How are you, son?"

Cooper intervened, saying, "He's alive, but he has no memory, sir. He doesn't know you or me or anyone else right now." She got serious and continued, "I will explain everything to you, but first I have to give a report to you and your superiors."

Buckley had never heard her speak to him like this before. She was quiet by nature, and knowing this, he knew she had something important to say.

Buckley escorted her to the other two men waiting patiently, saying, "Okay, Chief, let me introduce you to our commanding officer, Lt. Cmdr. Collins, the commanding officer of Eagle Corps. Over here is Mr. Dean Frederickson, chief of Newport Operations for the National Security Agency. He has authority over all civilian activity here. He also has direct access to the president of the United States."

Buckley stated, "I know you. You would not have asked to speak to the highest levels of command if you didn't have something important to report."

"Yes, sir, this is of the utmost importance."

Her demeanor changed. She became serious and said, "Gentlemen, let me introduce you to Richard, guardian to Dr. David Stack of New York, New York."

The men, already very curious about the spheres hovering before them, waited for something to happen. They now focused directly on Richard as he was strangely being introduced by Doc Cooper.

Richard did not speak. After a few seconds, they began to think that the chief petty officer was crazy.

Impatiently, Frederickson said, "What is this, some kind of joke?"

"No, sir, this is not a joking matter."

She turned and crouched down in front of the guardian and said, "Richard, I know I told you to be silent back when we met the soldiers, but now, I need you to speak to these men."

As if a switch was flipped, in a normal voice, Richard said to Cooper, "Thank you, Rachael Cooper, for giving me permission to speak."

The atmosphere in the room changed instantly. The expressions on the officials' faces went from annoyance to complete astonishment. Their mouths gaped open, and it was so quiet you could hear a pin drop.

"I am Richard, guardian of David Stack of the *Mist of the Atlantic*. I have been given the responsibility to inform the leaders of earth the intentions of the Aalzad, the people that I serve.

"I am here to tell you why we are on your planet and what it will mean to you."

Richard began his story, "Over one hundred earth years ago, the Aalzad's home planet, Aalzarada was dying. The planet's orbit around its star was deteriorating. It was suffering a slow death. The population had to escape a planetary catastrophe.

"The people of Aalzarada directed all their energy and resources toward a massive survival project. Already having the ability to travel in space, it took fifty of the hundred years to reach the point where they could commence interstellar travel. With interstellar travel available, it started exploration for a new home world."

"On liftoff of their first pioneer craft to find a new planet in a new system, the Aalzad had only the survival of the population in mind. After their early voyages, research and development was their number one objective.

"Technical breakthroughs happened, and interstellar travel occurred with more ease and regularity. Other technologies grew just as fast, as interplanetary travel was becoming commonplace.

"In the early years of exploration, the Aalzad were fortunate—they found a planet in a nearby galaxy that could support life. This news triggered a massive effort to employ newly built long-range transport ships to start evacuating the population. In the beginning, transports were slow by today's Aalzad standards. The drives were primitive, and they took years to reach the new planet.

"The effort snowballed into a battle against the clock to create bigger and better ships with improved propulsion systems. As progress was made, the process of transporting the population moved faster. Transports that left eight years earlier were still in transit when the newer ships had already landed on their new planet. They gave the planet the name Zome.

"Travelers on the older ships were transferred to the newer transports to finish their long journey. The earlier model crafts, emptied of their passengers, were left only with the crew to bring in supplies and resources from Aalzarada. The new arrivals wasted little time creating a new civilization."

Richard continued, "The Aalzad have come to earth because they have a need. There need is to take some of your abundant life-sustaining resources. At present, Zome has the ability to support a smaller population than Aalzarada, but the goal was to evacuate everyone. We were successful in many ways. On Zome, the lack of water and water-borne organisms was the most important issue to the new arrivals. An increase of both these necessities were needed to maintain the cycle of life to keep the atmosphere stable.

"We learned that in the nineteen sixties your president John F. Kennedy started the space program in response to the belief that another country was making an effort to control earth from space. The Earth program grew, leading up to men traveling to the moon. Then you had the shuttle program that never left the safety of Earth orbit."

"In the years that followed, your space program went into decline. Even though the space program transferred to the private sector in your twenty-first century, progress was slow. No important breakthroughs have been made beyond your one manned voyage to Mars and many unmanned voyages within earth's solar system.

"By comparison, when life was no longer sustainable on Aalzarada, eighty percent of the world's population managed to be successfully evacuated, traveling countless millions of miles from their home planet. That number was far more than was earlier estimated.

"Many of the people were still in transit when leaders realized that the evacuation was much more successful than originally planned. However, the more citizens that came reduced the time that Zome would be a viable planet. If they could not find water from another planet, they would have to transport the entire population to another world again. The search began for a second home planet with enough natural resources to support all the survivors.

"That's when exploratory probes to other solar systems revealed that there was a planet within comfortable range of Zome. This planet had all the resources it needed. In the scientists' estimation, there was more water than their new world's population could possibly deplete.

"It was determined Earth was that suitable planet. The problem was, as you know, it already has a sizable population. Relocating the population of Zome to a planet with population projected many problems and was considered impractical.

"It was decided the Aalzad would not colonize Earth but take resources that were needed, not interfering with the population. They also discovered that there was an ample supply of air on Earth that they could take to reinforce their own atmosphere. When the leadership met, they formulated a plan to take advantage of Earth's abundant resources.

"Before arriving on earth, the Aalzad were on the verge of developing wormhole technology. This will help them travel throughout the known universe, but space portal development had not yet been completed.

"They knew that they would have that technology in a matter of years. They couldn't wait for it to be achieved, so they decided to send two ships to Earth in advance of the day when wormhole travel was possible.

"The Aalzad came here forty-one earth years ago. They discovered the perfect location in the form of an undersea cave off the coast of your eastern United States. Their plan was to use this cave in support, as they isolated a small section of earth's surface, adjacent to its location in the Atlantic Ocean.

"The objective was to terraform small areas of land to place intakes for their subterranean air pumps. The plan called for a series of tunnels and vents under the Atlantic shelf. The vents would collect air from the islands in the region and offer access for tunnel maintenance. The heart of the operation are the twin portals.

"These portals are in the natural undersea cavern. The first one is a small incoming portal, entering the cavern from Zome. Once activated, its purpose is to bring Aalzad citizens and equipment to Earth. The larger and more important portal of their mission is built into the floor of the cavern. All resources taken from the Earth will be sent through this gateway.

"You must understand, the Aalzad are not asking permission to take these resources. They are taking a resource that you, the people of Earth, do not use to sustain life—ocean water. They intend to take enough ocean water and air to sustain life on their new planet."

The humans listening to Richard were amazed at what they were hearing. They knew that something was going on, but they never imagined there was underground work to this extent.

Frederickson interrupted Richard, "How can your leaders justify the theft of this world's resources?"

"No humans possess ownership of the oceans. You have many hostile factions here on Earth that dispute the ownership of these oceans, but none can legitimately claim them. The Aalzad reserve the right to take a small amount of your water on the basis that no one on this planet owns it. All people of Earth have access to it and use it, but it is a resource that cannot be possessed."

Frederickson continued, "When were you planning to tell us this? You have been here forty-one years."

Richard said, "I have told you what you need to know. My explanation was triggered by our first contact with human beings from the surface. This happened when Rachael Cooper found her way to the center of our world. I have come here to tell you what you need to know, nothing more. The Aalzad make no apologies for their actions."

Richard changed the subject. "Now to another matter. We have in the cavern with us almost eight hundred men, women, and children that were accidently caught up in our operation in 2015. They have stayed with us for the last ten years. All but a small number of them are alive.

"We would return them to you, but they will not survive on the surface of Earth for a prolonged period of time. Through the use of our technology, they have survived by artificial means and have not aged a day since that day ten years ago.

"Your citizens have used our regeneration device over and over for that time. The problem with using it is, the more you use it, the more dependent you become. They are hopelessly addicted to its power.

"Because of this addiction, they cannot lead normal lives on Earth without the regenerator. Without it, they would only live for a matter of months. If the process of regeneration is withheld, there organs will deteriorate at an accelerated rate, and they will die. It would be best for these humans to travel to Zome to maintain their quality of life.

"Because they cannot survive on Earth anymore, we accept the responsibility for their fate. Over time, your people will become productive members of the Aalzad society.

"When the first Aalzad citizens return to your planet, they will take them back when they leave. They will be allowed to live in peace as citizens of Zome."

Lt. Cmdr. Collins said, "When will your masters return to Earth?"

"The process was set in motion for the Aalzad to return when I came here with Rachael Cooper. When they arrive, they will immediately set in motion the collection of resources. The tunnels are not finished, but the portals are operational.

"For your own safety, I strongly recommend that you immediately leave this island. When the process begins, the tunnel will quickly transform into a conduit, carrying air down to the portal. Ships at sea in this area will also need to be alerted to leave the area as soon as possible. During the harvesting of water, they will be in peril from large whirlpools.

"I will leave Roger here with James Kelly to aid in his recovery. He will recover fully, but he has no memory of before the day we met. I will return to the cavern, and I will take a small delegation of your people with me to meet the Aalzad when they arrive. Your delegates will be under my protection and will be perfectly safe.

"We guardians and worker robots have no place on Zome. We were manufactured here on earth and will remain here when the Aalzad operation is completed. We will act as liaisons to the Aalzad people in the future if they choose to maintain contact with you. We can also act as guides to help your civilization update your technologies in the future."

With the conclusion of his speech, Richard went silent.

Frederickson gestured Collins to the door and said, "Commander, can I have a minute outside?"

When they left the room, Frederickson said to Collins, "What do you make of this, Commander?"

Collins replied, "This all seems a little crazy, but I think we have to take Richard seriously. It is necessary for us to locate the point where they will extract the water. Everything indicates its miles out underneath the ocean."

Frederickson, formulating a plan, said, "I'm going to forward this information to Washington and call for the evacuation of military personnel on Aquidneck Island. After I make my report, I intend to accept this Richard's invitation and go underground to the source and try to deal with the Aalzad. If we can't stop them, we should at least get exclusive treaty rights with them for the United States."

Lt. Cmdr. Collins suggested, "I want to take Falcon team and Harrier team as well as Corpsman Cooper."

Favorably, Frederickson said, "I agree, Eagle Corps should go, but I think we should leave Chief Cooper topside. She's gone through enough. She may also be under their influence. Either way, I'm sure she needs a break from all this. Include Lieutenant Buckley instead in your team. He has experience in the tunnels."

Lt. Cmdr. Collins replied, "Yes, sir."

Collins put in a call to Quonset to ready the unit. He wanted to take Falcon and Harrier teams, but he would take any member of any team that was ready. Within the hour, two choppers landed next to the Coddington.

Every healthy member of the two teams was there. Captain Steel was there with the functional members of his team. He and Falcon team came out of the trench right after the helicopters returned to Quonset with the body bags of their comrades. Lt. Cmdr. Collins's Harrier team was there at full strength. Lt. Buckley was ready too after quickly retrieving his gear.

Lieutenant Cmdr. Collins, the commanding officer of Eagle Corps, was directly below General Ray in the chain of command. He was an experienced officer with twenty-one years of service. Collins was successful at delegating authority and was perceived to be a desk jockey and too soft for field command.

Collins spoke to the group, "You'll need all your special equipment today, men. Wear your protective suits, but leave your helmets behind. Carry the small oxygen rebreather canister, just in case. We will make no threat toward the aliens, but we will protect ourselves in the case of hostilities against us. We may be called on to defend ourselves, our country, and perhaps our planet."

He continued, "When you're ready, stand by right here. We'll leave as soon as we can."

He turned to Cooper and said, "Chief, you're sitting this one out. You deserve a little R and R after what you went through. Before you stand down, do one more thing for me. Ask our new friend Richard to come down and join us."

Cooper nodded, then turned and walked back into the hotel to get Richard for the helicopter ride back to the tunnel entry point. She was relieved that she didn't have to go back.

Reaching the conference room, the lights were dimmed. When she entered, Roger and Corporal Kelly were still there. Medical staff was attending to him. Cooper approached Richard from behind.

Richard, sensing her presence, spoke, "I hope your people believe that the Aalzad have every intention of taking what they need to preserve their new planet."

Reluctantly, Cooper said, "I hope so too. I saw a demonstration of the advanced power of the Aalzad. The only thing is…" Rachael hesitated.

"You are worried about our civilization taking resources from your planet."

"It doesn't seem right."

"They wouldn't do it if there was another way."

In the background, the medical staff helped Kelly into a wheelchair and rolled him out. Roger dutifully followed.

Cooper enquired, "Is Roger staying here, or is he coming back to the cavern?"

"Roger will make sure James Kelly is properly taken care of and then slip back to base."

Now that they were alone, Richard's voice changed. It became low and direct. He said, "We can't wait, the Aalzad are coming to Earth now. You must come with me. The other humans can follow us later. Besides, I think that they are not as honorable as they appear. Their motives are to stop, not accommodate the Aalzad."

Richard moved to the door quickly, counting on Cooper to follow. He stopped at the door when he sensed hesitation. He hovered motionless, and after a long pause, he said, "Are you coming?"

THE TUNNELS OF EARTH

After another short hesitation, she moved to the door and followed Richard down the corridor. They avoided the elevator and took the stairs. Cooper running and Richard gliding down several flights of stairs, they heard the door on a lower level slam. It was on the first floor.

Someone was climbing the stairs two steps at a time, moving fast. Richard and the chief were between floors when they came face-to-face with the runner coming up. It was Lieutenant Buckley, her team leader, coming to find out what was taking so long.

Buckley stopped in front of Cooper, but Richard kept moving down the stairs. He was down a flight before Cooper started after him. She rarely saw her lieutenant speechless, but this was one of those times.

She reached the first floor, then out into the parking lot. She was being followed closely by Buckley. When both cleared the door, Richard was nowhere to be seen. Moving quickly around the corner of the building, they saw him gliding smoothly toward the causeway. Reaching it, he skimmed over the bridge toward Newport proper, or what used to be Newport Proper. They ran, trying to catch up.

Buckley, short of breath, running after the guardian, said, "What's going on, Chief? We were supposed to go with him as a group."

Cooper replied, "Change of plans, sir. He is making a getaway."

Approaching the other side of the causeway, they were gaining ground.

Richard has slowed down, Cooper thought. *He's letting us catch up?*

The far end of the bridge was in ruin. It was crumpled, twisted girders that presented no difficulty for the guardian. Richard flew off the end of the bridge, dropping to the black dirt, hovering at his normal height. He kept moving.

Cooper and Buckley didn't have it so easy. They had to climb down seven feet over the crumbling iron girders in a haphazard manner. They both fell at the bottom. Without missing a beat, they jumped to their feet and continued their pursuit.

On the bare black surface, Richard was out of sight again. Buckley looked in all directions and thought, *Where did he go?* The pair kept running, stopping, and then looking around, followed by running again. Ahead there was an indentation in the matte black surface.

"This has to be it!" Buckley said.

He jumped down into a crevice that was about six feet deep and descending. He landed hard, losing his balance on contact, falling face-first to the deck. Cooper was right behind him. She was a little more graceful falling and skidding on her butt. Again, they leaped to their feet, but they stood, looking up and down the north-south crevice.

Cooper said, "Which way?"

"This way," Buckley said, pointing south.

He was trying to get his bearings so they could get to the tower. It was miles away, but they had to go in the right direction to catch Richard. They rounded the first corner and abruptly stopped. There he was.

Richard was stationary, hovering quietly like in the conference room at the Coddington Hotel. The pair approached from behind, circling around in front of him. They were exhausted, completely out of breath.

Buckley, looking confused, glanced in Cooper's direction. "You were going with him, weren't you?"

In response, Cooper said, "I had no choice. He just took off without warning. I thought that I should maintain contact with him. That's when you came along."

Richard broke his silence. "Lieutenant Buckley, do you wish to join us to meet the Aalzad?"

"What about the delegation that we organized?"

"You and Rachael Cooper are a fine delegation."

Cooper almost sensed amusement from the floating guardian.

Part III

DELEGATION

Topside, the expeditionary force had assembled. They waited in the sunlight next to the pride of the naval services, the SH60 Seahawk helicopter. Falcon team led by Capt. Steel and Harrier Team under Lt Cmdr. Collins were waiting for the civilian Dean Frederickson, Lieutenant Buckley, and the talking hardware, Richard.

Collins Looked at his wristwatch and cursed under his breath. "Where the hell are they?"

Collins said, "Mount up, men. Get on the helicopters. I'm going to find the anchor. Both teams knew what he meant. Anchors weigh things down. They slow or disrupt a mission. Eagle Corps is used to moving fast and on a moment's notice." Collins thought, *This government chump can only be trouble.*

Collins stormed into the lobby looking for Frederickson. He found him in the manager's office. Barging in, he stood in front of him and looked at his watch. "Frederickson, we have to go, we have to go now!"

Frederickson, not ruffled by the Naval officer's rudeness, said, "Commander, relax, we are waiting for a physicist, an important scientist. He left Quonset ten minutes ago. That means he will be landing momentarily. Rejoin your troops, we will be there as soon as he arrives."

Not liking Frederickson's words but having no authority over him, he turned and stormed out. As he exited, he said in a loud, clear voice, "Five minutes!"

On his way back to the choppers, Collins was approached by Corpsman Brett Forster of Falcon team. He was alarmed.

Collins saw this and said, "What's the matter, Doc?"

"They're gone, sir!"

"Who's gone?"

"The robot and I think Lt. Buckley and Doc Cooper."

"How do you know this?"

"Captain Steel told me to round up Lieutenant Buckley and the robot in the hotel, but the conference room was empty."

"What do Lieutenant Buckley and the corpsman have to do with this?"

"Not sure, sir, they aren't anywhere to be found."

*****

Behind the hovering Richard, an elevator rose up through the earth. A panel slid open. Richard turned, entered, and waited. Cooper and Buckley again looked at each other, not sure what to do.

Buckley announced, "Richard, put down the red carpet, the American delegation is coming."

As the elevator descended back into the earth, Buckley realized that he was unarmed and had no special equipment with him. Everything he had for the descent was sitting on the helicopter pad with Eagle Corps. Cooper was now dressed comfortably in fatigues, not wearing her special protective suit. She finally had a chance to shower and change out of the space suit that she wore when she came out of the pit, six hours earlier. She didn't get a chance to follow Lt. Cmdr. Collins's orders to take this mission off.

Buckley said to Cooper, "Let's hope we don't run into that laser-carrying robot again."

Richard reassured Buckley, saying, "You are safe with me. You are protected guests of the Aalzad."

The lift stopped in a different subterranean passageway, not unlike the one Team Hawk traversed to the dome.

*****

THE TUNNELS OF EARTH

When the five minutes were up, Collins started yelling at the team members that hadn't entered the chopper, "Get on the chopper, men. We're leaving now, with or without the civilians!"

Collins within earshot of the manager's office yelled, "We're going, Frederickson!"

He turned and hustled toward the chopper.

When the pilot saw Collins coming fast, he started the engines. The rotors started to turn as he boarded and took up a position behind the pilot.

Once everyone was on the chopper, Collins yelled, "Let's go!"

The rotors turned, but the chopper didn't move. Collins jumped up and was about to reiterate his order to the pilot when he saw Frederickson and another man walking quickly to the helicopter. Collins sat back down. He was at a low boil.

The two men boarded the same chopper and, without a word, sat down next to him. The two helicopters lifted off and headed southeast.

It took less than ten minutes for the SH-60 Seahawks to touch down next to the trench. All the personnel deplaned quickly with weapons slung over their shoulders. Frederickson and the other man got out and moved toward the rim.

Collins approached them, and Frederickson spoke to him like nothing happened back at the Coddington, "Commander, this is Professor Julius Silver, professor of physics at Brown University. He is here to size up what kind of civilization we are confronted with. We know that they are vastly superior to our technology, so we want to see what advantages they have. If we can decipher some of their operating principles, this little trip could be very worthwhile."

Collins nodded and shook hands with the professor.

Collins said to both men, "Gentlemen, we are going into a very hostile place, and we are going in on our own. We will not have that talking robot to go in with us. It disappeared somewhere along the line. We have an invitation, so we are going without it.

"Only a few of us have been down there before, and no one other than the corpsman of Team Hawk knows where the Aalzad base is located. She appears to be missing as well. My men have a job to do. They will protect you as long as you are part of our group.

"When you start to stray, you will be on your own. I am responsible for these people so that would position me in charge of this expedition. I understand that you'll need to gather information and negotiate with the aliens if possible. I will get you in and get you out. The rest is up to you. I do hope that you know what you are doing."

The heavy Marine Corps CH-53K, capable of supporting a load of thirty-six thousands pounds, lowered the force on its three winches. When everyone was at the bottom, they started down the tunnel.

Captain Steel relished this moment, saying, "Stay alert, look for anything that doesn't seem right, and remember, they hit us in several ways. They hit us with high wind and then with a surging electrical charge. Not to mention they have the ability to take over our remote-control weapons systems and use them against us."

*****

The message brought by Richard was received loud and clear. On the surface, the evacuation was commencing. Aquidneck Island was evacuating the camps and military aircraft that were brought there quickly. Ships within a hundred miles of Narragansett Bay were diverted away.

High altitude aircraft flew over Newport, ready to capture events as they unfolded. Whatever information was becoming available would be gathered and sent on to the command center at Quonset. The commanders would then forward all that information to responsible parties around the country. Even satellites were poised in position to get a broader picture of events.

As a precaution Goat Island was evacuated. All the science was left in place. Most of it was highly classified, but onsite personnel had no time to remove substantial quantities of their data and equipment. The satellites kept an eye on that area as well.

THE TUNNELS OF EARTH

Quonset Point Naval Air Station was overflowing with personnel. Soldiers, sailor's airmen, and Marines were stuffed into the barracks, hangars, and office structures. Specialists were camped out around the workstations ready to gather data as it came in.

The civilian members accompanying E-Corps were on a three-pronged mission. The first objective they had was to contact the visitors and evaluate their strength. The second was to try to find a way to stop them from taking Earth's resources. The third was to try to negotiate a technology exchange if the aliens are too advanced and the mission cannot be stopped.

*****

On the move, Capt. Steel was on high alert; he remembered this part of the tunnel. *No surprises,* he thought. They reached the door where they left the casualties of Condor team but walked straight this time, right by the side door, down the tunnel on a true path.

Professor Silver was hardly dressed for a hike, but he didn't complain. He was in a button-down shirt with a medium sweater under his winter coat, chinos, and the one smart item he wore, hiking boots. He and Frederickson kept up, but it was obvious that they were not in the same shape as E-Corps.

Eagle Corps sensors guided their path. In some construction sections it was so black nothing was visible to the naked eye. Night vision goggles and flashlights were the order of the day. Other than small problems, everything was going smoothly…so far.

Petty Officer Second Class Mason Ross was on point moving thirty feet in front of the group. Steel, walking with Falcon team, listened intently on his earpiece. Just when he thought things were going too well, his headset came alive.

Ross reported, "I've got movement up ahead!"

Steel responded, "Can you identify?"

"No, sir, not yet."

"Stay put, we're coming up."

Everyone heard the communication and were waiting for orders. Steel said, "Falcon team, move ahead, Harrier, follow up slow."

This meant that his team, Falcon team, was taking the initiative. He was leaving Harrier team behind to protect their special guests.

Steel's team moved up quickly finding PO Ross crouched down, facing forward.

He dropped to one knee and asked, "What do you have?"

Ross replied, "Whatever it is, it's still coming."

Steel, whispering to the teams, said, "Stay sharp!"

Falcon team took up defensive positions, ready to fire on the approaching unknown.

As they waited, the blip on Ross's sensor kept coming. Ross said, "Fifty yards, sir."

Ross counted down, "Forty, thirty... It stopped, sir."

The team waited. After several minutes, Steel said, "Put some light on it!"

Five flashlights clicked on simultaneously. Hovering before them was a sphere, a guardian. It was completely motionless. Steel remembered what happened earlier when Condor team opened fire on the robot back at the passageway door.

He said, "Hold your fire, men. Stand up and drop back, s...l...o...w...l...y."

He overemphasized slowly; he didn't want to set this thing off. Falcon team got up and started to backtrack with their weapons trained on the sphere.

Out of the darkness, Lt. Cmdr. Collins shouted, "Don't fire! That's the sphere that was with the injured Marine in the hotel."

Collins moved ahead of the team and reintroduced himself, "I am Lt. Cmdr. Collins. We met back at the hotel with Mr. Frederickson and Lt. Buckley."

Frederickson approached and stood next to Collins.

"I am Roger, guardian of Rachael Cooper. It's nice to see you again. I have come here to escort you to the Aalzad's location."

Collins said, "You are Rachael Cooper's guardian? I thought you were with Corporal Kelly."

"I was escorting Cpl. Kelly because he couldn't return to your base by himself. It was my duty to help her in any way I could.

My task was to assist her and make her visit with the Aalzad as comfortable as possible."

Collins said, "Did she send you here?"

"No, Richard sent me."

Frederickson said, "Oh, you mean the robot that did all the talking. Where are Richard and Rachael Cooper now?"

"They are at the core waiting for the Aalzad's return. It is my duty to take you there as well. We must hurry because their return will happen very soon. Once here, they will initiate the process of gathering resources. You are to come with me."

Roger turned and led the teams down the tunnel at a quickened pace.

*****

Cooper and Buckley didn't know it, but the expeditionary force was behind them, moving toward the cavern. Guided by Roger, they were in a different tunnel, on foot. The boxcar would arrive at the cavern well in advance of the rest of E-Corps.

After the long ride, the cavern was in sight. To Cooper, it seemed much brighter than it was before. She tried to explain the ship in the background to Buckley and other things that were coming into view. The underside of the alien spaceship was now coming into the picture. Soon after that, the circle with its platforms directly beneath it were clearly visible. Buckley's enthusiasm caused him to ask a lot of questions that Cooper couldn't answer.

They approached the compound around the *Mist of the Atlantic*, and for the first time, Rachael saw a large number of passengers on the cavern floor. She thought it must be most of them, if not all! They were assembled, looking like they were anticipating something. Some had spheres with them, but most stood alone or in small groups. The boxcar stopped next to the courtyard where the crowd assembled.

When they got out of the boxcar, Richard spoke, "The people are waiting for the return of the Aalzad. Come this way please."

Richard moved toward the area beneath the looming Tropos Magra. Looking up, the human duo saw the enormous circle within the hull of the spaceship. Directly below the circle in the ship, Cooper and Buckley saw the closed drain in the floor. Reaching the edge of the polished black drain, they were led up onto a retracted gantry bordering most of the circular area.

Richard didn't offer any explanation about this structure, they just moved silently. From the gantry, they could see two openings in the wall on the far-right side of the circle.

A vertical cave was on the left and straight ahead, a smaller opening was dug out of the seabed wall. The larger vertical cave looked like a railroad tunnel that appeared to go deep into the natural rock. The smaller hole contained a heavy door. The trio climbed off the gantry and moved in that direction.

Standing outside the smaller cave, Richard finally spoke, "This is the area that will support the Aalzad once they return. In front of you is the control room. It is where they will coordinate the use of the portals."

Moving toward the vertical cave, Richard continued, "This is the portal that will bring the Aalzad back to earth."

Then directing their attention to the circle in the floor, he said, "We have just moved past the gateway that travels to Zome. It is a direct portal through space."

Walking toward the vertical cave, they saw what looked like a conveyor belt system coming out of the opening. Entering, they saw that it formed a long straight tube. The conveyor belt ran about three quarters of the way down the tube, which, by Buckley's estimation, was about seventy-five yards long.

Richard explained, "When this portal is activated, the Aalzad will be transported from the home planet and arrive on Earth in a matter of minutes. When they travel through this portal, they will be in a protective craft."

"When the craft arrives, it will come to rest on the conveyor. From there it will be carried out into the cavern. Because of the disorienting factor of traveling through a wormhole, robots will help the travelers from the vehicle while guardians monitor their health. When they fully recover, the Aalzad citizens will begin their work."

THE TUNNELS OF EARTH

Richard turned and led the pair to the control room. The door opened vertically, rising to the open position. Cooper and Buckley followed Richard inside.

Once more he began to explain the workings of the Aalzad system, "This is where all aspects of the harvesting operation will take place."

Cooper and Buckley looked around, but they were lost in the strange technology. They were special forces, not rocket scientists. Richard would point at something and explain its function, but it was far beyond their understanding. Nothing seemed mechanical. Buckley didn't think a rocket scientist would understand this highly advanced collection of panels.

Continuing the tour, Richard led the humans out of the control room and headed toward the ramp that moved up to the alien ship.

Reaching the base of the ramp, he spoke again, "When the Aalzad commence harvesting water, circular valves at the top and bottom of the Tropos Magra will open. This will allow the ocean to fall directly through and into the portal in the floor of the cavern. From there it will carry water through the earth, then on to Zome.

"When completely open, the portal can handle a rate of around one million gallons per second. A comparison that you would understand is that it is about two thirds of the amount of water that goes over your Niagara Falls in the same amount of time.

"If successful, the Aalzad will continue to let it fall for about two years, collecting enough water that could equal the amount of water in your Lake Superior. This means the accumulation of just over three quadrillion gallons of water. When the process is done, it will be enough to harden the water supply on Zome and lower your world's oceans just slightly.

"When the water is flowing, the Aalzad will open the air vents on the earth's surface. Opening the vents will cause some of the land to collapse around the tower. Other less prominent vents on smaller islands will open as well. The vents will draw in enough air to create a wind tunnel, conveying air at high speed down the passageways. One estimate is it will travel at perhaps eighty-five to ninety miles per hour at peak flow.

"If any of your people are in those tunnels or on the surface near the transformation sites, they will be in great peril with little chance of survival. On the seas, there will be whirlpools appearing and subsiding above the Tropos Magra's water intake."

Finishing his lesson, Richard said, "When the air is pulled into the surface intakes, it will travel into tubes all around the outside of the main portal. It will enter much lower in the earth and travel with the water to Zome."

Cooper spoke to Richard, "What will happen to the passengers of the *Mist of the Atlantic*?"

Richard replied, "They are now preparing for transport to our planet. When all the Aalzad's preparation is done, they will be transported through the main portal in the floor."

Not really understanding why they had to go to Zome, Cooper asked, "Why can't you leave them here?"

"As I told the leaders of your group, the passengers will not be able to survive on the surface of your planet. There bodily configurations have been altered by the regenerator so many times they will perish in your environment. Their bodies are more suitable to our planet now. If they stayed here, on the surface their bodies would try to revert to normal function. Unfortunately, they will age rapidly and fade away."

Cooper asked directly, "Did you give them a choice?"

"Why would we? It is logical that we give them back a semblance of normal living, and that would have to be on Zome."

"Maybe you should give them the choice."

"We are responsible for their lives. The choice that they have is to die on Earth or live on a new world where they will survive for a long time. We never thought that anyone would choose to stay. It is not logical."

Cooper persisted, "Not all human decisions are logical. Give them the chance to make their own decision."

"I will discuss this matter with the Aalzad on their return."

*****

THE TUNNELS OF EARTH

After several hours of waiting, the first sign of the Aalzad return was dozens of worker robots pouring out of every tunnel. They were moving down the ramp from the ship as well, heading for the circle. Another sign was the guardians began herding their human charges toward the main ship. The people moved quickly at the behest of their hovering protectors.

All Buckley could relate this to would be a high school fire drill. It seemed like everyone knew what they were supposed to do except him. Cooper seemed confused as well with the hustle and bustle going on all around them.

Richard spoke, "The time has come. We must seek shelter."

Richard led Cooper and Buckley to the control room and told them to wait inside.

Richard explained, "You can see everything that happens through these door windows. For your own safety, once I close the door, do not open it. I will return to get you when the process is complete."

The door lowered, leaving Cooper and Buckley alone as Richard moved away. Once the heavy door closed, Richard moved toward the tunnel. Several groups of robots gathered outside the vertical cave portal. Others were at stations around the circle.

While the robots prepared for the Aalzad's return outside the control room, the Navy SEALs had a chance to get a closer look at the instrumentation. There were strange consoles and screens with nothing remotely identifiable.

Snooping around, Cooper found an area around the corner away from the main controls with a huge panel that took up the entire wall. It appeared to be an operations map. Cooper could read this map. She deciphered the pit as it lay on the panel, and from there she figured out where the other main features were. She saw the incoming cave and she saw the representation of the *Mist of the Atlantic*. It was almost like a satellite view within the cavern.

Continuing to view the map, Cooper saw lighted color symbols dotting the surface. The chief looked out of the window and could place a symbol on the map for each robot on the cavern floor. Observing the symbols for a few more minutes, she could determine worker robots from guardians. She then made an astonishing discovery; looking closely at the control room, she determined that there was no representation of her and Buckley!

Cooper saw that they had no individual symbol. On what she made out to be the Aalzad ship, there was a large cluster of blips moving up the ramp that she knew represented the passengers and crew of the *Mist of the Atlantic*. She thought, *We are invisible!*

It all made sense to her now. All the time that she was hiding in the tunnel, moving around the station and hiding on the tram, the robots couldn't detect her. They couldn't see her because she was invisible to the network.

She thought, *If we get into trouble, this might be an important bit of information.*

With the robots in the cavern gathered by the vertical tunnel, none were in the control room. Cooper thought to herself, if the robots don't use the control room, then who does? That's when it all became clear. If the Aalzad didn't have to come back to Earth, why would they? They are in the control room where the Aalzad will be working to orchestrate the harvest of Earth's resources.

Looking out the window, Buckley and Cooper saw that all the humans were gone. They were secured in the Aalzad ship. Looking around the cavern, there was no activity. The robots were waiting, frozen in position.

They didn't have to wait long. The process started with a deep rumbling in the earth; the control room shook. Cooper had to hold on to the wall to remain stable. Her eyes were fixed on the portal through the window.

*****

Continuing down the tunnel, a deep tremor shook E-Corps. It came from the bowels of the earth, from the direction that they were traveling. Roger stopped. Everyone stopped behind him.

One of the shaken team members nearby asked, "Do you know what that was?"

Roger replied, "Yes, it's the forming of the portals. The Aalzad are here or soon will be."

Frederickson advanced to Roger's position and asked, "How much farther do we have to go?"

"Five miles to a side tunnel where we can connect with the transportation system."

"Are we going to miss the Aalzad arrival?"

"No, I don't believe you will miss the event, but for your safety we must move faster."

"Why? What is going to happen?"

"Once they arrive, they will begin the operation. This tube will then funnel air down to the portal. We don't want to get caught in either the air being pumped in from the surface, or the vent collapse."

Roger continued, "We must get to the transport tube and board a train. Riding the train will allow us to move faster and get us out of the upper structure. It does not extend up this passage, but we can board it where the tunnels merge. We must go now!"

Roger upped the pace, the others followed. In a short distance, the group started to string out, losing contact with the guardian. The teams were in front, followed by the civilians. Collins, recognizing the separation, ordered two of his team members to drop back to keep the civilians moving. Roger was a good distance ahead of the group, pulling away. Capt. Steel saw the possibility of losing contact, so he yelled in a booming voice, "Roger, stop!"

*****

The rumble got louder deep in the vertical cave where a point of light manifested itself. As the rumble grew, the light grew. With the light and rumble came a gush of wind. It came out of the cave as a forceful blast of air.

The light burst out of the portal entrance as the event reached a crescendo. The light flashed out, the wind stopped, and the rumbling subsided. All became quiet. After a pause, worker robots came to life, surging into the vertical tunnel. Moments later the conveyor belt slowly started to roll out of the cave.

From their position in the control room, Buckley and Cooper could see straight into the cave. It was dark, so when a large dark shadow appeared in the cave, they got close to the window. "What is that?"

Their question was quickly answered. A threatening ten-foot bipedal robot moved out of the darkness. There was no mistaking it for a worker. It was a menacing sight that held something that could not be confused with anything other than a big weapon.

That must be security, Cooper thought.

A moment later a second security robot exited the cave. One stepped off the belt to the left, and the second one stepped off the belt to the right. Their shiny metallic heads swiveled left to right and back again. There was no question that they were scanning the area for threats. When satisfied there was no threat, they stood perfectly still.

Nothing happened for about ten minutes. Then the same sequence started again. Rumbling followed by light, followed by wind. When the event subsided, the belt started moving again. This time a low blue capsule traveled down the belt.

It looked like a big pill—a time release capsule to be more precise. It traveled beyond the security robots to the end of the belt. The security robots lumbered up next to it and started scanning again.

Worker robots went to the capsule and lifted a hatch located in the front of the vehicle. There were two figures inside. They weren't moving. Were they unconscious? The worker robots stayed in position close to the open hatch. After a short period of time, one of the passengers started to move. He moved laboriously at first and then strained to get out of the vehicle, composing himself.

It must have been a side effect of travel through a wormhole. The second being started to move in a similar fashion. When he gestured to the robots that he wanted to get out of the capsule, they dutifully helped him to his feet. He had a human appearance.

They were smaller in stature than a normal-sized human, perhaps five feet tall with narrow shoulders and skinny arms. They were slender and had delicate skin and facial features that included very dark eyes. The most striking feature they displayed was their long flowing silver hair.

Worker robots moved the capsule off the belt to one side and assisted the Aalzad away from the portal opening. They were moving muscles and joints and straightening their backs.

Very human, Cooper thought.

*****

Roger stopped immediately on Captain Steel's command. While the teams were catching up, regrouping, a second deep tremor shook the tunnel. The ground shook again with the increased intensity. Frederickson came up next, breathing heavily but not totally exhausted. Dr. Silver and the two members of Harrier team were still far behind.

Steel asked, "Roger, do you know when the event you spoke of will take place?"

"It will happen sooner than I thought. I can't be sure when, because I don't know how many Aalzad will be traveling through the portal."

"Roger, I want you to go just fast enough so we can keep up so we all make it to the transport. We have to get everyone there."

"I will keep in contact with the group. We will only know the event has started by the commencement of air passing through this tunnel."

Roger moved off again, advancing at what Steel thought was about the same speed as he was traveling before.

Steel said to the teams, "We have to keep up with the robot, or we're finished! Drop your extra gear and go like hell! This is life or death!"

The group moved out fast. Frederickson was there, but the three stragglers were just catching up.

Steel waited for them, saying to the Harrier team members, "Get going. I'll stay with the professor."

Breathing heavily, one gladly responded, "Yes, sir," as they both moved off quickly.

Speaking to Dr. Silver, Steel seriously warned, "Doctor! You must keep up with me. We're running out of time. Something bad is going to happen in this tunnel following one of these tremors. I'll stay with you as long as you don't give up!"

The group moved forward with greater urgency. Eagle Corps could keep contact with Roger but with great effort. They were running, trained to push the limits of their physical ability. They were doing it.

Frederickson was next, He was moving as fast as he could, but in his midthirties, he was suffering badly. His desk job conditioning was letting him down. He knew that he had to keep up, or he would die. Coming up the rear was Captain Steel and Professor Silver. They were falling behind again.

Everyone ahead was pulling away. Silver, an older man, was badly out of shape, but he showed determination. He understood the consequences if he stopped.

*****

It all began again. The first empty capsule had been moved out of the way. Now the deep rumbling started. Moments later when the light went out and wind dissipated, a second capsule rolled out of the opening. The belt stopped and the robots stood by the passengers until they started to recover.

Two more Aalzad were escorted to the side of the tunnel. The first two looked more relaxed, fully recovered and communicating with Richard. Four Aalzad were now together recovering from their trip through the space portal.

Richard turned and approached the control room. The Aalzad were recovering thirty yards from where Cooper and Buckley looked out the window. When he was close, Richard remotely opened the door and entered.

In what could only be perceived as a stern voice, Richard said, "The Aalzad want you to leave the control room. I will escort you to a safe place."

THE TUNNELS OF EARTH

Thinking that they were there to talk to the Aalzad, Buckley said, "Aren't they going to talk to us?"

"I don't have that information. They just told me to escort you out of the control room."

He continued, "If they want to communicate with Earth humans, it will come through me or one of the other guardians. The guardians have never heard the Aalzad speak like you. With us we receive their messages in our minds and follow their orders. When we communicate with you, we do not get nonverbal messages like those from the Aalzad."

Richard turned and led the two Navy SEALs from the control room, away from the portals. He was leading them to the ramp. It appeared that the Aalzad wanted them to go up to the Tropos Magra with the others. As they moved halfway up the ramp, they stopped and looked down on the scene.

Standing a good distance away, they could still see the events clearly unfolding. All the Aalzad now seemed completely recovered. Together they walked toward the control room. Buckley and Cooper watched as one of the Aalzad stopped and returned to the capsule where he opened a side hatch. Someone else got out. It wasn't someone; it was something.

It was a different type of humanoid robot exiting the vehicle. It looked like a cross between a worker with its arms and legs, but it had that bulbous spherical body of the guardians. It was twice the size of its Aalzad companions. With no recovery time needed, this robot moved directly into the control room. With all the space travelers safe inside, the door shut.

Buckley asked Richard, "What's that robot?"

"That is the command robot or CR for short. It has a very important role—it possesses the entire knowledge base for this operation. It operates the systems while monitoring all information in the control room. It also has direct communication with Zome."

Buckley retorted, "That's a pretty important robot, what do the Aalzad do?"

*****

Eagle Corps was moving at a furious pace. A third tremor roared through the tunnels, distressing everyone.

The main thought among the men was *Not much longer, we're not going to make it.*

Out of the blue, one of the soldiers just stopped. He was exhausted and just stood, waiting for the inevitable. Steel and Silver came upon him and urged him to keep going, but he stared vacantly off into space. The officer and the scientist couldn't wait. Steel tried to verbally motivate the disheartened team member as he moved by.

Without looking back, Steel said, "You're not dead yet, Russel, keep moving!"

The words fell on deaf ears as they pressed on.

Roger stopped and informed the lead group that they were within two hundred yards of their goal.
Cmdr. Collins yelled back to the stragglers, "We're close, men, keep going!"
The teams, now near total exhaustion, surged forward again.

*****

On the surface, General Ray paced the floor thinking about the unit he sent down into the earth. Eagle Corps, plus the two civilians, had been out of communication range for hours. He was responsible for their actions and their safety. He now regretted sending more personnel down into the pit.

When the Aalzad event happened, there was a series of rumbles, like an undersea earthquake south of Martha's Vineyard. It was being recorded as far away as Alvin Canyon, in the open ocean. This was a surprise to General Ray because he thought that the tunnel couldn't possibly be that long. He figured it could not go beyond Cox Ledge.

THE TUNNELS OF EARTH

The cavern's location was much farther south than originally thought. The scientists were analyzing tremors in a location southeast of the Block Island Shelf Valley. This was the location of the seismic activity recorded at Goat Island.

At Quonset, they focused their attention on that area; sensitive equipment received another faint signal that a second earthquake happened. When the third earthquake occurred, it too was not a major event. Three minor quakes were recorded, if they could even be called that.

*****

Richard said, "The Aalzad are preparing the large portal for water transport. Soon they will begin."

The operation was commencing without delay. With the Aalzad at the controls, the hard cover to the cavern portal began rolling back. Eight curved horizontal sections retracted tightly into the outside wall of the pit. The gantry unfolded and rose from the cavern floor. When it reached a height of eight feet, it locked into place. It wrapped around the entire portal.

All remained quiet until high above the portal, a valve at the bottom of the Aalzad ship began to open. Water started to slowly spill into the open circle in the floor. The flow valve was less than 20 percent open when it stopped. It had reached a designated volume.

The water cascaded straight down into the center of the portal. There was no indication that it was filling up. Hearing a rumble from way down below, the surface of the portal started to solidify in a swirling electrified mass. The water fell straight down through it.

With a blinding burst of light from inside the portal, water was suddenly sucked down. The wormhole was open! Water was flowing toward the center of the Earth and beyond. With the successful opening of the portal achieved, the central valve on the Tropos Magra was opened completely.

As Richard had explained to the officials at the Coddington, millions of gallons were falling straight down into the open vortex. There was a deafening roar to the flowing water. It was a trickle when the door was partially open, but now it flowed like a massive waterfall. Dense mist filled the air.

Buckley in his youth remembered traveling to Buffalo, New York, to visit Niagara Falls. He remembered that he was amazed by the power of water falling over the edge of Horseshoe Falls on the Canadian side. This was a fair comparison in his mind. The door to the control room opened, and one of the Aalzad exited, moving to the gantry to inspect the flow.

He climbed a short ladder, walked to the edge, then leaned out far to get a good look into the vortex. When he was satisfied that everything was operational, he reentered the control room and closed the door.

There was nothing Buckley and Cooper could do but watch. Buckley realized that this was out of some science fiction story. This was the genre of books and movies that had amazing aliens demonstrating technological superiority, asserting themselves on lesser civilizations. He was living it!

A moment after the Aalzad returned to the control room, Buckley and Cooper could hear distant thunder up toward the surface. They knew what it was, as Richard foretold the opening of surface vents.

After the sound passed, there was a whirring sound at the edge of the cavern. They looked in the direction of the noise and noticed a building cut out of the wall. It was large, blending into the shadows. You had to be looking for it to see it.

It covered a massive section of the wall west of the circle. It was the pump house. Three gigantic tubes descended close to the cavern wall below a ninety-degree turn. They entered the pump house on the back side of this structure.

Cooper and Buckley hadn't noticed that area before, but now they recognized the tubes for what they were. Those tubes were the same tunnels that they had been traveling down to be here. The whirring of the pumps increased steadily.

*****

On the surface, satellites captured the massive explosions of the Aalzad air shaft bursting open. Down below, the ground inside the tunnel shook. Eagle Corps continued forward; their will to live forced them to carry on. Roger slowed down to move with the lead group. They were closing in on the exit, and he wanted to show them the way out.

Roger spoke, "On your right," indicating the location of the door.

Falcon team identified the opening and scrambled into it. They were followed closely by Harrier team, including Lt. Cmdr. Collins. Inside the door, everyone collapsed heavily on the deck. They made it. Collins picked himself up, moved to the door, and knelt on one knee looking for the trailers.

Then it happened—muffled explosions came from the upper end of the tunnel. Instinctively he looked at his watch. Everyone knew that it was coming from the surface. The ground quaked all around them. The door was at an intersection of two large air tunnels and a work shaft. The shaft would provide a highway, separate from the surging air. It would lead to the cavern below and keep E-Corps safe from the explosions happening at the surface.

Frederickson, still in the tunnel, was in an uncontrolled sprint. Drenched in sweat and his arms flailing, he raced clumsily through the open door and crumpled to the floor. Two Harrier team members partially recovered, grabbed him by the armpits, and dragged him deeper into the passageway.

Collins, still looking out the door, yelled down the tunnel, "We're in the side passageway, you can make it!"

There was no response. He shined his flashlight up the tunnel and saw nothing. There was another rumble, but this one didn't subside. It only got louder. With his light still shining up the tunnel, he saw two distant forms moving in his direction. It was Steel with his hand locked on Silver's arm, urging him forward.

Collins, understanding the situation, got up and sprinted out the door toward the distressed pair. The rumbling grew louder. The ungodly sound coming down the tunnel was gathering speed. Collins reached them, grabbed Silver by his other arm, and together with

Steel, hustled him down the tube. As they ran, he sensed a sudden change in the tunnel's air pressure.

Air, gathering speed as it came, rushed up from behind, moving toward the core. Collins and Steel got an unexpected assist from the increasing tailwind. The only problem was, would they be able to stop and get through the targeted doorway.

The door was coming up fast. Being closest to the door, Steel tried to work his way over to the side of the tunnel, but the wind speed was pushing them back toward the middle.

To compound the situation, debris was now being carried by the wind, pelting them from behind. This was it; with only one chance, Steel struggled over to the wall, holding Silver's arm tightly. Believing that if he missed, they would die, Steel lunged for the door.

As he was reaching in, arms were reaching out for him. Team members within the safety of the side tunnel grabbed him and held on. It was a human chain in a life-and-death struggle against the whirlwind.

Harrier and Falcon teams worked together to hold on to each other and the three men struggling to get in. With a gigantic tug, those inside the door pulled. It was working; the three caught in the wind tunnel were at the door. First, Steel was in, and then Silver was dragged inside.

Collins, giving one last push, let go of Silver's arm. He reached out for the edge of the door to add leverage so he could force the others to safety. Before he could get a good grip on the opening, a flying piece of jagged debris roughly the size of a baseball roared down the tunnel. It struck him on the side of the head.

No one could react fast enough. Without as much as a whimper, Collins went limp, his eyes closed, and his hands released his grip on the door. He had a peaceful expression on his face as he fell away.

His body tumbled down the tunnel, now encompassed by the turbulent wind and larger chunks of debris. Still holding out their hands in astonishment, the rescuers' grips had failed. In shock and with nothing more to do, the survivors closed the door. Lieutenant Commander Collins was gone.

*****

Cooper said to Richard, "Where is the air going?"

"The air is being pumped into the same portal as the water but hundreds of feet below the cavern surface."

Buckley asked, "How long do they intend to send water and air to your planet?"

"Only the Aalzad have the answer to that question. It will take as long as necessary."

All systems of the Aalzad mission were online. Millions of gallons of water were being transported to Zome as well as a lesser quantity of air. The door to the control room opened again, and the Aalzad exited together as if they were getting off their shift at work.

Cooper thought, *There was no getting around it—they are human, just like us.*

She said to Richard, "I want to speak to the Aalzad."

He replied, "You would need them to want to talk to you in order for that to happen."

Cooper, becoming upset, said, "That's not good enough. I have to talk to them."

Without warning, she bolted down to the base of the ramp. Running across the rough surface, she passed the location where the water fell steadily into the circle. Richard started after her, but she had a good head start. She moved directly toward the Aalzad standing outside the control room.

They saw her coming but seemed disinterested. They knew something that she didn't. As she got closer, the giant sentry robots came to life. They turned and faced the surprised corpsman, who was approaching fast. Their weapons came up and pointed directly at her. On seeing this, she stopped short in an uncontrollable skid and fell to the cavern floor on her back.

She jumped to her feet and called out to the Aalzad standing there, "I need to talk to you! Please let me talk to you!" The Aalzad were now curious; they approached but stopped at a safe distance behind the sentry robots. They were communicating among themselves as they watched her pleading with them.

When Richard caught up to her, he immediately spoke, "The Aalzad want you to turn around and go back up the ramp."

"I need to ask them a question."

"They are not ready to talk to you. They want to talk to your leader."

Buckley made his way up to Cooper's side and said, "I am her leader."

Translated by a guardian, the Aalzad seemed amused by that statement and turned to walk away.

Buckley said, "When will you talk to us?"

Richard repeated, "When they need to."

The robots stayed on high alert as the Aalzad reentered the control room, closing the door behind them.

Richard said, "There will be time to talk to them. You will have to wait until the time is right for them. Come with me to the Tropos Magra."

*****

Buckley and Cooper climbed the ramp and entered the Tropos Magra's vast hanger deck section. It was so large it could hold several medium sized navy ships within its walls. On entering they found the full complement of passengers and crew of the *Mist of the Atlantic*.

Their demeanor was nothing like the first encounter she had with them at the cruise ship and in the courtyard. There was an air of excitement in this large section of the hangar bay.

Half of the passengers had their spheres with them. Buckley noticed that the people were looking at them suspiciously. They had questions: "Who were these people, and why were they here now, of all times?"

Cooper and Buckley stood in a separate area from the ship's company. They saw individuals standing alone, families standing together. They also saw a religious service going on with a good-sized congregation. Richard joined a person that had to be Dr. Stack. The doctor seemed happy to see him.

Standing there, Cooper and Buckley shared an awkward feeling, having all these probing eyes on them. After several minutes, a familiar young man approached with a youthful smile on his face.

He said, "Hi, Rachael, remember me? George Field!"

"Of course, George, it's good to see you again. Are you all right?"

He responded by saying, "I'm fine, thank you. I can't remember feeling better. We are going to Zome you know. The Aalzad are going to take us with them so we can live with their people. I really want to go. I will grow up, and I will live out my life in another solar system. Maybe if I'm lucky, someday I will be able to come back and visit Earth."

Buckley introduced himself, "Hello, George, my name is Roger."

George smiled and said, "Oh you're the guy Rachael named her guardian after. Max told me all about it."

Buckley was confused. He looked at Cooper, but she ducked her head and didn't offer any explanation.

Cooper reminded the lieutenant, "That was Kelly's guardian I named, sir."

George interjected, "No, Roger was made for you. He is yours. He accompanied Kelly back to the surface to help you."

Cooper didn't know what to say about that, so she changed the subject. "Is everyone from your group going with the Aalzad?"

"Yes, we're all going."

"You're telling me that no one wants to stay on earth and return to their homes?"

"The people know that there is nothing left for them here, so we are all going to Zome together. Everyone is committed to this move. Our lives here on Earth have been taken away. The Aalzad want to make up for their mistake of cutting our lives short here.

"We all know that we couldn't live six months on the surface after using the regenerator for all these years we have been down here."

Buckley spoke, "George, is there a leader among your group? I would like to talk to him if I could."

"We have no official leaders here. We don't need leaders. We all have guardians to help us with any problems we might have. The leader when we were on the *Mist of the Atlantic* was the captain, Captain Larsson. Since the accident though, he has had no influence on anything."

*****

Last Stop

Once at the tram tunnel, E-Corps caught a ride the rest of the way down to the cavern. Now they were at the proverbial end of the line. The tram stopped a good distance from their destination, so they had to hump the final mile down the tube. Steel, in the last section of the empty tramway, walked down in advance of the group. In the distance he could see an expanse of light growing across a large empty cavern.

They were tired and beat up. Most of their weapons and equipment were gone. Half of the team members had their side arms and only one rifle remained. Harrier team's Lance Corporal David Moreno held on to his sniper rifle. He thought he was useless to the teams without it.

Most of the backpacks, weapons, and equipment were gone, discarded for the sake of speed. Moving with Roger down the last bit of tramway, it was slow going. All were exhausted, but they had no choice but to continue. They were moving toward the light, dead ahead. Roger exclaimed that this was their destination.

Frederickson said to Roger, "Will we meet the Aalzad now?"

Roger replied, "I don't know if the Aalzad are ready to meet you yet. You will need to have your questions ready when you do because they have no patience for unpreparedness."

Roger said to the group, "Until the Aalzad want to speak to you, I will escort you to their ship where the members of the *Mist of the Atlantic* are assembled. You are free to talk to and ask them any questions that you have."

THE TUNNELS OF EARTH

Frederickson stepped in next to Steel and spoke, "Captain, let your sniper and spotter slip away from the group and take up a position at the entrance facing in the direction of our movement. They can keep us covered in case of a problem. Don't let the guardian see what you are doing."

Frederickson moved away. Steel didn't like the plan, but he followed orders. He grabbed Moreno and pulled him to one side.

The rest of the group walked out into the giant cavern. It was well lit with panoramic views. They could clearly see the *Mist of the Atlantic* propped up near the dark underside of the alien ship.

From their vantage point, they saw mist rising as water poured down into what appeared to be a giant hole in the ground. To their left they could hear the whooshing sound of air being pumped through monstrous pipes.

E-Corps could see ramps and walkways from a long way off as they proceeded deeper into the cavern. They could see dozens of trams parked off to their right. Now in the open, they walked down a distinct path toward the alien ship. As they got closer, they made out the forms of the giant security robots facing their direction with weapons at the ready.

Capt. Steel said to Roger, "Are they anything we have to be concerned about?"

Roger replied, "You should not have anything to worry about if you stay with me. They are Aalzad high security and will deal with any threat that may arise. It could be in the form of a threat to the Aalzad citizens or the operation."

Now in command of Eagle Corps, Steel said, "Stay close together, men, and don't provoke those things."

He turned to get a look where Moreno and his spotter were setting up. He was satisfied that he couldn't see them.

They passed between the security robots and the *Mist of the Atlantic* and started up the ramp. Looking down over the side, E-Corps could now clearly see the portal. They could also see the side tunnel and the control room with figures moving inside the windows. More figures were outside of the control room, dozens of them.

*****

Buckley said, "George, will you introduce me to the captain?"

George agreed and escorted Lt. Buckley across the room to a small group of people that looked like the crew. Some wore old white pseudomilitary uniforms that ship personnel wore. They were speaking to each other and their guardians in Swedish. The pair approached the man in his still tidy formal uniform.

George stopped and said, "Hello, Captain Larsson, this is Roger Buckley. He would like to speak to you."

Captain Larsson, facing away, turned and faced the newcomers. He smiled warmly and said, "Hello, George," then he turned to Lt. Buckley and said, "Hello, you are one of the surface people that have come down to rescue us?"

The crew chuckled.

"What can I help you with?"

Buckley asked, "You are the captain of the *Mist of the Atlantic*?"

"I was."

"Then you are the responsible individual for the safety of passengers and crew."

"I have not been responsible for anything in a long time. How many years has it been?"

"Almost eleven years, Captain."

Larsson smirked and said, "Eleven years, and I am still forty-five years old. Not bad, wouldn't you agree?"

Buckley, losing patience with Captain Larrson, said, "If you aren't in charge here, is there someone else that you consider the leader, someone that I could talk to?"

Larsson laughed and called out for Sven. The crew turned and looked in anticipation to see Buckley's expression when he saw Sven and what would follow.

To Buckley's left, he heard a voice reply in electronic Swedish. Captain Larsson responded in Swedish and then for Buckley's sake spoke in English, "Sven, I need you to do something for me. This gentleman wants to ask you some questions. I would like you to answer them."

Sven responded in English, "I will answer this gentleman's questions."

Buckley turned back to Larsson. "I don't want your guardian to answer my questions. How will I know that he is telling me the truth?"

Larsson, glaring at Buckley, said, "Sven will answer your questions truthfully. He has no reason to lie. He is so superior to you that he has no fear of telling you anything. He has vast amounts of information, and he will share it with you at your request."

Buckley stared back at Larsson then turned to Sven. "What is going to happen to the people of the *Mist of the Atlantic*?"

"The passengers and crew of the *Mist of the Atlantic* will travel through the wormhole to Zome, where they will become members of Aalzad society."

"What will they do on Zome?"

"They will be productive members of society."

"Doing what?"

"Whatever they want to do. They will live under no restrictions."

"Will the Aalzad give them jobs to do?"

"If they want jobs."

"What kind of jobs?"

"It will depend on what they can qualify for. For example, Captain Larsson, with training, could become a galaxy ship commander if that's what he wants to do."

Amazed, Buckley said, "Could that really happen?"

"There could be a chance of that becoming reality with the help of command robots. He has the individual skill of commanding a large ship. It would not be that different for him. It would just be on a larger scale."

"Will the Aalzad ever make them work?"

"Only in an emergency situation, when everyone works."

"You've evacuated your home planet. Wouldn't you consider that an emergency situation?"

"Yes, that would be considered an emergency, but there are already many Aalzad citizens doing the work now, setting up our civilization. A lot has changed on Zome in the last fifty years. Don't worry for your people. They will not be forced into labor."

Buckley changed the focus of his questions. "What if they don't want to go to Zome?"

"That would be suicide. Any member of the *Mist of the Atlantic* that stayed here on earth would die within months of returning to the surface. Regeneration has changed them. The climate of the cavern was adjusted to provide optimal living conditions for your people. Special compounds were added to the air similar to the present atmosphere on Zome. That is why they are so healthy in these artificial surroundings.

"Those ingredients are not present in the natural atmosphere of Earth. In essence, your people have become dependent on them. They cannot survive on the surface for long without them."

Buckley asked, "Have you given them the option of staying?"

"No, it is believed that no one would stay just to wither and die while they could continue to live well on Zome."

Cooper said abruptly, "Ask them if they want to stay! Don't force the ones that don't want to go to travel against their will."

Sven calmly answered Cooper's demand, "It's not up to guardians. We only carry out the directions of the Aalzad. The decision has been made that it is best that they go."

"I want to talk to the Aalzad to request that those people that want to stay have that option."

"You do not have authorization to talk to the Aalzad. Besides, why do you think there are passengers that even want to stay?"

Cooper shouted, "Then you talk to the Aalzad and convey my message!"

People broke off their conversations and stared in the direction of the disturbance. Sven simply moved away, leaving Cooper alone in her angered state. Cooper helplessly looked at Buckley with tears welling up in her eyes.

Cooper had finally come to the realization that all the people were going to Zome. Their lives on Earth were behind them. It would be fatal for them to stay. She and Buckley moved to wait in an isolated area away from the passengers and crew.

Water was crashing into the portal while the air hissed down individual tubes into the pit. Guardians were floating near their charges that were milling around in anticipation of leaving. Anxiety levels were high, while off to the side, Cooper noticed how much more alert they were than she had previously observed.

*****

Temporarily assigned to Falcon team, Army Ranger Vince Blackwell recognized them as the same kind of humanoid that exploded inside the door back in the tunnel near the surface. They pressed on, up the ramp, into the Tropos Magra.

Entering the main hangar where the passengers gathered, Roger led the group to an open side of the room away from the people. He said, "You can rest here. The Aalzad will address you when they complete their work."

Frederickson looked around the room and noticed that no one was paying any attention to them. The teams removed whatever little gear they had and slumped down to rest.

Steel said to Roger, "Why are these people so indifferent?"

"They think you are here to take them away."

"How can we reassure them that that's not the reason why we're here?"

"I will signal the other guardians to pass on the message that you are no threat to their humans. Once I communicate that, I think that the people will relax and not fear your motives any longer."

Roger transmitted the message to all the guardians, and after a few moments, Steel saw a noticeable change in the room. Just as Roger explained, the guardians communicated the message to their charges. Steel could see the people start to relax.

An hour went by, and the new arrivals passed the time sharing the rations they had left. Captain Steel was observing the new relaxed atmosphere in the room when Frederickson approached with Professor Silver.

"Captain, did you take care of what we talked about?"

"Yes, sir. Our sniper and spotter were deployed somewhere on the outskirts, near the entrance. They will shift as needed and position themselves anywhere in the cavern. Depending on the situation, they will use their training for effectiveness and act independently or on my signal. I hope we don't need them. If we do, that would indicate we're in deep shit!"

Frederickson continued, "Captain, I don't think you know what the purpose of this mission is. Dr. Silver and I are here to try to stop the Aalzad operation. I know that you have met the doctor but not exactly under the best conditions. Captain, this is Dr. Julius Silver, professor of physics at Brown University. He is here to size up the Aalzad's strength and perhaps act as a technical liaison with them."

In a grateful voice, Silver said, "Captain, I want to thank you for saving my life. I would never have survived back in the tunnel without your help. You and Lt. Cmdr. Collins gave me the strength to make it to the door. I feel terrible about what happened. He sacrificed his life for me."

Steel shook his hand and said, "It's nice to meet you, Professor. I'm glad you made it, and you're right about Lt. Cmdr. Collins. It's the class of man he was. It all came down to doing what he had to do. In that respect, you are dealing with a whole group of men who would do the same thing."

In a caring voice, Steel finished his thought, "I am grateful to him too. We never would have made it to the door without his help. He wouldn't just let us die."

Steel changed the subject. "What do you think you can accomplish?"

"I'm not sure. I can negotiate and give them alternatives to taking our resources. We have identified a number of planets and moons where they can fulfill their needs for water. In other solar systems, there are a large number of planets. Here in our own solar system within a stone's throw of Earth, by their standards, we have moons of Jupiter and Saturn."

*****

THE TUNNELS OF EARTH

Patiently waiting for what happens next, a guardian moved in Cooper's direction. It seemed familiar, not like the ones personalized by their passengers. Yet there was something about it. Waiting for it to pass, she was startled when it stopped directly in front of her.

The guardian spoke, "Hello, Rachael Cooper, I am Roger, your guardian."

"Hello, Roger, I'm surprised to see you again. The last time I saw you, you were with Corporal Kelly at the hotel."

"Yes, I left him with the medical staff. I also accompanied your delegation from the surface to this place."

Buckley saw Cooper speaking to this guardian and got up from where he was sitting to move close enough to hear what they were talking about.

Seeing him approach, Cooper said to him, "The delegation is here from the surface."

A little surprised, he said, "Where are they?"

Roger spoke up, "They are across the ship on the other side of the water core."

Buckley replied, "How did you find us?"

"Two guardians had direct contact with you earlier, so I learned that you were here through their collective thoughts."

"Thoughts?"

"Not exactly, it is more a shared memory that all of the guardians are connected to. I believe that the word you would use is interface."

Roger continued, "The reason I sought you out is to tell you that the Aalzad will meet with you and the delegation soon. You need to join the others and wait to be summoned."

Cooper, half joking with Roger, said, "Are you sure the Aalzad are in charge, not you?"

Not having a sense of humor, the guardian replied, "We serve the Aalzad, but they do need us."

Buckley asked, "How does that work?"

"We advise and guide them. We make them formidable. Without us, they would be more like you. The difference between you and the Aalzad is that you make decisions for yourselves. Quite often you make good decisions where the Aalzad do not try. Come, the time is approaching."

Roger escorted Lt. Buckley and Chief Cooper to the spot where Eagle Corps and the two civilians rested.

Seeing Buckley and Cooper coming, Captain Steel stood up from his not-so-comfortable resting place on the floor and said, "Well, look who's here. I wondered if we were going to see you down here. What's your story, Lt. Buckley? What happened to you?"

"Sir, Richard the guardian made a run for it. I found Chief Cooper following it down the stairs at the Coddington. I thought it would be best to follow after him as well. We chased him outside toward the causeway. When he crossed the structure, he slowed down to let us catch up. He wasn't coming back, so we were persuaded to go with him."

Steel turned to the corpsman, "What do you have to say about this, Chief?"

"The lieutenant got it right, sir. The guardian wanted to go, but he wanted me to go with him. If I didn't go, he would have gone anyway. Lt. Buckley intercepted us in the stairwell and saw what was happening. It was a no-brainer. We had to follow after him."

Steel replied, "Okay, we'll talk about your vanishing act later. What can you tell me about what's happening here?"

Buckley responded, "After we arrived, the Aalzad came through a portal to their base. Their first action was to open the bottom of this ship, the Tropos Magra, to allow ocean water to fall into that hole in the floor, a wormhole. From what the guardian told us, the water is falling across the universe to their home planet."

He pointed in the direction of the pump house and continued, "They are also sucking the atmosphere through those gigantic pipes over there. We tried to talk to the Aalzad when they arrived, but they wouldn't talk to us. I think that is about to change. Roger here tells us that we are about to meet with them."

Confirming what Roger told Buckley, Steel said, "We got a heads-up a few minutes ago." Moving closer to Buckley, Steel lowered his voice, "Lieutenant, how do we stop these guys?"

"I don't know, sir. They're much more advanced than we are. What they lack as individuals is made up by their guardians. It appears that they have a strong dependence on them."

Hovering close by, Roger said, "It is time. Your delegation will now meet with the Aalzad. Please follow me."

Leaving the Tropos Magra, Eagle Corps, led by the two civilians, started down the ramp. They were surprised when they saw worker robots preparing trams. They were being assembled close to the exit portal. Fifteen trams were being moved into special positions around the pit. As they watched, several more were being brought out of the upper tunnels.

Each tram looked like it would hold no more than twenty people. After making some simple calculations, Professor Silver came to the conclusion that they were far short of the number of trams they would need to bring every passenger and crew member of the *Mist of the Atlantic* to Zome.

Passing the giant security robots, Steel said, "These machines look badass. Have you seen them in action?"

Buckley replied, "On the Aalzad's arrival, they guarded the pods that they were in. They were ready to fire on us when we made a move to communicate with their bosses."

They approached the control room and waited. Buckley continued to describe to Captain Steel everything that he observed.

Mr. Frederickson talked to Dr. Silver, "Doctor, how do we stack up against these aliens?"

"I'm not sure. There are so many amazing things down here, but I don't have the slightest idea how they work. I want to hear what the Aalzad have to say. Perhaps I can gain some insight. I hope we can deal with them. They have so much to offer."

Frederickson said, "If we can't, are you aware of our backup plan?"

"Not exactly, but I know that the Aalzad gave away their location when they arrived through the wormhole. All the seismometers on the east coast must have been tripped, pinpointing our location. What they will do, I don't wish to speculate."

Frederickson said, "We have a few tricks up our sleeves, but we need to wait and see what develops. As you say, the Aalzad have a lot to offer us. If nothing else, we might be able to stay in front of the rest of the world in obtaining new technology. I can only hope."

The security robots came to life and moved into positions on either side of the control room door.

Frederickson to Silver with a wry smile, "I want one of those!"

The door opened, and a single figure emerged. Except for Buckley and Cooper, the delegation was startled. They saw a man, a man of slight stature with long flowing hair. His skin was smooth, and his features were delicate. He had no facial hair.

He was wearing a suit made of a tight-fitting silver material. He wore boots that were of similar design, silver with black soles. Other than his clothing and hairstyle, he looked like a diminutive malnourished human being.

The Aalzad moved out of the control room, striding toward the gantry above the portal. The intimidating robots kept pace, gliding next to him. On reaching the gantry, he climbed to the top and looked down into the pit.

At the base of the gantry, on high alert, the robots turned and faced the group. Guardians assembled around the single Aalzad. Frederickson, Silver, and the members of the E-Corps standing at the base of the gantry looked up at this figure in anticipation of what was to come next.

Speaking through one of the guardians, he said, "My name is Florzo Lox, ambassador of the Planetary Government of Zome. I am here to speak to you, the representatives of Earth." Pointing to the civilians with Eagle Corps, he said, "I will speak to you now."

Dean Frederickson and Dr. Julius Silver nodded, then climbed the gantry ladder, approaching Florzo Lox.

Frederickson spoke first, "I am Dean Frederickson. This is Professor Julius Silver. We are the representatives of the United States government."

Lox said, "Are you the leader of the United States?"

"We are authorized to act in their interests."

"You will convey what I am about to say here to those who are your leaders?"

"That is correct."

Lox gestured positively to the two men.

Lox looked beyond the two men and began to speak to the entire group from the surface as a whole, "First, let me tell you that we the Aalzad have nothing to gain by communicating with you here today."

Through the guardian, he continued, "We do it in good faith to quell any fears that you may have about our presence. Next, we are not here to be your friends. Conversely, we are not your enemies. To us, this is a mission to save our planet. Nothing is more important to us.

"If you want to stop us, you are welcome to try. For those of you with short memories, I will remind you that when we first made contact, you tried unsuccessfully to destroy our starship. None of your weapons had any effect on our defenses. If you thought that we were powerful then, we are far more powerful now."

Lox continued, "There is absolutely no reason why we need to stay in direct contact with you. Ninety-nine percent of our operation is entirely under your ocean. We will operate here, in seclusion, until we have met our needs.

"For the time being, we will not offer you anything that you can turn around to use against us. We may from time to time offer solutions to your worldly problems that you have no answer. We may also help in other unspecified ways.

"When we are finished here, depending on your leader's cooperation, there is a chance for diplomacy between our worlds." He smiled and pointed out into the cavern, saying, "We have almost eight hundred potential ambassadors between our worlds."

Lox paused a moment then said, "In the final analysis. I am sure that we will be friends.

"Our science and technology have advanced exponentially in the past ten Earth years. While observing your civilization, we have not seen very much progress. As you have been told by our emissary robots, we have come here to tap into your abundant resources for our newly colonized planet. We are here not to interfere with the activities of your planet but to ensure the survival of ours.

"Our home world has died, consumed by its dying sun. Our entire population was displaced, and a new home had to be found. When we found our new world, we gave it the name Zome. This name was given after one of our early primitive gods. Ironically, Zome was our sun god.

"In many ways, our new planet is like Earth. There are mountains and valleys, forests and oceans. However, based on our population, it is smaller, and it has limited resources. Your planet surface reminds me of Zome.

"When we arrived on Zome, our leaders discovered that the planet would not sustain life over an extended period. The natural resources were limited. Our oceans were too shallow, and our atmosphere was too thin. This created a dilemma because we spent years transferring the bulk of the population from Aalzarada.

"Our planetary leaders met to find ways to assure that our civilization would survive. Our alternatives were to gather resources from off world sources or find another world where we could move our population again. Our decision was to try to make our initial move work. Earth was discovered with its abundance of water and air, thus establishing our goals.

"The Aalzad had been on Earth undetected for three decades. In that time, we created a series of tunnels and passageways under your seabed. Only ten years ago we began to condition some small islands off your mainland. As you know, we sent the smoke to New England islands in preparation to acquire enough land on the surface for our purposes. The newly exposed structures at the end of the tunnels were built to draw air into the underground facility.

"Our first contact with humans was not as smooth as it could have been. The people of the *Mist of the Atlantic* cruise ship have suffered greatly. We owe them much. We welcome them to renew normal lives on Zome. I'm sure you would like to know details of what happened that day.

"We arrived at our target over your ocean and made our descent to the sea. Our first ship entered the ocean without incident. It rode down along a beam that parted the water in its path. When our second ship descended to the ocean, it accidentally captured the *Mist of the Atlantic* in its beam. The *Mist of the Atlantic* dropped from the ocean's surface into the hole that we created.

"When the Aalzad commander realized what he had done, he tried to correct the situation by protecting the ship's plunge by cocooning it within the beam. When we lodged the Tropos Magra in the seafloor, we continued to protect the cruise ship, bringing it within our ship's central core. This is where the water is now passing through. To ease their trauma, all the passengers were rendered in a highly sedated state for their own protection until the cavern was stabilized.

"Many of the people on the *Mist of the Atlantic* had died and others had been badly injured. We were able to save most of them. Unfortunately, some passengers were thrown from the ship in the fall and were never recovered.

"We are now sitting about forty-five miles southeast of the island of Nantucket, below the continental shelf.

"Our original strategy was to create a diversion so the people of Earth would not comprehend what we were really doing. We transformed several of your islands into unusable places. We wanted you to believe that we were terraforming them for future occupation. We also wanted you to believe that we were very different from you.

"It was a complete fabrication because as you can see, there is little difference between us. We need the same elements as you to live. As far as we know, there is little difference in our physiology. We must breathe air, drink water, as well as eat food for their nutrients. We could not live on those islands either.

"Our strategy was not to hurt the population of the islands. When we bombarded them, it was done in a pattern so your population had time to recognize the danger and leave.

"The real mission of the smoke was to finish our base, right here, under the ocean. We spent that time building this subterranean complex to gather air from the surface and construct the two space portals that you see."

He pointed to the side tunnel in the cavern wall. "One is for incoming movement and one for outgoing movement. Back when we arrived, we didn't have the technology to use space portals, so creating the caustic nature of the environment of the island was needed to give us time. Now we are back. The portals have been finished and are finally functional."

Florzo Lox finished his explanation. "Can I answer any of your questions?"

Professor Silver asked, "Yes, how much water do you plan to take from the Earth?"

Lox replied, "In understandable terms, the amount of water we are taking could lower your oceans approximately one inch worldwide. We believe that this amount will create a stable ocean system on Zome.

"We have approximately that amount of water on our planet now. The additional water with all its microscopic life, phytoplankton and zooplankton, will stabilize our environment. Hopefully they will be enough to produce a sustainable ecosystem. It is important that we will be able to create our own oxygen supply from the enhancing earth water."

Lox again turned and faced the falling water behind him. The talking guardian said to Frederickson and Dr. Silver, "The ambassador would like you to meet with him privately in the control area."

Lox turned and gave a friendly arm gesture to Frederickson and Dr. Silver to join him. Together they moved to the control room door, closely shadowed by the security robots.

E-Corps remained in place below the gantry. They could clearly see everything in the cavern from where they stood. Standing facing the pit, they could see the spectacular waterfall cascading down, saturating the air with moisture. Behind them and to the left, they could see the *Mist of the Atlantic* looming nearby. To their right was the Aalzad cave portal, and to their right rear was the control room, now closed with the security robots back in position.

Cooper's guardian Roger spoke, "Rachael Cooper, please have your group move to the left of the cave portal. You will be out of the way of the *Mist of the Atlantic* group departure. It is a good place for you to observe the proceedings."

Cooper conveyed the message to Lt. Buckley, who then ordered the teams out of the way. They moved slowly to the left of the portal, well out of the way of the cave opening.

Set back away from the pit, worker robots were preparing the trams. They were moving the bus like vehicles in the direction of the portal. The gantry formation was being reconfigured to allow each tram to glide snugly into a slot around the big drop. The tram noses were placed at a slightly downward angle, hugging the edge.

The first six trams were being moved into place. This would be a drop that would make the highest roller coaster in the world seem tame. When loaded with people, the trams will be moved forward into position. When each vehicle's turn came, they will drop directly into the pit, falling straight down and out of the solar system.

Cooper looked up the ramp leading to the alien ship and saw the procession of passengers moving down. She sadly conceded that it was time for the people to go to their new homes.

In the distance, Moreno and his spotter Lance Corporal Bailey were watching the activities in front of them. During their deployment, they marked down ranges to all parts of the cavern. They determined that the team was not in immediate danger, but Moreno stayed on the scope watching.

The passengers and crew of the *Mist of the Atlantic* walked down the ramp like a huge living mass. They moved in absolute silence in this final procession. Anticipation was etched on their faces. They knew their options and selected the one to live. Unlike the delegation from the surface, they had been in the Aalzad sphere of influence for a decade.

They held on to the belief that they would be treated as citizens of their new world. Most embraced the opportunity to start their lives anew. All had the knowledge that their lives ended on Earth many years ago.

Reaching an area close to the edge of the pit, they stopped and waited patiently for the boarding to begin. Soon it would be time for them to board one of the departing trams.

The control room door opened, and a different Aalzad individual left the entrance, dramatically approaching the humans. The security robots did not move. He stopped in front of the subdued orderly crowd.

A guardian moved in next to him and spoke, "My name is Zeglor Bl [pronounced Bull]. I am the leader of the Aalzad expedition to Earth. I am so happy to meet all of you."

He extended his arms and continued, "I welcome you, our newest citizens. The moment that you have been waiting for has arrived. Prepare yourselves for your wonderful new lives.

"Today you will embark on a journey across space to the newly colonized planet of Zome. Do not be afraid, our citizens feel a great indebtedness to you and your people for the gift you have provided."

One of the older men in the crowd took exception to that remark and said, "What gift! This is not a gift. For it to be a gift, someone must give you something. You're just taking."

Mildly annoyed, Bl folded his arms then sarcastically said, "Perhaps gift is not the right word. Perhaps sacrifice would be a better term."

Recouping his enthusiasm, Bl continued, "Either way, a great adventure awaits you. Please prepare yourselves for a very short journey. Follow your guardians' directions and begin to enter the trams. They will be transports to your new lives."

Bl turned and walked back to the control room. When he entered, he passed the area where a discussion was taking place between Ambassador Lox and the two Americans.

Frederickson, attempting to coax Lox, said, "You must give us something for our natural resources. It would only be fair."

Lox responded, "You are in no position to bargain. We know of your planetary conflicts, and we know that your country is one of great power and influence. By our standards, your civilization is unstable. Many years ago, Aalzarada was a similar world.

"Nothing brings a planet together faster than knowing that your world is in its final stages of existence. We matured quickly. We came together to save the people of all our so-called countries. You will need to correct many of your shortcomings in order to negotiate as equals with the Aalzad."

Silver joined the conversation. "You insist on taking this planet's water. Are you aware that there are many unpopulated planets and moons well within your interstellar travel capabilities? We know they're out there, but we can only see them with our powerful telescopes and satellite feeds. However, I am surprised that you chose Earth over some of the moons of our solar system's gas giants. Through our unmanned exploration, we determined that Europa, orbiting Jupiter, possibly has more water than we have here on Earth."

Lox replied, "We know of this moon now. In the desperate search for locating a suitable planet, we failed to detect Europa. When we discovered it as a water source, our program to create wormholes to and from earth were too far advanced. Another reason we will continue with Earth is we need atmosphere as well."

Silver asked, "Will you ever try to switch your efforts to Europa?"

"Unfortunately, by the time we altered our efforts, we would already be finished with our collecting resources from Earth. It took us ten years to establish our operational wormholes. It would take the same amount of time to change our efforts to your moons or another source.

"Rest assured that in the future if we need resources, we will go elsewhere, such as Jupiter's moon, to collect water if necessary. But for now, we are here, and here we will fulfill our needs."

Unsatisfied, Silver asserted, "You've really not given me answers that I hoped for. Because I can't get the information from you, I feel the need to travel to Zome with the passengers of the *Mist of the Atlantic*. There I will talk to someone in authority that can give me some reassurance that Earth will not be harmed by your efforts."

Lox scowled as the guardian translated, "I discourage you from doing that. We want no other human's hurt by our actions."

Assertively, Silver said, "Ambassador Lox, it's too late for that. I am ready to go."

Lox nodded reluctantly. "Very well, if that is your decision. I will not stop you. Join the others by the trams."

"Thank you."

The door opened, giving a clear indication the meeting was over. Frederickson and Silver exited into the cavern.

Frederickson stopped Silver outside the door and stated, "You know I have to go with you."

"I was hoping you'd say that."

Walking toward Eagle Corps, Frederickson said, "I'm going to look for a few more volunteers from the teams."

Silver had reservations about Frederickson's last remark. "I don't think that would be wise. They are military. They could be perceived as a threat."

Frederickson smiled and said, "I hope that the Aalzad are nice enough to send us back when we're done."

They walked across the open space between the control room and the line of trams and joined the waiting flock. The first group of humans were strapped in on the first six trams. The worker robots had been busy, hastily installing harnesses to the once "standing room only" vehicles.

From their position next to the cavern wall, E-Corps watched as the first tram went over the edge. It drifted forward with the nose stretched over the side of the abyss, causing the tail to kick up until the tram was straight up and down. It was a rapid process.

People screamed as they tipped toward the portal. Some screams were in utter terror, but some were the sounds you would hear at the first big drop on a roller coaster. It didn't last long as the tram dove into the wall of water, disappearing.

The screams drowned out, leaving only the sound of rushing water. The second, third, and then the fourth tram went over the edge. A few passengers were laughing, as "Geronimo!" could be heard as they slipped over the edge.

The first six trams were gone, dropping one by one into the vortex. Worker robots methodically moved the next six trams into position. The line of humans moved again toward the newly assembled vehicles.

Cooper watched the people shuffling forward in turn. Her eyes scanned the crowd and stopped at a familiar face. It was young

THE TUNNELS OF EARTH

George Field. He was standing patiently in line with Max and his family.

She moved quickly to his side and called his name, "George!"

"Hi, Rachael, are you coming to Zome too?"

"No, George, I'm not. I am just waiting for our negotiator, and then I'm going home, I hope."

Now excited, George said, "I'm ready, Rachael. I want to go. I want to grow up and become an adult like you. I don't want to continue life as a child or to die here on Earth... Besides, my family is going."

In a sad tone, with his head lowered, he added, "Rachael, there is really nothing left here for me. I need to start a new life."

He lifted his head and gave her a poignant smile.

Upbeat, Cooper responded, "It's okay, George. You have your whole life in front of you. You will grow up in a society far advanced to Earth. I am happy for you."

She gave him a big hug.

Once again, the group of trams launched one at a time. The screams were less, while the cheers and yelps increased. George was getting closer to one of the trams. As they continued to fall, people shuffled forward to fill the next empty one put into place.

Cooper asked, "Is Max going with you?"

"No," he responded. "He can't go with me. None of the robots or guardians manufactured on Earth are going to Zome. He has never been to Zome. As a matter of fact, he has never been off the Earth. We were told there will be new ones there for us."

George said to Max, "Thank you for your help, Max. I wish you were coming with me."

Unemotional, Max stated, "I will be useful here supporting the operation, and I will help your human friends return to their homes."

George replied, "That's great. Take good care of them. They're nice people."

"I will do my best."

The third round of trams were moving into position as the line of people moved forward again.

George's turn had arrived. He walked to the closest tram, where he was directed to a harness near a side window. Cooper could see him. When he was securely strapped in, he turned and looked out the window.

When he saw Rachael Cooper, he had a big smile beaming on his face and a tear in his eye, as the tram pitched forward and dropped out of sight. George was gone. Max was hovering nearby, just facing the pit. In a human sense, he seemed lost.

Rachael said to Max, "What will happen to George now?"

"I don't know. Only his actions will determine his future. He is young, but he is smart. I was there for him, but he functioned very well without me. He is different from the Aalzad. They are dependent on us. He is not. That is their weakness. The Aalzad are good people, but they have flaws.

"They are very intelligent. They engage in space travel, and they have created a high-functioning society. The ones you see here are some of the finest citizens of our planet. They still, however, are reluctant to make important decisions on their own. Your people going to Zome will make a positive impact on the population, if they get the chance."

Cooper probed, "What do you mean?"

"Many of the passengers have accepted the influence of their guardians and may not wish to make decisions on their own again."

"What about George?"

"George is special. He listened to me, but he was not overly influenced by me. He made his own decisions on most things. He asked me questions. I was only his teacher. He learned well. He is fearless, he will go far on Zome."

Cooper looked around and saw that there were only three more trams being led to the launch area. The people saw the same thing and became unsettled.

An unidentified guardian calmed the crowd by saying, "Do not be concerned, there are more trams coming down from the tunnels, and others will be returning from Zome."

The vocal guardian directed the remaining people to move out of the way of the cave entrance. He said that to ensure the returning trams would not injure anyone in transit. Four hundred and twenty people had departed. Three hundred and sixty-six remained. They were anxious. They were beginning to doubt the Aalzad and became suspicious about what was going on.

Lieutenant Buckley, Chief Cooper, and Captain Steel observed the unrest and wondered why the Aalzad were not more efficient transporting the people to Zome.

The waiting passengers' fears were diminished when a tram came out of one of the tunnels. It was loaded up with another twenty people and sent on its way. The process continued that way for the next several hours. Trams appeared, and people would continue to leave. However, none of the trams had returned from Zome yet. It continued to be a waiting game.

Captain Steel approached Lieutenant Buckley and told him that Dean Frederickson and Dr. Silver were planning to go to Zome to communicate directly with the leaders of that world.

"When they leave, we leave. Mr. Frederickson passed the word along to me that Eagle Corps have been exclusively selected to be permitted to return to the cavern in the future.

"When we get to the surface, we will have to formulate a rotation for the teams to be posted down here at all times. Perhaps two- or three-man teams would work best. I'm pretty sure it would prevent burnout. It's a tremendous responsibility for such a small number of servicemen and women."

Buckley heard the familiar sound of the deep rumble from the earth. The cave portal was activating. Guardians moved quickly to keep the people back, away from the entrance. The crowd moved out of the line of the opening in anticipation of the arrival of more trams.

The rumble increased in strength. The floor of the cavern started to shake, wind started to billow out of the cave and then the familiar flash of light. Once the flash and wind passed, the conveyor started to roll.

To the relief of the people, a tram rolled out of the cave. It crept out of the darkness and stopped at the end of the belt. Robots moved efficiently to prepare it, shifting it into position in one of the gantry slots.

Buckley, looking intently, observed that there was someone sitting perfectly still on the tram. After several moments, this new figure unsteadily stepped down onto the cavern floor. It was another Aalzad. He was dressed in the same manner as his companions, but his hair was short and neatly quaffed. Except for his clothes, his height, and his pale white complexion, he looked like he fit right in with the passengers.

Much like his comrades, he needed a few moments to fully recover from his trip through the portal. Buckley watched as the personality of this Aalzad slowly surfaced. He shook off the jet lag and seemed to perk right up. Climbing down off the tram, he approached the curious crowd.

He started to address them, "Hello, friends, my name is Tretorn Glor. It is so nice to meet all of you. I am here as the new ambassador between your planet, Earth, and my planet, Zome."

He was speaking English! He spoke without any accent, using good inflection. It was a little strange to see an Aalzad not speaking through a guardian.

Glor laughed and said, "Our acquaintance will be short due to the fact that you are leaving. I, however, have come to Earth to coordinate the relationship between our worlds.

"I have good news, the trams are lined up on Zome ready to return. You will soon be joining your friends on our world. They have already been made to feel welcome. The same awaits you."

Glor moved around the crowd with great energy, He was smiling and friendly toward every person he came in contact with. His presence had a positive effect on the people. It seemed to cheer them up while they waited their turn.

Trams started to arrive just as Glor predicted. Robots dutifully moved them into position for the next load of passengers. He moved through the crowd still pouring on the charm. Passengers that had been waiting for hours started to show signs of easing tension. When everyone seemed content that it was just an unscheduled delay, Glor stepped away from the crowd and approached the Aalzad commander at the control room door.

THE TUNNELS OF EARTH

Standing with E-Corps, Lieutenant Buckley watched Glor work his magic on the passengers. Zeglor Bl acknowledged Glor's presence, and to Buckley it seemed that Bl was mocking his appearance. Glor didn't react to the chiding. They communicated for a brief moment, and then Bl returned to the control room. Glor cheerfully walked back to the group of passengers, continuing to talk to the people as he helped guide them onboard.

Buckley said to Steel, "Sir, do you see that guy over there? He's an Aalzad that thinks he's a game show host." They both laughed.

Steel replied, "I did notice him. He arrived on one of the trams and has been working the crowd ever since. I'm sure we'll know who he is very soon."

The crowd had dwindled down to about fifty people. People that were ready to go hours ago were waiting as patiently as they could. Walking among the group, Glor worked to keep morale high. He made the passengers smile. He was different from the other Aalzad, a real oddity.

Another rumble started, and the crowd eagerly anticipated the arrival of another tram. This rumble didn't feel right. It wasn't the same as the previous ones. It grew in intensity, and the shaking was amplified compared to the earlier tremors. There was no wind and there was no flash of light.

Steel said to Eagle Corps, "That was different. It felt like an earthquake."

Buckley, still watching the show, saw that Glor, too, was aware of the difference in the rumble. Glor turned and looked to the control room and saw the door open with the other Aalzad looking curiously out into the cavern. None of them seemed amused.

The leader Bl standing at the control room door indicated for Glor to come over. He wasted no time complying. Buckley could see concern on their faces and could only guess that the last shaker had something to do with it. After a moment, Glor returned to the group, smiling again with some information related to him by his leader.

Glor had an announcement, so he called everyone together. He turned toward the pit and waited until the latest tram descended into the darkness. When it was out of sight, he turned, smiled, and addressed the crowd.

"I have been asked by Commander Bl to make this announcement. Please do not be alarmed. I need to tell you that we must temporarily stop the trams from coming back through the cave. We detected a tremor in the surrounding seabed.

"It had nothing to do with our operation. It was located somewhere to the east. We want to make sure that it doesn't affect the safety of our transporting you to Zome. Our commander will wait a reasonable period of time to make sure that it doesn't happen again. When he feels that there is no further danger, we will begin importing trams again."

Once again, there was concern on the faces of the waiting passengers. They had waited for what seemed like an eternity, and now they were on hold again. Thirty people were left plus Dean Frederickson and Professor Julius Silver.

Glor added, "Please return to the Tropos Magra and wait. We will send for you when we feel confident that we can continue our transfer."

People grumbled as they turned and walked back toward the ship. It was unknown what the Aalzad were going to do next. What Glor did next was quite unexpected. He walked directly over to Captain Steel and Lieutenant Buckley and said, "Perhaps you heard me introduce myself as Tretorn Glor to the people. I was sent here to create a liaison between your leaders and the leaders of Zome. I was told by our Commander Zeglor Bl to escort your group back to the surface and establish diplomatic relations in the interest of both of our worlds."

Steel replied, "Yes, we heard your introduction. What about your duties here?"

"My job is finished here. I can do nothing more for these people. They will be gone soon thus changing the focus of my mission."

Steel questioned, "I heard you tell them that transport was suspended. Is there a problem?"

"Our commander doesn't think that it is serious, but he wants to wait and see. The tremor was different from our transport rumble. He doesn't want to put anyone in danger.

"Travel through portals are controlled and don't exceed certain intensity levels. This one was five times more powerful than the strength generated by our transport. If we lose the cave, we won't be able to bring anything here to earth. The portal returning to Zome is working perfectly, so we can always leave, but the cave is our support line."

Now in a more congenial mood, Steel said, "Where do you want to go, Mr. Glor?"

Glor replied, smiling, "Take me to your leader!" After a hard laugh, he said, "Let's get to the surface where I can plan to meet your leaders. And please, don't call me Mr. Glor, call me Ted."

Steel nodded and then said to the teams, "Okay, people, time to saddle up, we're going home."

E-Corps painfully rose to their feet. Their morale was high because they knew that the missions end was in sight.

Steel said to Glor, "I was told that the members of E-Corps are the only people allowed to come here from the surface. I want to start by leaving two members here for now and then rotate two members in and out every five days. Will this be satisfactory to the Aalzad?"

"We trust your judgment. If it works for you, it works for us."

Glor turned and left the group, heading for the control room.

Steel talked to the teams, "Who wants to volunteer to stay down here for a few days?"

No one volunteered, so Steel named two members from different teams.

He said, "Petty Officer Ross, you and Lance Corporal Moreno have the first watch. It will be the shortest. When we get topside, we will do a quick turnaround and have someone back to relieve you in two or three days. After that we go in five-day rotations. We have limited manpower, so this must include officers and medical personnel as well."

Steel said to Buckley, "Signal Moreno and Bailey to get down here. We don't know how much time we have before we leave."

It was a moment the teams were just standing around waiting to leave. Steel left the group and caught up with Frederickson and Silver walking back toward the ship.

Reaching them, he said, "Are you sure you are ready for this?"

Dr. Silver responded cheerfully, "I can't wait to embark on this adventure. The opportunities to gain knowledge are boundless. I don't know if Dean here shares my enthusiasm."

Frederickson seemed resigned to go with Dr. Silver. He felt enormous responsibility for him. In his mind, he went where Silver went.

Frederickson said, "We should be back soon enough, that is, as long as they fix the earthquake problem. Who knows, if we have another earthquake, we may not get there at all."

Shaking both their hands, Steel said, "Good luck, gentlemen, we'll be monitoring activities down here, so we'll know when you get back. I hope we can get updates on your activities from the Aalzad." Chuckling he added, "Maybe we can send you a message in a bottle down the waterfall."

The two government men smiled politely and said their goodbyes.

Steel turned away and returned to his troops. When he arrived, Ted Glor was there, anxious to head up the tunnel and out into the world. He was alone but technically he had several guardians accompanying him. Roger, Chief Cooper's guardian, and Richard, no longer assigned to David Stack, were now available to assist with the exodus. The third one had to be his personal guardian.

Glor explained, "We have to go up this tunnel on foot for a while, and then we can board the last transport left in the complex. It is much smaller than the ones taking your people to Zome. It will fit six people on board or four people and two guardians tightly. It will take us to the elevator, closest to your command island. Four trips will be necessary to get everyone to the elevator and out."

Leading the way, Glor stepped lightly on his feet up the path toward the tube.

Before starting up the tunnel, Steel turned and said to the two SEALs staying behind, "Someone will be back to relieve you in two or three days. Just keep an eye on things down here and report to me when you get topside. Try to find a spot we can set up our HQ."

PO Ross replied, "Yes, sir."

Ross and Moreno watched the team moving away and wondered exactly what they were supposed to do in this strange world.

Ross said to Moreno, "I hope it's quiet for the next few days. I have no idea what we are supposed to do if something happens." Ross turned and was startled when he saw a guardian hovering next to him. Neither of the men saw it approach, and they were surprised by its appearance.

The guardian spoke, "I am Max, former guardian of George Field. Now I am the guardian of Eagle Corps."

Moreno said to Ross, "Maybe he could show us a place where we can sack out. Nothing else is going on."

*****

Captain Steel, Lt. Buckley, and Tretorn Glor were on the first boxcar ride. It was a long trip up the tunnel. An hour elapsed before they reached the hatch to the elevator.

Making the ride tolerable, the boxcar avoided tunnels where air was being carried down to the cavern. Taking the elevator up to the surface, the first thing they saw was not the familiar smooth black soil, but instead there was a sheet of white from an early snowstorm.

Everywhere they looked there was a six-inch-thick level coating of snow. It was quite a contrast to what they were used to. The elevator was roughly two hundred feet away from the causeway.

Once on the surface, Captain Steel noticed that there was a slight glow around the Aalzad liaison. His body was outlined with a subtle halo.

In a low voice, Steel said to Buckley, "Am I glowing?"

"No, sir, it's just him."

Steel said to Glor, "Mr. Glor, are you aware that you are glowing?"

"Yes, I have a temporary shield surrounding my body to protect me from your environment. When it activates, it gives off mild radiation and a subtle amount of light."

"Why do you need something like that? Your commander said you are just like us in every way."

"This is true, but I have no immunity to your planetary microbes. I will easily fall prey to illness if exposed to them. I must shield myself with this protective screen. I have taken an antimicrobial potion prepared over the years by the guardians. It is made up of artificial earth microbes. They will take full effect in several earth days, so until then, I need the shield until they activate."

"I see. Here on earth we call that nanotechnology. Nanobots circulate in the body and cleanse the blood of bacteria."

"That is very similar to our system, but our nanobots, as you call them, have the ability to search out harmful microbes and destroy them. Don't worry, Captain. I won't be glowing very long."

*****

Over the course of the long day, the remaining members of the teams arrived back at the Coddington. Helicopters were waiting to bring them back to Quonset Point.

Reopened after the earlier evacuation, Goat Island was back in business. Tretorn Glor met Maurice Millius and took up residence at the hotel. Overwhelmed by the opulence, he was assigned to stay in a first-class hotel room. It was Frederickson's old room.

In the beginning, when the NSA man arrived on Goat Island, Millius and Frederickson became good friends. He had originally been here as a young agent in 2015. It started from the time Frederickson helped separate Millius from his office. Since that time, he had been in the hotel on and off for the last ten years.

Because he was there so often, Maurice Millius always gave him the best room available at the time. On his last visit, he got the bridal suite. He never checked out. Glor was now in the suite trying to adjust to his new accommodations.

Surprised by the magnificence, he said to his guardian, "This is more room than most people on Zome would be allowed to live in."

The guardian telepathically responded, "Zome doesn't have people spending nights in hotels. Your homes are small and very utilitarian. Nothing is wasted, and there is no excess. Judging from this hotel, everything is the opposite of Zome."

*****

Moreno relaxed on the balcony of his stateroom, high on the top deck of the *Mist of the Atlantic*. He leaned forward on the railing thinking that this duty wasn't too bad. There was no sunset, but he could use his imagination watching and listening to the water flowing steadily down into the portal.

Max took care of all their personal needs. He was a wealth of information on everything, and he brought them plenty of food— tasty robot-prepared food. He and Ross seemed to be the only ones who were happy in the cavern. The thirty or so people, plus Frederickson and Silver, were still waiting to leave.

It had been twenty-four hours, and the people waiting to go to Zome were still here. They had abandoned their cabins on the *Mist of the Atlantic*, so they were just rummaging around in the Aalzad ship.

Ross was returning to the *Mist of the Atlantic* after getting a midnight snack. He had talked to Frederickson and Silver and learned that they were going to bring back the next tram within the hour. While exiting the enormous spaceship, he saw one of the Aalzad officers standing alone near the edge, halfway down the ramp.

This was the first time he saw any of the Aalzad away from the control room. He was surprised to see him, but he didn't let on. Keeping his composure, he nodded to him as he walked by.

After passing the Aalzad, heading back to the *Mist of the Atlantic*, a guardian came up beside him and spoke.

It said, "Engineer Menzo Shoog would like to meet you."

That announcement made Ross nervous, but he tried to maintain self-control. He nodded and then turned to walk back to where the Aalzad stood. The engineer seemed delighted to meet Ross.

Shoog spoke through the guardian, "I am Menzo Shoog, engineer and first officer of the Aalzad expeditionary unit."

"I am Mason Ross, petty officer second class, United States Navy SEALs, sir."

"You are the first human I have met. You seem very much like a person from my planet, yet you are, as I would imagine, very different. I hope that does not offend you, my calling you different."

"I am not offended, sir. You're the first spaceman I've ever met, so I don't know what to make of you either. You're not like anybody I ever met back in Tennessee."

"What is Tennessee?"

"It's a place, a state. There are fifty states in the United States, and Tennessee is one of them. That's where I live."

"I see, of what social class are you?"

"What do you mean class?"

Shoog elaborated, "On Zome, there are structured social classes. Starting with the highest category, you would have the royal class. That would include those descended from our former royal family, the former king's family. We have not had a king in two hundred years, but even though they are dead, the family bloodline continues to this day. Not as kings and queens but as royals. They have vast wealth, and they use it for the good of the population.

"Below the royals is the government class. These devoted people make our society work. They form the backbone of society, and they are among the most caring among us. They make and enforce the laws of our planet."

Ross said quizzically, "The most devoted to society, huh. That's not like here."

"Next you have the intellectual class. These are the academic leaders and professional people. I would be considered in this class because I am an engineer and a star traveler."

"Below these knowledgeable individuals there are the industrialists of society, working closely with the government to make our new planet livable. Next there is the skilled worker class or the guilds, then the warrior class and the laborer class. I suspect that you are in the warrior class."

Ross said, "Yes I think that if we had classes, I would be in the warrior class, but I think that I could be in any class that I strived to be in. People in the United States are not restricted to classes."

"That is very interesting. There are no classes in your system?"

"That's right. Don't get me wrong, people do have restrictions. People may have limits in their abilities or their motivation, but everyone in our country has the opportunity to better themselves. Some people would consider themselves to be in a class, but they can move up or down depending on their willingness to improve themselves. I don't know about the rest of the world."

"Thank you, Mason Ross, for talking to me. I have reevaluated my opinion about what class I think you are in. I think you belong in the intellectual class."

"That's very nice of you, but I'm not so sure about that. Thank you anyway, I enjoyed talking to you as well. Can I ask you a question?"

"Of course you can. I will happily answer anything."

"What class will the Earth people going to Zome be in?"

Shoog thought about the question then said, "I don't know where they will fit in as individuals, but I think that they will be in a class by themselves. Depending on the group, they could be anywhere on the chart. Personally, I think they will do well. Some will excel and others will not. Either way they will be held in high esteem by our people."

Ross hesitated then asked, "I saw your undersea vehicles in your ship. Would it be possible to get a closer look at it?"

"Yes, you can do anything you want here in the cavern as long as you have a guardian with you. You have the freedom to see and do new amazing things."

Ross, now smiling broadly, said, "I appreciate that, thank you."

*****

The Marine corporal and the Navy SEAL could hear that familiar rumble again coming from the cave. In his suite in the *Mist of the Atlantic*, Ross moved to the window to see the next tram sliding out on the belt.

He yelled to Moreno, "It looks like they're back in business!"

The worker robots started to position the tram for the next group. People walked down from the Tropos Magra toward the pit once again. Twenty more people moved to the tram. They took their positions, and the tram moved forward, dropping over the edge.

Eight more to go! It would take one more trip to get all the passengers to Zome. Still waiting with the final six passengers was Frederickson and Silver. It was unknown when their tram would arrive.

*****

Twenty-four hours later, Moreno was sitting in his usual spot on the balcony taking in the view. This time he had his feet resting on the rail. The sound of water falling into the pit was a constant reminder of what the Aalzad were doing.

The giant tubes sucked air down from the surface, but the whooshing sound it made was drowned out by the millions of gallons of water dropping through the cavern into the pit. In the distance at the tunnel entrance, someone was moving into the cavern.

*****

Changing of the Guard

It's Wednesday," Buckley said to Ross waiting at the hull entrance of the cruise ship. "Cooper and I are here to relieve you."

Cooper was beginning to think that she and Buckley were connected at the hip. Captain Steel decided that they would be the next pair down. They were Team Hawk, and perhaps he thought Cooper would be better off with an officer than of one of the enlisted men. She thought, *I guess he thinks I can't handle myself with these guys*. Anyway, they were working together again, and Cooper was okay with that.

They had two and a half days off. Cooper spent her time sleeping in the barracks back at Quonset. As far as she knew Buckley caught a nap, took a shower, and returned to duty. There was a lot to do, and he was in the thick of it. He met with General Ray and Captain Steel to coordinate the duty roster. He helped assemble the schedule and then sat with the enlisted men to see if they had an accurate picture of the subterranean world.

On one of the days, they had a guest. The guest was Tretorn Glor. Although he was physically present, he was little help. He was not an engineer, and he felt terribly ill. Because he had just arrived himself, he could not help with an understanding of the layout of the tunnels. He said the general needed to talk to the resident engineer or one of the guardians.

Glor, looking a little green, didn't last long at the meeting. He was finding that the nanotechnology swirling around his body was doing more harm than good. The glow was gone, but he was sick and spent most of his time in his suite. His cameo appearance at this meeting was the first time anyone had seen him since they surfaced.

*****

Buckley said to Ross, "Do you have anything to report?"

"Sir, the final group of civilians left yesterday. It was made up of six remaining passengers, Mr. Frederickson, and Dr. Silver. Three of the Aalzad left as well, but they left in their own vehicles. One Aalzad is still here.

"He spends most of his time in the big ship. He occasionally goes down to check things out in the control room. I think this whole operation is run by the command robot. There's not a lot of other activity going on. Since the final trams left, the worker robots are nowhere to be found. Once in a while you will see that big command robot leave the control room and go to the ship, but most of the time it stays put.

"We've been left on our own ever since the team surfaced. It's been a very interesting experience. As long as Max was with us, we could go anywhere in the cavern or tunnels. I mean anywhere! We've done a lot of exploring already. We have entered places that I would think that if this was an American installation, it would be considered off limits. I mean really top secret."

Ross was giddy when he told Buckley and Cooper what he and Moreno had done.

"Sir, we used an undersea vehicle, a submarine!"

A confused Buckley said, "What do you mean undersea vehicle? You left the cavern and went out in the ocean?"

Ross said with a giant smile, "Yes, sir, we were cruising the bottom of the Atlantic Ocean."

"The Aalzad let you do that?"

"Yes, sir."

Buckley was speechless.

Cooper, hearing this, skeptically said, "You drove a submarine?"

Ross replied, "I didn't say I drove it, Chief." Pointing toward the guardian, he said, "Max did. He's our ticket to everything."

Buckley said, "It sounds like you had a pretty good time down here. Show us where you set up shop. Then you guys can head up to the surface. Max will go with you up the tunnel then return in five days with the next team."

Buckley, pointing to Cooper's guardian, said, "Roger here will be with us."

Ross said, "We are staying in the *Mist of the Atlantic*. You can have any room you want. It's an old ship, but there are many great rooms to choose from."

"The boxcar is up at the entrance of the cavern and will take you within a couple of hundred feet of the Goat Island causeway. You're within an hour of eating hot food and taking a shower. A thirty-six-hour pass is waiting for you as well. After that, you'll be placed back on the duty roster for a trip back down here. I don't think you'll mind coming back when your turn comes around again."

"No, sir, this is pretty good duty."

Standing at the base entrance to the *Mist of the Atlantic*, Moreno said, "The best rooms are near the top above the main deck. They are staterooms with balconies. The head doesn't work, but the passengers rigged up a good latrine system. Guardians call in worker robots to deal with that. Other than latrines, its five-star accommodations, and you get a panoramic view of everything in the cavern. For a sniper like me, it's the ultimate high ground."

*****

Sixteen members of Eagle Corps were taking part in the rotating duty schedule. In the last month, eight pair had stood watch with nothing eventful taking place. With rides in the undersea vehicle now off limits after Ross told Lieutenant Buckley, the teams had little excitement.

Three days earlier, Buckley and Cooper on their second rotation replaced Ross and Moreno. They had little else to do but walk around the cavern checking out its features. On the second day, Cooper with her guardian Roger took a walk to the deepest, darkest section of the cavern.

It was the narrow end that seemed to come to a point in the darkness. There was a meager waterfall on the far wall with water trickling down into a narrow crevasse just big enough to crawl into. It was a dark cave that extended down below the floor of the cavern. On closer examination of the water, she tasted it to determine the salt content. To her surprise the water had no salinity whatsoever. It was fresh.

On her walks she found many fascinating gems and rocks. She took some of the small loose ones to have analyzed. She was hoping that she had something of value to boost her modest military salary.

Although there were amazing things to see and do in the cavern, the custodial duties of Eagle Corps were pretty boring. It was interesting that Ross and Moreno told them the truth about free access to everything, but that didn't help. The one thing they could always do was catch up on their sleep.

That night Buckley couldn't sleep. After tossing and turning for hours, he staggered out of his bed. He decided to take a walk. The room he was sleeping in was one flight above the main exterior deck. This was the pool deck, where sun worshippers gathered. On this deck, there was, at one time, full exposure to the sky. Buckley envisioned beautiful bikini-clad women baking slowly in the hot sun. Here in the bowels of the Earth, the deck was lifeless and utterly grim.

The main feature of this deck was the large swimming pool surrounded by several hot tubs. Although the pool was dry, it looked structurally sound. Everything about it looked functional. He imagined holding a hose, filling it right up, and then diving in for a swim.

As he continued his stroll, he saw various booths where trendy cocktails were crafted and food was prepared. He could see clearly in his mind, waiters and pool staff scurrying around, serving drinks and catering to the needs of the passengers.

The treadmills that lined the rail, bolted to the floor, looked brand new. The only exception was at one end, three were ripped from their position, leaving only the supports attached to the deck. Other damage was now clearly in view. Upper components of the poolside rigging were damaged, and next to an old sign that said Parade of Nations, the flagpoles were bent and drooping down. It was eerie to think that this area once thrived with a party atmosphere.

Reaching the stern of the ship, he descended another dark stairwell leading to the main concourse. It was a deck lined with shops in a wide atrium that retained its majestic high ceiling. This deck was nothing like the pool deck. The pool deck was clean and tidy. This deck was picked clean of every item in every shop. It was obvious the passengers and crew looted every bit of merchandise over the course of their stay in the cavern.

Meanwhile, in her stateroom, Cooper, having a sense of uneasiness, sat up straight in her queen-size bed. She had no idea what woke her up. Getting out of bed, in her fatigue uniform trousers, she wiped the sleep from her eyes and threw on her heavy khaki shirt. She then went out on the balcony to look around.

It was quiet, just like all the other times she looked out. There was no sense of time in the cavern, so she looked at her watch. On the surface it was four in the morning. E-Corps units were ordered to keep normal hours to stay oriented with the rest of the east coast time zone.

Buckley's walk was interrupted by a tremor causing him to head back to his stateroom. He decided to check with Chief Cooper and see if she felt it.

Cooper heard a knock on the door, hearing Buckley say, "Chief, did you feel that?"

Cooper moved to the door and opened it, "No, sir, something woke me up, but I don't know what it was. What did you feel?"

"It was a tremor. I looked over the railing to see if something was coming through the cave, but nothing happened."

Roger, nestled in the corner of Cooper's room, moved forward to where the conversation was taking place.

Buckley said to Roger, "What just happened?"

"There was a small earthquake of short duration and low intensity."

Interested, Buckley said, "What will the Aalzad do?"

"Menzo Shoog will monitor for more tremors, and if they reach a certain level, he will have to shut down the portal."

Buckley said to Cooper, "Chief, go out on the balcony and watch for a reaction from the Aalzad engineer. I'm going down to the cavern floor to take a look around."

He turned to Roger. "Come with me, we're going to take a little walk."

Buckley and Roger moved to the dingy stairway and started to descend to the cavern floor. At the bottom, he walked directly to the pit where he noticed it was wet around the gantry. Other than that, he found everything seemed to be operating normally. He moved past the control room. The large security robots didn't move, so he looked in the window and saw the command robot burning the midnight oil. It was sitting at the console. There was no way of knowing if it was reacting to a problem or not.

"Roger, do you detect anything unusual here?"

"Nothing unusual."

Buckley walked toward the ramp that went up to the ship, and the cavern started to shake again. This tremor was more intense; he had trouble keeping his balance. He didn't fall, but he had to crouch down low, close to the surface, and put his hands down to remain steady. He could see the water falling in erratic waves, rhythmically missing the portal, splashing down on the gantry.

Again, it was short. Buckley stood up and looked around for problems. Dust and light debris fell from the cavern roof, but no major damage could be detected. On his feet and moving again, he continued toward the ramp to the Aalzad ship.

Coming down the ramp, riding on a hover craft, was Menzo Shoog. He had originally seen this kind of machine on that first day in the dome. Shoog was moving fast and had a concerned look on his face.

He came up next to Buckley, stopped, and then spoke to him through Roger, "You must get out of the cavern if you can. If the earthquakes continue, I will have to shut down the water flowing through the Tropos Magra and then shut down the portal to Zome. Once all of those tasks are completed, I will secure the ship.

"If I don't time the closing of the pit precisely, there will be massive flooding here. The worst case would be the seal around the Tropos Magra could break and water flooding the cavern. We haven't reached that point yet, but if you wait too long, you will have no time to escape."

As Shoog finished his warning to Lieutenant Buckley, the ground shook again. It was bigger and more powerful than the previous ones. Dust continued falling from the roof with amplified shaking. Shoog was thrown from the speed craft, and Buckley again hugged the ground. Roger was still hovering, but he was rocking back and forth to the rhythm of the quake.

From the cruise ship, there was a horrible sound of twisting metal. Buckley and Shoog looked toward the *Mist of the Atlantic* as it began to break free and list in their direction. Buckley couldn't see Cooper on the balcony and hoped that she was getting out.

As the quake subsided, the *Mist of the Atlantic* hung with the main deck leaning toward the interior of the cavern. Buckley thought, *Another quake will surely bring it down.*

With his own problems, Shoog left his speeder where it lay and ran down the ramp, between the security robots, into the control room. Buckley got up and ran toward the cruise ship.

As he ran, he yelled, "Get out of there, Chief. The ship can't survive another quake!"

No sooner had he finished that statement when the ground shook again. Buckley had to decide whether he wanted to run under this rocking unstable ship. He stood fast and kept yelling, "Chief, get out of there!"

Buckley thought, *This is a big one!* Forced down on the deck again, he crawled back to a position where he thought the ship could not fall on him. Roger didn't stay; he glided across the courtyard and disappeared into the shadowy hull entrance.

Soon after Roger had gone up the stairs, metal creaked and began to twist. An unnatural rumble followed, and the mighty *Mist of the Atlantic* started its plunge. Buckley started to rethink his position and tried to get farther away. He crawled awkwardly as the ground rose and receded under him, shaking intensely.

At the crescendo of the quake, he turned and stared at the falling ship. In slow motion, the enormous *Mist of the Atlantic* tilted, dropped, and crashed in a heap. The force of the fall crumpled the starboard side hull on the cavern floor. The deafening noise subsided just as the quake ended. Thick dust darkened the cavern completely.

Buckley stood up but could barely see. The dust was blinding. As it cleared, twenty yards away, he was facing the main deck of the *Mist of the Atlantic*. As visibility increased, he saw one of the two smokestacks breaking away from its base, crashing to the cavern floor.

When all the wreckage stopped moving, giving the stack a wide berth, he ran toward the ship. He found himself standing next to the crumpled main deck; it was perpendicular to the ground. There was no way for him to climb up to a door.

The nearest door was fifteen feet above his head, horizontal to the ground. He ran around the bow and tried to gain access by climbing up the side of the broken hull. Dust and debris still fell all around as he tried to find a way up.

The keel didn't rest on the ground; it was well above his reach. He frantically kept looking, trying to gain entry. He yelled to Cooper but heard no response. He didn't give up, couldn't give up. He had to get her out.

Part IV

RESCUE

At the Goat Island facility, the seismic equipment registered several small to medium tremors. General Ray had been alerted and entered the situation room just as a fourth tremor hit.

Speaking to a geologist housed in the hotel, he asked, "What's going on down there, Professor?"

The geologist pointed to a chart on the table and said, "There is strong seismic activity in this area in the middle of nowhere, south of Martha's Vineyard. To this point, we count four tremors. They were at a magnitude of around four to six point five on the Richter scale.

"We can categorize them as medium earthquakes. The ones that have already hit have the capabilities to cause some damage. Nantucket, Martha's Vineyard, and Block Island have already reported higher seas, causing minor damage.

"I can't predict what is happening to the seabed. We don't know how this system of tunnels and chambers affects the stability of the seafloor. It is possible that they could lead to larger and more damaging quakes."

General Ray said, "Thanks, Professor, let me know if anything else happens." He turned and told his aide, "Get Captain Steel in my office ASAP, and get our Aalzad guest down here from the bridal suite. Maybe he can finally be of some use."

His aide saluted the general and said, "Yes, sir."

After ten minutes, Captain Steel entered the general's office. A few minutes later, Tretorn Glor entered the room with his guardian.

He was scheduled to leave for Washington, DC, several days earlier, but he was still having a reaction to nanobots. For days, he was so ill that he couldn't get out of bed. It took weeks, but today, he was feeling better and was glad to be forced to think about something other than how terrible he felt.

Ray said to Steel, "Captain, get Eagle Corps ready. We have to send a rescue party to get our people out of the cavern. I want all available members of your team here on Goat Island ready to go, ASAP!"

Steel acknowledged the general's order and left the room to get things rolling.

Turning to the Aalzad, he said, "Ambassador Glor, we need your help. We need a way to get vehicles into the cavern to evacuate our people. I was told that if we get a few more tremors like the last one, it could start to bring down parts of the cavern.

"It's not confirmed, but we think that some of the air vents have been breached and water is entering the system. Of course, if you still have people down there, we will get them out as well."

Glor responded, "General, you are right in everything you are saying. Although I don't have direct contact with the engineer, the matrix of guardians is reporting damage and flooding in two of the three air intakes.

"Because the integrity of the cavern is in jeopardy, the intake from the ocean will be suspended. I have no information on whether the portal to Zome is open or closed. More information indicates that the *Mist of the Atlantic* has collapsed to the ground. I was also informed that your people are safe for the time being."

"Ambassador Glor, I need this kind of information here at headquarters, so please stay and keep me informed with any further information that you get from your guardians."

"I will keep you informed, General, but I insist on going with your team down into the cavern."

"Ambassador, I need you here in the command center! I need you to pass on updates from your sources. Because of your special knowledge of this matter, I need you to advise me on the condition of the tunnels and what course of action we need to take."

THE TUNNELS OF EARTH

Glor explained, "General, you don't need me here. I will be more of service to the people down in the cavern. I will leave my personal guardian with you and take the one called Max with me."

As convincing as he could, Glor said, "I'm the only one that understands the Aalzad technology that could allow me to close down the system if necessary."

"Will your guardian be able to communicate with us?"

"Yes, of course. He speaks perfect English. He speaks several other languages as well."

"Okay, you've got your wish, Mr. Glor. I don't have time to argue. Good luck."

After a little over an hour, the teams were assembled. Captain Steel was in the office getting a final briefing with the general and Ambassador Glor. Glor's guardian provided an updated report from the underground tunnels and air vents. It provided the group with two options to enter the pit. It had to consider speed and safety.

The first option would be to drop down the familiar route, the active air vent at the tower. This would give direct access for a vehicle. If they go that way, they will have to contend with high winds and then a transfer through the side tunnel to the safer main tunnel.

Steel said, "In our experience, going through the side tunnel will give us direct access to the main entrance, and most importantly, there won't be wind."

The second option would be to breach the island dome. This was the same dome that Team Hawk was confronted by the robots. Its location is approximately five hundred yards west of the main air tunnel. The island dome was under the surface and would have to be breached with explosives.

Glor said, "There are problems with both plans. The tower tunnel would afford quick access, but it is carrying winds at a steady ninety miles an hour. The dome has its own unique problems. First, it has to be located in a timely manner, and secondly, it has to be breached without collapsing too much of the surface above it. If successful, it will offer a quick, easy, and more direct access to the cavern, skirting the wind."

After examining the virtues of both entrances, General Ray decided that there were more risks involved in going in through the wind tunnel, but it would take too long to prepare the dome for entry. His decision was to go down the pit.

General Ray said, "We're going in against the wind, but we can go right away. I have just the vehicle for the job. It's being transported from Quonset at this very moment.

"You're going down the wind tunnel, at an entry point you are very familiar with. We will be using an amphibious vehicle ready made for this kind of job. Its heavy in weight, and it has the ability to drive on hard surfaces then transform into a boat to travel through deep water. It can move fast on land, up to fifty miles an hour. Those attributes make it the perfect vehicle for this mission."

*****

Buckley stopped and listened. He heard faint banging, coming from the interior of the ship. He followed the noise around to the top deck where the sound grew louder. Above his head, a metal sculpture crashed through a set of double doors on the main deck, falling to the ground. It was a heavy statue. It was Neptune, god of the sea, lying facedown with his trident bent.

Buckley looked up and called to Cooper. There was no response. He could hear shuffling of heavy things within the superstructure. Next, a thick firehose unfurled and dropped to the ground. Totally unfazed, Cooper leaped and was hanging out over the edge below the doors, looking down on her CO. She slid down the fire hose landing directly in front of him.

Roger was next. When he jumped, he was in freefall. Looking like he was going to crash and splat on the cavern floor, instead, he slowed down in flight and broke his fall about three feet off the ground, never touching. He hovered there, in his natural position.

Buckley said, "Are you okay, Chief?"

"I'm okay, I was in the central passageway trying to get to the ground when the ship fell. I held on and rode it down. I found myself near the exit at the base of the hull when I had to reverse course and go back up to the top deck to get out.

"Roger here is a pretty handy guy to have around. It was pitch black in there, but when Roger found me, he turned on all kinds of body lights. With some kind of powerful pocket laser that popped out of his side, he burned through twisted metal blocking our way. He's better than a Swiss Army knife."

Concentrating on rescuing Cooper, Buckley didn't notice the stream of water coming down the ramp from the Tropos Magra. It was about eight inches wide and about a half inch deep. Cooper noticed it first and then noticed the considerable flow of water coming down the main tunnel. It was a much larger stream than the one sourced at the ship.

Cooper said, "Lieutenant, was this water flowing when you came down to investigate?"

"No, it must have started after the last quake. I spoke to the Aalzad, and he told me to get out of here. He doesn't know if he can control what's happening."

Buckley and Cooper watched as the water flowed steadily down the ramp. Water rushed out of the tunnel entrance, pooling at the lowest points in the cavern.

When the pair heard a metallic sound coming from the Aalzad ship, they looked toward the pit. As they watched, the waterfall started to dissipate. The water door in the Tropos Magra was closing. Menzo Shoog was securing the cavern. *Once he gets that done,* Buckley thought, *he will close the space portal in the pit to lock down the area.*

*****

DUKW

The DUKW amphibious vehicle was a converted vintage GMC truck. It was used during important beach landings in Europe and the Pacific during World War II. It was referred to as a duck boat because of its designation D-U-K-W. The D stood for the year 1942, the U indicated utility, the K referred to all-wheel drive, and the W signified that it had two rear driving axles.

It was a big heavy vehicle. Thirty-one feet long and almost nine feet wide, its capacity accommodated up to twenty-five fully equipped troops or a payload of about two and a half tons of cargo.

General Ray had lined up this vehicle from the Navy Seabee Museum at Quonset Point for just this kind of situation. He called his friend, the curator, as soon as he felt the first tremor. In the past the two men discussed the practical application of this World War II-era relic in relation to the situation on Aquidneck Island. They agreed that it would be more suitable for infiltration into the underground world than a strictly land-based vehicle.

Having never served in combat, the museum DUKW was around seventy-five years old, but it was in good serviceable condition. It had been completely overhauled several times over the years. The last time was just before it came to the expanded Quonset Seabee museum in 2021.

The only official function it had was every fall, in the spirt of good community relations, the museum broke out the DUKW for local events. Part of its demonstration included a short cruise around Wickford Harbor with the Cub Scouts or Little League teams riding in the back. It was a big hit.

*****

Lieutenant Buckley and Chief Petty Officer Cooper saw that the window of opportunity to escape up the tunnel had passed. It was simply out of the question. The water flow into the cavern increased with each tremor. The main tunnel was a fast-moving river. There was no going against it.

They stayed on the ramp near the main entrance to the ship, watching the cavern fill slowly with water. After the last and largest quake, Menzo Shoog exited the control room and waded through the rising water toward the portal. He looked frustrated. He climbed on the gantry above the pit and watched as flood water overflowed the edge and poured into the portal. The water was rising with no signs of slowing.

Shoog was baffled; he couldn't shut down the portal to his home world. Part of the problem was, water shot out under pressure from the damaged air intakes deep down below the top of the portal. Rising air came out of the unblocked tubes. The water became trapped, bubbling up to the top.

As water entered the portal, it mixed with air from down below, preventing it from leaving smoothly through the wormhole. With extra water not falling through the portal, it clogged, causing water to back up. It wasn't a geyser; it was more like a toilet bowl overflowing.

The Navy SEAL pair saw that Shoog had no solution to the problem. They moved down the ramp to Shoog's position to find out if they could help. Wading through the waist-deep water, they approached him on the gantry.

Buckley asked, "We can't get out through the tunnel. Will we have a chance to go through the portal and go to Zome?"

Shoog replied through his guardian, "That is not an option anymore. If you jumped into the portal under normal conditions, you would go directly to Zome and probably survive, but because water flowing out of the air vents is backing up, you would drown before you left the Earth. Of course, if that happened, we would bring you back to life. But as you know, you would not be you anymore."

Buckley, speaking through Shoog's guardian, asked, "Do you have an escape plan?"

"Our main option at this time is to go to the Tropos Magra and secure the doors. We will be safe there for an indefinite period of time."

"Are the sea crafts functional? Can we use them to escape?"

"It is possible, but there may be a better option. We could take the entire ship to the surface."

Cooper jumped in, "If that's an option, we should use it."

"There is one problem. I am not qualified to fly a starship. It would take a pilot-class Aalzad to do this."

Quizzically Buckley asked, "Won't you try if our lives depend on it?"

Shoog nervously said, "Yes, I will try. I have to try. Go to the Tropos Magra and wait for me. I must make the effort again to shut down the portal and bring the CR to the ship before we go. It is imperative that I do this."

Cooper asked, "What will happen if you can't close the portal?"

"If this unrestricted flow continues, it will cause a disaster on my home world. Water will drain to Zome, and if unchecked for a long time, it will flood the nearby cities. It must be closed for the sake of both planets."

Buckley offered, "Can we help?"

"No, I must do this alone. Go to the ship. I will be there soon."

Buckley and Cooper waded back to the ramp; the water was noticeably deeper. They were tired when they reached it. The base of the ramp was on a higher level of the cavern. At its base, the water was only ankle-deep. Many of the other areas of the cavern were already filled with water that was over their heads.

Water continued to flow unabated from the main tunnel. The depth was steadily increasing. The pair climbed to a point above the cavern floor toward the Tropos Magra's entrance. where they stopped to watch Shoog.

From the safety of the ramp. they watched him open the door to the control room and go inside. Several minutes later. he reappeared, frantically trying to close the door behind him. It was jammed open. The water was too deep to close it. He was in too much of a hurry to worry about it now.

He timed his movement precisely to the pit, avoiding being caught in the overflow. The waves were forceful, but they were predictable. Water flowing back over the top of the portal spread through the cavern quickly and then drained back into the pit when the air broke the surface.

The SEALs watched as Shoog moved to the gantry. He climbed above the pit where he looked in again. He stood there for several minutes staring off into space. It was obvious to them; he didn't know what to do!

As he stood there, frothy bubbles overflowed the lip and receded several times. Shoog needed to return to the control room.

He needed to time his next move carefully. He hesitated, and then he jumped. It was an awkward leap down off the gantry. Slipping, he lost his balance, sinking below the surface.

Attempting to stand up, the lightness of his body caused him to be knocked over like a feather by the next incoming wave from the pit. Still unable to stand, he was being carried by the wave away from the portal. Submerged, the backflow picked him up and carried him back toward the waterfall. All his struggling was in vain; helplessly he went right over the lip and into the portal.

Alarmed at what they had just seen, the two Navy SEALs ran down the ramp toward the spot where Shoog disappeared. The water was deeper now at the base of the ramp, slowing their movement. It had been over a minute, and there was no sign of him. They timed the overflow and waded to the gantry and climbed up. Looking over the side into the pit, Shoog was nowhere to be seen.

No water came up from the depths for half a minute. On its return, they heard the forceful rush of water. It was bubbling up fast. Cooper and Buckley braced for impact, but there was none. Water simply flowed below them, pushing away from the gantry spreading through the cavern. Reaching the outer point, it forcefully returned to the portal. No Shoog.

They watched as the water drained down the pit again. There was no sign that he was carried back up to the cavern. Did he go through the portal? They were looking around the newly formed lake with Shoog nowhere in sight.

Buckley said, "We have to get to the Tropos Magra and close the door. At this point that's our only hope. Maybe we can operate the small watercraft with Roger's help."

"Lieutenant, the water is rising. We should wait until it recedes again. We don't want to wind up like Shoog."

The water rose then receded, allowing Cooper and Buckley the opportunity to struggle through the water back to the ramp. From there it was an easy walk up to the ship.

*****

Blackhawk helicopters landed near the Aalzad air tower. Twelve members of Eagle Corps disembarked and assembled near the vent opening. Since the explosions, the moat had grown to double its former circumference. Stationed in the center of the moat was the familiar pillbox standing tall. A new sucking sound was heard coming from the depths. Air was being pulled down by the enormous pumps deep within the cavern.

The first landing helicopter contained Falcon team, led by Captain Steel. His team was the only one fully intact. Falcon Team was comprised of Doc Forster and Petty Officers Mario Flores and Mason Ross. Attached to Falcon Team for this mission was the Sniper Lance Corporal David Moreno, the only member not in training with the newly forming Harrier team. Steel wanted him there because he was exceptional at his trade. By far the best shot in Eagle Corps, he also proved himself as a patient professional sniper in the cavern.

The second helicopter contained the combined Team Hawk and Condor team. On the chopper were Petty Officer Brewer and SSgt. Torres from Hawk, while Condor team was made up of Army Rangers Vince Blackwell, Tom Benson, and Charlie Weber with Master Sergeant Delbert Brown.

The combined team was led by Army First Lieutenant Kyle Uber, now fully recuperated from the wounds he sustained by the explosion in this same tunnel. Waiting for the group was General Ray and Tretorn Glor.

The teams were fully loaded down with their personal equipment. The heavy protective gear of the previous mission had been shed for khaki field uniforms with PASGT (personnel armor system for ground troops) DuPont Kevlar vests, and helmets. Many of the SEALs carried the SCAR assault rifle (Special Operations Forces combat assault rifle).

Moreno carried his trusty bolt action Barrett fifty-caliber sniper rifle while Ross's primary weapon was the Eagle Corps Squad automatic weapon or SAW. Tucked away in a pouch on his hip was his pirate gun, as it was known to the Navy SEALs. It was a modified M79 grenade launcher with the barrel shortened and the stock cut short. This made it look like a weapon straight out of a pirate movie.

Brewer carried sniper gear, the Remington MSR MK21, but he also liked to carry his M4A1 carbine as back up.

Blackwell and Benson were carrying a new unproven pulse rifle as well as the trusty SCAR as backup. All carried nine-millimeter semiautomatic pistols, mostly Sig Sauer P226. Doc Forster carried a full medical pack, while each man had an issue of three grenades.

Staff Sergeant Torres and Master Sergeant Brown had packs loaded down with claymore mines and C4. The general thought that if the portal was open when they got there, E-Corps might be able to close it with high explosives. In addition to explosives, Torres also carried an M4A1 Carbine. All team members were issued hooded field jackets and goggles for protection in the wind tunnel.

A different kind of heavy-lift helicopter was standing by for the insertion. It was a bigger more specialized helicopter than the CH53. It wasn't a military helicopter at all; in fact, it was bright yellow with two-foot-tall lettering on the tail fuselage forming the words Mcgovern Air Crane.

This mighty machine was built for lifting cargo, raising tall structures, and providing support fighting forest fires. Its lifting capacity was twenty thousand pounds, and with its long cables, it had the ability to insert the teams efficiently to the bottom of the moat.

The Mcgovern Air Crane (SE-64 Sikorsky Skycrane) was in the area working on the offshore wind farms that dotted the ocean around Block Island, Martha's Vineyard, and Nantucket.

General Ray thought that its precision cargo control would be perfect for this job. It carried a crew of three pilots, two sitting in the traditional cockpit and one sitting in a section viewing the cargo to stabilize the craft when tight control was required.

The bulky DUKW was cradled on the end of the heavy cables. To these young men, the amphibious vehicle looked ancient. None of the men were over the age of forty, so it was like preparing to enter a time machine back to World War II.

It was covered in olive drab paint, had big oversized wheels, and a canvas cover over the metal ribbed passenger/cargo hold. One would imagine that it looked like a Conestoga wagon from two hundred years ago. This heavy canvas cover was Eagle Corps' only protection from the hostile environment they will soon be dropped into. What really looked out of place was the big navy-blue block letters on the side spelling out "Seabee Museum."

Captain Steel said to the teams, "Circle up, gentlemen. The general has a few words for you."

The men complied, surrounding the general.

Pointing toward the DUKW, General Ray said, "This duck boat may not look like much, but it's the perfect versatile transportation for this job. It's heavy enough to be stable in the wind tunnel. It is also a worthy amphibious vehicle that will allow you to travel on hard surfaces and in deep water. When you reach your objective, you will bring out your fellow team members and the Aalzad personnel.

"Men, this is one more dangerous mission that Eagle Corps must undertake. It's a very important mission, and you are the only men I trust to carry it out. You must insert then navigate the tunnels not knowing their condition. I have been told that there is flooding in different areas.

"You must also make sure that the Aalzad portals are shut down. Get in, do the job, and get out. If all goes well, it should take around twelve hours.

"Okay, men, board the duck boat. You can't board it down below because of the wind tunnel effect. It may be strong enough to carry you away."

Steel said, "Mount up, men, let's get this show on the road." Steel fell in behind the teams walking toward the DUKW when he heard the general say, "Captain, I need a word with you."

Steel returned to the general, who said, "Captain, I have a package for you to take with you in the duck boat. It's a crate full of some additional weapons. The weapons will be stored in the back of a MX6 combat robot prototype that's already on the duck boat. I know that there are a couple of menacing robots down there, so I want you to have enough fire power to take them out if necessary."

Sitting in the cargo space of the DUKW was the olive drab MX6, a metallic unmanned ground vehicle. It has the ability to act autonomously or by an operator with a handheld controller. It's small enough to fit in the back of the DUKW with dimensions of four feet high, four feet wide, and eight feet long. It sat atop a mini tank chassis with sturdy duel treads. Its usefulness on this journey was apparent to General Ray. It can support various interchangeable weapons. On different occasions, it could be fitted with a laser or a mini gun, but today a sixty-caliber machine gun adorns the body of the MX6.

Some of the MX6's less deadly features are cameras arranged to give the operator 360-degree vision. In the rear, a storage bed can carry supplies, extra equipment, and wounded soldiers, if necessary. On this mission however, it was carrying the toys General Ray brought them.

The general described what he brought, "In the crate are AT4s [single-shot recoilless smoothbore antitank weapons]. There is also a case of smoke grenades and flares. If you can't kill those things, maybe you can hide from them.

"Keep them in the crate unless you need them. We don't want to start an intergalactic war. Glor doesn't need to know that you have them unless it's absolutely necessary. Good luck to you, Captain." He extended his hand. "Bring our people home."

Shaking the general's hand, Steel said, "Thank you, sir, we'll be back at the completion of our mission." Steel saluted General Ray and then turned to mount the DUKW boat.

Employees from the Seabee Museum worked to finish attaching the canvas securely to the ribs on the vehicle. A pay loader lifted the large mysterious crate in its bucket into the MX6's cargo space. It wasn't a fancy accommodation in the DUKW, but everyone managed to find a place to sit on the bench seats running along its outside walls.

Everyone tucked in under the canvas tarp securing their personal leg room for this trip. There was plenty of it because the DUKW was capable of holding twice the number of troops on this ride.

Glor and Max were the last to board. Glor found an empty part of the bench near the back of the vehicle and sat down. Max just hovered in the rear corner. Looking around the cargo area, it seemed comfortable enough, but that feeling would end when the mission started.

The vehicle, not airtight, would allow wind to swirl through the cargo area. It was going to cause problems. Nonetheless, E-Corps believed that they were physically safe in the thirteen-thousand-pound vehicle.

Steel moved up into the seat next to the driver and was surprised to see a man in his mid- to late fifties in camouflaged pants, a black sweatshirt, and a pair of old jungle boots. On the front of the sweatshirt was a rendition of an angry bee. The bee was facing to the right in a sailor cap, holding a machine gun with its front legs while its back legs held a wrench and a hammer. In big letters below the embroidery were the words Fighting Seabees.

Ed Carter with a big smile, thinking Steel was a naval officer, said, "Hello, Lieutenant, I'm Ed Carter. I will be your chauffeur today."

Steel was surprised and quite dismayed to see a civilian in the driver seat of this hulking antique military vehicle. *Why would General Ray put him in danger?*

Steel politely asked the civilian, "Sir, are you sure you're supposed to be here? This is a military operation."

Carter, still smiling, said, "Damn, Lieutenant, I'm the only man in the State of Rhode Island that can handle this beast. Besides, I consider myself military. I spent thirty years in the Navy, and after that I've worked for the Navy department, managing military properties, including my present position at the Seabee Museum in Davisville."

"Well, sir, thirty years in the Navy goes a long way with me, but—"

Carter cut him off with a smile, "Don't you think an old guy can drive a truck?"

"Yes, sir, but this trip could get ugly."

Carter, more serious, looked Steel in the eyes and said, "Lieutenant, I cut my teeth on ugly."

The Seabee employees finished preparing the DUKW and stepped away. Loaded with the Rangers, Navy SEALs, Marines, Ed Carter, Tretorn Glor, the guardian Max, plus the MX6 and the big mysterious crate, the yellow Air Crane lifted off, hoisting the DUKW

THE TUNNELS OF EARTH

boat off the ground. Reaching altitude, the helicopter slowly spun around moving to its position over the deep air-sucking trench.

Whether Steel liked it or not, Ed Carter was their driver. The winches kicked in, and the DUKW was lowered slowly toward the darkness. Carter turned on the lights, causing the trench to be bathed in luminescence. Everyone hunkered down behind the driver seat in anticipation of a very uncomfortable ride.

A cold blast of air was immediately felt as they descended below the surface and out of sight. Only a few men could actually see what was happening out the windshield. Tretorn Glor felt better and was trying to engage anyone in conversation. He didn't seem to relate danger to this trek.

There was a creaking sound as the suspension on the DUKW pushed down on the hard surface at the bottom of the trench. Dropping down into the tunnel brought hard winds, but now at the bottom, it was like being in a hurricane. Explosive bolts released the DUKW from its umbilical cord to the real world.

Visibility was good as Carter adjusted his goggles and slipped the transmission into gear. The DUKW lunged forward and started to move down the tunnel. The headlights showed the size and uniformity of the travel space. It was nice and wide for the large vehicle to maneuver. Carter worked his way through the gears, and before long they were moving along at an acceptable thirty-five miles an hour. Master Sgt. Brown was monitoring distance traveled and announced, "One mile."

Nothing unusual happened at the beginning of the journey. This was enough to ease everyone's minds, allowing them to relax. Glor finally got a conversation going with, of all people, the no-nonsense Master Sergeant Brown.

Glor showed that he had the gift of gab, and with his charm, he could break down anyone. After a few minutes with Master Sergeant Brown, he got the humorless top Sergeant to crack a smile and then laugh out loud. Noting his dress and his mannerisms, Brown said out loud, "Aalzad, my ass, Ted here is a comedian."

Quickly back to his duties, Brown said, "Three miles."

Webber took a message coming in from the surface. It was General Ray. "Give me Captain Steel."

"Yes, sir. Captain, General Ray's on the horn!"

Steel moved in next to Webber. Taking the secured handset, he said, "Yes, sir."

"What's your status so far?"

"Nothing but heavy winds, sir."

Brown shouted out, "Four miles."

Not keeping with the mission, Ray asked, "Did you meet your driver yet?"

"Yes, sir, Mr. Carter, civilian. I'm a little worried about him."

"You don't have to worry about Ed Carter. I know him personally, and I would count on him in any situation. What do you know about him, Captain?"

"I know that he was in the Navy for thirty years and now he works for the Seabee Museum."

"Did he tell you anything else about himself?"

"No, sir."

"All I am going to say to you is be sure to call him sir."

With that the receiver went dead.

Steel's curiosity was now peaked regarding Ed Carter, but it was secondary for the time being. He was satisfied that they hadn't seen any burst pipes or cracks in the subterranean structure. He hoped that it would stay like this for the entire trip.

Brown reported, "Seven miles."

As they moved down the tunnel, the wind was relentless. The DUKW had plenty of stability because of its size and weight; it moved forward with no noticeable resistance. As a matter of fact, a tailwind gave the vehicle a nice push, but in the back, the occupants were having a rough time. The wind was a constant irritant coming in under the canvas and through the vehicle, making the ride very unpleasant. Their nerves were starting to fray under this environmental stress.

Brown said, "Mile eighteen."

Glor resumed his conversation with Master Sergeant Brown. "Do you like being in the military, Mr. Brown?"

"I love it. It's what I was born to do. It's hard on my family, but they are very supportive of my career."

"I am happy to hear that. It is nice that you can make career choices. On Zome, you are born into a career, and you are never allowed to stray away from your place in society."

Brown leaned in closer to Glor and said, "I'm curious about Zome. What's it like?"

Glor replied, "It was a primitive world when we arrived, nothing like our home planet, Aalzarada. I actually remember Aalzarada. Even though we left that world over fifty years ago, the beauty of its majestic mountains and plush forests, I remember it like it was yesterday."

He said with remorse in his voice, "It's a dead world now. I imagine just a burning cinder.

"Over the years after our arrival, we transformed Zome into a global society. The city where I live is the capital city on the planet. It is modern and beautiful. It is a growing metropolis."

Brown said, "I live in a big city, Chicago, Illinois. How do you define beautiful?"

"Chicago—yes, I know about Chicago. Sirilo is a beautiful city. As a matter of fact, if you were to take a ride through the portal, you would empty out of a cave at a constructed reservoir in Sirilo. The reservoir is perhaps half the size of your Narragansett Bay. Wide deep canals travel in four different directions out of the city.

"Three of the canals drain into the largest planetary ocean, and the fourth goes directly to a pond serving a series of water treatment plants. Those plants desalinate and purify it. We have tall buildings and deep underground structures. As I said, it is very modern."

At mile twenty, Steel thought the insertion was going too well, but things were about to change. Arriving at a debris field at mile twenty-three, Carter reduced speed to around twenty miles an hour. The tunnel was so wide he could easily weave around the chunks that had fallen off the wall and ceiling. Farther down the tunnel the piles were getting bigger.

As the DUKW maneuvered through the rubble, it covered larger lateral expanses of the tunnel bed. So far, the trek was nothing the

DUKW couldn't handle, but the driving was getting more difficult. Carter zigzagged back and forth, driving over the smaller mounds of debris.

Brown reported, "Mile thirty-two."

The ride was getting bumpier. In the truck, warriors trying to sleep were having a difficult time. They tried to put the discomfort out of their minds. One thing about these men was they were all experienced in stressful and dangerous situations. In their minds, this wasn't even close to the worst situation they had experienced. Most of them served in combat situations, while others served in difficult humanitarian relief efforts.

Glor said to Brown, "I know Zome has fewer people than Earth. I know that the Aalzad people live mostly in the new cities. People here on Earth move around, living in cities, the country, and in the remotest places. I think that by living in our cities, we are consolidating our resources. We have no choice. Perhaps your people can learn from us in that respect."

Brown said, "People of Earth like to make their own choices. Here, many people want to get out of the cities."

Directly ahead, visibility remained good. They were close to their exit. When they reach it, the DUKW would leave the wind tunnel and enter a side passage leading to the main access to the cavern.

Glor pointed out that there were several exits, but the first would allow them to reach the main tunnel faster. Not to mention the fact that it will finally give the battered passengers relief from the wind. That sounded good to everyone within earshot, so there was a collective sigh of relief when they approached the turn out.

To keep the mood light, Ed Carter put on his right turn signal. The DUKW moved through the hatch without difficulty and moved in the direction of the main tunnel. Within this new tunnel, it didn't take long for the DUKW to stop in its tracks. They were parked in front of a large pile of rock. The walls of this tunnel had collapsed.

Steel said to the team, "I want to check this out. Be ready to go on a moment's notice."

He wanted to take a look to see if there was a way through to the other side. He approached the rocks and shined his flashlight on the top edge. The light went beyond the debris over into the next section.

Steel called out to one of Team Hawk's members to take a look.

"Brewer, bring your flashlight over here."

Brewer responded immediately.

Steel said, "Take your light and have a look over the top of this pile of rock. See if there's a way through. If so, we can blow a hole to get through."

Brewer climbed up and shined the light over the debris.

He said to Steel, "Sir, you need to see this."

Steel climbed the rocks and looked over the top. As soon as he looked, he knew that they weren't going this way. A steady stream of water was shooting straight out of the side wall under high pressure, much like a city water pipe bursting under a street.

The roof of the tunnel was on the deck, and water flowed down the tunnel. Steel thought, *Even if we blew this wall, we would be in the same situation again farther down the line. Not to mention, we will have to contend with water as well.*

Steel called out to Brown, "Top, how many miles are we in now?"

"Thirty-eight miles, sir."

"How many miles left to reach the cavern?"

"Twenty-seven miles or so, sir."

"How long would it take us to walk it?"

"With all our gear, going three miles an hour, with clear sailing, it will take around nine hours, sir. We can't walk this way, and we definitely can't walk in the wind."

Steel asked Glor, "How many miles to the next turnout?"

"Eight miles."

Steel made a decision and ordered, "Back in the truck, men!"

He approached Ed Carter and said, "I hope this beast has reverse. We are going back into the wind."

"I'll see what I can do, Lieutenant."

Steel had enough of being called lieutenant, saying to Carter, "Sir, there are differences in the rank structure between our branches. I am a Marine officer. I am a captain, not a Navy lieutenant."

Carter smiled at Steel and said, "Of course there is captain. Being in the Navy for thirty years, I served with many fine marines."

Puzzled by Carter's response, he sat down along the wall of the DUKW and braced himself for the return to the wind.

Back in the tunnel, things quickly became uncomfortable again. Even though they didn't get through the first side tunnel, they were moving again at an acceptable rate. The wind was as strong as ever, but they were moving, and that was a good thing.

Brown said, "Mile forty-six."

With five miles to go to the next side tunnel, the tube shook hard, throwing the occupants of the DUKW boat around under the tarp. They just experienced another large tremor, and it struck with no mercy. The DUKW kept moving forward, but now there were sections of the tunnel cracking and falling. The ride was bumpy, but there was no indication that Carter was going to slow down. He was increasing speed.

He said to Steel, "We better get to our destination as fast as we can. The conditions here are deteriorating, and I'm afraid they're not going to get any better."

There was no turning back. Carter's reasoning was to go fast, and if something happened, they will at least be closer to their destination, just in case they had to hoof it the rest of the way.

Carter and Steel, looking ahead, saw that there was a distinct change in visibility. It was a change amplified by the wind. The wind up the tunnel had a rushing sound that made a consistent hiss. The men had become used to it. But now there was a change. Ahead they could hear a different amplified sound. It was the hiss of water, spraying under pressure.

Cracks in the ceiling were spraying pressurized water down into the tunnel. As soon as it hit the wind, it blew horizontally down toward the cavern. Carter could see the sheet of water clearly now as a translucent wall developed straight ahead. As they entered the mini monsoon, the team's misery increased sharply.

The ride coarsened, but the DUKW boat was still moving—that was the important thing. After the last big tremor, Steel noticed that the wind was slowing down. The horizontal rain completely stopped, and visibility cleared. Long rivulets of water continued to flow under the tires. That wasn't enough to slow down the DUKW boat. The vehicle with all its tires in contact with the tunnel floor moved on.

Looking down the tunnel, Carter became aware of something in the tunnel. It was shaded, but he could make it out to be a large obstacle. The closer the DUKW got, he realized that it was a mound of debris that had fallen from the roof. To the passengers, it seemed more like a mountain. It was a blockage that contained debris from above the tunnel and remnants from the apex of that section. Carter stopped the vehicle sixty feet from the mound.

There was no sound other than the DUKW idling. The wind had completely stopped. There was no telling why, but with all the water traveling down the tunnel, it was easy to surmise the air intake down below must be blocked. The debris obstacle climbed a third of the way up toward the ceiling. It rose twenty feet.

The men in the back of the DUKW threw back the cover and looked out. What they saw was Captain Steel and Mr. Carter standing outside the vehicle, knee-deep in water, looking at the tall mound of debris. Water flowed under the DUKW and proved to be getting deeper at the base of the blockage.

Steel said, "I think we have to leave the vehicle and walk the rest of the way to the next passageway."

Carter replied, "That's one plan, Captain, but look at the water coming down the tube. My thought is that if we wait a little while, the water will rise, and we can float up to the top of the mound in the vehicle, drive over the top, and then power down the other side. From there we can continue to the next turnout."

Steel looked at the speed of the rising water and thought that Carter's idea might work Agreeing with Carter, he said, "We have had good luck with this machine so far. I think we should trust her a little while longer."

Carter nodded his head affirmatively. "Good! Captain, let's get back in and see what happens."

Steel thought to himself that Ed Carter was a cool customer. He took each situation as it came and kept each one in perspective and dealt with them logically.

Returning to the vehicle, Glor moved up between Ed Carter and Captain Steel and said, "Max has informed me the next transfer door is not far beyond this obstruction."

The crew in the DUKW boat didn't have to wait too long. Water rose under the vehicle, lifting it off solid ground, causing it to float freely. When the tires lost traction, the vehicle drifted toward the pile of debris. Steel saw the situation and ordered two men to jump out and keep the bow off the rocks.

Ross and Webber responded to the call, jumping over the side, holding the bow at arm's length off the rocks. As the water slowly rose toward the crest, the men in the water were up to their waist. Every minute or so they would step up and back on the slippery debris to keep the boat from going over the top of them. As the water kept rising, everyone in the back of the DUKW leaned over the side, watching the plan develop.

Carter spoke to the team, "We only have one shot at this, so when I give the word, I want everyone back in the boat holding on. When the water flows over the top, I am going to gun the engine.

"I'll power the DUKW over the debris and see what happens. I don't know if I will be able to control the descent down the other side. It's steep, and it might be slippery, so I'm going to count on the all-wheel drive, put my head down, and go straight."

It took forty-five minutes to reach the point where the water was inches from the top.

Carter calmly said, "Get in, gentlemen, it's time to go!"

When the front tires came in contact with the chunks of debris near the top, Carter throttled up. At first the front tires jumped, slipped, and skidded sideways without gaining traction. He nursed the gas, being patient not to spin the tires.

He craned his neck over the side to watch as the water level rose to the point where it started to cascade down the other side. Finally, the DUKW reached the point where it couldn't go any higher. He throttled up, urging it forward.

The vehicle jumped, caught an outcropping, shifted to the left, and charged forward. The other side of the mound angled down sharply, but it was maneuverable. The men in the back were in free fall as the DUKW barreled down the far side, hitting a boulder, jerking to the right, and skidding down the rocks at a forty-five-degree angle.

Smashing into more debris nearly broadside, Carter spun the wheel, straightening the DUKW out, bringing it back under his control. Moving forward and down, it slammed into one more pile of rubble, denting the right rear quadrant of the vehicle, knocking out a taillight, then blowing the rear tire.

The DUKW reached the bottom of the mound, moving fast, barreling forward and down the tunnel. Relieved, Carter applied the brakes to slow down a bit. It looked like smooth sailing ahead.

Just when he thought they were in the clear, he heard a disturbance behind them. Turning in his seat, he saw the mound of rock and debris they just scaled start to break apart.

He watched as the pile started to separate and crumble under the tremendous weight of the water pushing from the other side. Carter turned around and gave it the gas. The DUKW raced down the tube, but before it could create enough distance between it and the mountain of debris, the mound burst under building water pressure. The forceful mass of water obliterated what was left of the wall.

Carter yelled, "Brace yourself; this is going to be rough."

It took only seconds for the rushing wall of water to reach the stern of the DUKW. It shuddered and lunged forward, bobbing up and down in the rushing water. They were sideways, floating in the tunnel. Carter had no control. He flipped a switch, and the power was diverted from the axles to the propeller. He hoped that he could regain some control, but for the moment, they were at the mercy of the floodwaters. With some effort, Carter managed to maneuver the bow of the DUKW forward.

Carter yelled, "How far, Mr. Glor?"

"About a mile on the right!"

"This isn't the last door, correct?"

Glor shouted, "No, we have one more chance after this! It's not that far. We should aim for the first one, if possible!"

Carter yelled back, "The water is moving too fast for me to get into position to exit cleanly!"

The DUKW boat raced down the tunnel. It was helplessly caught in the turbulence. No matter what Carter tried to do, he couldn't gain control. The power output of the boat was less than the speed of the surging water. The helm was unresponsive.

Glor cried, "Three quarters of a mile to the door!"

Carter realized he wasn't going to gain control in this surging water. He called for Captain Steel's attention. "Captain, prepare to abandon ship! If we get out early, we might be able to get the team to swim to the sidewall. Those that don't make it through the door can be pulled in by those that do. If that fails, they will have one more shot down the line!"

Steel yelled to team, "Prepare to abandon ship! We have no rudder control, the boat is finished!"

The team tethered themselves together with rope and then lined up at the stern, prepared to abandon ship.

Steel yelled, "Swim, swim as hard as you can to the wall! Once you get there, try to grab the door or anything you can get your hands on to prevent being swept down the tunnel. If we can latch on to something, we'll be able to work our way to the doorframe!"

What the Marine officer was saying sounded crazy to the teams. It sounded crazy to him too, but they had little choice. If they were able to get to the wall, grabbing and latching on to something might be possible. These men were trained to deal with desperate situations, he believed they had a chance. Once attached to the rope, the men tested their links to each other then gave the thumbs-up.

"First man, go!"

Blackwell was on the end of the rope and the first to jump off with a splash. The rope played out, and the next man jumped in; it was Ross. They were the strongest swimmers in Eagle Corps.

THE TUNNELS OF EARTH

The water was cold and choppy as they inched their way toward the sidewall. The water was slightly over their heads. This allowed them to push off the bottom and bob toward the sidewall.

Next was Benson, another strong swimmer. Three men were now in the water tethered to the DUKW. Flores was checking his knot on the rope, preparing to make the plunge when another tremor hit. It was the biggest yet.

Violence shook the tunnel again. Water churned all around Blackwell, Ross, and Benson, forcing them to fight for every breath. The helpless DUKW rocked in all directions. Giant cracks formed in the tube, and chunks of debris were falling all around them. Flores stayed in the boat, holding the rope tightly attached to his comrades in the water. This tremor seemed endless.

As the tremor died down and with no warning, the left side of the tunnel shell cracked and fell away. It didn't crash down on the DUKW. Instead, it collapsed outward into a giant fissure beyond the tunnel. It was swallowing everything on the left side of the passageway.

The seabed was exposed. Water under the DUKW boat cascaded over a cliff and down into what seemed like a bottomless pit. Miraculously the water that captured the DUKW was draining off from the tunnel. Not only did the fissure drop down, but it extended upward, high above the roof of the tunnel as well.

Water that rushed down the tube immobilizing the DUKW boat was now falling over the edge into the crevasse and away. The DUKW drifted toward the edge but abruptly skidded to a halt as the tires reestablished contact with the hard surface. The men, struggling in the water, were violently swinging around the stern from right to left.

They were being swept toward the waterfall. Carter saw his one chance to save the vehicle. He stepped on the gas and hurtled toward the approaching door. He thought, *There's a very small margin of error. We'll either make it through the door or we'll be caught in the raging water and carried down the tunnel to our deaths. The door was close, and it was open.*

Blackwell, the last man on the rope, was gliding fast over the water, pulled toward the precipice. In horror, his feet swung out and dangled for a split second over the falls. He was sure that he was a goner when he was yanked clear of the falls by the accelerating DUKW. He skimmed on top of the water away from the fissure.

Seconds later, his body was dragging on solid ground. Flores yelled for Carter to stop. When Steel saw what was happening to his men outside the vehicle, he echoed Flores's command to Carter: "Carter, stop!"

Although understanding that they could be engulfed in water again momentarily, without hesitation, Carter jammed on the brakes. Steel moved to the rear of the vessel, offering a hand to help get the men back in. The tethered team members struggled to get to their feet and started trudging toward the vehicle.

Steel yelled to Carter, "All ahead, slow!"

Carter responded precisely as ordered, moving forward.

Blackwell, Ross, and Benson were now on their feet running toward the DUKW. Benson grabbed on, and the others were getting close when the bottomless fissure filled with water, bubbling over the rim and back into the tunnel.

It flowed toward the fleeing men. Trying to reach the boat, Ross and Blackwell were knocked down again as water swept across the floor, taking their feet out from under them.

Seeing this, Steel yelled to Carter, "Give it the gas, we have to go!"

Carter gunned the engine with the men, again caught in the swirling water behind the DUKW. Leaning over the side, extra hands held on, trying to save the men in the water. Team members in the vehicle held on to Flores and Benson. They, in turn, held the rope attached to Ross and Blackwell.

The left side wheels were under water when Carter went up the short ramp in front of the door. Coolly he took the sharp right-hand turn, not thinking to use the turn signal this time. There was relief on board when the nose of the DUKW boat roared through the exit door.

THE TUNNELS OF EARTH

The DUKW was through and out of the tunnel, but the team's work wasn't done yet. Ross, still in the raging rapids, drifted past the door first, followed by Blackwell. Everyone prayed that the rope would hold. Team members untethered themselves and jumped down from the DUKW to aid their comrades.

Carter slowed down after passing through the door, causing the rope to be pulled in at a much slower rate. First Ross reached the door but couldn't stand up in the rushing water at the entrance.

He had to be lifted by his belt and shirt collar into the side tunnel by Brewer and Doc Forster. Blackwell was the last man to save; he was on his stomach trying to swim against the rush of water, getting plenty in his mouth and down his throat. When finally assisted out of the water, he stood up, acting like it was no big deal.

The water hurtled down the tunnel like a raging river. Looking out for the last time, Steel saw that the giant fissure next to the tunnel had been filled and absorbed into the fast-flowing river. He couldn't see how far up the fissure went, but if it gave way, all the Atlantic Ocean would come crashing down, crushing everything underneath it.

In the minds of the group, they were no longer on a rescue mission. It had become a survival mission. No one would say it, but none of them believed that they would make it out alive.

*****

Topside, the biggest tremor shook Aquidneck Island and the surrounding communities. The Coddington remained standing, but smaller buildings and infrastructure around it were damaged. Telephone poles that hadn't been used in years sagged down. Roads and former parking areas were cracked, leaving crevices so large they were impassable.

All the military and scientific personnel spilled outside into the parking lot, moving away from the buildings. They were anticipating big aftershocks. No one was in a hurry to go back inside.

Maurice Millius burst out the front door and moved quickly toward the throng of people standing around. He was looking for General Ray.

Millius cried, "General Ray, General Ray! The communication officer is monitoring disturbing chatter on the radio. A cargo ship ten miles off the coast identified what they think is a huge tidal wave. The captain said that it was heading toward the southeast coast of Massachusetts and Rhode Island."

General Ray yelled, "Everyone, a tsunami is heading this way! We need to get to high ground. Get to the top floors of the hotel!"

The crowd instantly came to life, pushing and shoving to get inside. The stairs were jammed with people, crushing each other to get to the highest levels. Being the last person to enter the building, Ray climbed to the observation deck on the ninth floor with Millius. They were on a deck at the peak of an architectural structure where the roof angled down on four sides.

The view that they had was of the once spectacular Newport Harbor. Most of the Coddington was a three-story hotel connected to higher towers on each end, north and south. The south tower was ten stories, with Glor's suite on the top. It loomed above Goat Island with its sharply angled roof complete with a series of balconies. There were additional floors on the north-facing end.

Standing on a flat surface above the sloping roof, General Ray raised his binoculars. He was looking for any unusual activity to the southeast.

Millius queried, "General, have you heard from Admiral Carter or Captain Steel?"

Ray replied, "Not a word, Mr. Millius. We've had some major earthquakes here on the surface. I can only imagine the intensity they're feeling down there. They're close to the epicenter, so I'm not optimistic about the condition of the tunnels."

Millius pointed to the southeast. "General, do you see that?"

Ray turned and looked in the direction Millius was pointing. He lifted his binoculars and said, "My god, I hope this building is tall enough."

Ray was referencing a wall of water approaching Aquidneck Island from the southeast. It was coming like a freight train, and through his binoculars, Ray saw the tsunami crash onto the smooth surface on the south side of the island, picking up speed.

Water rose to great heights, moving fast over the low friction of the island surface. General Ray had a clear view as the wall of water came sweeping across the island. The observers were fixated on the water as it surged across Newport harbor, hitting the south end of Goat Island and then moving north on the island at a sharp angle.

In a matter of seconds, the destructive force plowed into the hotel. It ranged upward three stories. The hotel's huge windows and sliding doors buckled below the angled roof, forcing the weaker side of the brick structure inward.

The undermined upper stories tilted then buckled. People were launched from the balcony as floodwater crashed through the hotel's facade. In the maelstrom, portions of the Coddington were swept away into the angry bay. Anyone on the collapsed balcony sections that were going to survive struggled for their lives, carried into the waters of Narragansett.

Up to that point, the tsunami destroyed everything in its path. Slowed down by the flat surface of Aquidneck Island, the tidal wave continued across the east passage of Narragansett Bay. Reaching the low hills of Conanicut Island, the wave dissipated, slowing it down as it crossed the west passage of the bay. Most of the coastal communities beyond Conanicut Island were spared. The destructive wave concluded.

After the devastation, local emergency services had their hands full, struggling to aid the oceanside communities.

*****

It took several individuals using all their strength, but after a long moment, the heavy tunnel door swung shut. Team members got to their feet and moved back to the boat. They were about to enter the second leg of their journey. It was through a dry side passageway leading to the calm main tunnel. From there, the finish line, the cavern, would be in reach. The reliable engine of the DUKW started up, and the vehicle moved off again.

Glor said to Steel, "If this passageway is still intact, it will be a smooth trip. I can only hope the tremors are over."

Steel had to admit to himself that this was the right vehicle for the job. They would never have reached this point in a jeep or on foot. A Jeep would have been destroyed a long time ago, and trying to walk in these conditions would have been suicide.

The DUKW was up for the challenge. It had a flat tire in the right rear quadrant and the taillight on that side, crushed. Other than that, the reliable antique DUKW boat was able to continue toward its destination.

The team crossed the service tunnel without a problem, entering the main tunnel and finally heading down toward the cavern. Breaks in the tunnel above caused the main tube to flood. It was wide open and free of debris. Entering the tunnel was like entering a water slide. There was a slight drop down into the water, and off they went. They were floating down the main tube.

The DUKW hadn't been in contact with the floor for quite a while. From what they could gather, the water was about six feet deep, with the angle of descent less steep than the upper tunnel. The engine was running, and Carter had control of the helm. The propeller kept the craft moving just a little faster than the flow of water.

Most of the team finally had a chance to rest, while Steel and Carter prepared for the next step. It had been a rough trip, and all the stress and excitement had taken its toll. Steel was exhausted, but he didn't leave Carter's side. He thought, *If I am this tired, I can only imagine how Carter feels*. He was cheerful and didn't show any signs of fatigue. One would never know Ed Carter was the helmsman of the ship to hell.

"How are you holding up, Mr. Carter?"

"As you would imagine, I'm very tired, but I'm okay. I can rest later. I'm sure you understand, Captain, being in the position of command. You have men's lives in your hands, and you can't let anything get in the way of protecting them until you successfully complete your mission. Like you, I'll rest when we get there."

Steel was now very curious. "Mr. Carter, I have never served with a more squared away member of the Armed forces. You're calm under fire, and your immediate response to orders, even when you didn't agree with them, make you the perfect military man to me. If I may ask, sir, what were your duties in the Navy? General Ray told me to address you as sir, and as far as I am concerned, you deserve that courtesy."

"Captain, it's not necessary for you to call me sir. As a matter of fact, I would prefer that you just call me Ed."

*****

Arrival

The hard trip was coming to an end. The tunnel opened up into the wide expanse of the cavern. The DUKW slid down and out of the tunnel, splashing down in open water. The cavern was starting to look like an underground sea. The dangerous voyage was over, and it finished like an amusement park ride. Unfortunately, it was a perilous amusement park ride; they weren't out of danger yet.

Team members that had seen the cavern before were shocked to see how it had transformed. The *Mist of the Atlantic* was no longer the majestic backdrop standing in place. The floor of the cavern was now a lake. Everything was different.

The feeling of relief of making it there alive was put out of their minds when Staff Sergeant Torres said, "What's that over there, floating in the water?" Under power Carter guided the DUKW over to where the object floated, partially submerged. Glor was the first to identify the clothing of his compatriot.

He spoke up, saying, "It's the engineer, Menzo Shoog. What could have happened to him?"

Benson and Flores jumped over the side to retrieve his body. The water was over their heads as they passed Shoog up to other members of the team. As carefully as they could, they placed him in the center of the cargo deck in the DUKW boat.

Lieutenant Uber asked no one in particular, "If he's dead, who's running this place?"

Glor replied, "There are no Aalzad here now. It's operating on its own."

Glor stood up and listened. He was slightly alarmed, saying, "The portal to Zome has not been shut down. We must get over to the control room immediately. If we can't shut it down, there will be major problems here on Earth and on Zome."

Carter guided the DUKW in the direction of the control room. He noticed that there were waves hitting the boat in short intervals. He looked in the direction that the waves were being generated.

Carter spoke to Captain Steel, "Captain, you've been down here before. Where is the portal that Mr. Glor is speaking of?"

Steel pointed over in the direction of the control room door, which was now almost completely underwater, and said, "Over there to the left of that door by the gantry."

"Do you see the waves coming from that direction? Could they be from the portal?"

"Yes, I think that is exactly where they're coming from."

Just as he spoke, a large bubbling mass of water crested the portal, pushing out in all directions. It happened at precisely the spot that they were talking about in the floor. Moments later, there was a loud sucking sound pulling the water back into the portal.

Steel asked, "Can we get over there?"

Carter replied, "I don't know. We need to see how far apart those surges are. If there is enough time in between the waves, the answer is yes. If they are close together, we could be dashed up against the rock wall, or worse, we could be sucked down the portal. Let's take a second to see if there is a consistent pattern."

"Let's move over to that ramp and unload the crew. You and I can handle this."

Glor said, "Don't forget me and Max. I'm not an engineer, but I am somewhat familiar with the technology, and more importantly,

I can order the command robot to help. Max will be helpful communicating directly with the command robot from the boat."

Steel said to team, "Okay, Mr. Carter, Mr. Glor and I will make a run for the control room. Before that, we will drop the rest of you off at that ramp."

Lance Corporal Moreno spoke to the team leader, "Sir, what about those big security robots?"

Everyone that had seen the robots before swiveled their heads around in the direction of the control room door. No robots!

All eyes nervously scanned the cavern. If they were not there, where were they? It would be hard to miss them at ten feet tall, but as they searched the cavern, the robots were nowhere in sight.

Looking toward the portal through binoculars, Lieutenant Uber said, "Over there by the portal, by that raised gantry post."

Captain Steel asked, "What do you think you see?"

"Not sure, sir."

All heads turned, directing their attention to an unidentified metallic object in the water, attached to one of the lower sections, on the far side of the gantry.

Steel said, "That's one of them. It looks trapped in the water by the portal."

In the distance, they were looking at one of the robots on its side, with its vise-like hand clamped to an upright section of the gantry. The head was 75 percent submerged facing up, and the right side of its torso was partially exposed. The one arm that was exposed was engaged in a rigid death grip in the surging water.

Steel said, "Let's find the other one. If we're lucky, we won't have to deal with either of these things. I hope it went to Zome in the flood."

Part V

HIDE AND SEEK

Not that far away from the newly arrived E-Corps, up the ramp, inside the Aalzad ship, Cooper did the low crawl over to Buckley's hiding place.

In a quiet voice, she said, "Can you see it?"

"It just went around the center chamber," Buckley replied. "We might be able to get to the door before it comes back."

After Menzo Shoog disappeared down the pit, the security robots came to life and began stalking the humans as intruders. Through intercommunication with the abundance of worker robots, the security robots were aware that Buckley and Cooper went up to the spaceship. They moved in pursuit, trudging through deep floodwater, toward the ramp. It was difficult for them. They were terrestrial robots, not built for aquatics as they struggled forward in the deep tidal pool.

Once again, the pit bubbled over and surged outward. The robot closest to the pit was jostled by a wave affecting its balance. When the next wave hit, it tumbled forward, down under the water. Unable to regain its footing, it thrashed, suspended under the surface, trying to get a traction.

Like every other wave sequence, it was drawn back toward the portal. Stretching and scraping along the bottom in the receding water, the robot was helpless. With no way of gaining a foothold, the robot drifted under the gantry. As time was running out and it

THE TUNNELS OF EARTH

was about to hurtle over the edge, the robot's right hand shot out, latching onto the last vertical gantry support.

Without any visible concern over its companion's dilemma, the second robot clumsily slogged toward the Tropos Magra. After moving through the difficult water, it stepped up onto the base of the dry ramp. Single-minded, the lone security robot moved toward the ship where Cooper and Buckley were not expecting company.

*****

Resting in the ship, Roger was alerted to the sentry robot's approach.

It said to the pair, "You are in great danger. The security robots are coming for you. They have a directive to protect the operation if it is in jeopardy. You are a threat now, and the robots are programmed to eliminate all threats. Hide!"

At the realization that the robots were hunting them, they heard a large door on the Aalzad spacecraft open. Cooper and Buckley ducked down quickly and then quietly moved to the interior of the ship. They needed a place to hide, and they needed one fast. They found themselves in the area Cooper recognized as the kitchen. They found a couple of tables and crawled under them.

With several guardians and robots nearby, they didn't know if their position would be compromised. The SEALs slipped away into the main chamber looking for another better place to hide. They settled on a wide partition that was three feet from the wall, extending twenty feet. It was open at both ends. They thought there was enough space behind it. Cooper and Buckley slipped in and moved to the midpoint, where they crouched down.

After several minutes, staying low, Buckley crawled to the other end of the partition and glanced out. He couldn't see the robots, but he could hear what he thought was two robots moving deeper into the craft, crashing into things and knocking them down. He returned to the safety of the center of the partition.

Apprehensive, Cooper whispered, "Let's get out of here while we can."

Trying to stay cool, Buckley said, "We have nowhere to go. Let's stay put for now."

The lone security robot had been sweeping through the Tropos Magra for twenty minutes. There couldn't have been many other places that the robot hadn't searched. At that moment, this was one of the few times the SEALs couldn't hear it.

Buckley said, "Maybe while the robots are deep in the ship, we can get to the *Mist of the Atlantic* and hide there."

Cooper agreed. "It's worth a try. Sooner or later they're going to search this area."

Cooper and Buckley worked their way to the end of the partition, closest to the main door. Because they couldn't hear robot activity, they slipped quietly out and moved toward the ramp. The door was closed when they reached it, but with Roger's help, it opened.

Running out onto the top section of the ramp, they were surprised to see their rescue team down below at the base. Steel and the others looked up to see what was happening.

They were greeted by Buckley yelling, "Get into the boat! Get into the boat, let's get the hell out of here!"

Confused but without hesitation, everyone scrambled into the DUKW boat and waited for the pair sprinting toward the vehicle to get in. It didn't take long. Carter immediately shifted into reverse and splashed down off the ramp.

Buckley yelled, "We have angry robots after us!"

Steel said to Carter, "Take us over behind what is left of the cruise ship."

Steel said to Buckley, "What happened here?"

Buckley responded, "Shoog was sucked down the pit activating the security robots." To Carter, he said, "Can this thing go any faster?"

As he turned toward the *Mist of the Atlantic*, an annoyed Carter said, "This is not a thing, young lieutenant. It's a DUKW amphibious vehicle."

Carter kept motoring toward the collapsed ship at what felt like a snail's pace.

Falcon team member Mario Flores, looking toward the top of the ramp, yelled, "There it is! It's coming out of the ship!"

THE TUNNELS OF EARTH

Carter couldn't get any more speed from the DUKW boat. It was already at its maximum water speed. It was moving toward the bow of the crumpled cruise ship at a paltry six knots.

Reaching the bow of the *Mist of the Atlantic*, Carter turned the wheel, making a controlled left turn. As they motored around the bow, a powerful fireball glanced off the hull of the cruise ship, deflecting behind the DUKW boat. The robot had fired on them from the ramp.

To anyone that would listen, Buckley said, "Where's the other one? I thought two of those things were after us."

Ignoring Buckley for the moment, Steel called Moreno over and said in a controlled voice, "See that low point in the keel up ahead? We are going to drop you and Mr. Glor there. You are going to blast that thing with the Barrett, and Glor is going to tell you where to aim."

Glor heard what was being said and tried to protest, but Steel sharply clarified, "We don't have time to argue about this. Go with this Marine and tell him how to stop this thing. If he can stop it, great. If he can destroy its sensors, I'll take that too. We need to neutralize that robot, and we need your help."

Answering Buckley's previous question, he said, "The other robot's over by the pit, clinging to the gantry. We don't have to worry about it right now."

The DUKW approached the lowest point of the crushed keel. It lay there at a forty-five-degree angle. Moreno didn't hesitate to jump onto the ship's hull, while Glor reluctantly followed. When he leaped, Moreno was there to break his fall. Both tumbled down on the hull. With two hands, Ross tossed the sniper rifle up to Moreno. Once they were on the *Mist of the Atlantic*, Carter gunned the engine to get clear of the structure. The sniper and the Aalzad scrambled up the warped broken hull to find a good firing position.

Steel turned to Roger. "Do you know where the robot is?"

"'Yes, it is following our path, coming around the bow of the cruise ship attempting to catch us."

"Are you using sensors?"

"Yes!"

"Does it have sensors too?"

"Yes, it has sensors, better sensors than I have."

"Is it gaining on us?

"No, it is not catching up. It is moving very slowly through the water."

"Can we get back to the ramp before it sees us again?"

"You can get to the ramp, but you won't get to the top before it has you in sight again."

Steel shouted out, "We need the smoke and flares!"

To Lieutenant Uber, he ordered, "Open that crate, pass out the AT4s."

Uber looked confused but didn't hesitate to go the back of the MX6 to crack open the crate. He was astonished to see the small arsenal of weapons provided by General Ray. He started passing out the antiarmor weapons.

To Sergeant Major Brown, Steel barked, "Grab the smoke canisters and flares and get ready to drop them out the back!"

Steel said to Carter, "Ed, get us to the ramp!"

"Top, when we hit the base of the ramp, start dropping smoke."

"Flores, get on the M60 and start firing as soon as you see it come around the corner!"

Right about now, Steel thought that General Ray was a genius. Sending the smoke and flares was a brilliant plan. The smoke would hopefully block the vision of the robot if it uses optics, but the flares could be much more effective, throwing off sensors and acting as countermeasures for heat-seeking weapons.

Ed Carter did everything he could to get the most out of the weighty six-and-a-half-ton vehicle. They were still burning up the water at almost six knots.

After the difficult climb up the side of the ship, Moreno and Glor were both out of breath. Standing on the side wall of the superstructure, they looked for and found a firing position at the railing near the bridge. For the moment they were concealed, but that didn't make them feel safe.

Moreno said to Glor, "What part of the robot should I aim at to stop it?"

THE TUNNELS OF EARTH

"I am not an expert on this type of robot. I think that it is heavily armored on all parts of its body."

Composed, Moreno took out a single fifty-caliber round, showed it to Glor, and then chambered it. "I've got armor-piercing ammo. I'll start with the head."

The deadly security robot was moving below them. It would soon be moving around the bow of the *Mist of the Atlantic*. Moreno was lining up his shot just in advance of the sharp edge of the bow. He was hoping that after he shot, the robot's momentum would carry it around the bow, unable to return fire.

Glor tried to enlighten Moreno on the potential of these mechanical threats. "Be careful, the weapons on this robot can destroy a small army. It has an array of lethal burn weapons on each arm that kill its enemy. One uses a super-hot fireball to kill, while the other is a powerful laser that can pierce the layers of vehicles, giving the occupants nowhere to hide. We are in a very vulnerable position if the robot chooses to use its laser."

The giant robot lumbered into Moreno's sights; he squeezed off one round. Glor saw it smack into the side of the robot's head—a temple shot in human terms. He couldn't tell if it caused damage because just as he planned, the robot disappeared around the bend beyond the bow.

Getting up to find another place to fire, Moreno urged Glor on, "Let's move. If he comes back, we won't have a chance."

Ducking inside the wheelhouse, they stood on the side window observing the instruments resting vertical to the cavern floor. They climbed through a horizontal hatch moving into the chart room, standing on the wall. They waited to see what happened next.

Ed Carter powered up to the base of the ramp where he had to stop. He had to stop to transfer power from the propeller to the wheels. It was a quick process, but any time wasted could affect the chances of escape. Carter was efficient getting the DUKW moving again. It could move faster now, so the team felt positive that they were going to reach the door of the Tropos Magra.

Steel looked to Lieutenant Uber. "Lieutenant, start dropping flares. The smoke may not blind it, but maybe the flares will throw off its sensors."

Flares and smoke were being dropped off the stern. Smoke was released as quickly as Brown could puff it. By the time the robot reached the stern of the cruise ship, there was plenty of concealment of their movement. Flares were being dropped intermittently. Steel was looking toward the stern of the *Mist of the Atlantic*, but he could only see the smoke billowing up, hiding them visually.

Steel turned to Roger. "Can you detect the robot through the interference screen?"

"I generally detect the robot, but I cannot pinpoint its exact location."

"Good, let's hope that it sees us with the same clarity that you see it."

*****

Moreno was able to line up a second shot from a position on the collapsed hull near the railing. He was fully exposed in the prone position, but the robot was going the other way, toward the ramp.

When he fired, the round hit and bounced off its heavy outer shell, kicking up the water to its left. On impact, the robot spun around to face its assailant. Seeing this, from his position straddling the railing, Moreno hopped up and managed to leap over it as the robot shot a burst of hot fire in his direction in retaliation.

Escaping over the rail wasn't an easy move. He had a ten-foot drop to the bulkhead below. Glor tried in vain to catch him as Moreno landed hard, unable to feel his left leg.

Surprised, Glor said, "That fireball was weak."

Moreno, wincing in pain, said, "It didn't feel weak to me."

"It should have melted the plates on the ship. I wonder if the saltwater is weakening its power. That would at least give us a fighting chance. Let's see if we can do more damage to it."

"I don't think I can move."

"Let me try. I can get in a good position on the railing."

THE TUNNELS OF EARTH

Moreno offered a quick tutorial. "Look through the sights, line up your target, control your breathing, then slowly squeeze the trigger. If you're lucky, you'll hit what you're aiming at."

Glor climbed up to a spot where he could get a clear view in the direction of the ramp.

The DUKW was halfway up the ramp when Steel heard another shot ring out from the cruise ship. He knew that Moreno was creating problems for the security robot. Once again, they heard a follow-up blast coming from the robot's weapon. It must be firing at the duo on the ship; he hoped that Moreno and Glor were okay.

Steel said, "Hold the smoke, Lieutenant."

Flores spoke to his captain, "Sir, I can't see the robot to fire on."

"Be patient, you'll see it soon enough."

To Carter, Steel said, "Move high enough up the ramp to get above the smoke, Ed. We need a clear shot to blast this thing out of the water."

Carter complied and drove forward. Flares continued to be thrown off the stern to prevent the robot from acquiring its DUKW boat target. The vehicle reached a point high enough to where they could finally get a glimpse of the robot laboring through the water. It was making slow progress near the stern of the *Mist of the Atlantic*.

It was time to get the AT4s into the fight. Steel said to Benson, "Bring up your AT4." Everyone, knowing of the back blast that would be coming, shifted their positions to get out of the way.

"Stand by to fire on my command."

The robot could be seen in the distance through wisps of smoke. It was turned away, facing the *Mist of the Atlantic*. Everyone shifted, getting low on the deck or up next to the bulkhead to avoid the deadly back blast.

Steel yelled, "Benson…fire!"

Benson fired; the eighty-four-millimeter heat warhead was away, in the direction of the robot. In a blur, the rocket smashed into its metallic body and exploded. The slow-moving security robot was blasted sideways then went down under the water.

Unlike the first robot, it ominously surfaced, turning back toward the ramp. The robot returned fire, but its aim was far below

Eagle Corps. The flares were working. It started to move toward the ramp again.

Steel commanded, "Flores, open fire and keep it hot!"

Flores leveled the sixty-caliber machine gun on the approaching security robot. Water splashed up all around, with most of the rounds bouncing off its body.

Benson retrieved a second AT4 and repositioned himself to fire on the stern of the DUKW.

Steel said, "On my command!" The crew shifted again. "Fire!"

Benson fired, and another direct hit jolted the robot. It managed to stay upright. It kept coming.

Steel said, "Mr. Carter, all ahead full."

At that distance, Steel couldn't tell if the robot sustained any real damage. The smoke was again rising, blocking their direct view. The machine gun stopped firing when visibility collapsed. The DUKW was getting close to the door when the next blast from the robot's weapon fired. Once again, the impact was a safe distance away from them. The passengers on the DUKW were relieved when Carter drove through the door into the Aalzad ship.

Steel yelled, "Everyone, on the ground! Take up firing positions." The Navy SEALs, Marines, and Army Rangers, acting accordingly, jumped off the amphibious beast and prepared for battle. The only team member still on the DUKW was Flores, manning the machine gun. From inside the door, Sergeant Major Brown took the final flare and threw it down the middle of the ramp.

Torres, using the handheld controls, powered the MX6 down the short ramp from the DUKW onto the ship's deck. He moved it closer to the door, giving Flores a good line of sight on the advancing menace.

Steel said to Brown, "While we have time, set up the claymores outside the door along the wall facing left, toward the edge of the ramp."

The ramp was not narrow, but at the outside edge, there was a cliff dropping straight down seventy-five feet. It was Steel's intent to blast the security robot off the ramp with the hope of neutralizing it.

Like the AT4s, there is a dangerous back blast associated with the detonation of the claymores. The directional antipersonnel mines send out a deadly blast, releasing seven hundred steel balls that can travel up to one hundred meters. The teams set up deep inside the door, well away from the sixty-degree radius kill zone. The troops, prepared as well as they could be, knew that the indestructible robot was moving up the ramp.

Steel commanded, "Webber, bring up the last AT4 and wait for my command."

Everyone waited. The smoke was dissipating, and the robot remained concealed within it.

Steel calmly said to Webber, "Wait for my command."

Through the thick smoke, the torso and head of the robot came into view. When it cleared the smoke and was fully visible, Steel commanded, "Fire!"

The AT4 fired at the same time Flores started up on the machine gun again.

As the machine gun peppered the robot and the AT4 launched its HE round, simultaneously, with the warhead away, the robot fired its own weapon. Cries of pain came from the left side of the battle line inside the spaceship door. Two team members were down! Sergeant Major Brown was hit, alongside Benson, screaming in pain.

Steel looked down the ramp. The robot was down, writhing on its back at the edge of the smoke. Its limbs contorted in the effort to stand up.

Buckley yelled, "Corpsman, get up here!"

The men had severe burns. Brown lay quietly, while Benson, with burns down the right side of his body, screamed in terrible pain. Buckley feared the worst.

Cooper and Forster moved quickly to the casualties, first to Brown, whose lifeless body lay quiet. Cooper then moved to Benson's side. With Forster's help, they carefully moved him back deeper into the Tropos Magra. It was clear to everyone watching the corpsmen work; Sergeant Major Brown was dead.

Forcing himself to concentrate on the task at hand, Steel said to Torres, "Are the claymores set to go?"

"Yes, sir, set and ready to go."

Assessing the situation, Steel thought that this must be the final blow. He said, "I don't think the claymores will be enough. We need more firepower. Sergeant Torres, while the robot is down, set up the C4."

Ross removed his pirate gun from his pouch and fired, trying to suppress the robot's recovery. He started firing high-explosive rounds, while Torres dashed forward toward the center of the ramp. He wasted little time dropping the C4 in front of the claymores. It was a quick trip as he wanted to get back to the safety of the ship. Ross gave Torres the time he needed to deposit the C4 and get away from the floundering robot. This was it.

Steel pointed out, "The blast from the claymores should set off the C4. I hope that does the job!"

The security robot attempted to rise but kept losing its balance. It stumbled and fell backward again and again until it was obscured by the smoke. E-Corps knew that it was badly damaged but not finished. Four claymore mines were set up close to the side wall, with two bricks of C4 placed in front of them.

In the smoke, the robot was being assailed relentlessly by Flores peppering it with the sixty-caliber machine gun and Ross sending in HE rounds from the pirate gun. Everyone thought, *The mechanical giant must be taking a beating.*

Steel said to E-Corps, "This is going to be big. Move deeper inside the ship!"

Everyone dropped back and took up new positions. Steel had a protected view of the ramp behind the DUKW. Time seemed to stand still, waiting for the robot. He didn't dare send anyone up to see where it was; instead, everyone waited in place, under cover. Smoke still rose in the foreground as the collection of warriors stood by, waiting to finish this fight.

The time had come. Out of nowhere and to everyone's surprise, the robot fired its weapon again. A ball of fire rocketed into the ship, smashing into the MX6. Flores, still manning the machine gun, was launched backward onto the hard deck. He lay there badly burned.

THE TUNNELS OF EARTH

The MX6 was engulfed in flames. Everyone close to it managed to scramble away.

Steel was relieved that none of the weapons in General Ray's crate were still on the MX6. Had the AT4s, claymores, or the C4 still been onboard, the explosion would have wiped everyone out. Fortunately for Eagle Corps, they had all been used. The robot was coming again. This was the final battle.

Through the smoke, the top of the robot's head came back into view. It moved unsteadily with its bad mechanical limp. The damaged torso was now coming into sight. Its big scary weapon became visible as the robot staggered toward the door.

Steel said to Torres, "Get ready to blow the claymores. Wait for my signal! It's not there yet."

To the team, he commanded, "Stay down, don't give it a target!"

The security robot was now fully exposed to the defensive positions. After a few more erratic steps, it was lined up with the claymore mines.

Steel yelled, "Light her up, fire in the hole!"

Staff Sergeant Torres detonated the entire array of ordinance together. A thunderous explosion rocked the ship, and visibility was reduced to zero. Debris, smoke, and fire blasted across the ramp.

As the smoke settled and the air cleared, no one could see the security robot. There was no motion in the ship. Everyone remained perfectly still, anticipating another attack from the ten-foot robot. None came.

Pointing toward the entrance, Steel said to Uber, "Take one man and check out the ramp."

Uber grabbed the first person he saw. "Webber, come with me!"

The two Rangers cautiously worked their way to the entrance, hugging the inside wall. Uber poked his head out around the door and saw that the cliffside third of the ramp had collapsed. On the wall side, rocks were blackened by the intense back blast of the claymores.

The robot was gone. Lieutenant Uber and Sergeant Webber moved out to the edge of the ramp and looked over the side of the cliff. From their position above the collapsed section, they couldn't see straight down to the water.

Moving farther down the ramp to a point where it was still intact, they carefully peeked over the edge. Uber did a quick glance and pulled back. When he looked a second time, there it was, the mighty security robot was in the water on its side in two pieces.

The head, still intact, was looking straight ahead. The torso was flattened out by the blast, and its right arm was connected but dangling loosely by its side. One robotic leg floated away from the body, with the other still attached but twisted in a grotesque angle at the hip. Uber watched as the robot slowly sank beneath the surface. He sent Weber back in to tell Captain Steel that the robot was finished.

Everyone made their way out to see the results that the incredible explosion unleashed on the robot. Steel thought to himself, *If this thing is not destroyed, at least it can't pursue us.* After being told personally by Lieutenant Uber that the security robot was destroyed, he relaxed just a little."

Steel said to the team, "Take care of the casualties."

*****

Moreno passed his sniper rifle down to Brewer and then gingerly slid down onto the DUKW boat. It was bobbing up and down in the water like a rough afternoon on Narragansett Bay. Glor was next. He jumped, lost his balance, and slipped, landing on some bags at the rear of the cargo bay.

He got up, brushed himself off, and noticed that divers Blackwell and Brewer were glaring at him. He couldn't imagine what he had done. Then he turned and looked at the bags behind him.

It dawned on him by the size and shape of the bags that they contained bodies, bodies of Eagle Corps members. He had an expression of shock on his face, and when he looked back at Blackwell and Brewer, the smooth talking Tretorn Glor was speechless.

Watching closely, Steel wanted to defuse the situation. "Mr. Glor, I need to talk to you."

THE TUNNELS OF EARTH

Glor worked his way forward in the rocking boat. To get to the front of the DUKW, he walked by the divers, who now put the incident behind them and were helping the injured Moreno.

Shocked, Glor said, "Captain, you lost men to the robot?"

"Yes, we lost Master Sergeant Brown and Petty Officer Flores. Your engineer is in the other body bag."

Visibly moved, Glor said, "This is awful. No one should have died here. I am glad that you destroyed the robot. I don't know why, but it was weakened by something. Potentially if the robot's weapons were at full strength, we wouldn't have made it around the bow. The fireball would have melted everything in its path. Its deadly laser never fired, perhaps it was disabled."

"Mr. Glor, we're glad too. I'm also glad I didn't have this information when we were fighting it."

The DUKW was moving slowly back to the base of the ramp to drop off Moreno, who needed treatment. Once that happened, Steel, Carter, and Glor would endeavor to get to the control room with the two swimmers.

Steel explained to the Aalzad, "Mr. Glor, as you can see, we have a problem. The door to the control room is completely submerged. The water in the cavern has risen another four feet since our arrival, so entry into it must be done by divers."

"I have some outstanding swimmers here, and I think with your input we can find the control and shut down the portal. You said that the guardians can help with the command robot. What can they do?"

Trying to be helpful, Glor disclosed, "They can communicate with the CR directly and order him to close the portal. They can do it from the boat. There interconnected abilities should be enough to get the job done. The swimmers will not be needed."

"Is the command robot functioning underwater?"

"Yes, of course, the CR can work in many vastly different environments. It can work in far-ranging temperatures as well. High temperatures are found on other planets, and it can also work in the coldness of space.

"The robot has a similar shield to the one I used when I went to the surface. The difference is that it seals the robot completely from the surrounding environment. Once it shuts down the portal, we need to bring it out of the control room and bring it up to the Tropos Magra. We will need this robot for our survival."

Personnel not needed for the operation remained on the ramp. Tom Benson, still feeling intense pain, walked under his own power to a place up against the wall, away from the craft. Brewer and Blackwell stayed on board to serve as divers just in case they were needed to help get the Command Robot out of the control room.

Glor said, "When we get to the entrance, both Max and Roger will send this message to the command robot: 'This is Tretorn Glor of Zome representing Engineer Menzo Shoog of Zome. I require you to shut down the portal to Zome and then exit the control room to board the awaiting boat.'"

Ed Carter moved the slow amphibious vehicle toward the control room, keeping close to the vertical cavern wall to the right of the portal. He carefully navigated away from the area where the immobilized security robot was submerged. He gave it a wide berth.

The flow of the water cycle had changed; it didn't bubble over anymore, but instead it cascaded down the portal in a circular waterfall. Air was no longer passing through any of the tubes; they were all blocked and inoperable. The boat eased over to the door and stopped. Carter had to work the controls to prevent the DUKW from being drawn toward the pit.

The guardians started transmitting Glor's message to the command robot. Immediately the command robot replied.

Max, speaking for the CR, said, "Glor of Zome, the portal is locked open. I have no ability to unlock it. All other controls are inoperable. I will exit the control room now."

Moments later, the CR broke through the surface and bobbed up and down. Brewer and Blackwell went over the side to secure a rope so it didn't drift away and go over the falls.

CR said through Max, "Why are humans here? Humans should not have control here."

Thinking fast, Glor said, "I am in charge, not the humans. They are working for me."

The CR went silent; Glor thought that was good enough for now.

The DUKW boat climbed the ramp and had to stop forty feet outside the spaceship door. The ramp continued to deteriorate to the point where the vehicle could no longer pass. There was a four-foot ledge that the team members could easily traverse on foot, but the DUKW needed at least another five feet of width to enter the ship.

"Okay, let's get everything off the DUKW we need." Pointing to the body bags, Steel ordered his men to do the gruesome job. "Brewer, you and Webber grab a bag. Blackwell and Ross, come over here and take this other bag." Once the first two body bags were removed off the vehicle, Lieutenant Uber and Doc Forster removed the third one.

Ed Carter shut off the engine for the last time and held back from the others entering the ship. He felt disconsolate but also had a sense of satisfaction leaving this hardworking vehicle that got them through all those extraordinary challenges.

When he entered the Tropos Magra, he realized that he was in the large hangar bay. The hangar's inside wall stretched around the center of the structure. It was vertical, going straight up in the center, where it met the curved roof that moved down to intersect the floor at the outer wall. This was all new to Carter; the rest of the team had experienced this large familiar room before.

No sooner had they entered the first twenty feet of the hangar when the CR glided over to the inside curved wall and opened a mechanical sliding door. The wall moved out and slid to the right behind the partition Buckley and Cooper used to hide behind. It revealed what looked like the main control area of the Tropos Magra. It was filled with work panels.

There was absolutely no indication that this area existed when it was closed. At the center of this circle was another rounded wall. Beyond this wall was the conduit where, when open, water from the ocean passed through the flow valve to the portal.

Glor spoke to Captain Steel, "Have your men set up an area where they can rest. I am ordering the robots on the ship to prepare food for them. You and Mr. Carter may enter the control room with me. Have your men bring the bodies of your countrymen in as well. We will attempt to bring them back."

To the men, Steel said, "Bring the bags in here. Mr. Glor will tell you what to do."

Located in the back of the room were two metallic tables enclosed by a wall of glass. Glor led the morbid procession to that area. Strange alien lettering was on the instrumentation panel, located just to the right of the opening.

Glor said to Brewer and Webber, "Please remove the body from this bag and place it on the table."

The SEALs, following Glor's directions, revealed the badly burned body of Master Sergeant Brown. He was barely recognizable. Chunks of his uniform were burned away, and some of the material was melted to his skin.

These were hardened warriors, but the sight of Brown's condition made them nauseous. He was a big man, as they worked hard to lift his body onto the table. He was heavy, but they were as gentle as they could be under the circumstances.

Glor said, "Back away and shield your eyes."

He explained, "This machine will restore our friend, Mr. Brown's life. First his internal organs will be repaired, restoring life. When that is done, the Magno will reconstruct the outer shell and his skin. That procedure will take longer, but in the end, it will completely repair his body."

Following Glor's instructions, the men stepped away, thinking that this machine was unbelievable.

Glor stepped to the glass panel and lowered a visor to protect his eyes. Turning to the side panel, he ran his hand over the bank of instruments, switching on an intensely focused light. Everyone covered their eyes or turned away from the concentrated lights. The beam moved slowly over his body, crafting repairs.

Speaking to Blackwell and Ross, Glor moved to the second table. "Bring your companion over here." He directed them to a similar device off to the right. Shielding their eyes as they walked by the first machine, they placed Mario Flores on the next table and then turned away.

Flores's body was in a similar condition to the master sergeant's. The glass side came down, and the next light was engaged. Glor gestured to the four servicemen to move to one side, away from the retina-burning light.

Explaining the process, Glor said, "This is the machine that allows the people of Zome to live very long and healthy lives. Yes, it will bring people back to life when necessary, but its main purpose is to allow the population to maintain a youthful existence.

"Over the course of an Aalzad's life, they will use this regenerator many times. It restores health to the sick, and it inhibits the aging process. Unlike your friends who are deceased, a living person that uses it will not be deprived of their memories. It maintains their minds and renews their bodies.

"In the case of your friends, the regenerator is operating on its maximum settings to restore life. A normal healthy Aalzad using it would be set on panel adjustments that are much lower. The less healthy you are, the higher the settings."

Lieutenant Buckley overheard the whole talk by Tretorn Glor. He said dramatically, "For ages man has searched for the Fountain of Youth, and now we have found it in the form of a machine."

Glor proudly said, "We didn't find it, we created it."

Brewer said jokingly, "Where can I get one of those tables of youth?" There was a low chuckle by the others.

Lieutenant Buckley noted that there were only two of these regenerators on the bridge and said to Glor, "You are taking care of our people before your own?"

"Yes, they have not been lifeless as long as Menzo Shoog. I will try to revive him once your men have returned. In his condition, he may have been gone too long to be fully restored. I chose to go first with those with the best chance. Remember, they will be revived, but they will have no memories. Here on Earth, in that state, perhaps they would be better off remaining dead."

Buckley responded, "Why do you say that?"

"Do these men have families?"

"I know that Master Sergeant Brown is married with two teenage sons. I don't know about Flores."

In a soft voice, Glor said, "Master Sergeant Brown will not know them. Memories of his former life have been erased. It's not a process of the machine to restore it. If there is no memory when placed in the machine, none can be reestablished."

Buckley said, "Under those circumstances, I have to agree with you. It's sad, but it might be better if they remained dead.

"It is unfortunate that the families will know them, but they will not know their families. The only proven way for a loved one to regain the victim's trust and love is to bring that victim back into the family as soon as possible. It's almost like introducing a new baby into the family. When the affected person starts to relearn things and identify his family members, it will be easier to integrate them back into the family group.

"That's why it is important they are taught by their spouse and family. The family bond can be restored under those conditions. It's not a guarantee, but it has worked on our world. Lives have been fully restored within a range of recovery levels provided by their family group. It doesn't always work that way."

After a few minutes, on the table where Master Sergeant Brown lay, the blinding light stopped. Summoned by Glor, a group of four worker robots entered the bridge, moving directly to Brown. The glass lifted, and Brown sat up straight. His eyes looked vacant and distant. A robot assisted him to his feet.

He was alive, but he was still badly burned. None of the burns had healed. It was hard to look at him as he silently walked by. His appearance was like a hideous movie monster. He showed no recognition of any his subordinates.

A door opened, and he disappeared with his contingent of robots. Moments later, the second light went out, and the same ritual occurred with four new robots helping Flores move toward the door. Everyone watched the process and discussed what would happen next.

Glor, realizing what the group's conversation was about, intervened, saying, "Your friends' lives have been restored. However, they will need treatment in our Magno machine. This machine will close their wounds and then replace the dead skin with fresh new skin. This process takes time."

Buckley said to Glor, "Will they get their own guardians? I ask because Roger here helped another member of our team. That member was killed in our first encounter with your worker robots. He, too, was brought back to life."

"Yes, these men will be temporarily assigned guardians. Guardian assistance will have an impact on their early recovery." Glor continued, "If you have seen the results of our machine before, then you know that it will take years for these men to rehabilitate. I will make arrangements for guardians as soon as we solve our bigger problem—survival."

Sitting on the ramp just outside the door, Moreno watched the steady transformation of the cavern. Water was rising at a measured rate as the portal continued to drain off world. The waterfall was gone, filled in by a lake. Periodically, small whirlpools were spinning around the portal, only to disappear under the water again.

He also noted that the water, leaking from the roof of the cavern, had grown in volume dramatically as it streamed down the ramp. The draining was being outpaced by the increased water coming into the cavern from various sources.

When the flooding reached a point ten feet below the ship's door, he reported to Lieutenant Buckley inside the control room, "The security robot by the gantry is gone."

Amused by what he saw, he continued, "I watched the gantry collapse and float over to the edge where it was swept into a whirlpool. The robot held on to the stanchion with its metallic hand to the bitter end, as it was swept down the hole. The one we blasted to pieces is in an eddy next to the ramp, bobbing up and down."

Buckley said, "We are about seventy-five feet above that section of the floor of the cavern. The water has risen sixty-five feet. Let me know when it's around five feet below the door."

"Yes, sir. Captain Steel is with Mr. Carter at the door monitoring that process."

"Good." Changing the subject, Buckley asked, "Lance Corporal, you and Ross took a ride in the underwater craft, didn't you?"

"Yes, sir."

"Is it big enough to get everyone to the surface?"

"Not all at once, sir. It's only big enough to carry four people at a time, and that's without a guardian driving it."

"Ask Captain Steel if he will join me here in the control room. It's time to explore our options of what we have to do to evacuate."

Moreno limped out of the control room, favoring his banged-up left leg. He proceeded to the ramp, where most of E-Corps were lounging around just outside the door. Some were asleep, while others were fascinated by the slow rise of water. The cavern was still an amazing sight. The *Mist of the Atlantic* was almost entirely submerged, disappearing at an astonishing rate.

Standing by the door, Steel approached the thoughtful ex-Navy man and said, "It's too bad we can't save her. No one would have gotten this far without such a versatile vehicle."

Carter nodded. "I agree, it's an incredible machine. I don't know if anything else could have handled this job."

Moreno approached Captain Steel and said, "Sir, Lieutenant Buckley requests your presence on the bridge."

"Thank you, Marine."

Steel said to Carter, "Maybe you would like to be in on this."

"Yes, I would."

The Marine captain and the thirty-year Navy man entered the bridge. When they arrived, they observed Lieutenant Buckley in serious discussion with Tretorn Glor.

When Buckley saw his superior approaching, he interrupted his conversation and said, "Sir, I've been talking to Mr. Glor, and he is ready to close the main door. He also mentioned several options we might implement to escape. These options have varying degrees of risk.

"Mr. Glor said our first option is to close the outer door and live in the big ship until we are rescued. Because our military doesn't have technology readily available to save us, we'd probably have to wait to be rescued by another Aalzad ship."

Buckley continued, "The second option is to send the Aalzad underwater craft to an island to contact a land base. Once we have ships overhead, we can evacuate small groups to the surface. Third, with the highest degree of danger, is to separate the main ship and let it rise to the surface."

Captain Steel called to Glor, who had returned to his workstation. He invited him to join the conversation. "Can we get any additional input from you on what we need to do to get out of here?"

On his arrival at the small circle of men, he said, "You know I'm not a pilot, but yes, I believe we are limited to the three choices I discussed with Lieutenant Buckley."

Steel said, "Mr. Glor, go ahead and close the door. We certainly aren't going out the way we came in."

Carter interjected, "I have a question about separation. How difficult would it be to separate from the seafloor?"

Glor thought about it and said, "If the Tropos Magra is intact, we should be able to separate without a problem. If there is any damage to the ship from the earthquakes or if the superstructure is buried by avalanches, we could rip open and flood."

Steel asked, "Is there any way you can determine if the ship is damaged?"

"Yes, I will instruct the CR to evaluate the condition of the ship to determine if we can separate successfully."

"How long will that take?"

"I don't know. Starship command is new to me. Please have your men move inside, away from the main door. I will close it when you are ready."

Steel said to Buckley, "Clear the door area and move the men inside."

"Yes, sir."

Carter said to Buckley, "I'll go with you, Lieutenant. I want to say goodbye to my old friend."

The two men exited the bridge, joining team members still gathered near the main door.

Buckley passed along the order from Captain Steel, "Eagle Corps, move inside. Mr. Glor is going to seal out the water and seal us in."

Carter moved toward the door, staying just inside. He crouched down, looking out at the vehicle that did so much work under such challenging conditions. He watched as water crept up, partially submerging the rear tires. The DUKW was finished now, not because it couldn't perform but because the environment was closing in around it, leaving it at its final destination. He stood up and stepped back as the large door moved down into its closed position.

The Aalzad ship's bridge was now alive with military personnel moving around trying to find the best place to sack out. They figured that they were going to be here for a while, so a nice private area out of general traffic would be a great find. Returning to the bridge, Buckley and Carter saw Glor standing next to the CR at the main console.

Steel took a moment to rest at a nearby Aalzad crew members' workstation. It was a tight fit, but somehow, he got comfortable. He was waiting for the CR's verdict if the Tropos Magra could detach successfully from the seabed.

Menzo Shoog was out of the regeneration machine and was being escorted away by a single guardian. He looked bad; he looked the same as when he was dredged out of the water. He followed his guardian like a puppy to the Magno room, much like the military men did earlier.

Buckley said to Carter, "I never planned on living in a submerged spaceship for a hundred years."

"I don't think that it will be that bad. We have the small underwater vehicle that can travel to the surface. Judging by what I've seen in Aalzad technology, I would guess that the crafts range would allow us to reach land without too much difficulty."

"I hope you're right."

The two men watched as Glor approached Captain Steel. They waited a moment, and then Steel turned, gesturing them to join the conversation. The captain's face didn't give anything away, so Buckley was curious.

Steel spoke, "Gentlemen, Mr. Glor has determined that the Tropos Magra can be safely detached from the seafloor."

Turning to Glor, he said, "Mr. Glor, please explain to Lieutenant Buckley and Mr. Carter how this can be accomplished."

"What I found out from the CR was this: we can complete the task of removing the Tropos Magra by simply reversing the embedding procedure. It's done with intense heat jets on the underside of the ship. When directed into the rock, they will cause the rock to melt into a molten state. By melting the rock, the Tropos Magra can break free and rise from its present position."

Steel responded, "That sounds good. Will we rise to the surface?"

Glor boasted, "Captain, we can do more than that. The CR can fly us to shore, where we can step off on dry land."

Steel enthusiastically responded, "That sounds even better. What are we waiting for?"

Carter intervened, "What happens to the portal when we lift off and open it up to the ocean?"

"Unfortunately, there will be an uncontrolled flow of water to Zome until another ship can come to close it. It will flow at a higher rate than Zome can safely receive. I surmise that a ship from the fleet is already on its way."

Thoughtfully, Carter said, "Gentlemen, think about this. We are in a craft that can control water flow through the center of its structure. What if we melt the rock below us and move down into the cavern and land, covering the portal? We can fit the ship over the portal with the valve and portal aligned. If the Tropos Magra lands with the portal open, there won't be any resistance. If we can seal the ship over it, we can control the water flowing to Zome."

Skeptically, Glor said, "We could try that, but I don't know if, during the process, the power of the wormhole would crush the ship with us on it."

"That could happen if the flow valve is closed. If the valve is open, you can cover the portal and then close it down slowly."

Steel cut in, "I like the plan, but I don't like having so many SEALs, soldiers, and Marines on the ship when it happens. I suggest that we use the underwater craft to evacuate E-Corps."

*****

Moreno, Ross, and Lt. Uber were assigned the task of using the underwater vehicle to get help from the surface. The plan was to notify authorities and then get help to remove the members of Eagle Corps and Mr. Carter.

Once the team was gone, Captain Steel and Tretorn Glor would stay onboard having the CR execute the plan of burning the Tropos Magra out of the rock. Once free, it would drop down and use the heat jets to enlarge the crater. This would allow the craft to lower into the chamber to seal the portal.

Moreno and Ross were selected because of their experience in the Aalzad submarine. Lt. Uber was there to provide some authority when they contact the Navy or Coast Guard topside.

Max was the driver. Like all guardians, he was clearly qualified to captain this craft. He proceeded flawlessly out of the hatch of the large ship and off to the surface. It was topside in several minutes. The Tropos Magra was imbedded 250 feet below the surface, far less than anyone suspected.

The strange craft moved northeast, on a direct course to the island of Nantucket. It was an unsightly water vehicle. Its shape included a tapered nose cone that was attached to a craft that had a rounded rear fuselage, much like the vehicles that brought the Aalzad to Earth.

There were oval glass windows all around the upper half of the vehicle, so it had the appearance of a very strange nautical craft. It moved at a good pace in the water without any drag, even with its odd shape.

In the late afternoon, with the sun in their eyes, the reluctant seafarers saw their destination on the horizon. Nantucket was the lucky island. It was the only major island not afflicted by Aalzad smoke. For some unknown reason it was spared.

Treated in the same manner as Aquidneck Island, Martha's Vineyard and the Elizabeth Islands south of Cape Cod were destroyed and rendered uninhabitable by the smoke. Only the black silhouettes remained in those places. However, Nantucket was another story.

Reaching the island on the east end, they navigated around Great Point at the Nantucket National Wildlife Refuge. From there, on the northern coast of the island, they traveled parallel to Great Point Road. At sunset they passed through the breakwater at the entrance of Nantucket harbor. Traveling south, the craft powered past the lighthouse at Brant Point and into town.

On arrival at the municipal dock, they were met by the irate steamboat authority manager. He was ready to shoo them away until he looked down and saw the very alien craft. Moments later Lieutenant Uber was on the phone to the Navy.

*****

Steel entered the quiet room that contained his recuperating men. They were repose on what looked like normal hospital beds, encased in tinted glass. Sgt. Major Brown's skin was looking much better. It definitely showed significant signs of healing, even though there were still sites on his body covered with soars and blisters that had not healed because of the depth of his wounds.

Once he checked on Brown, he moved to Flores. He, too, was recovering. Captain Steel was startled when Flores turned and looked at him, showing no sign of recognition. Steel smiled and nodded to his subordinate before turning to the third reborn individual.

Menzo Shoog didn't look so good, compared to his men who showed improvement. Shoog was pale, and his breathing was slow and labored. Steel turned to Glor, who had entered the room, and said, "Is he getting any better?"

"He was gone for a very long time. I don't know if he will recover. All Aalzad reach the point where they cannot regenerate. Perhaps this is Menzo Shoog's time. If he does not show considerable improvement soon, he will have to be let go.

"He has lived a long life, so it would be all right. That decision will have to wait though. Your people have arrived at the island of Nantucket."

There was another person in the room. It was Benson. He was smiling and conversing with a guardian.

Steel spoke to him, "How are you doing, son?"

"Sir, it's a miracle. I feel great! I'm completely healed. All my burns are gone.

"That's amazing. Do you feel up to leaving with the teams?"

Benson, still smiling, replied, "Yes, sir, I'm ready."

"Alright, join E-Corps and prepare to leave."

The underwater craft returned with only Lt. Uber and Max on board. As soon as it docked and the water in the vehicle bay drained, Uber went directly to the bridge. He saw Captain Steel and approached him.

"Captain, we have a destroyer and a Coast Guard cutter steaming above us. They're ready to start receiving our people."

"Very good, Lieutenant. If they can be moved, start with Brown and Flores and one of the medical guardians. Then you can coordinate the rest of the evacuation."

"Yes, sir." Before he left, his tone changed. "Sir, I was told that Goat Island, including part of the Coddington, was washed away by a massive tidal wave. Many of the military tenants have been recovered alive. General Ray is still missing."

Steel, with no change in expression, replied, "Thank you, Lieutenant."

Uber left to start the evacuation.

Steel looked around for Ed Carter. He was sitting on the floor in contemplation, on the far side of the bridge. He walked toward the ex-Navy man with a heavy heart and a difficult message.

Steel said somberly, "Ed, I have some bad news."

"Really, Captain? What kind of bad news."

"All the earthquakes that we suffered here in the underground spawned major tidal waves topside. One took out Goat Island and much of the low-lying areas around it."

Concerned, Carter said, "Are there casualties?"

"Yes, I don't know how many, but I can imagine that with a tsunami of the size that can take down the Coddington, there will be many casualties."

Steel paused then said, "General Ray hasn't been accounted for. He was in the hotel when it collapsed."

Impassioned, Carter said, "Oh no, not Bob. I hope that they find him safe."

Carter, visually upset, didn't say another word. He slowly turned and walked away.

Stopping him, Steel said, "Mr. Carter, we are getting out of here. You're on the next shuttle."

Carter nodded and kept walking.

*****

The last shuttle left for the surface with only Captain Steel and Tretorn Glor still onboard. With the CR at the controls of the main ship, they would be the ones to release the Tropos Magra from its lock on the seafloor and ultimately descend over the portal.

Max brought the underwater craft back and docked it in its bay. Steel and Glor were surprised to see Ed Carter had returned. He had ascended to the surface but, after second thoughts, chose to return to the Aalzad ship.

Carter entered the bridge and said, "Seeing it was my idea, I figured I should be here."

Captain Steel, showing no sign of surprise, nodded to him and said, "I'm surprised you left in the first place."

Ronald (Rex) Steel learned that Ed Carter was a dependable ally. His presence could only be a positive in this situation.

Glor was communicating with the CR while Max told the men what was going on.

"The command robot will close the door to the bridge and then start heating up the bed rock beneath the Tropos Magra to its melting point. When it is released, it will rise above the cavern, allowing it to flood completely. The ship will then burn its way down through the remaining seabed fringe. Once that is complete, it will precisely line up above the portal for its final descent."

Carter questioned, "Won't the water pressure above prevent the ship from rising? It seems to me that the Tropos Magra is like a big plug under enormous pressure. Shouldn't you flood the cavern first to relieve the pressure?"

"That will not be necessary. The ship has the ability to displace water. It can move the water out of the way, right up to the surface of the ocean. The Tropos Magra will create a hole in the water, and we will fly within that hole."

"When we complete that maneuver, water will fill the cavern below, allowing us to descend over the portal. Once we lower over the original resting place, the jets in the hull will burn through the rock surrounding it. Once enough room is created to pass through the hole, the ship will land, melting into the floor, adhering to the portal, creating a permanent seal."

Glor said to the men, "We are about to begin. Please sit down and hold on." He pointed to the tight little crew chairs.

Steel and Carter squeezed in, sat down, and held on.

The command robot began the process by moving its mechanical arm over a portion of the controls. Outside on the underlying hull, steam bubbled up, and the hull began to glow from the intense heat. The robot touched another part of the console, and a wide beam of light scattered the water aside from above the ship.

The Aalzad ship separated from its connection to the bedrock and lifted off. The sea rushed in, dousing the hot molten slag, cooling the area in contact with the seabed. Water rushed into the air-filled cavern. As the water rushed in, the lonely DUKW, abandoned on the ramp, was instantly swept away by the onrushing flood of water.

The higher the Tropos Magra rose, the quicker the water rushed in. When it was completely clear of the hole, the dry cavern was no more. The only known air-filled cavern beneath the oceans of Earth was now history. It was just one more underwater cave dotting the globe, albeit the largest.

The command robot moved to another console and followed a similar procedure to fully open the valves at the top and bottom of the ship. This procedure would allow the water to pour through, as it did prior to the earthquakes.

Before the CR could process water through the ship, it had to shut down the beam displacing the water above. Finishing that step, the ocean closed in around the Tropos Magra. The CR proceeded to open the valves, permitting water to fill the now wide-open center chamber. The final step was to lower down over the return portal to Zome.

With the heat jets reengaged, bubbles rose up from the seafloor turning red again. The Tropos Magra was burning its way through the remaining rim of its previous resting place. Slowly and precisely the CR guided the ship through the molten rock until its underside was completely in the cavern.

Pressing straight down into the chamber, the ship centered over the interstellar portal. It was far bigger than the tube through it; however, the dimensions of the Tropos Magra were easily large enough to completely cover and seal the portal all the way around. If any part of the portal was exposed to the water-filled cavern, the ability to shut down the flow of water to Zome would fail.

If it could apply to robots, the CR was taking great care placing the Aalzad ship directly over the portal. The outside hull was burning hot as it seated on the melting floor. The control room went silent when the propulsion system of the spacecraft shut down. It was in position, completely sealing the outer edges of the portal. The efficiency of the CR was precise. The procedure was over in ten minutes.

Max spoke again to Admiral Carter and Major Steel, "With the ship sealed to the cavern floor, the CR will now attempt to close the valves, thus closing the portal."

Continuing, he said with no implication of danger, "If the Tropos Magra's valves close and the portal stays open, the suction will cause it to break apart and be sucked down the pit."

The CR began closing the check valves while monitoring the integrity of the ship. The falling water began to taper off as the valve moved toward its closed position. Halfway closed, the CR stopped the process. It looked at a panel then communicated with Tretorn Glor. Glor acknowledged the CR and walked over to the men sitting nearby.

Glor, not as calm as Max, said, "This is the critical point. If the command robot closes the valve and the portal does not shut down, the suction on the ship will be so great that it will break apart, sending us all to Zome. The command robot gives us a seventy-five percent chance of success."

Hearing that, Carter said, "Should we go to the getaway vehicle?"

"No, we need to monitor what happens. If the portal closes, we can take our time and leave when we want. If the portal does not close, we might have enough time to get out…or we might not."

Steel said, "What are you waiting for? Let's do this!"

Glor nodded and turned back to the CR, directing it to continue the process. Once again, the valve crept toward the closed position. That was when the shaking started.

On the bridge, the men noticed small vibrations growing in strength underneath the ship. Glor and the two Earth men had to hold on to remain stable. The vibration transformed into a steady shaking.

Steel thought to himself, *This is it!*

The quaking continued as the valves approached the closed position. The trembling became so strong that the men were forced down in a prone position on the deck. They were holding on to whatever they could reach to remain secure. From the bridge, they could hear loud crashing in other parts of the ship. Whatever was not tied down was falling over.

The ship was holding together, but how long could it possibly last? During the final stage of the shuddering, Carter blacked out, followed closely by Steel. His final thought was *We're not going to make it!* He then slipped into darkness.

*****

The fog cleared from Steel's head as he gradually returned to consciousness. He awoke in the same quiet dark space on the bridge, but now he had a severe headache. It was pounding after the repeated banging on the floor during the event. Carter was sitting at the controls where the CR remained at his station.

Carter turned and said to him with a smile, "Welcome back, Captain. According to Mr. Glor, the shuddering stopped when the portal fizzled out and closed. It worked. It all worked."

Steel rubbed his head and smiled. "I've got the worst hangover of my life. Can we get out of here now, Ed?"

Carter smiled and said, "Mr. Glor is readying the underwater craft as we speak."

Carter held out his hand assisting Steel to his feet.

Steel, looking at the command robot, said to Carter, "It did a hell of a job."

"Yes, he did, his work is done for now."

"What do you think will happen to the CR now?"

"I think he will stay with the Tropos Magra, at least for the time being."

*****

Eagle Corps lifted off the USS *Zumwalt*'s duel helipads en route to Quonset Point Naval Air Station. The two SH60 Seahawks headed west in the morning sun.

Ed Carter observed the scene inside the chopper. It was quiet, very quiet. The team members were all in somber moods. Their thoughts raced, thinking about the bizarre events that they just experienced. Carter could see the chopper's reflection on the ocean's surface, himself thinking about the amazing adventure this small band of Marines, Navy SEALs, and Army Rangers had shared.

Captain Steel looked back on the mission and felt that E-Corps had done an outstanding job. Flying over the black surface of Martha's Vineyard, he could see tiny people exploring the barren island. They had no idea of what just happened to the south of the island, 250 feet down in the Atlantic Ocean. He was tired. He turned away from the window and closed his eyes.

Glor was thinking about what just happened as well. Reality was sinking in. He had been an enormous help to the mission in the cavern, but he felt more of an outsider than before. He was alone, the only functioning Aalzad citizen left on Earth.

His ambassadorship was a joke. With all the problems that he had, it was essentially over before it began. Earth's resources had stopped passing through the portal. Nothing was being sent to Zome. Until it flowed again, Glor had nothing to do. He thought sadly that he may never return to his home planet. Dejected, he thought, *Have I been forgotten?*

Aquidneck Island's smooth black surface was instantly recognizable from a distance. Their ETA was fifteen minutes, and as the pair of Seahawks flew low over the ocean on approach, no evidence of earthquake or tsunami damage could be seen. Captain Steel strained to see the condition of the Coddington Hotel up ahead.

When the SH60s made landfall, the hotel was finally in sight. It was not immediately discernible the condition it was in, but as they got closer, they saw that the upper floors on the south side of the hotel had imploded. The balconies on the east side of the structure were gone, the upper floors smashed downward with only the exterior walls on the first floor partially intact.

The central three-story section of the Coddington looked structurally sound, but all the windows were blown out on the lower levels. The north end lost only a section of its southeast wall. Looking around the rest of Goat Island, Steel could see it was largely swept clean of structures. The old Goat Island Marina building was still there, but it was smashed in with the roof resting on the interior floor. The empty brick condos to the south of the island were standing but also badly damaged.

Flying over the west passage of Narragansett Bay en route to Quonset, the team witnessed tsunami damage in the low-lying areas of Jamestown. Neighborhoods were wrecked. Flashing lights of emergency vehicles and cleanup crews could be seen dotting the island.

Flying above the Jamestown Bridge and turning north, Quonset clearly came into view. Familiar structures on the base looked like they sustained little tsunami damage. On final approach to the airport at Quonset, a formation of three helicopters could be seen passing them going in the opposite direction toward Aquidneck Island.

Looking out the forward window, Ed Carter thought it strange and said to himself, *What is this?* He leaned back on the bench seat. "We will probably find out what is going on when we land. At least it doesn't involve us.

Part VI

INQUISITION

The tight formation of Rhode Island Air National Guard helicopters flew across the bay, landing near the original site of the pillbox and trench. On this occasion those structures were unseen. Resting on top of them was a new different Aalzad ship. It was a perfect fit, resting in the surface indentation.

The officer in charge adjusted his uniform and disembarked from the lead helicopter. He got goose bumps from excitement when he looked at the spot where the pillbox had once been visible.

Before him was a massive flying disc. It was as black as the surface of the island, blending in perfectly with its surroundings. Other than the wind blowing from the southeast, it was very quiet. The Aalzad have returned.

Standing before the new Aalzad spaceship was General Nicolas Teranova, the commanding general of the Rhode Island Air National Guard. He stood facing the ship without a speck of knowledge about what was going on. This duty should have fallen on the shoulders of General Robert Ray, commanding general of Eagle Corps. General Ray, however, was swept away by the tsunami and presumed dead.

General Teranova now stood in front of a delegation that was hastily thrown together to meet the new arrivals. No one knew what to expect. Only the personnel on Goat Island had clearance to deal with the alien presence.

*****

Back at Quonset, the two helicopters set down on the cracked runway. The SEALs, soldiers, and Marines couldn't get out fast enough. First, they would report to Hangar 11 to drop their gear. It still showed damage from Hurricane Enzo.

The corrugated steel hangars were not affected by the tsunami. Once members of Eagle Corps signed out, some would be free to go home to their families, while others, just happy to be back on terra firma, would go to the NCO Club for well-deserved adult beverages.

Brown and Flores got out with the help of Cooper and Forster, with the guardians staying close by. An ambulance waited nearby to take the regenerated men to the base infirmary. Steel had to find a place where he could report in. He saw the one-story communication center across the runway was still there, so he started in that direction. Ed Carter followed along, needing to use the phone.

Tretorn Glor assisted the physically diminished Menzo Shoog out of the chopper. He had a guardian as a helper. Not knowing what else to do, Glor, with Shoog, just stood by the side of the helicopter. They only moved when a crew chief shooed them out of the way of the Seahawk lifting off. He found a place on the edge of the grass and remained there.

*****

General Teranova had been waiting outside of the newly arrived ship for about fifteen minutes when a large door on the side slid open. Several more minutes elapsed with no sign of life. The suspense was broken when from the delegation's position, they saw a single figure exiting the door.

It was a person in an Aalzad space suit complete with helmet in place. This individual walked directly to where General Teranova was standing. Two military policemen began to block his path in response to the potential threat. They were stopped by a quick wave of the general's hand.

The humanoid stopped five feet in front of the general and removed his helmet. He was human. The delegation looked around at each other to see if there was any recognition of this stranger. There was none.

He walked up to the general, extending his hand, and said, "I was hoping General Ray would be here to meet me, sir. My name is Dean Frederickson. I was chief of station at Goat Island until I traveled to Zome."

General Teranova shook the hand of the man claiming to have just arrived from another world.

"Where is my superior, General Ray? I expected to see him here."

"Unfortunately, no one has seen the general since the giant tsunami smashed the Coddington Hotel."

"The general's dead?"

Frederickson, looking very concerned, said, "General, I hate to drop this on your lap, but we have a situation here. The highest officials in the Zome government feel that we have sabotaged their operation here on Earth."

Teranova, looking very confused, replied, "I don't know anything about sabotage. Goat Island was a very secretive place. Yes, I would get bits and pieces of intelligence about the goings on there, but that's all."

Pointing toward the delegation, Teranova said, "Furthermore, no one here knows anything about the Goat Island operation."

Frederickson continued, "General, I have to tell you, inside this ship is a panel of Aalzad officials. You will be facing an inquiry. The Aalzad demand a representative of Earth's government to explain what happened to their facility.

"You, General, being the ranking official, will be expected to answer their charges. At the Aalzad's request, I traveled from Zome to offer assistance. Because I thought General Ray would be here to answer the questions, I didn't hesitate. General Ray would have had all the information required to set things straight. I'm afraid you must go in his place. It's not going to be easy."

Teranova replied, "I will go in, but as I told you, I have no pertinent information about any incident that might have happened." Nervously, Teranova raised his index finger and said, "Give me one minute. I want to see if I can find someone back at the base that has more information."

Frederickson said, "Good idea, General. Find someone. The Aalzad are not in a good mood."

The general turned to his aide. "Jeffers, take my chopper and return to Quonset. Find someone that can help us. If there are any survivors with knowledge of Goat Island activity, get them over here. Jeffers, this is serious, notify Washington too."

Jeffers turned and mounted the lead helicopter as ordered and told the pilot to take him back to base ASAP.

Back in the Quonset communication center, Captain Steel was looking for the officer of the day; he was nowhere to be found. After supervising the team checking out at Hangar 11, Lieutenant Buckley was making his way to the main parking lot to see if his car was still there.

When he heard the big Navy Seahawk helicopters taking off, he turned to watch. Instead of watching the chopper's departure, he caught a glimpse of the sad spectacle of Tretorn Glor with the shell of Menzo Shoog and their two guardians standing at the edge of the tarmac. Feeling bad, he walked back to where they stood.

"Mr. Glor, do you have anywhere to go?"

"No, Lieutenant, we don't. The hotel that I was staying at no longer exists."

"Why don't you come back to my place with me for the night? We can sort things out tomorrow morning."

"We accept your offer. That is very kind of you."

Looking out the window of the comm. center, Steel saw Lieutenant Buckley with Glor, Shoog, and the company of guardians walking toward the parking lot. He thought about calling them over but was distracted by the duty sergeant.

At the radio, the duty sergeant called out to Steel and Carter, "Sir, did you just get off that Seahawk from Nantucket?"

The sergeant had received a message from an approaching chopper. It read, "Find anyone attached to or having any knowledge of the operation on Goat Island. Have them report to the comm. center."

Tired and in a bad mood, Steel responded, "Who wants to know, Sergeant?"

Keeping his military bearing, the desk sergeant said, "General Teranova wants to know, sir."

"Where is the general?"

"He's on Aquidneck Island."

Steel perked up. "Okay, Sergeant, you have my attention. I was on the helicopter."

"Please wait here, sir. The general is sending transport for you. There is something going on over there. They need personnel that were attached to Goat Island."

Cruising over the bay, the helicopter carrying Major David Jeffers approached the landing zone at Quonset. Landing, he ran directly to the comm. center and asked the desk sergeant if he found anyone that fit the description that he forwarded.

He pointed in the direction of Captain Steel and Ed Carter. Jeffers acknowledged the sergeant and approached the two men. He started to speak to Captain Steel, but he was startled by the presence of Ed Carter.

Jeffers respectfully spoke to Carter, "Admiral Carter, how are you, sir? It's me, David Jeffers, adjutant to General Teranova. Are you involved in this Goat Island affair?"

Carter, recognizing Major Jeffers, replied, "I'm fine, Major. Yes, I am involved to a certain extent. What do you need?"

"Sir, I need you and anyone else that was stationed on Goat Island or involved with that situation to come with me."

Steel joined the conversation. "What do you know about the operation, Major?"

Slightly annoyed and in a low voice, Jeffers said, "All I know, Captain, is that there is a big black spaceship sitting in the middle of Aquidneck Island with its occupants accusing us of sabotage."

"Why didn't you say so? Let's go."

The trio boarded the general's helicopter and headed toward Aquidneck Island and the new Aalzad threat. Steel couldn't remember the last time he had a minute to himself. The endless hours that he put into this mission reminded him of the campaign in Cuba.

THE TUNNELS OF EARTH

In the warzone, he had little time to himself. There were no breaks. Here in Eagle Corps, there was little difference. Steel had to put that out of his mind for now and find out what was going on. In his mind he could see an army of ten-foot security robots surrounding the Aalzad ship. That would not be good.

*****

Escorted by Dean Frederickson, General Teranova reluctantly entered the enormous craft with his entourage of minor government diplomats in tow. This was the group that was available at the time of the Aalzad landing. There didn't seem to be any reason why these particular officials were picked, but nonetheless, this was what he had for support. He only knew one of them by name.

Moving into the interior, they were met and escorted by smallish humanlike beings to the large bay where a group of Aalzad officials waited. It was a strange arrangement. It was a big empty room with absolutely no furniture. The Aalzad assembly was made up of seven individuals dressed in silver robes. They were standing under spotlights in the center of the space. They were in a line facing the human procession.

As the group entered, it was stopped near the edge of the room by Aalzad security—humanoids, not the dreaded ten-foot robots. Only General Teranova was escorted to a position directly in front of the Aalzad tribunal. He sheepishly looked around, noticing a number of robots lining the interior walls of the chamber. They were worker robots, but to him they looked threatening.

Mr. Frederickson took up position next to the general and said, "I have a guardian, a robot that will translate the Aalzad language for you. It will tell you exactly what the panel is saying, and it will translate anything that you say in response."

Frederickson continued, "General, I have some knowledge of what is going on here. I was in the cavern when one of the earthquakes hit. I think I have more knowledge about what happened down there than anyone in this room. I want to help you if I can."

"I don't have a complete picture of the situation in the cavern in the aftermath because I traveled to Zome before any of the real problems occurred. That's the main reason I hope that your message to Quonset is heeded.

"Let me help you, I have good rapport with the Aalzad."

Speaking through the guardian, the central figure of the Aalzad brought the room to order. "I am Dulf Rapp, high judge of Zome. I am here to conduct an inquiry about the events that led to the destruction of our facilities under your ocean.

"At this moment the people of Earth stand accused of destroying our operation to harvest water and air for the preservation of Zome. You are also accused of flooding the Aalzad base and closing the interplanetary portals. You are also accused of having the ultimate responsibility for harming our engineer and destroying our security robots. What is your defense?"

*****

Sitting next to Ed Carter on the helicopter, Steel smiled and turned to him, "Major Jeffers addressed you as Admiral. I knew I should have shown you more respect!"

Carter smiled and said, "It's been a few years since that title applied. People that knew me back then still call me that out of habit. You, however, need to keep calling me Ed. I am your friend and not your superior."

"I am honored to be your friend, sir."

Carter responded, "Ed! Not Admiral and not sir, just Ed."

"Yes, sir—I mean, Ed."

Both men smiled and turned their attention back to the mission. Before long the Aalzad ship appeared in the distance.

With the smile gone from his face, Carter said, "Will you look at that! Our friends are back."

Steel grumbled, "Will this nightmare ever end?"

As they closed in on the familiar landmark, the pillbox and the trench, there was an Aalzad ship sitting in place. It was twice the size of the one they had just left under the Atlantic Ocean. Steel wondered why he didn't see it when they were flying back to base.

*****

General Teranova was sweating; he had no idea what this individual was talking about. He said, "Sir, I do not have a response to your accusation about the incident of which you speak. I have sent my aide to find someone that knows of the circumstances behind your charges."

Looking to his side, he said, "Perhaps Mr. Frederickson can shed some light on the matter."

Dean Frederickson nodded to the general and then spoke, "Judges of Zome, General Teranova has spoken truthfully. He does not have a security clearance for the specific information that you seek. There is only a small group of people that have any knowledge of your presence here on Earth.

"My knowledge about the incident in the cavern is firsthand. I was there when the first earthquake struck. I entered the tunnel when your portal was operational, and I was there when secondary earthquakes shook the cavern.

"The latter earthquakes seemed to be caused by the activation of your entry portal. When you sent a craft through the portal from Zome, the seafloor shook. When I was in the cavern, there was only one secondary earthquake, but it was enough for your engineer to suspend the incoming tram operation."

Frederickson stopped and turned to see what the disturbance at the ship's entrance was. Rex Steel and Ed Carter entered the chamber under escort. Frederickson excused himself and approached them as they came in. After a quick greeting, he hustled them directly to General Teranova's side.

Frederickson said to Dulf Rapp, leading the proceedings, "I have an officer that was present when the portals were operational and knows what happened after I left for Zome."

Steel self-consciously said, "That's not exactly true. Our team arrived when the cavern and tunnels were falling down. In any case, I will try to answer your questions."

Rapp asked, "With whom am I speaking now?"

"My name is Ronald Steel, captain, United States Marine Corp."

"You are of the military class?"

Steel said proudly, "Yes, sir, I am."

"I see, Ronald Steel, did you ever see the operation of the portals?"

"Yes, I saw the portal taking the passengers and crew of the *Mist of the Atlantic* to Zome. Everything was working well until the earthquake struck. At that time, water was still flowing from the Tropos Magra into the exit portal to your planet."

Something came to Steel's mind and he said, "Excuse me a moment." He turned and said to Jeffers, "I have two team members that were actually present when the Aalzad came through the entrance tunnel, and they were there when the destructive secondary quakes occurred. We need them here! My information can't cover the timeline of the quakes. You need to find them and get them over here."

Jeffers asked, "Who am I looking for?"

"You are looking for Navy Lieutenant Roger Buckley and Navy Corpsman Rachel Cooper."

He remembered and said, "We also have two Aalzad citizens over there somewhere. Bring them too if you can find them. They could be the answer to our problem."

"I'll get right on it."

Steel turned back to the Aalzad panel and said, "I'll try to answer any other questions you have."

Rapp asked, "What was your mission down in the cavern?"

Steel replied, "We were on a rescue mission. We went down to save our team members and your engineer. We had your ambassador Tretorn Glor working with us."

"Our ambassador?"

*****

THE TUNNELS OF EARTH

Buckley found his apartment building across from the base access road just the way he left it. Dishes were piled up on the counter, and clothes and uniforms were all over the furniture. The good thing was there was no indication that the tsunami hit anywhere in the vicinity.

He directed Glor to bring Shoog into the living room. He moved some magazines and then gestured for them to sit down on the sofa. He opened the refrigerator door and noticed a pungent smell; something didn't smell right. He grabbed a beer and closed the door.

No sooner had he popped the top on the can when he received an electronic message on his phone to report to the comm. center at Quonset Point immediately. It also said that if he knew the whereabouts of Chief Petty Officer Rachel Cooper, Tretorn Glor, and another Aalzad, have them there too. He guzzled down the beer and said to the Aalzad citizens, "We have to go back to the base. Something is happening, and they need us there." Buckley worked his phone, relaying the message to Cooper.

Buckley said, "Back in the earth car, boys."

The Aalzad citizens looked like a couple of pathetic homeless men. There shiny uniforms didn't hold up well after the cavern experience. Not only that, Glor looked confused, while Shoog clutched his arm with a blank expression on his face.

*****

Steel was out of answers. He and Frederickson had exhausted all their knowledge about the flooding of the cavern.

He finally said, "If we can stop these proceedings until our individuals with firsthand experience of the catastrophe arrive, I'm sure that would be worthwhile to everyone concerned."

*****

Cooper was waiting when Lieutenant Buckley arrived at the comm. center with the Aalzad duo, plus guardians in tow. She looked exhausted. The same sergeant that spoke to Captain Steel directed them to a helicopter waiting on the runway. The crew chief waved them on board, and they quickly lifted off.

Buckley said to Cooper, "Do you know what this is all about?"

"All I got was the message from you, sir."

*****

Rapp changed his point of questioning. "I am going to ask you some questions regarding something you should have knowledge. You were there when the portal to Zome closed?"

Steel replied, "Yes, I was there when the command robot closed the portal by lowering the Aalzad ship over it, then closing the flow valves."

"Do you expect me to believe that our command robot, the one that communicated that you upset the operation, destroyed our security robots, and killed Menzo Shoog, the same robot that we sent to Earth to manage the operation, would be the one to terminate it?"

"That's what happened. This was all done with the cooperation of Tretorn Glor, ambassador to Earth from Zome."

Aggravated but curious, Rapp looked to his colleagues and said, "Who is this Ambassador Tretorn Glor? I know nothing of this citizen. Go find out who this mysterious Aalzad is."

The second Aalzad to Rapp's left bowed and dismissed himself moving to a door to the left of the room. Communication between Rapp and his colleague was not translated through the guardian interpreting the proceedings. Steel, Frederickson, and the others asked for a translation, but none was forthcoming.

Rapp raised his voice and continued the questioning, "You destroyed a security robot. Why?"

Composed, Steel responded, "Your engineer Menzo Shoog drowned in the flooded cavern. As far as I know, this is when your robot became hostile. We neutralized it before it destroyed us."

"I am amazed that your simplistic earth weapons could stop our elite security robots." In a condescending tone he said, "Perhaps we underestimate you. The engineer, you say he drowned. Is he dead?"

THE TUNNELS OF EARTH

"Not exactly, he was brought back to life on your ship by Tretorn Glor, along with two members of our team."

*****

The Seahawk landed outside of the massive ship. Glor was excited when he saw it from a distance. He would be reunited with his people. What this also meant was that he did not have to deal personally with the demise of Menzo Shoog.

Glor knew Shoog was not going to recover this time, so the official action would be done by those trained in such matters. However, that wasn't the reason why they were here. They needed to go inside the ship to find out why they were summoned.

The two humans and the two Aalzad entered. Roger, Max, and one other guardian were right behind them. Dean Frederickson greeted them at the door and explained the gravity of the situation. He told them that they must tell the Aalzad what they know about the flooding of the cavern and the closing of the portal.

Meanwhile, Rapp continuing his questioning of Captain Steel, said, "You had access to the regeneration machines?" Looking to the side door where the second Aalzad had disappeared, he said in a loud voice, "Have you found out the identity of this Tretorn Glor yet?"

He got his answer from the main door as the group entered. Frederickson escorted the four individuals with their guardians to the crowded center of the room next to Captain Steel and General Teranova.

Rapp spoke now through multiple translating guardians. Roger and Max were there, as well as the previous translator. "Please identify yourselves."

Buckley said, "I am Lieutenant Roger Buckley, United States Navy."

Cooper answered, "I am Chief Petty Officer Rachel Cooper, United States Navy."

Stepping forward in front of the others, Glor said, "I am Tretorn Glor of Zome, Aalzad ambassador to Earth."

Rapp leaned forward and spoke to him in the Aalzad language, "Who are you, Tretorn Glor, and why are you standing with these humans against us?"

"I was sent here when the harvesting operation began. My primary function was to help the humans traveling to Zome feel comfortable with the transition. I learned English back in the early years when we first visited Earth from a guardian skilled in that language. Being a language specialist, fluent in many languages, I was prepared to make the new citizens of Zome welcome. When our new citizens were on their way through the portal, I went to the surface to act as a liaison with the Earth's leaders."

"Really? What leaders did you talk to?"

"None, I'm afraid. I never left the island hotel on the surface."

Rapp sarcastically complained, "What kind of ambassador doesn't travel to meet with leaders?"

"I was scheduled to go to the Capitol to meet with high officials, but the earthquakes caused me to join a rescue mission to the cavern. I arrived when the problems started. It was important for me to stay and help."

"Are the Earth humans responsible for the destruction of the water and air transfer operation?"

"Absolutely not! It was a natural disaster. Earthquakes occurred under the ocean. I think it was because the incoming portal upset the balance in the earth's crust."

"How do you know that?"

"I was present when the first tremor occurred. It happened right after the trams started returning from Zome. Over time it became bad enough to start a series of earthquakes that cracked the cavern's protective shell, flooding the tunnels and the base."

"Were you present when the secondary earthquakes happened?"

"No, I was not, but I was in the tunnel with the rescue team moving toward the cavern." Pointing to the Navy SEALs waiting in the background, he said, "These two Navy SEALs were there and witnessed everything."

Rapp looked up and said, "Navy SEALs, step forward!"

Buckley and Cooper joined Tretorn Glor in front of the Aalzad panel.

"You are of the military class, are you not?"

Glor spoke up, "These Navy SEALs do not fit in a military class description like those on our home planet. These are young leaders in their organization."

Rapp said in an annoyed tone, "Tretorn Glor, let the humans speak for themselves."

Buckley, speaking for the pair, said, "We serve in the military."

"You are warriors?"

"When necessary."

"Why were warriors in an Aalzad installation?"

"We were investigating the pillbox and trench on the surface and found our way in."

Rapp, looking confused, asked, "Pillbox and trench?"

"Yes, your air intake tower and large vent."

"Did you communicate with the Aalzad crew present in the cavern at the time?"

"Only the guardians at first."

"You were down there to destroy our operation, were you not?"

"That was not our mission. Only Chief Cooper made initial contact. She was the first individual to enter the cavern, and that was purely by accident."

Rapp called out, "Chief Cooper, what do you have to say?"

Looking nervous, Cooper took a step forward and began speaking, "I was lost in the tunnel and thought I would never get out. When I found the cavern, I met humans that had been down there for years.

"Then I met guardians. I was amazed when I was welcomed in the cavern. There were no Aalzads at the base when I arrived. After talking to a group of guardians, one of them traveled to the Earth's surface with me to establish contact with our society. It met with officials and then invited a small delegation to meet the Aalzad in the cavern, on their return."

Rapp turned his attention back to Buckley. "If you did not destroy our operation, tell me what happened."

"It was a natural disaster triggered by the operation of the entry portal."

"What happened to our engineer, Menzo Shoog?"

"When the cavern was flooding, Menzo Shoog, trying to stop the flow of water, was pulled down into the exit portal. Somehow the air tubes were blocked by the flood water, preventing the air flow from escaping down the portal. Prevented from escaping, air was forced back up and bubbled over into the cavern. When the air escaped, the water was free to go down the portal. Menzo Shoog was caught when the air was released and was trapped in the backflow of water returning to the pit."

"You saw this?"

"Yes, but we were high on the ramp."

"When you found his body, what did you do?"

"We didn't find his body. We thought that he went through the portal."

"I still find it hard to believe that any of this happened the way you say. You are of a lowly class that must not be believed without confirmation of a superior. Do you have such a superior backing up the story?"

Taking a half step forward, Steel was about to speak, but Ed Carter moved up and touched his arm, asking if he could step in. Steel nodded and then took the half step back.

"I think that I can help Lieutenant Buckley in that respect. My name is Edward Carter, rear admiral, United States Navy (retired). I was on the rescue mission that entered the cavern after the initial earthquakes."

"Are you military class?"

Irritated, Glor jumped in, "He is in the intellectual class of the highest order! He is a leader of leaders!"

Rapp, now losing his patience with this unknown Aalzad, raised his voice and said, "You must refrain from these outbursts, Tretorn Glor!"

Rapp turning back to the man in the center of the room, he said, "Please speak, Edward Carter, rear admiral, United States Navy, retired."

THE TUNNELS OF EARTH

"I don't know anything about being in the intellectual class, but I would like to help. You refer to these fine Navy SEALs as being in a low class. Perhaps that is true on your planet, but here on Earth, they represent the finest qualities that the military has to offer. They are leaders whose word should be accepted as honest and factual.

"I was a member of the rescue mission that found Engineer Shoog's body. He had been under water a very long time. I was told by Lieutenant Buckley that before your engineer drowned, he bravely tried to close the outgoing portal. Unfortunately, he was caught in a backflow of water and went down the portal.

"These Navy SEALs tried to save him, but they thought he had gone to Zome. Not realizing it didn't happen that way, they gave up the search. What they didn't know was a surge of water brought his body back up to the top of the portal. From there, his body was swept across the cavern to a far sector. He was carried close to the main tunnel where our rescue team found him."

Rapp spoke to all of them, "None of your answers prove that the disruption of our operation was a natural disaster. Because Menzo Shoog cannot speak for himself, we cannot rule out sabotage."

Rapp's attitude softened when he realized that Menzo Shoog was standing there. Shoog was in the background, standing frailly with the delegation. His mind was gone; he was beyond regeneration. Rapp stepped forward from his prominent position in front of the group and walked up to him. With great sympathy, he placed his hand on Shoog's shoulder. Rapp turned and waved his arm for assistance.

Rapp, speaking to his unresponsive compatriot, said, "You have had a fine productive life, Menzo Shoog. You are a hero to our people, and now it is time for you to rest." Two compassionate underlings came up to gently escort him by the arms away from the group.

Rapp visually moved, turned his attention back to the gathering, and said, "Let us stop these proceedings for a moment to pay tribute to our lost hero." The Aalzad around the room stood up straight with their right arms across their chests. Together as one, they spoke respectful words in the Aalzad language. The human delegates stood by quietly and respectfully.

As a tribute, Rapp then led the group in a song. At the same time the song was ending, Menzo Shoog was escorted to his final rest. He disappeared through a door behind the tribunal. It took several more minutes for the ceremony to end. Once the memorial service was over, the whole room turned their attention back to Rapp and the matter at hand.

Rapp, composing himself, said, "It appears to me that we cannot draw a clear conclusion on what really happened here without Menzo Shoog's testimony. The presence of humans in the cavern, for whatever reason, violated the integrity of our operation. Because of my personal reservations after listening to all the human stories, I am authorizing a strong security force to come to Earth to protect our interests."

Glor spoke, "No! You have no proof that the humans had anything to do with the destruction of our base. I have testified that the humans had nothing to do with the flooding. It was an accident, and I can prove it."

"It is obvious that you are taking the side of the humans. You have turned against the judgment of your leaders. This will not help you."

"I said I can prove that the cavern was flooded by a natural disaster."

Rapp smiled wryly and said, "Very well, Tretorn Glor, prove it."

"This will require us to travel back to our submerged Tropos Magra. Once we are there, I can prove to you that the humans are innocent."

Surprised by Glor's statement about the cavern, Rapp said, "What are you saying, Tretorn Glor? Are you saying that the Tropos Magra was not destroyed? It was my understanding that everything was destroyed."

In a loud angry voice, Glor said, "That is where you are mistaken, high judge of Zome! The Tropos Magra is intact and fully functional!"

Rapp looked flustered and said, "Don't try to trick me, Tretorn Glor. You will be severely punished if you are lying."

Rapp became distracted by the tribunal member returning from his inquiry into the identity of this defiant citizen, interrupting the heated exchange. During the conversation, again the translation was not offered. However, Glor listening intently understood every word.

He shouted in the Aalzad language, "Are you now satisfied about my identity, Dulf Rapp? Do you still think that I am lying in behalf of the Earth humans?"

Steel and company saw a new Tretorn Glor emerge as he became aggressive, brimming with confidence. He spoke again loudly, "Do you now know who I am?"

Rapp's demeanor changed, from the stern inquisitor to a man struggling for words. He looked afraid.

He sheepishly said, "Yes, sir, I am now aware of your identity. It was ignorant of me not knowing who you were before. Forgive my disrespect, sir. I believe everything you say."

Not really knowing what was transpiring, Earth's delegation looked at each other in total confusion. One minute Rapp was a fiery inquisitor and the next he was a submissive little kitten.

Rapp said to Glor with deference in his voice, "This must have been an unpleasant experience for you. I know you must be tired. If you would like, come with me and rest in the dignitary's suite. You certainly need some Aalzad hospitality, perhaps some rest and refreshment. I apologize for not believing you. Your word cannot be questioned."

Tretorn Glor replied, "Thank you, Dulf Rapp. I would like to use the cabin to rest. It would be most pleasing to me. Now that we have an understanding, we need to talk about the disposition of our operation openly and what we need to do to fulfill our resource requirements."

"I would be honored to hear your account of what happened and to discuss the future of our program."

With no explanation to the humans, they started to walk away together. Near the exit door, Glor suddenly stopped, turning back to the Earth delegation, leaving Rapp standing alone. He approached the Americans riveted in position, not having a clue about what just happened.

Glor advanced to the small forward group, including Carter, Cooper, Buckley, Steel, and Frederickson. "You will have no further problems with this high judge of Zome. Thank you for your help. Goodbye."

Glor turned and walked back to where he left Dulf Rapp. The attentive high judge showed adulation over Tretorn Glor as they walked off together through the side door panel, disappearing from sight.

Just like that, the inquest was over. Glor had a big secret that no human or Aalzad that was present knew. Through their investigation on Glor's identity, the panel member uncovered some information that Rapp was visibly afraid of.

Cooper turned to Roger and asked, "What just happened?"

Roger replied, "It appears, Rachael Cooper, that Tretorn Glor is a member of the Aalzad royal family. Although he is an obscure royal figure, he is a royal nonetheless. Your Earth delegation just saw what his power and influence has on all the Aalzad present. Apparently among the Aalzad, he is of a station in society, not to be trifled with. Dulf Rapp wanted no part of challenging him.

"In the private discussion between Dulf Rapp and the other Aalzad, I heard that Tretorn Glor is a direct descendant to the last king of Aalzarada, Rogu the Great. This last king has been dead for five generations, but his ancestors live on maintaining the highest social standing."

Cooper said to no one in particular, "There was more to this guy than meets the eye. It looks like he just saved Earth!"

The large chamber emptied out. The Aalzad panel and security filed out of the many different doors. The human delegation was left standing as a group in the center of the chamber. Realizing that they were being left alone, it dawned on them that there was nothing else. Knowing that the proceedings were truly over, they filed to the exterior door.

Once outside, they were captivated by the beautiful December afternoon. It had been a brisk day. The sun suspended low over the horizon where the winter sky turned from blue to gray. The delegates talked quietly as they walked to the three waiting helicopters. General

THE TUNNELS OF EARTH

Teranova had his own chopper, so he and his staff got on board and were the first to leave. Cooper saw Dean Frederickson mount the second helicopter with the other dignitaries.

She thought, *I've got to ask him!*

She ran the extra twenty-five yards to the second chopper. She yelled, "Mr. Frederickson!"

The rotors turned faster, and the noise level was rising as Frederickson barely heard Chief Cooper's call. He turned from the entryway on the Seahawk Helicopter and saw Cooper waving at him. The crew chief gestured for him to sit down and strap in; they were taking off. Looking at Cooper, he shrugged his shoulders, holding out both hands, palms up, as if to say, "What can I do?" The second chopper took off.

By the time she got to the third helicopter, she was the last to board. Once in her seat, the chopper headed home. She craned her neck to see if the other choppers were heading toward Quonset. On the flight, over the west passage of the Bay, the lead chopper turned north toward Providence. The other was on direct approach to Quonset.

The first helicopter that landed at Quonset was emptying out when the one carrying Chief Cooper landed two hundred feet away. She saw Frederickson walking toward the comm. center. He was fishing for something in his pocket when the enthusiastic Cooper caught up to him. She startled him, but he turned and smiled.

Smiling, Frederickson said, "What's on your mind, Chief?"

Cooper, out of breath but very excited, said, "What was it like? What was Zome like?"

Frederickson, with a big smile, said, "You wouldn't believe me if I told you."

Cooper pressed him. "Try me. You have to tell me."

"I'm sorry, Chief, I can't explain it." Without hesitation, he turned and walked away.

Disappointed, Cooper turned to leave. A moment later she heard Frederickson say, "Chief!"

She turned as he approached with a concerned look on his face.

"Chief, I don't know why I said that. I can't remember a thing about my time on Zome. What I said to you before must have been a canned response placed in my subconscious mind. My time on Zome has been blocked. I actually felt good about that response I gave you."

Shaking his head, he said, "I was brainwashed."

Frederickson said goodbye, turned slowly, and walked away, not feeling as good as he did before he talked to Chief Cooper. Thoughts raced in his head, but memories of Zome weren't in there They were erased from his mind.

*****

It was dusk when the flight took off from TF Green airport in Warwick, Rhode Island. It was a commercial flight traveling to Washington, DC. Chief Cooper, Lieutenant Buckley, Captain Steel, and Dean Frederickson were among the people summoned to a conference with a congressional delegation to discuss what had happened on and below Aquidneck Island over the past months.

Once airborne, Nationwide Airline routinely flew over Narragansett Bay on its southern route. Over the intercom, the flight attendant eagerly pointed out the strange black island. There was a carnival atmosphere in the cabin as everyone anticipated seeing this unusual site from several thousand feet up. Cooper strained her neck as well to get a good look.

Standing alone on the southern plain, at the corner of Bellevue and Narragansett, was the giant Aalzad spaceship.

When the Earth delegation left the ship and returned to Quonset in December, it remained quietly in position. When the doors closed for the last time, it adorned a dull white glow.

Up to now, there was no further contact with the Aalzad. There was plenty of speculation about what happened to them. One school of thought was that the crew was still onboard waiting for the next step in their operation here on Earth. Others believed that the crew of the spacecraft was using the damaged tunnels to bring water up and through a portal on this new Aalzad ship.

In her heart, Rachael Cooper knew that the surface ship was empty, the crew transported out to some off-world location. Did they go to Zome? She didn't know, but she was positive that she was looking at a vacant ship.

As the Boeing 767 aircraft gained altitude, Cooper observed the soft glow outlining the spacecraft. She knew that glow. She had seen it before. She saw it around Tretorn Glor when he visited earth's surface, and she was told in a conversation with Captain Steel that the command robot had a similar shield protecting it from harsh environments. Now she saw the glow protecting the Aalzad ship.

With the sun below the horizon, Racheal looked around the cabin. She saw the awe on the faces of the people looking out of the windows and heard the excitement in the rows behind her. This was all because of the strange glow on the even stranger monument standing alone on Aquidneck Island.

Rachael Cooper could only believe that contact with the Aalzad had only just begun and that she, a Navy Corpsmen and Eagle Corps, would play some future role in dealing with this advanced civilization, the Aalzad from Zome.

The End

About the Author

Born in Columbus, Ohio, Frederick Carpenter is a graduate of the University of Rhode Island. Before attending the university, he served in the United States Marines for two years during the Vietnam Era. While in the Marines, he served aboard an American aircraft carrier, the USS *John F. Kennedy*, and at the Naples, Italy, NSA (naval support activity). He finished his enlistment at Camp Lejeune, North Carolina.

After his discharge, Carpenter completed his education and went on to work as a secondary school teacher and an interscholastic league soccer coach. After coaching soccer for twenty years, he was elected to the Rhode Island Soccer Coaches Hall of Fame.

Retiring in 2011 from the Exeter-West Greenwich Regional School District, Carpenter took up writing. Through his writing he incorporates his experience in the Marines with his love for science fiction.

He is married to his wife of fifty years, Jan. They have two adult children and a chocolate lab named Jesse.

This is Carpenter's first work of science fiction.

CPSIA information can be obtained
at www.ICGtesting.com
Printed in the USA
BVHW031526090321
602112BV00005B/269